About ...

Born in the UK, **Bec**... interminable wanderlust from an early age. She's lived and worked all over the world, from London to Dubai, Sydney, Bali, NYC and Amsterdam. She's written for the likes of *GQ*, *Hello!*, *Fabulous* and *Time Out*, a host of YA romance, plus three travel memoirs – *Burqalicious*, *Balilicious* and *Latinalicious*. Now she blends travel with romance for Mills & Boon and loves every minute! Tweet her @bex_wicks and subscribe at beckywicks.com

Tara Pammi can't remember a moment when she wasn't lost in a book, especially a romance which, as a teenager, was much more exciting than a mathematics textbook. Years later, Tara's wild imagination and love for the written word revealed what she really wanted to do: write! She lives in Colorado with the most co-operative man on the planet and two daughters. Tara loves to hear from readers and can be reached at tara.pammi@gmail.com or her website tarapammi.com

Double winner of the National Readers' Choice Award, **Kira Sinclair** writes passionate contemporary romances. Her first foray into writing fiction was for a high school English assignment, and not even being forced to read the love story aloud could dampen her enthusiasm...although it did make her blush. She lives in North Alabama with her two amazing daughters and their pet hedgehog.

Postcards from Paradise

January 2023
Caribbean

April 2023
Costa Rica

February 2023
Brazil

May 2023
Australia

March 2023
Hawaii

June 2023
Bali

Postcards from Paradise:
Bali

BECKY WICKS

TARA PAMMI

KIRA SINCLAIR

MILLS & BOON

First Published in Great Britain 2023
by Mills & Boon, an imprint of HarperCollins*Publishers* Ltd,
1 London Bridge Street, London, SE1 9GF

www.harpercollins.co.uk

HarperCollins*Publishers*
Macken House, 39/40 Mayor Street Upper,
Dublin 1, D01 C9W8, Ireland

Postcards from Paradise: Bali © 2023 Harlequin Enterprises ULC.

Enticed by Her Island Billionaire © 2020 Becky Wicks
The Man to Be Reckoned With © 2015 Tara Pammi
The Sinner's Secret © 2020 Kira Bazzel

ISBN: 978-0-263-31935-4

This book is produced from independently certified FSC™ paper
to ensure responsible forest management.

For more information visit: www.harpercollins.co.uk/green

Printed and Bound in the UK using 100% Renewable Electricity
at CPI Group (UK) Ltd, Croydon, CR0 4YY

ENTICED BY HER ISLAND BILLIONAIRE

BECKY WICKS

To my rock star boyfriend Konrad, who is by now quite used to long periods of keyboard tap-tap-tapping before I stop and ask him worrying questions like, 'How much do you think a facelift would cost on a remote island near Bali?'

#grateful

CHAPTER ONE

MILA RICCI SWIPED at her thrashing hair as the waves jumped and frothed around the speeding boat. The exclusive transfer by Dr Becker's private yacht from Bali to the island of Gili Indah wouldn't have been quite as bumpy as this, she mused, as a tourist shrieked behind her, but she'd missed it. She'd been advised by an elderly lady with a twinkle in her eyes to sit on the roof of the tourist boat for the next best thing.

The tree-dotted hills in the far distance were pale swathes of varying greens, shrouded by a thin veil of fog in the morning light. The island looked like a painting—just as Annabel had once described it.

Gathering up her red dress, Mila copied the backpackers next to her and dangled her legs over the edge of the roof, resting her arms on the railings. It didn't seem entirely safe by the standards she was used to at home in Britain, but she wasn't worried.

Travelling in potential peril had been standard practice during her time in the Army—especially out in Afghanistan. A few bumpy waves were nothing compared to the time she'd had to take a convoy in the middle of the night and go past the place where the insurgents had burned the bodies of the soldiers they'd shot dead on the bridge.

The direct route to the nearest air station had been just eight miles straight, but they'd gone over a hundred miles around it to escape. Two of the trucks had broken down in the first hour. She'd hitched a ride on another truck and they'd hidden in the sand dunes, listening to the mortar rounds being fired at the vehicle they'd just fled.

Mila rubbed her face. She was tired. She was thinking too much about the past. She couldn't be further from a war zone now if she tried. This was a new start. There was nothing to fear on a paradise island...except maybe a tsunami.

She rolled her eyes at herself at the thought. Why did she always fear the worst?

You know why, she reminded herself. *Because you can't always prepare for the worst, even when you think you can.*

On the deck, an Indonesian man was playing with a rescued baby monkey. Mark would've got a kick out of that, she thought now, acknowledging the stab of guilt that told her she hadn't ended things with him too well.

She'd been so busy wrapping things up before she'd left the London hospital where she'd devoted herself to her work since leaving the Army. She'd barely had a moment even to think about him since she'd broken things off. He was a good man, but maybe a little too soft for her. He didn't know how to handle her.

What was it Mark had said before he'd left her flat? *'You don't need a man right now anyway, Mila. You need to figure out who you are."*

He was probably right about that. She hadn't come home from Afghanistan the same person. She'd learned quickly out there who she really was. She was part of a team and she couldn't fail. She was eyes, ears, instincts. She was ready for the worst—always.

She could still hear the whirring rotors of the helicopters infiltrating the hot, sticky night air. When she least wanted to she could conjure up the smell of dust and the acrid stench of wet blood on inconceivably terrible wounds. The agonised moans of broken soldiers still made it into her dreams some nights.

It had been more than her twenty-four-year-old self had known how to handle at the time she'd been deployed, though she'd never admitted that to anyone. It had only been after her twin Annabel's death, eight years later, that she'd truly fallen apart.

Mila watched two Australian lads making faces at the monkey, but she wasn't really paying attention. She was dreading the anniversary of her sister's death all over again. It was almost three years ago now since the accident.

She'd been home on leave for a few weeks when it had happened. Annabel had been trying to lift her spirits, keeping her one step ahead of depression after her latest posting to Afghanistan. But for all of Mila's Army training, and everything she'd endured in combat, she'd still frozen on the spot when she'd come across her mother's twisted, unrecognisable car, smashed just like the motorbike Annabel had hit before wrapping the car around a tree.

Those wasted seconds she'd spent, willing the steel of the car to unwind, willing the clock to go back, might have been the difference between her sister's life or death. The worst thing had happened and she hadn't been prepared. She'd failed to get Annabel out alive.

'There they are!'

Mila blinked as a voice shrieked excitedly behind her. A backpacker in a red football shirt was pointing at the islands, coming ever closer to them. They were headed for the largest of those several small bumps in the ocean, which jutted like camel humps ahead of them.

Adrenaline spiked in her veins. She willed herself not to think about Afghanistan, or the accident. But she knew Annabel would be here too; she was everywhere.

Annabel had actually come to Gili Indah without her years ago. She and her twin had planned the trip together, but Mila had come down with an unfortunate case of laryngitis just before the flight. She could still remember that crackly phone call from her twin.

'You've got to see it one day, Mila! The most beautiful mountain views...the blue of the water...it's unreal! And there are loads of hot men here. You're missing out, I can tell you.'

Was it a coincidence that this opportunity to spend the next couple of months or so at the prestigious Medical Arts Centre there—or the MAC, as it was known—had appeared in her online searches, just last month?

The MAC hadn't been there at the time of Annabel's visit, six and a half years ago. It would have been a mere gleam in the eye of its founder, the billionaire Dr Sebastian Becker. He'd left his whole celebrity surgeon lifestyle behind in Chicago only three years ago, to set up this exclusive facility.

Mila watched the monkey peel its own banana, its tail wrapped around one of the Australian guys' forearms.

What was he like? she mused. This man Dr Becker?

Her friend Anna back at the hospital in London had told her a little about him, but only what she'd garnered from watching him on TV.

The Becker Institute—Dr Becker's revered plastic surgery practice in Chicago—was the base for a globally popular reality TV show focused on the lives of its patients and their various cosmetic surgery procedures.

Dr Becker had only starred in one season, with his brother Jared Becker, before leaving the show to concentrate on building the MAC. Anna had said he'd really left because the media circus had got too much for him. Something about an ex-girlfriend, threats, scandal...

Mila had stopped her there. She hated listening to gossip. And it had felt wrong to poison her mind about a man she'd never met—especially a man who was doing such remarkable work.

Dr Sebastian Becker had pioneered what was now the world's leading method of scar tissue surgery, blending the newest innovative laser treatment with a simplified but highly effective surgical procedure. This was the first time he'd offered an opportunity for another experienced surgeon to come to the clinic for a short-term placement and observe his techniques.

It had sounded fascinating to her—the chance to learn something new at his exclusive private island clinic—and she hadn't hesitated to hand in her notice at the London hospital.

Indonesia was surely bound to be a far nicer setting than an overwhelmed city hospital or a military hospital in the Middle East. She was done with all that. She'd come for something completely different—a new focus, a change of pace, even if it was only temporary.

She couldn't even recall what Dr Sebastian Becker looked like, or the name of the TV show he'd so briefly starred in. She'd never had much time for TV, and she didn't ever bother with social media. Hopefully the man was agreeable, at least; they'd be working in pretty close proximity.

Mila smoothed her red sundress and held her hair back as the wind wrestled with it. She wished she could have asked Annabel what to expect from this place beyond the gorgeous guy she'd met when she had been here. What had she said his name was? Bas…or something like that?

Sebastian Becker hauled the last remaining tank out of the water and eyed the speedboat heading his way. He reached down to help the first of his dive group back onto the boat. Getting them all on board before the next intake of tourists whipped up the water was imperative if he didn't want his students flailing in opposite directions within seconds.

'Give me your hand.'

Gabby, a British woman in her early twenties, pushed her mask down to her neck and grinned up at him from the water. 'I'll give you whatever you need.'

He helped her up the ladder and she fell against his chest, heavy and wet in her tank and vest.

'Sorry,' she muttered, so close to his face he could feel her breath on his skin.

She wasn't sorry. This girl had been flirting with him all morning.

He helped the others up. Checking his students were seated and had disposed of their flippers in the right place, he yelled, 'Ketut, start the engine!' and bounded up the three metal rungs to the roof.

Alone, he unzipped his wetsuit, letting the thick wet fabric unfold around his middle. The sun sizzled on his skin.

Maybe tonight, when the last scheduled surgery was done, he'd take Gabby out for a drink, somewhere with candles and a sandy floor. She'd be gone in a day or two. Why not give her something to talk about, once her plane deposited her back into her boring existence?

Those had been her words this morning, not his.

'My life is so boring compared to yours. I should stay here and just go scuba diving all day with you...what do you think?'

He hadn't encouraged her. Why tell a stranger that he wasn't only a scuba diver, either? Why tell a tourist he would never see again that he was actually living here because he'd pioneered a way of operating on the facial scarring of accident victims which minimised their scars often to near invisibility?

He thought back to last week, satisfied. Lasers were incredible things. Trevor Nolan, a forty-two-year-old wedding singer from Dakota, had grappled with his young son to prevent a firework going off in his face and the poor guy had taken the hit himself. After six months of surgery and a month of crowdfunding by his friends he come to him at the MAC for what all the medical journals were calling 'revolutionary treatment.'

Trevor had left with his chin almost the shade of the rest of his face, instead of raw red and stretched in scars. Best of all, he could sing for people again without it hurting.

'Mr Diver Man, come down here!'

Gabby was calling him from below. He stayed put. The sun at this time of the day was perfect. Not too hot. He liked to soak it up while he could, before he put his hospital scrubs back on.

Sebastian assumed most people visiting the island's clubs and bars and dive shops didn't even know the MAC was on the other side of it, and if they did most of them didn't know what happened there.

He always let word of mouth bring his clients in now. He wasn't famous on Gili Indah. He wasn't followed and he was barely recognised. It was too small an island and he was too out of context, he supposed—a world away from the Institute in Chicago and all those cameras.

He still had to be careful on the mainland of nearby Bali, though.

He'd left the hugely successful *Faces of Chicago* show back home. He'd left Klara behind, too, he told himself, furrowing his brow at the horizon. Now all that mattered was his team, and having his patients walking away looking and feeling better than when they'd arrived.

The speedboat was close now. A few faces stood out— locals, friends. And lots of new arrivals. But none for the MAC. *His* staff came in on *his* boat.

All but Dr Ricci, he remembered suddenly, raking a hand through his hair. She'd missed her transfer, which wasn't uncommon—the traffic on the mainland was a nightmare.

He stood, scanning the other boats around the bay. He'd been too swamped at work to search online and put a face to the name of his latest employee, but he knew she'd worked in trauma on deployment with the Army in Afghanistan, so she was likely looking to add a new scar treatment string to her bow.

He considered what it must be like to spend months in a war zone, seeing soldiers with their limbs blown to shreds. All those gunshot wounds, severed bones and bombs exploding...

Some of the things he'd had to fix himself had been far worse than Trevor Nolan's chin after his battle with a rocket in his backyard. But to be in a war zone—that was something else.

The boat jolted and he heard a tank flip downstairs. He shot back down the ladder. This woman, Dr Ricci, must be some kind of special breed. What was she looking for, exactly, here on such a remote island?

He set the tank upright again and watched Gabby make a show of resting her bare pink toes on it to keep it in place. Ketut threw him a look from behind the wheel, and Sebastian took a seat as far away from her as he could.

Was Dr Ricci running from the horrors of war and looking for peace, like he had been? But he'd been running from the media explosion after starring in the TV show and from the guilt that had racked him over what had happened to Klara. Hardly the same thing.

Sebastian realised he was scowling at the horizon, thinking about Klara again.

He couldn't have known what would happen after filming started. No one could have anticipated so many photographs, so many camera lenses zooming in on his every move, in and out of surgery. All those headlines and sub-headlines...the crazy stories people had sold or made up about them just to get their clicks in.

Letting cameras into his surgery had invited the whole damn media circus in—which had squeezed every last remaining shred of joy out of his relationship with Klara.

All she had ever wanted to do was be with the kids at her kindergarten school and live a simple happy life with him. She had been so broken by the invasion of her privacy, and everything people had said about them both as a couple, that at the end she'd left without saying goodbye.

He put a hand down to the ocean spray and let his

thoughts about her go—like he did every time he went diving. Diving was a workout for his brain…a place to switch off from other thoughts. It was only when he was on the surface that the memories came back.

He knew Klara wasn't in Chicago any more. She'd already got married—someone she'd met in Nepal. He didn't know where she was now, but he was happy for her. Sometimes.

Right now he would much rather be living here, somewhere beautiful, fixing Trevor Nolans and kids with burns the size of basketballs on their cheeks, than go back to having camera flashes and the paparazzi's car tyres screeching in his wake, and performing endless boob jobs in Chicago. Although he wished he could see his family more often—especially his brother Jared and Charlie… He smiled thinking of his nephew.

The tourist boat slowed. A line of excited people craned their necks from the roof to the turquoise shallows. Everyone was in awe of the colour of the water here.

A slender woman in a bright red sundress had her hand on her brown hair, trying her best to tame it, and a memory flickered across his mind.

He lifted his sunglasses and squinted to see better.

She was leaning on the railings now, elbows out. Her sundress was catching her ankles in the wind. He gripped the side of the boat even as Gabby tickled his calf with her toes. It looked *exactly* like her. Must be six or seven years ago now… A British woman dancing drunken pirouettes on the sand, back when he'd been here for the first time—long before he'd even had the idea to build the MAC.

What was *she* doing back here?

Mila's eyes followed the diver right until his boat rocked out of sight. His abs were like a digitally enhanced ad for a diving school. She'd seen men like that at military hospitals, trained for fighting but battered and blue. Never this colour.

The diver's skin was a warm shade of caramel—as if he'd earned that tan with a life outdoors over a long, long time.

Her boat bobbed in the shallows as people leapt from the sides onto the sand. Mila followed, taking the ladder down. She hoisted her sundress further up her legs as an eager Indonesian boy no older than eight or nine helped her down into an inch of crystal-clear water.

'Terima kasih!' she told him. She'd already mastered a few basics.

The warmth of the sand rose to meet her toes in her flip-flops and she breathed in the scent of the air. Flowers… maybe jasmine…or was that an incense stick? The local market on a dusty path ahead told her she wasn't exactly in Robinson Crusoe territory.

Mila stood still. When was the last time she'd stood in the ocean? Probably back in Cornwall, about twenty years ago. She'd been with her mum and Annabel, and they'd bought Cornish pasties and prodded jellyfish in the sand. That had been a good day.

'Can I help you, miss? You need room?'

The kid in front of her now looked about seventeen, and he seemed to want to deny her the pleasurable personal moment of feeling her feet in the ocean for the first time in twenty years. He waded over purposefully and helped drag her case away from the shore.

She studied his tattooed wrists as he flashed a ring binder at her, showing coloured photographs of accommodation options. 'Oh, no, thank you. I have a hotel for tonight.'

'I have better one!' He flicked to a page with a photo of a shack on it. It looked basic, to say the least.

'Tomorrow I move to the MAC,' she explained, wading onto the beach. Tiny bits of coral prodded at her heels and toes.

Mila took her case back quickly. She had probably divulged too much information already. It was never good to trust strangers on a first encounter unless in a medical situation. Besides, she already knew Dr Sebastian Becker kept a low profile.

He encouraged his staff to do the same.

For protection, when it comes to our clients' anonymity.

He'd written that in a welcome email.

'Taxi?' she said in vain as a horse and cart trotted past her on the dusty street.

'Watch out!'

The teenager was back. He caught her elbow and yanked her to the side of the path just as another horse and cart rattled past at full speed. It almost struck her.

'Thank you, I'm fine.'

She picked up her fallen sunglasses. She wanted to tell him she could take care of herself but she refrained. He was only being chivalrous and she *had* been caught off-guard. She hadn't slept in almost two days.

Frazzled and sweating, she wheeled all her worldly belongings along the thick, dusty, potholed concrete that constituted a street.

Street food vendors were mixing noodles and jabbing straws into coconuts. Girls were swigging beer, pedalling bicycles in bikinis. The salty air was already clinging to her forehead. No one else offered to help her but that was OK. She'd done this before, in worse places. She just hadn't imagined the island would be this crowded...

Through the jet lag she remembered that she'd come in on a tourist boat, to the tourist side of Gili Indah. The MAC was on the west side. That part of the island was exclusive territory—just for patients and staff. She couldn't wait to dive into a swimming pool. She just had to wait until tomorrow...

Mila was about to hail the approaching horse and cart when a noise from the shore made her stop in her tracks. A shriek. Someone thrashing in the waves.

Squinting through the throng, her eyes fell on a girl a few metres behind the speedboat. She saw the yellow dive boat she'd seen before, from the water. Something must have happened.

'Snake!' Gabby screamed. 'It bit me! Ow, it hurts! Sebastian, help!'

'OK…it's OK. Let's get you back to shore.'

Sebastian looped an arm around her waist, turning his head in all directions, looking at the shallows. Where was the snake?

One minute Gabby had been heading back from the boat right next to him, after their second dive, the next she'd been toppling over in her half-undone wetsuit.

He made a grab for her mask and fins before they were swept out of reach, and threw them to another guy in their group.

'There it is!' Gabby sounded horrified.

He followed her pointing finger to the thin, yellow and black stripy body of a sea snake. It wriggled past him, heading for the deep beyond the reef.

Sebastian tried to wade faster. Gabby's face had turned pale. She wasn't making this up.

'Where did it bite you?' He kept his voice controlled, not wanting to panic her. Her head was heavier every time it landed on his shoulder.

'On my foot…my foot!' She was sobbing now, barely able to breathe.

'Ketut!' he yelled.

Gabby's legs seemed to crumple underneath her on the sand. He caught her before she could fall and lowered her gently to her back on the sand. She was whimpering now, trying to clutch at his arm. Her face was almost white.

A frenzy of people crowded around. Some were even snapping the scene with their cameras.

'Get back,' he ordered gruffly, as the familiar surge of

contempt for this kind of privacy invasion consumed him. 'Ketut!' he called again.

But someone else was already sprinting over.

'I'm a doctor—how can I help?'

The lady in red from the boat. The British tourist. It was definitely her…the woman from a few years ago. Speechless, he watched as she dropped to her knees.

'Snake bite,' she noted out loud, before he could explain. She put a hand to Gabby's ankle.

'Yeow!' Gabby clamped her hand around his wrist in a death grip.

Easing her fingers away, he helped his new partner adjust the bitten leg and support it on an upturned rock.

'We need pressure immobilisation,' she told him—as if he didn't know.

She started pulling things from her bag. Her sunglasses were pushed high on her head, sweeping back the kind of thick honey-brown hair he'd bet smelled good wet, right after she showered…

He caught himself, racking his brain for her name.

They hadn't done more than flirt a little back then. If his memory served him right there had been no chemistry between them whatsoever. She'd been a drinker, he hadn't, and she'd been intent on partying every night until she dropped.

But he never forgot a face. Had she really forgotten his?

'Do you know what to do?' she asked him.

Her wide-set eyes were a vivid blue in the sun, over high, freckled cheekbones.

'There's anti venom at the clinic,' he said.

'At the Medical Arts Centre?'

He lost his voice for a second. Up close, he smelled the coconut waft of her sunscreen.

'No, the other one—the Blue Ray Medical Clinic on the strip.'

Didn't she recognise him at all? Was it even her? But,

yes, it had to be. Her eyes, her face…they were all so familiar. He just couldn't remember her name.

'What will you do to me?' Gabby cried out.

'You need to keep as still as you can,' he said. 'Stop the venom circulating.'

The Brit…what *was* her name?…raised an eyebrow. Her blue eyes gave his body a swift appraisal in his wetsuit.

'You're a doctor?'

'You could say that.' He watched her pull an elastic bandage from her bag. 'The clinic's next to the Villa Sunset Hotel. It wasn't here before.'

'Before…?'

Her hands worked quickly, wrapping the elastic bandage around Gabby's leg with deft efficiency, starting from her toes, moving swiftly up to her thigh.

He sprinted to the restaurant right by the harbour. Their fence was made up of pieces of piled-up driftwood—just the right size for a splint.

'Use this,' he said, dropping back down next to her.

'Perfect—thanks.'

She was impressively fast. She *looked* like the girl he'd met before, but she sure as hell wasn't *acting* like her. Her red dress was catching dirt but she didn't look as if she cared or even noticed as they loaded a sobbing Gabby into the back of a cart. His eyes lingered on the curve of her shoulder as one strap fell down to her arm. She caught his eye and yanked the strap up.

'Come with me, *please*,' Gabby begged him.

The Brit answered instead. 'I'll go with you. We need to take the pressure off your leg as much as possible in this cart, though. Can you work with me on that?'

'I'll try.'

'I'll help you.'

She was good with her patient. Sebastian helped her arrange the leg, waiting for any hint that she might remember him.

'The driver knows where to go,' he told her. 'I'll follow on my bike. Tell them I sent you.'

'And your name is…?'

'Sebastian Becker?' He said it like a question as he slid the lock shut at the back of the cart.

Her blue eyes grew wide in shock. 'Dr… Becker?'

Finally. He opened his mouth to say something about the coincidence of another encounter all these years later. But he couldn't exactly admit to her that he'd forgotten her name.

It was only after she'd disappeared in a cloud of dust that he finally remembered it.

Annabel.

CHAPTER TWO

'SHE NEEDS ANTI-VENOM,' Mila called out, hurrying through the doors of the Blue Ray Clinic.

She flashed her security card at a man in the small, busy lobby. The bearded Indonesian man in his mid to late fifties sprang into action. The name badge on his white coat read *Agung*.

In a white room off the hallway, the tiled floor squeaked under her flip-flops. 'Sea snake,' she told Agung. He was already observing the bandage. 'She needs anti-venom. Dr Becker will be here any second. I'm Dr Mila Ricci—I'm new at the MAC. I just met him at the harbour.'

That scuba diving poster model in a wetsuit—that *doctor*—was the surgeon she'd soon be working with.

She was still in shock.

She closed the door behind them, noting the fresh paint on the cream walls and the Indonesian art hanging by the window. A palm leaf tapped at the glass from outside.

They helped the still dripping girl to a bed and onto fading sheets. Her breathing was laboured—probably due to her writhing around, not to the venom spreading too much. But then, she hadn't stayed very still in the jostling cart, even with Mila's assistance.

A rush of air-conditioning blasted her face as the door swung open to admit Dr Becker. 'Agung, how's she doing?'

He was pulling on a white coat, arm by long, bulked-up

arm, and striding towards the bed in black sports sandals. He was every bit as striking in the white coat as he was in a wetsuit.

He made to pass her, then stopped, placed a hand on her shoulder. 'Thank you for what you just did.'

'You're welcome.'

The words came out smoothly, calmly, as she'd intended, but she didn't feel calm. The look he was giving her now had suspicion all over it.

'Put this on,' he told her, throwing her a white coat from a hook on the wall. 'Nurse Viv is with another patient, so I hope you won't mind staying a bit longer. I need you to cut the suit,' he said, motioning to the pair of scissors on the tray.

Mila snipped carefully at the girl's wetsuit and discarded the flimsy material. She was following commands when she'd usually be giving them, but that was OK. She wasn't a hundred miles away from base in Ghazni. No one had been blasted by shrapnel from a rocket-propelled grenade, There were no wounded soldiers crying out for attention. There was only this one girl…right here, right now.

She put a gentle hand to Gabby's leg and soothed her as Dr Becker administered the anti-venom and the meds kicked in.

Agung's pager made a sound. 'Excuse me, Dr Becker… Dr Mila,' he said.

He left the room and instantly the air grew thicker. Sebastian was appraising her again.

'Mila?' he said in a surprised voice, as soon as it was only the two of them. He stepped towards her.

'She looks much better,' she told him, looking up to see his eyes narrow. 'I think we got to the bite just in time. She just needs to rest now.'

He folded his arms, towering over her. He must be at least six foot two inches to her five foot three.

'Why Mila? I thought your name was Annabel?'

All the breath left her body.

'I couldn't remember at first…back there. It was at least six or seven years ago, right? Before this clinic or the MAC existed,' he said. 'You were late to our snorkelling party—you'd had too much to drink, remember?'

He grinned, laughing at a memory that wasn't hers.

Tears stung her eyes. She could have wrestled him to the ground when he reached for her wrists, but his long, tanned fingers ran gently over her scars and she felt bolted to the floor.

He was turning her arms in the harsh overhead light, studying the faint silvery lines as if they were clues to a mystery game. 'You didn't have these before,' he said, frowning. 'What happened to you?'

She bit her cheeks as the tears threatened to spill over. *He'd met Annabel.* This must be the guy her sister had come back talking about all those years ago. Bas. Sebastian. It made sense now. Dr Sebastian Becker was Bas. And she had to work with him?

She had to set him straight. This was unbearable.

'I'm not…not who you think I am,' she managed. The room felt suddenly way too small. She took a step back, pulling her arms away. 'Dr Becker, I'm Dr Mila Ricci. I've come to work at the MAC for a while and learn your techniques. I would have met you earlier, but I missed my transfer. I apologise for the confusion.'

She watched him rake a hand through his hair as she struggled for composure.

He paced the room, then stopped. 'Am I going crazy here? I did meet you before, didn't I? Did you change your name?'

'I'm not Annabel,' she said through a tight throat. 'Annabel was my twin sister. She's dead, Dr Becker. She died three years ago. It was her you met—not me.'

* * *

The cat padded her way across the bar towards them, its black shiny fur glowing pink under the LED lights. Sebastian ran a hand along her soft back. 'I'm so sorry about the mix-up this morning,' he said to the woman in front of him, his newest albeit temporary employee.

He'd been thinking about her all day. He'd sent Mila to her hotel to get some sleep and had somehow kept things on schedule back at the MAC, even though his mind had been whirring. He'd even checked in quickly on Gabby, back at the Blue Ray, who was fine. She'd found the strength to ask for his number, but he had no intention of entertaining her now. He just wanted to clear things up with Mila.

'It's not your fault. It's a coincidence and a surprise, that's all. Annabel talked about meeting a guy called Bas—I just didn't put the pieces together.'

Mila's legs were crossed in his direction on the swing seat beside him.

'What's her name?' she asked, watching his fingers stroke the length of the cat's tail.

'This is Kucing. I found her when she was a kitten. Someone dumped her in the garbage can down by the bottle store. Nice, huh? She was in a real sorry state—weren't you, girl?'

Kucing rubbed her nose against his fingers and promptly sat down to lick her tail.

'She likes it here. The guys give her tuna from the can on Wednesdays.'

He watched Mila reached out a hand to rub the cat's ears. The scars across her wrists glinted in the light of the candle in a coconut shell.

'Why is she called Kucing?'

'It's Indonesian for cat.' He shrugged. 'We like to keep things simple around here.'

Reggae drifted in from the speakers outside on the palm trees. Ketut's wife, Wayan, slid two empty glasses across the bar towards him, followed by a jug of ice water. It wasn't a fancy bar, more a rustic boho shack, but it was usually quiet—which was why he liked it. He hoped Mila was OK. It was hard to gauge how his new recruit was really feeling about this mix-up.

'It was brief. Meeting your sister, I mean,' he said.

She nodded, her eyes still on the cat. It was surreal. She looked absolutely identical to Annabel. He still couldn't believe it. He didn't recall Annabel ever telling him she was a twin—not that they'd really spent much time together.

'How did she die? Is it OK if I ask?'

'She went out one night to a party,' Mila said slowly, without looking at him. 'She was driving our mum's car…'

'You mean she died in a car crash? I'm so sorry. Was she alone in the car?'

Mila stiffened, picked up her drink. 'I don't really want to talk about this now, if that's all right with you. I'm here to work, Dr Becker, to focus on what's here and now—not on what happened in the past. What's the deal with the Blue Ray Clinic, by the way? Do you work there too?'

'I drop by if I'm needed. And I've done some work on the place. It was more of a shack when I got here,' he said, admonishing himself for prying. 'Look, we don't have to talk about the accident if you don't want to.'

'Thank you.'

Mila had changed from the red dress into a long, pleated pale blue skirt and a low-cut white top. He assumed her slender frame would look good in most things—including an Army uniform. She had an air of sophistication about her, he mused. And a bluntness, too. It was unequivocally British—like her accent.

He'd only met her twin a few times when she was here, but Annabel had been very different. She had danced in a skin-tight dress and drunk tequila shot after shot, hogging the microphone on karaoke night. He couldn't picture *this* woman doing that, somehow.

He felt a slight awkwardness between them as she petted Kucing. 'You don't have to call me "Dr Becker", by the way, Sebastian is just fine,' he said, to break the silence.

'OK—Sebastian.' She smiled slightly, tucking her hair behind her ear. 'So, you also teach scuba diving? Sounds like you have a lot on your plate.'

'That's what happens, I guess, on an island. You kind of end up taking on a little bit of everything.'

He ordered them both a smoothie—the house speciality. He didn't think of his efforts at Blue Ray as anything different from his work at the MAC any more. He was just living his life, doing what was necessary to keep things moving.

He still harboured some small hope that one day Jared would leave Chicago and join him here, but that would mean the rest of his family giving up the show and all the fame that came with it.

His brother was a little different from him where that was concerned. Jared and his wife Laura hadn't come under half as much scrutiny as he and Klara had. He assumed that because they'd already been married a while they weren't as exciting. They had never been splashed on magazine covers or stopped for trick photos outside jewellery stores.

'From what I know about your background, I could probably learn some things from *you*, Dr Ricci,' he said now, shoving away the thought of the time he'd been stopped by someone pretending to be homeless just so that someone else could get a photo of him reportedly shopping for an engagement ring. Up to that point he hadn't even considered proposing to Klara, but the pressure from the public had been on after that.

'Call me Mila, please,' she said, scanning his eyes now with her vivid blue ones. 'What do you know about my background, exactly?'

'I know from your résumé that you risked your life in Afghanistan,' he said.

She looked vaguely amused. 'I was safe most of the time.'

'And I know you know your way out of an awkward situation.'

She paused, a half-smile still playing on her lips. 'Well, I'll let you think you know about me for now. So we don't make things even more awkward.'

Were they *flirting*? For a second it felt as if she was flirting with him. With any other woman it would already feel like a date.

'So, why did you sign up for the Army?' He poured ice water into her glass, watched Kucing nuzzle her chin and then snake around the coconut shell candle. 'Did you always want to end up out there in a combat zone?'

'I joined the Army reserve for money, plain and simple.'

She twirled the ice cubes in her glass. He noticed her nails—plain, neat, unpainted. Her earrings—tiny silver studs.

'I thought it would help me to pay for medical school. I was only twenty-four and my plans were rock-solid—you know what it's like when you're young.'

'Did you have any choice when you found out where you were going?' he asked curiously. He hadn't met too many women who'd spent so long in military service.

'I didn't question it. I knew what I'd signed up for. We trained for four months before we left for Afghanistan and I was sent to two forward-operating bases as part of a mobile surgical team. Straight in at the deep end.'

'You only trained for four months?'

She nodded. 'Four long months of saying goodbyes and firing hand grenades…'

Sebastian felt his eyes widen.

'You think I couldn't still fire a hand grenade if I really needed to?' she teased.

He found the idea vaguely arousing, somehow. He cleared his throat, took a sip of the smoothie Wayan had presented him with.

'Annabel was out of her mind when I told her they were

placing me close to the frontline,' Mila continued. 'We all thought I'd be on the base in Bagram—not some tiny outpost. On the plane it kind of hit me like a bomb—no pun intended… That's the only time I thought I might die out there.'

'How do you even train for something like that?' he asked, watching her lips close around the bamboo straw in her smoothie. She looked at him over the rim of her glass.

'We had to kick down doors, do escape and evasion stuff, urban combat manoeuvres—a lot of things that were probably unnecessary, now that I think about it.'

'Like the hand grenade lessons?'

She shrugged. 'Those actually came in handy. I just wanted to be the toughest soldier and the best trauma surgeon I could be—and it didn't feel like more than I could handle to be both those things. I enjoyed the training. I wanted to be the face of resilience and strength, you know? I wanted to be the one who could keep her cool in the middle of all that…' she paused. 'All that horror…all those soldiers with devastating wounds. So devastating, Sebastian. So pointless.'

'I can't imagine,' he said.

Her lips were pursed, as if she was trying not to let any more emotion than necessary escape with her words.

'Every patient that came to us was critical,' she said. 'I do miss that type of patient care sometimes. The teamwork out there is like nothing else I've ever experienced. The things you go through you're not going to go through anywhere else.'

He found he was listening intently, as if she was taking him on a journey. He almost forgot where he was.

'It's an adrenaline rush, you know? But you're still human at the end of the day. I exercised it out—all the excess trauma that felt like it was spreading from them straight into me. I ran miles on the treadmill every day to get it all out, but I still cried every night in the shower.'

Sebastian was silent. What the hell could he say?

'You never really stop seeing it,' she told him. 'I'm not going to lie to you: it took a lot to get over that stuff. But not as much as it took to get over my sister's death. I was home on leave when the accident happened, and after that I got out as soon as I could.'

Mila ran her hands through her hair, revealing those scars again. He didn't dare ask again how she'd got those; she'd recoiled from him in horror when he'd examined them before.

'Like I said, I'm here now to be *here*—present. I don't see why the past should affect what I'm doing,' she said, sitting up straighter.

He wondered if she really believed that.

'So, tell me something about *your* life, Dr Becker. Why did you move your skills so far away from Chicago and from the States in general?'

He sat back. He hadn't been expecting such directness. 'You don't read the news?'

'News always finds me eventually, if it's important.'

'Interesting perspective on communication,' he said dryly. She was fascinating. 'But, seriously, you never even looked me up on the internet after I hired you? You don't know about the infamous, record-breaking, highly rated— or should I say *overrated*—TV show *Faces of Chicago*? Or how the "scorned Becker brother" left town after only one season, all alone…?'

She slowly spun her glass on the bar, with one finger on the rim. 'I don't follow celebrity news or social media.'

'I don't have social media accounts any more,' he told her, wondering what it was, exactly, that was making him feel the need to earn her respect before he left this bar stool.

She met his eyes. 'I know about your work. I know you've spent three years revolutionising your facial scarring reduction procedure out here—mostly alone. I know your skills had brought unprecedented fortune to The Becker

Institute in Chicago even before the TV show brought you fame. Was it your father's practice?'

'Late father,' he said. 'He passed away.'

'I'm sorry.'

'Thank you.'

She didn't ask how, or when it had happened, but she looked for a moment as if she wanted to.

'If I'm honest,' she said, and sighed, 'a friend filled me in on some things about your personal life which may or may not be true... I always prefer to ask people about this sort of thing to their face, if I need to. I wasn't anywhere near a television when your show was on.'

'I'm sure you had better things to do than watch me and my brother performing tummy tucks on spoilt pop stars anyway.'

'I'm not sure that's true...' she said thoughtfully.

Kucing leapt back on the bar and padded straight towards Mila, almost knocking over her smoothie glass. She caught it deftly, avoiding any spillage.

'It would have been nice to switch off and see what else was happening out there in the world. Some nights the silence was worse than the sound of the guns firing.'

Not for the first time in her company, Sebastian found himself speechless.

'Sorry,' she said, shaking her head in bewilderment. 'Talking about this is a bit of a Pandora's box. I don't want you to think I'm always like this. I'm just tired. Back to you?'

He was stumped. There was a lot he wanted to say, but he didn't know where to start. So he just said, 'I very much look forward to working with you, Mila. I just hope the island and the MAC live up to your expectations.'

'I try not to have any preconceived expectations,' she told him. 'So... I'm guessing you really didn't like being on that show?'

Sebastian tipped the ice cubes in his glass to one side

and back again. She had a lot of questions. 'It wasn't so much the show I didn't like—more the way the media ate us up. They're vicious out there...hiding in the shadows, waiting to pounce.' He made his hands like a cat's paws and she smiled.

'I know a bit about people like that,' she said.

He hoped she wouldn't talk about Klara, but even if she knew anything about her she didn't ask.

'So you still take the high-paying clients if they seek you out here? The celebrities?' she asked.

'Yes. They like the luxury of the island. But I do also have plans for a place over in Bali—a wellness centre for trauma patients in recovery. Something a little less...expensive. We have to start reaching more people.'

'You seem to have things under control,' she said. 'Your brother Jared—is he involved here too?'

'He's still busy being a television star,' he said, hoping he didn't sound as if he begrudged his older brother the life he'd chosen in the spotlight. 'We should get a snack— I'm hungry.'

He ordered them chips, then moved the topic to a patient who was heading in for a routine penis enlargement. Anything seemed better than bringing up his family issues. They were small fry compared to what this woman had been through.

So she talked, and he listened, and Sebastian couldn't even remember when he'd met a woman quite like Mila. She was definitely going to keep him on his toes.

CHAPTER THREE

'I'M OPEN TO SUGGESTIONS, Dr Becker. What do you think might improve…this?'

The woman in the plush leather chair opposite them stretched out the skin on her cheeks with her fingers. Mila watched Sebastian push his glasses further up the bridge of his nose.

'Turn to the left, please,' he said. 'Now the right.'

Incense swirled from the polished window ledge of the cosy, bamboo-panelled consultation room. It floated about his thick dark hair as he studied their patient's face. Mila fought not to look too long at his handsome profile in the sunlight.

It was already a week since she'd first stepped through the high-arching, intricately hand-crafted doors of the Medical Arts Centre, and she'd been transfixed by everything in it ever since.

This facility was a world away from the Blue Ray Clinic, which she'd noticed still looked a little rough around the edges in places. Everything about the polished marble floors, the potted palms and golden vases spoke of peace and control. It was the least traumatic place for a trauma victim she'd ever seen. It was as if she'd fallen asleep in the back seat of a convoy truck, been pelted with an AK-47, and then woken up here.

Rachel, their bubbly radiology technician, who had a

penchant for wearing pink sandals around the place, had told her they hadn't remodelled the entire Blue Ray Clinic yet because Sebastian was funding everything himself.

'Rumour has it there are problems in the Becker family, and it all started with the show. Did you know his brother Jared has never even been out to visit the island?'

Mila had remained quiet—she wasn't about to join in gossip. But she had found something else the other woman had said rather intriguing:

'I heard that Dr Becker was so devastated about his ex-girlfriend after she left him that he used to fly out of here every weekend to go and try to find her.'

There was a lot of gossip going around this island about everything, she'd noticed. And she couldn't help wondering what was true about Sebastian and what wasn't. She'd enjoyed their chats so far—he was interested and interesting...certainly not the flashy ex TV star she'd imagined.

Sebastian was absently tapping a pen against the side of his black-rimmed glasses...clearly thinking. 'Have you considered a general lift instead of going under more knives?'

Their patient was a fifty-seven-year-old California-based criminal lawyer called Tilda Holt. She'd lost over one hundred pounds and needed some help smoothing things over. Tilda didn't like what she called her 'bingo wings', and even though she was already booked for a brachioplasty she was intrigued by the work other people were having done on the premises and had come to find out more.

'Can he give me a face that reflects my young soul, do you think, Dr Ricci? Or is that too much work?' Tilda was looking directly at Mila now.

'Dr Becker's work is some of the best I've seen,' she said tactfully. 'I think you can count yourself lucky you found your way here. How did you hear about Dr Becker's work, can I ask?'

Tilda was back to looking at him in admiration. 'I saw him on the television. I said to my husband, That's the guy for me. He can help me.' She took Sebastian's hand in hers across the table. 'You always had a way of really *seeing* people, Dr Becker, that's why people loved you on that show.'

Mila caught the flicker of embarrassment in Sebastian's eyes as he looked at her over his glasses. She smiled at him. She couldn't help a flutter of affection.

She'd noticed how he gave every consultation himself—in person or via video call. He went to the mainland a lot, too, for people who couldn't travel this far. He wanted to know everyone who walked through his door.

He must know his personality still counted for a lot, she thought, no matter how he appeared to dislike his own celebrity label. And he allowed these patients in, along with their money, because it was helping the island.

Sebastian was leafing through a brochure with Tilda. 'No filters necessary on your photos after this particular procedure. At least, I don't think so. How it works is we fire ultrasound energy into the muscles you'd usually get tightened in a face lift…here, here, here…so no knives and no needles.'

'No knives?'

'Absolutely zero. We get new collagen forming under smoother, brighter skin. Sometimes the cheekbones look more sculpted and defined. I had a patient last month email me to say she hadn't enjoyed wearing make-up for twenty years until she had this procedure.'

Tilda let out a groan. 'I used to love make-up.'

It amused Mila, the way Sebastian could turn these procedures into scenarios that sounded almost exciting. He knew just how to keep a patient's attention—maybe he'd honed that skill on television.

She'd been expecting to find this man a bit spoilt—arrogant, maybe, even flashy. She'd thought maybe he'd come with all the trimmings of a reality TV star. But he was none of those things, from what she'd seen so far. She thought of Annabel and wondered if her sister had felt this same attraction to him when they'd shared their brief encounter.

At the bar she hadn't asked him about what had happened between them. It had been too much even to think about it at the time, reminding her of Annabel and the accident.

There hadn't been time to talk privately since then either. Too many meetings, introductory briefings and shadowing surgical procedures. And in between all that calming breaks spent sipping green tea out in the sun with the staff.

It was beautiful here, and the patients were appreciative and relaxed after their treatments. It was everything she'd hoped for when she'd boarded that plane at a blustery Gatwick Airport. But it was a little unnerving that she was thinking so much about Dr Becker when he wasn't there—especially as he'd only been completely professional with her.

'So, these muscles come up here, and the brow comes up here, and the whole face and neck treatment takes about thirty minutes. It'll cost you less than surgery—a lot less.' Sebastian was back in his swivel chair. He was wearing blue sneakers with jeans under his white coat: trademark Chicago boy.

'Would *you* do it?' Ms Holt asked Mila.

'Only you can decide if you want this procedure, Ms Holt,' she said, blinking herself back to the moment, 'But I can assure you if you choose to do so you'll be in good hands.

'What happened to your arms, Dr Ricci?'

Tilda's question came out of the blue. The woman was studying her scars over the frangipani flowers and candles. Mila felt obliged to leave her wrists facing up on the desk, so Ms Holt could see them. It wasn't the first time she'd been asked about her scars.

'It was an accident,' she said simply. 'I don't really notice them now.'

OK, so that last part was a lie.

Tilda looked sympathetically at Mila. 'Can't you fix them? Someone like you? Can't *yo*u fix them, Dr Becker?'

Sebastian coughed and stepped in quickly, before Mila could even answer. 'I'm afraid our appointment's almost over, Ms Holt. I'd just like to add that with the ultrasound treatment there's no downtime at all—not like with surgery. You'll just look a little suntanned for an hour or so. But that's nothing new around here. We'll let you think about it.'

He stood and ushered her politely towards the door, talking about seeing her on the MAC's private beach in a few days' time for the sea turtle sanctuary fundraiser.

Why did he have to step in? Mila thought in annoyance. He wasn't her protector. She didn't need one.

She'd earned her high position in combat support hospitals, where she'd trained medics on the military camp in spite of her age. She'd even taught a fresh medical team to handle trauma victims her first time in command. In fact, she had excelled at everything she'd ever done—without any guy stepping in on her behalf.

Maybe she was being unfair... He probably assumed she was embarrassed whenever someone mentioned her scars because she hadn't elaborated on how she'd got them. Men often thought they had to protect her because of what she'd been through.

'So...'

Sebastian turned to her when Tilda Holt had gone. Sunlight was streaming from the window across the polished floor onto his sneakers. She was still a little annoyed with him...but he looked really, really good in those glasses.

For a second she thought he was going to come right out and ask her again how she'd got her scars. He must have been wondering ever since he'd first seen them, back when he'd thought she was Annabel. He probably thought she'd got them out on deployment—most people did. Would he ever imagine she'd got them trying to pull her twin sister through a smashed-in car windscreen?

She felt sick even thinking about it. She didn't want him to imagine that. He had his own clear picture of Annabel, whatever that entailed. She wouldn't ruin a nice image of her beautiful sister for anyone.

'Will we see *you* at Friday's fundraiser, Mila? We've got some pretty fun live music lined up. And the turtles could do with your help.'

She caught herself. 'Friday?'

'Yes—you didn't forget about it, did you?'

She wasn't about to tell him, but she *had* totally forgotten.

Sebastian's phone was buzzing on the desk. His brother's name flashed on the screen before he swiped up. 'If you'll excuse me?'

'Jared? Your brother?' she said, remembering how he'd never been to visit—if indeed that rumour was true.

'More like my nephew Charlie on Jared's phone.' He touched his hand lightly to her shoulder. 'I really do have to take this. It's his birthday and he needs to tell me all about his presents—you know how it is.'

He left the room, chatting to his nephew in an excited voice she knew he probably reserved only for him, and Mila felt her unfortunate soft spot for her current employer soften just a bit more.

'When he gives you that look you can see in that moment *exactly* what millions of viewers saw, watching Dr Sebastian Becker on television,' Rachel sighed. 'Do you know the look I mean? You've seen it, haven't you?'

Sebastian stopped in the shadows at the sound of his name. He couldn't see their faces, and they couldn't see him. But Rachel was what he would call *swooning*. Mila was saying nothing.

'Watch out, Dr Ricci! The Becker boys can change your face and steal your heart,' Rachel enthused, gesturing to Mila's heart with a glass of wine.

They were at the turtle fundraiser, standing on the MAC's beach in the light of a flaming torch stuck in the sand.

'What did I steal?' Sebastian knew his voice would make them both turn around.

'Oh, God.' Rachel covered her face with her hands. 'I'm sorry,' she mumbled through her fingers.

Mila was biting back a smile.

'It's OK, I promise not to steal your heart, Rachel,' he teased, but he couldn't help his eyes lingering on Mila and her curves in a blue dress which swooped at the back in a low V.

'I should go and check on the turtle cake,' Rachel muttered, gathering up her skirt to walk hurriedly in the direction he'd come from.

In the next moment it was just Mila in that dress, and him, and the buzz of the fundraising crowd behind them.

'Catching up on the island gossip, are you?' he asked pointedly. 'I thought you weren't into that.'

'I think Rachel likes to talk.' Mila shot him a sideways glance. 'I was put in an involuntary listening position.'

He swiped up a seashell and led them both down the beach, turning to look over his shoulder and see Rachel watching them from the buffet table.

'She told me she watched every single episode of *Faces of Chicago* before applying to the MAC—all in the name of research,' he disclosed.

'Of *course* for research,' Mila replied, a smile playing on her lips.

She waded out a foot away from him into the shallows, bunching up her dress. He watched the breeze playing with her hair and the silky blue fabric as she inhaled long and deep with her face to the sky. She looked as if she was breathing in life from the water. He wondered if she'd ever been diving.

'So, I heard your big speech earlier,' she said, when she had taken her moment. 'You've been raising tiny turtles till they're big enough to thrive around the coral which you are regenerating with electromagnetic technology? Is that right?'

Her accent was so great when she said, *'Is that right?'* He liked a British accent. Annabel's had been the same, but again it struck him how Annabel had been so very different from Mila.

'That's correct. We're hoping for seventy per cent regeneration in the areas where we've invested. It's early days yet, but we'll keep on monitoring it.'

'Is there *anything* on this island you're not involved in?' she teased, wading with him towards a wooden swing.

'Maybe a couple things,' he consented. 'There's always something to do.'

He held the swing so she could sit on the polished driftwood—and so he'd be able to admire the slope of her shoulders and the backless cut of her dress from behind when he pushed her. He had the swing put here—had even done most of the work himself, with a little help from Ketut. He wouldn't tell Mila how he'd sat here most nights before the MAC had even been built, from sunset into dusk, trying to count the reasons not to jump on a plane, to go and look for Klara.

'Most things are a team effort in a place like this,' he told her, pushing her out on the swing and watching her toes skim the surface. 'And it has to start with ocean conservation—that's what keeps us all afloat on this island.'

'No pun intended?'

'None whatsoever.'

He let the waves lap his calves as she dug her feet into the sand again. The wind picked up strands of her hair and they tickled his face as he tightened his fists around the swing's ropes.

'Have you ever been diving, Dr Ricci?' he asked over her shoulder. Her hair smelled good…like the incense that swirled on the MAC's reception desk.

'No,' she answered on a breath. 'Not in the ocean. Describe it. The feeling—not the technique.'

He considered this. 'It's like a cranial cleanse,' he said, loosening his fists around the ropes. 'When you're down there it's possible to completely switch your mind off. You have no internal chatter—nothing pressing, at least. It's just you and the sound of your own breath in your ears.'

'It sounds magical. Like the very best kind of meditation.'

'It is. Close your eyes.'

One strap of her dress tumbled down over her shoulder in the breeze. She left it there and obeyed him.

You're drifting with the current,' he told her. 'Like you're breathing with the earth itself. In. Out. In. Out. You don't need your hands much, just your eyes, and it's all about controlling your breathing.'

'You're really selling this to me,' she said after a moment.

Her eyes were still closed and her head was tilted back slightly, almost against him, not quite touching.

'Maybe I'll try it…'

'I'll take you,' he told her. It surprised him how much he wanted to show Mila Ricci all the things he loved most about the ocean. 'I can't believe in all your Army training, you never went scuba diving.'

'I did dive a couple of times in a lake, but I was always too busy up on the surface throwing hand grenades to put it into practice in the ocean.'

She was smiling as she turned the swing around to face him, making the ropes twist tightly above her. Her bare legs were locked between his for a second, or maybe he pulled her there…he wasn't sure…

'Hello? Dr Becker! Hello!'

A man with blue hair was waving a coconut at them from the shoreline.

Sebastian released the swing's ropes and Mila was almost thankful for the interruption. Sebastian had placed her under some kind of spell and she'd been momentarily transfixed by what he was saying and his presence in general.

She was supposed to be shaking off this attraction to him—they had to work together. Not to mention his previous…whatever it had been…with Annabel. But it was pretty hard to stay away when he had that…*thing*… Rachel had been talking about. Magnetic appeal.

The man with blue hair greeted Sebastian with what she could only describe as reverence and seemed not even to notice her presence. She recognised him from the patient files: Hugo O'Shea. He must have just arrived for his treatment. She believed it was a routine penis enlargement.

According to Rachel, the man was a renowned internet gossip queen. 'He loves gossip more than I do,' she'd told Mila, which Mila found hard to believe.

Hugo's board shorts were a patchwork of colourful bananas. 'Beautiful evening! I'm sure the turtles are as grateful for your work as I am, Dr Becker.' He raised an eyebrow at Mila.

'Apologies, Hugo, this is Dr Mila Ricci,' Sebastian said smoothly. 'She'll be with you during your surgery.'

Hugo swivelled his entire body towards her, extending a hand with a flourish. 'I don't mind a woman's touch,' he said as she shook it. 'But I think we both prefer Dr Becker's—am I right?'

He winked and leaned into her, fanning his face.

Mila smiled politely.

'Can I get a photo of you both? Just the one? The moon behind you is perfect.'

'No, not tonight,' Sebastian said curtly, before she could reply, and turned to leave. 'Enjoy your night, Hugo.'

Mila considered letting Sebastian go alone, and ending their conversation entirely, but she realised she wasn't done yet. She shouldn't let a pushy patient come between them—that much she knew—but it was something else that spurred her legs into action and made her follow him away from the crowd, up the rocks to the viewpoint.

This side of the island was quieter. The waves lapped at the rocks with big, loud sloshes and ahead the black night sea was like a blanket rolled out by the mountains in the distance.

'You really don't like anyone taking your photo, do you?' she said cautiously, lowering herself to the sandy rocks beside him. Up here, they were safe from prying eyes on the beach. She knew that was what he was most afraid of.

'O'Shea signed an NDA,' Sebastian said. 'He knows we don't let cameras in the MAC.'

Mila pulled her knees to her chest. 'Is this about what happened in Chicago?' she probed gently. 'I know you were stalked by the paparazzi. But I don't know the exact details…'

'They followed me and Klara everywhere—relentlessly,' he told her. His jaw was clenched now, his shoulders stiff and tense, as if even the memory was painful to contain. 'They caught her getting out of the car once, outside the Valentine's Gala on Lakeshore Drive. It was windy, and Klara's dress was—unfortunately—blown into a highly compromising position. The paps were all over it: zooming in, pointing out all the things you wouldn't want anyone pointing out. You haven't heard all this from anyone else?'

Mila put a hand to her mouth, shaking her head. The humiliation. She couldn't bear it. The poor woman…

'It was the worst possible outcome for a kindergarten teacher,' he continued.

'She was a teacher?'

'We were different,' he admitted. '*Very* different. I guess I liked it that she wasn't part of my world. I met her through my nephew Charlie. I went to collect him from school one day. Klara was there, stacking all these tiny plastic chairs…'

He trailed off, as though he realised he was telling her too much.

'Some of the kids' parents got together…made a huge deal out of the photo,' he said. 'They made out she was unfit to be around their kids. She *loved* those kids,' he stressed. 'They were her whole world. She was devastated. Then one publication…' he paused to sit up and make quotation marks with his fingers '"…*revealed*" that she was seeing another guy, which made it worse. He was a colleague—the principal of the kindergarten—but they printed photos of them talking outside the school. His wife got all suspicious, and then she was dragged into it…'

'This is horrifying!' said Mila.

He nodded slowly, his eyes on a night dive boat chugging out into the blackness.

'The principal offered her a sabbatical, to get away from it all. I quit the show. I thought maybe I'd go away with her, but she wanted to go alone. She got a volunteer position at some school in Thailand, deleted all her social media accounts, changed her number… She wouldn't even see me before she left.'

Mila pulled her eyes away from his biceps as he leaned back on his elbows with his face to the sky. 'Not at all?'

'Not even to say goodbye. I guess she thought I might show up with a bunch of photographers behind me. I couldn't really blame her.'

'But you had no closure?'

She realised this was probably getting far too personal now, but she couldn't help wanting to know. She would rather hear the truth from him than some rehashed version of the story on the rumour mill.

Mila remembered now how Rachel had told her he'd used to fly from Bali every weekend to try and find Klara. She didn't ask if it was true, and Sebastian didn't mention it, but the look on his face told her that he must have really loved this woman.

She felt a flicker of envy strike unannounced at the

thought. She hadn't ever loved anyone like that—she might not *ever* love anyone like that.

'I guess I found closure here,' he said. 'I brought a skeleton team out with me and we worked bit by bit on renovations at the Blue Ray while the MAC was being built. I signed up to teach people to dive, set up the turtle foundation with Neesha and her husband—you'll meet them later—and spent a lot of time just getting to know the locals. That's important in a place like this. We had to ease our way in slowly on the island…build the trust. Then we opened the doors to the MAC and it's been non-stop since then, pretty much.'

'And what about the show? What happened when you quit?'

Sebastian bristled, once again examining the distant fishing boats. 'I half expected Jared to call it quits too, and follow me out here. He saw what I went through with Klara, and he knew they could have done the same to him and Laura—that's his wife.'

'Why didn't they?'

He shrugged. 'They were married, they were stable—influencers for the perfect family life. Laura has a cooking blog and she does a podcast for mums. Maybe that's not so titillating for readers? I don't know. You can't tell who they'll make their next target, or what lies they'll choose to spread, but I guess they chose me and Klara because we were younger, we went out more—we gave them more chances to pair their headline-grabbing stories with photos. They took *so many* photos!'

Mila was shaking her head, still hugging her knees. This was all news to her, and she wondered what it must have been like for him and Klara, living in the eye of a media storm. She supposed it wasn't dissimilar to being in Afghanistan in some ways—living in fear, priming herself for things that might not even happen.

'The network wanted to try another season,' he continued. 'They found a replacement surgeon, so Jared wouldn't have to, and threw more money at us. They basically made it impossible for him to leave. The show took off again without me, and Chicago's media found something else to do instead of ramming their camera lenses into my business. Life goes on.'

He tossed a pebble over the rocks, dragged a hand through his hair and shot her a sheepish smile.

'I don't know why I'm boring you with all this, Mila. It's not exactly a life-threatening issue.'

'You're not boring me. It's nice to get to know you,' she said truthfully. 'The man behind the surgical mask.'

She watched the way his shoulders relaxed suddenly, as if in relief.

'What does the future hold for you, then?' she pressed. 'Do you want to stay here for ever? Don't you want a family of your own?'

He turned to her. 'Why can't I do that here?'

Mila paused. For some reason she hadn't expected that. 'I can imagine there would be a lot to inspire kids growing up here...' she told him carefully, and realised she was picturing it herself now.

A future here, teaching kids how to love the ocean, seeing them running around the island barefoot, taking reading classes on the sand... That all seemed pretty good to her, even though she'd decided a long time ago that she was never having children.

'There would be worse places to raise a family, don't you think?' he asked.

'I don't know... I don't really think about raising a family anywhere.'

He studied her with interest for a moment. She was ashamed to admit it, but she was afraid to have a child herself. What if she lost it or something happened to it...? Or what if something happened to the father? She couldn't bear the thought of enduring that kind of emotional loss a second time round.

'Well, I'd rather do it here than in Chicago,' he told her. 'I'm not saying I never go back there to visit—in fact I'm heading back soon for my mother's birthday. But, between you and me, I never wanted to do that show in the first place. The further I am away from all that now, the better.'

Sebastian's shirt was open…four, maybe five buttons. It was the most she'd seen of him outside his scrubs since the last time they'd talked properly, like this. The breeze was teasing his thick brown hair and she wondered momentarily what it might be like to touch it.

'Why did you do the show then?' she asked.

'Mom wanted it—she thought it was something that our father would have done if he'd still been here. Jared wasn't sure, but he saw the potential for attracting new clients. It was closer to home than my idea anyway…which was to set up this place here.'

He gestured around them.

'This place was always my passion—not theirs. It was on hold for a long time while the show was taking up all my time. I wanted to quit as soon as they started sensational-ising everything. We all knew Dad wouldn't have wanted *that* kind of attention on the institute—all those cameras that never turned off, the ones that started following me and Klara home. But it took that photo getting out for me to quit for good. Maybe Klara thought I'd quit too late.'

He picked up a stone and smoothed it between his fingers.

'She wouldn't have wanted to stay here anyway. She was always a city girl, really. And I guess this place was always going to steal me away, sooner or later. I mean—look at it.'

He gestured at the sweeping ocean ahead of him, then turned to offer her his full attention.

'When are we going to find the time to take you on your first ocean dive, huh?'

Mila took the opportunity he was giving her to change the topic, and soon they'd both lost track of time talking about manta rays and shipwrecks, and Charlie's school projects, and their very different school days, their very different preferences in clothing back in the nineties, when they'd taken their boards for Surgical Critical Care certification...and how they'd both somehow grown up having never seen *Star Wars*.

Sometimes Mila saw Annabel in her mind's eye, sitting there with them on the lookout, daring her to ask Sebastian what had happened between them when she was here.

Why couldn't she do it?

Mila knew why. She just found it hard to admit. It was the same reason something prickled inside her when he spoke about his past with Klara.

She was starting to really like this man. And it frightened her.

CHAPTER FOUR

'YOUNG GIRL, EIGHT years old.' Dr Fatema Halabi looked harried. 'We're vaccinating for rabies, but she's going to need more than a few stitches. We brought her straight here from the Blue Ray.'

Dr Halabi was a new recruit on the MAC's medical residency training programme. She'd done three years of general surgery in a practice in Charlotte, North Carolina, and now she was filling in with general duties around her plastic surgery training under Dr Becker's guidance.

She'd wheeled this patient into the light, airy, jasmine-scented treatment room before Mila had even pulled on her gloves. The unfortunate dog-bite victim was a French tourist—Francoise Marchand. Her mother was close behind.

Mila peeled back the huge bandage that was struggling to soak up the blood and surveyed the damage. She saw immediately the lacerations to the child's nose and lips. It looked pretty bad, but not as bad as she'd anticipated... considering the last dog bite she'd had to treat.

'How big was the dog that bit you?' she asked the little girl.

'It was some kind of Alsatian—big, very huge!' her mother cut in, in broken English. Her chin wobbled, as if she was struggling not to cry as Fatema applied fresh cloths to the wound. 'The crazy dog! It was lunging at her!

It should have been tied up! What is wrong with this place? It's just not safe for children here…'

'Mrs Marchand, I can assure you the island *is* safe,' Mila informed her, wondering if the statement was indeed correct. 'The dog *should* have been tied up, I agree, but we're here now. We're going to help Francoise, OK?'

Francoise sniffled, watching Fatema, who was the picture of calm. Mila knew she had to stay the same—as much for this mother as for her child, who was still conscious and in pain. Francoise's long blonde hair was matted with blood. So was her watermelon-patterned T-shirt. She was being braver than her mother, though.

'Francoise didn't m-mean to upset the d-dog,' Mrs Marchand stammered, clutching the side of the bed. 'She was just trying to get to the puppies. The mother dog must have thought she was too close… She just went for her… There was nothing I could do… This island is *not* safe!'

Mila put a hand to her shoulder and led her to the leather chair in a corner of the spacious room. It all made sense now, she thought with a frown. Approaching a mother dog and her new puppies without the owner's consent was never a good idea. This might have happened anywhere.

'This is not your fault, OK?' she said, although it wasn't true. 'I need you to stay calm, for Francoise's sake.'

The frazzled-looking woman swiped at her watery blue eyes. Mila knew it was imperative she stay calm. Her daughter was absorbing her panic like a sponge and amplifying it.

'Maybe you'd like to wait outside? We'll come and get you when we're done.'

Mila walked Mrs Marchand to the door. She needed to focus. The periorbital oedema was obvious around the girl's left eye—severe bruising that must have come from her struggles. She'd noticed lacerations to the soft tissue around her upper lip too, and to the skin across the lower left jawbone. Hopefully there wouldn't be any nerve damage.

Fatema excused herself and Rachel ran the X-rays.

Mila found she was waiting for Sebastian. His trademark treatment would be needed here. The new revolutionary thread dissolved faster in the skin, meaning there was no need for removal and less visible scarring on the lips, face, or mouth. Francoise and her mother likely didn't know how lucky they were that this had happened here. Not that she should be using the word *lucky*, really.

'You're being so brave,' she soothed Francoise, and the kid almost smiled—before wincing again in pain. She was handling the injections and the clean-up well, thank goodness.

Mila knew that dog bites accounted for thousands of facial injuries every year, and that over half the victims were children. She'd seen a few dogs around the island. She'd never thought to fear them.

She studied the X-rays on the computer monitor, but she couldn't help the flashbacks. Last time she'd dealt with a dog-bite it had been even worse than this. The German Shepherd had been terrified when they'd found it. It had been chained to a fence at a tiny military outpost. His paw had been a bloody mess, slit by razor wire.

He'd lunged as they'd approached the body of his owner—an Afghan officer who'd been shot in the back. She could still see his face, and the dog, too. The poor thing must have been there a while, listening to the blasts and seeing the shrapnel raining down, watching his owner lose his fight for life just feet away. No wonder it had launched itself at them and almost torn her colleague Neil's face off.

'Are you OK?'

Mila looked up from the screen with a start. Sebastian was looking at her strangely. She hadn't heard him come in. He was clean-shaven, wearing a red shirt and jeans with black sneakers.

'I'm fine,' she answered, though she knew her heart had sped up.

He pulled on a white coat and she caught a whiff of sun-

screen and a new cologne she'd never smelled on him before. She briefed him quickly on the situation, noting how
her palms were clammier than they had been before he'd
walked in.

She resented this sudden rush of nerves at performing
the revolutionary treatment Dr Becker had perfected. This
would be her first time using the lasers, but it was him more
than the notion of performing that unsettled her.

'I have it under control,' she told him, looking him square
in the eyes.

Of course Mila was in full control. But Sebastian kept
throwing her speculative looks, as if he was monitoring her
mood as well as her capabilities.

An ER doctor over at the Blue Ray could stitch up a
wound, maybe even conceal it pretty well, but it took a surgeon's work to stop a person living with noticeable scars
for the rest of their life. She had to block him out—or at
least pretend she wasn't so damn attracted to the man that
she physically felt his eyes on her wherever she moved in
the room.

Mila woke with a jump. 'No, no, no…' she muttered to herself, reaching for her phone. It was only midnight, but she'd
had the dream again. She knew she wouldn't be able to get
back to sleep now.

Flustered, she lay back down under the fan, trying to
let the cooling air work its magic, but images were coursing through her brain at a million miles an hour, as usual.

She squeezed her eyes shut. No, she couldn't bear it any
longer.

Wearily she threw back the cotton sheets, splashed some
cool water on her face in the bathroom. Looking at herself
in the mirror, she let out a long sigh. *Why* was she still having the dream?

She pulled on a dress over her underwear and stepped out
onto the porch. The moon and the stars were bright above

the waving palm trees. She considered lying in the hammock there, trying to go back to sleep out there in the safe confines of the MAC's staff quarters. But maybe a short walk would clear her head.

She slipped into her sandals and set off into the warm, muggy night, taking the path around the MAC's grounds.

The dream played on in her head, no matter how she tried to block it by appreciating the island scenery. It never got boring to her—the mountains glowing in the moonlight, the twinkling lights on the bobbing boats, the gentle lap of the waves on the shore. But the dream was a nightmare every time. It threw her right back to the night of the accident. There was Annabel, slumped over the steering wheel.

Mila stopped at the swing in the water, settled on the heart-shaped seat. She couldn't even stop the dream invading her memories now that she was awake.

In reality, on the night it had happened, Mila had known she was going to be too late to help her twin the second she'd seen her—maybe even before that. She'd sensed it somehow…the lack, the loss. Maybe that was why all her years of training had flown out the window and she'd frozen.

But in her dream Annabel's car was in Afghanistan, not rural England. Mila was heaving her out through the windscreen on her own, just as she had in real life. Rocket-propelled grenades blasted all around them. Fire blazed and flames lapped the blown-out windows of a tall building. Women were screaming in the dust from the fallout, staggering over to her with their wounded children, begging for help.

Mila couldn't save Annabel and she couldn't save anyone else either. It was stress, grief, guilt—all of it tangled up in one dream. She'd had it over and over again since she'd arrived here on the island.

The ocean helped a little, she thought, letting the ripples wash over her ankles. Maybe going on a dive with Sebastian would help even more. He seemed to think diving was like switching your brain off for a while. She could do with some of that. They hadn't managed to squeeze it in yet, though—they'd just been too busy.

Mila was walking back towards her room, thinking of Sebastian, when the sound of the dog barking close by made her jump. She was probably on edge, after what had happened to Francoise, but she hurried on, back towards the staff quarters, hoping it wasn't the same dog that had bitten the child.

Hadn't Sebastian said that someone had removed the animal and her pups and put them somewhere safe?

It couldn't be the same one, she thought. But it didn't stop a spike of adrenaline flooding her veins anyway.

The barking tore up the night again. At first she couldn't see a dog. Then it appeared on the sandy path, right in front of her. Mila stopped in her tracks. There was no one else around. The dog was big and stocky, speckled with black and white spots. It was staring straight at her, not barking any more, just looking at her inquisitively.

She took a tentative step towards it, taking a calm approach. 'Are you lost, buddy?' she asked softly. His tail was the longest she had ever seen. This was a real Bali Dog, she observed, wondering if it was friendly or not.

'Bruno!'

Mila spun around at the voice.

Sebastian was sprinting towards them. The dog met him in the middle of the path, jumping up at the Chicago Cubs sports shirt he was wearing, pressing his big paws against his chest. Sebastian was wearing board shorts and flip-flops too, looking the most casual she had seen him since the day they'd met. She couldn't help running her eyes up and down his body.

'Hey, Mila… Sorry, did he scare you? He got out through the gates—someone must have left them open by mistake.'

Someone?

'This is your dog?'

Mila smoothed down her dress, embarrassed suddenly by her un-brushed hair and just-out-of-bed look. She hadn't even cleaned her teeth. She watched Sebastian crouch to the ground and ruffle the big dog's fur lovingly. The dog repaid him by licking his cheek, arms and neck…everywhere he could reach.

'He's only with me till we find him a new home,' he disclosed, laughing at the dog's enthusiasm. 'Mila, meet Bruno. Bruno is…a handful. He wouldn't hurt anyone, though, if you were worried…?'

'I wasn't,' she said, maybe too quickly. 'What are you doing up so late?'

He stood up straight, fixed her with a piercing gaze. Damn him for looking so good—even at midnight.

'I could ask you the same thing,' he said.

'I couldn't sleep,' she confessed.

'Something on your mind?'

She nodded, and walked with him along the path, past the swaying palms. The sea was still swooshing behind them. His private home was only metres away, but she realised she had never seen beyond the tall wooden gates before. He kept them locked, as if his house was like some kind of ivory tower. Knowing a little about his past with the paps, she could understand why.

They stopped when they got to the now open gates. Bruno charged back inside and Mila caught a glimpse of Sebastian's place for the first time. Modest. Small. One level. No swimming pool. Nothing like what she'd been expecting. She'd thought it would be something more extravagant, reflective of his fortune, maybe.

He put his hand to her arm gently, looking at her in concern. 'You looked like you had something on your mind today, when that kid with the dog bite came in. Are you OK? We're not overworking you, are we?'

'No, Sebastian, I'm used to hard work.'

'Well, I *know* that.'

She looked down at his hand on her bare arm. The warmth of it flooded through her, and with it came a surge of emotion that threatened to turn into tears. She swallowed it back, looking away.

'It's just…sometimes I dream about her, you know… Annabel. It's the anniversary of her death, soon. I guess she's just been on my mind more often than usual. Don't worry, it won't affect my work. I hope it hasn't—'

'Hey.'

He caught her chin for a second, guiding her eyes to his. His features wore a look of pure concern now. She felt her lungs tighten and her breath catch.

'Mila, your work is not what I'm worried about.'

She fought not to let those tears spring from her eyes. She shouldn't have told him about the anniversary—it was way too personal. But it had just slipped out. She was so exhausted and his kindness was killing her.

'I want you to be happy here,' he added.

He looked as though her happiness was genuinely important to him. Mila's heart swelled just a little bit more.

'I love it here,' she told him honestly, pulling her eyes away. 'It's everything Annabel said it was. Better.'

For a moment she considered asking him what had happened between her sister and him. She should just ask him, so she could let it go either way. But it made her feel like a paranoid teenager, which was certainly not the impression she wanted to give him. Whenever she plucked up the courage to ask whether he and her twin had been intimate or not, the thought of the ensuing conversation, focused on Annabel and the way she'd died…because *she'd* been too frozen to help her…was just too much. She couldn't do it—not yet.

Behind him she could just make out the living room of his place. The decidedly non-ostentatious, cosy-looking room was lit up softly and the door was open, as if he'd left in a hurry to chase the dog. The huge window revealed some gym equipment, a black sofa, and a coffee table with a bottle of wine on it.

She could see two wine glasses, both empty. Her stomach started churning.

Had he been drinking with the same 'someone' who'd left the gates open?

'Do you want to come in? I have some tea…' Sebastian paused, looked a little sheepish, as if maybe he knew it wasn't very professional to be asking her that.

But now she just couldn't help wondering who'd been drinking wine with him so close to midnight. She felt him watching her, seeing her looking at his lit-up living room and the wine glasses. Embarrassment flushed her cheeks.

Why did she care if he'd had a guest over?

'I should probably be getting back,' she told him, hoping he wouldn't see how this was affecting her. 'See you at the MAC. Goodnight, Sebastian.'

CHAPTER FIVE

'HE WAS ADVISED against XXL, so he's going for extra-large,' Dr Halabi confirmed out loud, reading from the notes on the monitor.

Sebastian winked at his resident trainee. 'Extra-large is enough for this guy. If he had XXL he'd fall over,' he said, and Fatema giggled.

Hugo O'Shea was almost under. His eyelids were fluttering. His blue hair seemed even bluer in the surgery lights. The long, slick piece of silicone they'd insert into Hugo's currently not so prized manhood floated promisingly in a beaker of antibiotic solution next to them.

Sebastian had done this procedure hundreds of times—on and off camera, he thought wryly. He'd done it so much he could probably do it with his eyes closed, but he still loved teaching others these skills. Fatema was a keen student. Soon she'd be doing the routine procedures herself, while he got back to scar repairs with Mila…and the million other things that demanded his attention.

There was a knock on the door. Mila stepped in.

'Sorry to interrupt, Doctor,' she said. 'Is it OK if I grab that light?' She motioned to the mobile surgery light in the corner.

'Of course, Dr Ricci.'

He let his eyes linger on her bare ankles as she crossed the floor in her white sneakers. She was wearing her brown hair in a bun, pinned to the top of her head. It reminded him of Annabel for a second. Annabel had worn her hair like that…he was sure of it. Sometimes it still blew his mind that he'd met Mila's twin first, but the two were completely different women in his mind. They looked alike, but that was all.

Mila was an entirely new species.

He still couldn't figure her out.

He hadn't seen her outside of the MAC for the last few days. The last time they'd spoken without other people around had been outside his house in the middle of the night, after she'd come across Bruno. He'd asked her inside, but she'd hurried off. He assumed he'd made her feel a little awkward. They were colleagues after all—and he never invited colleagues from the MAC home, nor patients.

He'd realised when he'd gone back inside and seen the wine glasses on the table that she'd probably seen them too, and had maybe thought he'd been entertaining a woman.

Not this time. It had been just Neesha and her husband Dan—his friends from the turtle sanctuary. They'd been adding up the profits from the fundraiser and planning where the money should go, along with a little extra donation from his own private funds for some new tanks for the baby turtles. Neesha had poured wine for herself and Dan. He'd had a herbal tea himself.

In one way he liked it that seeing those wine glasses might have evoked a stab of jealousy in Mila; it wasn't as if he hadn't been admiring her work…and her eyes…and her body…but in another way he couldn't deny that he was concerned for her.

She clearly thought about Annabel a lot more than he did, and more often than she was letting on. Coming here was reminding her of her twin—especially because he'd met her here, too. He knew how grief could flare up when you least wanted it to. He'd been through it after his father died.

Mila went to leave the room with the light she'd come in for, without looking his way.

'See you later?' he asked her as she reached for the door.

She turned back to him and he saw Fatema glance up at them over Hugo.

He cleared his throat, hoping Mila hadn't forgotten. 'The dive centre this afternoon?'

It had taken ages to get a slot when both of them were free.

Mila blinked. Her phone buzzed in her pocket. Distracted, she fished it out as she said, 'Yes, Doctor... Sorry for disturbing you—excuse me.' And she left the room.

When she'd left, Fatema couldn't get her words out fast enough. 'Diving? You and Dr Ricci? Better not tell Rachel about that. She likes to pair people up, and I think you're both on her hit list. Young, single, beautiful, tortured... It's like you belong together. Sorry, Doctor, am I speaking out of line?'

Fatema flushed a little at the realisation that she had just called him beautiful and tortured. Sebastian fought to stop the amusement from showing on his face; he'd been called worse things in his time on the show.

'Shall we begin?' he suggested.

His afternoon off couldn't get here fast enough.

'How's it going over there? It's been a while since I've spoken to you...'

'Sorry, Mum,' Mila said, sinking down onto the low stone wall outside the MAC and observing the patients lying around, reading or chattering in the grounds. 'The time difference here is crazy—plus we've been so busy.'

She heard her mum let out a sigh down the phone. 'I figured as much. I won't keep you.'

'No, no, it's OK. I have a few minutes. Dr Becker is training someone at the moment, and then we're in for a scar repair. It really is non-stop around here, but I'm sorry I haven't called you as much I should.'

'I don't expect you to, darling. I'm fine over here.'

Mila wasn't so sure. Her mother had a way of putting on a brave face. 'Are you really fine? What have you been doing?'

Her mum paused. 'This and that. I watched a couple of episodes of that show your famous doctor used to be in. *Faces of Chicago*. Is he married?'

Mila shook her head at the sandy ground. Trust her mum to ask that. 'No, he's not married.'

She pictured Sebastian a few nights ago, outside his house, all smiles and moonlit muscles and charm. She was still so embarrassed at having shown her weaknesses around him. She knew she'd appeared overly emotional, telling him about her dreams and then hurrying off after seeing those wine glasses. The man was entitled to entertain whoever he wanted. He must think she was crazy.

She'd been so mortified about it she'd been keeping away from him whenever possible. She wasn't used to men stirring up her emotions. It made her feel far too vulnerable for her own liking. Besides, she wasn't here for *him*, technically speaking.

'Well, I was just calling to say I've posted you a letter,' her mum said.

'A letter? That's delightfully old-school of you, Mum. What's in it?'

'It's just a few photos. I found them in Annabel's drawer. I thought you might like to have them over there with you as keepsakes.'

Mila's throat felt tight. 'You were looking through Annabel's drawers?'

'I… I was missing her. And you. I think I needed to do it.'

'Oh, Mum.'

Mila could picture her mother at home, curled up with her legs under her at her usual end of the sofa, a book on the arm. Maybe a cup of her favourite tea. They had both cried together on that sofa for days after Annabel had—

No. She couldn't think about it again. She felt guilty for being so far away. And now her mother had started going through Annabel's things without her.

'I saw someone else wearing her clothes the other day,' her mother continued. 'That yellow dress with the black spots—remember it? The one she ordered from the Japanese warehouse?'

Mila swallowed. 'I remember.'

'Annabel loved that dress.'

'I know, Mum.'

She and her mother had made the mistake of taking some of Annabel's clothes and shoes to the local charity shop a few months after the accident. Their good deed—intended as a method of coping with their grief—had backfired badly when they'd started seeing women around the town wearing the donated clothes. Her mother had come home in tears several times, thinking she'd just seen Annabel.

After that neither of them had been able to bear to go back to her things. There were boxes and drawers of her personal items that hadn't been touched since.

'Let me know when the letter arrives,' her mum said. 'I don't know how long it will take to reach you out there, but I thought you might appreciate something on the anniversary…you know. You will call me, won't you?'

Mila's heart ached. She fixed her eyes on the ocean. Someone was swinging on the sea swing where Sebastian had first offered to take her diving. 'Of course I'll call you.'

Her mother sounded concerned. 'You won't be alone on the day, will you?'

Mila bit her lip. 'I won't be alone, I promise. *You* won't be alone, will you?'

'I might have company. Either way, I'll keep busy. Maybe your famous doctor can distract you, Is he as good looking as he is on the television?'

She rolled her eyes, smiling now. 'He's an inspiration, Mum. He's even taking me scuba diving.'

'Really? He dives, too?'

'He pretty much does everything on this island.'

'Did he take Annabel diving? You said before that he met her. I still can't get over that—what a coincidence!'

Mila felt the usual stab of envy, confusion and nausea. She felt it whenever she thought about Sebastian and Annabel together—which was often.

'I don't know, Mum. I haven't asked what they did when Annabel was here. It's none of my business, is it? I have to go. Thank you for sending me the photos. I love you.'

She was determined not to let her emotions overwhelm her with people around, but her mother was still talking.

'When you finish your stint out there and come home we'll go through the rest of her things together, OK? It's time, Mila.'

The coral reefs surrounding the islands were home to some of the planet's most diverse marine life. Sebastian watched Mila admiring the brown and white stripes of a solo lion fish with a look of total awe as he floated beside her.

She'd said she'd done some diving training before, in her Army days, but she'd never been in the ocean. Looking at her now, he couldn't believe it. She exuded confidence—more than many of his other students on their first dives. She'd followed Big Al, one of their rescue turtles for a good ten minutes, and he'd got a little kick out of the way her eyes had lit up just at drifting along, observing his barnacle-speckled shell, his scars and his wise hooded eyes.

Damn, she was beautiful with her hair down...and up.

He usually couldn't remember his thoughts after a dive, but when they finally climbed back onto the boat he realised he'd spent most of the dive both admiring her and worrying about what she might be thinking.

'So, did you switch off completely down there?' he asked, watching her shake out her hair.

He'd reserved the boat just for them, but his buddy and driver Ketut was watching them intently, just like Fatema and Rachel were clearly doing behind their backs. Maybe next time he'd take her out alone.

'I don't actually remember.' Mila looked pensive as he placed her heavy tank back in its holder and signalled to Ketut to start the engine. 'But it's true what you said. It's so peaceful down there. I really needed it. Thank you, Sebastian.'

He stepped closer, softly brushed a strand of damp hair back behind her ear. 'You're welcome.'

Ketut cleared his throat at the steering wheel and Mila looked uncomfortable for a second, then broke contact by stepping back.

'That turtle...' she started. 'The big one...'

'Big Al? Yeah, he's a pretty special guy.'

'What happened to him? I saw his fins, with all those scars.'

'He got into a fight with a boat propeller. That's what we think happened anyway.'

'He does look sad,' she mused, following his eyes to the jagged slashes across her left inner forearm. 'But he's so beautiful.'

Sebastian tossed their fins into a box along with the masks and snorkels. 'So are you, in case you ever doubt that. Turn around,' he instructed.

He lifted her wet hair and released the zip of her wetsuit slowly, noting the shape of her shoulders, the contours of her body as he helped to pull it down to her waist. Mila was tense, though.

'I should tell you...that dive was so much more enjoyable than the lake dives we did in training, pulling all those...' She grimaced as she turned around in his arms.

'All those what?' he asked curiously.

'Fake bodies,' she replied. 'They had us helping rescue divers treat the bodies so we'd know how to handle it if it really happened. I don't need to tell you this was a thousand times better.'

He motioned for her to follow him up to the roof of the boat—his favourite place. Her bare midriff was taut and toned. He caught her appraising him too as they stood there on the roof of the bobbing boat.

His hours in the home gym had paid off, he knew that, but Mila had probably always been this way. She'd worked her brain and her body equally in the Army—he had probably only heard about a fraction of the things she'd done and seen. It was eternally fascinating to him. Her scars were beautiful to him. She was beautiful inside and out.

'Maybe next time we'll go to Shark Reef,' he told her, taking a seat on the hot wooden roof and rolling his own wetsuit down to his waist. 'It's a little further out...off the next island. The current has to be just right.'

'I thought you said there aren't any sharks any more?'

He dangled his legs over the side and folded his arms over the railing. Mila's wet hair caught the afternoon sun as she sat beside him. Their bare arms brushed on the hot metal.

'Not many, and it's a gift if you actually get to see one. We donate to the shark nursery off Lombok, so the numbers are rising slowly.'

'Sharks, turtles, dogs, humans...is there anything you're not saving on this island, Dr Becker?'

For the first time in days Mila offered him a real, genuine smile and he felt a weight lift from his shoulders.

'Talking of dogs, thank you for walking Bruno home with me the other night. My friends Neesha and Dan came over—they must have forgotten to shut the gates. They did have a little wine while they were at my place.'

Mila looked indifferent, but he swore he saw her cheeks flush just a little. He didn't have to explain himself—he knew that. He could have anyone he liked over to his house. He could have a woman over if he wanted. But he didn't. Not any more. It surprised him, this need for Mila to know he wasn't playing around.

'You know,' she said, letting out a sigh, 'this is where I first saw you—up here on this roof, the day I arrived. I'd be lying if I told you that you didn't get my attention, looking all...like that.'

She pulled a face and motioned to his bare chest and wet hair, and he laughed.

'Is that so Dr Ricci? Well, I'd be lying if I told you I didn't see you then, too.'

'But you thought I was Annabel.'

Mila rested her head on her arms as he floundered for words.

'It's OK. I wonder what she'd say if she could see us now, working together...diving together.'

'She would probably think it was a pretty funny coincidence. Wouldn't anyone think that?' he asked, slightly annoyed with himself for his initial mistake over her identity. It still bothered him, the way he'd confused the two of them and been so vocal about her changing her name.

'I don't know. I can't speak for my twin. She's not here. I wish she was.'

'When is the anniversary, exactly?' he asked cautiously.

He'd sensed her tense up the second he'd said he thought Annabel would find it amusing, knowing Mila was with him there. He shouldn't have put words in her mouth. It had clearly bothered Mila.

'You mentioned it was coming up to three years since she died?'

She closed her eyes to the sun. 'It's in a few weeks. I might take a day off, if that's OK—do something nice for her. I don't know yet. I haven't had a chance to really think about what I'll do besides call my mother. It's a tough day for her, too.'

'I'm sure. Is she alone over there?'

'You mean, does she have a man? I don't think so. There hasn't really been anyone since she divorced my father. She has a lot of friends, though.'

'I can help you think of something to do here, if you want…to take your mind off it.'

She seemed to contemplate his offer for a moment. 'Thank you. I don't know if *anything* will take my mind off it, but I appreciate that, Sebastian.'

Colleagues or not, the urge to touch her, to reassure her that he was here for her, was overpowering. He couldn't help it. He reached his hand to the back of her head and drew her gently against his shoulder, keeping his hand in her soft damp hair.

They rode back to shore like that, in silence.

Thank goodness it was only a short boat ride back to the beach. Mila could practically feel the sparks flying between them on the roof. It was getting more difficult to ignore their obvious chemistry. Even resting her head on his comforting shoulder felt as if he was rolling out the red carpet, inviting her further in.

What had possessed her to admit she had noticed him on day one, before she'd even got off the boat? She didn't know. But something about his presence was comforting, and real, and he'd seemed to want her to know he hadn't been entertaining anyone in his house lately except friends.

No. She couldn't go there.

Would Annabel really think their meeting was a funny coincidence?

She had asked that very question out loud and sent it off on the wind, many times, longing for an answer. All she'd got in return were more bad dreams that woke her up in a cold sweat.

Sebastian had taken care of returning the dive equipment. It was after four p.m. now, and the afternoon sun cast a flattering light on his biceps as he ordered them both takeaway smoothies at the dive shop bar.

She was trying and failing to find an excuse not to spend the rest of her afternoon with him when a child in blue denim shorts tugged at her shirt from behind. It was Francoise, the French girl who'd come in with the dog bite.

'Hey, you!'

Her mother was hovering at the entrance to the dive shop, waiting for her daughter. They raised their hands at each other from afar.

'I was on my way to find you,' the child said, in excellent English for her age. Her big round eyes observed Mila's wet hair, the beach towel sticking out of her bag. 'Have you been snorkelling?'

'I was scuba diving...with Dr Becker.'

Sebastian appeared with the smoothies. His tall frame threw the young girl into shadow.

'Well, if it isn't our brave canine-fighting superhero. I see you found us.'

'Hello, Dr Becker!' Francoise beamed from beneath her red sun hat. 'My *maman* saw you here. We go home today— back to Bordeaux.'

'Your wounds look much better already, Miss Marchand,' he told her, crouching down to her level to inspect Mila's handiwork on her jaw. 'You'll only have a small scar there, if anyone can even see it at all.'

'I'll be more like a stripe, for braving your ordeal,' Mila followed up.

'Like *your* stripes.' Francoise placed a finger softly to the scars on Mila's left wrist.

'A bit like mine,' she mused aloud.

She didn't pull away. She didn't mind Sebastian looking either. It wasn't like he hadn't been looking at them ever since they'd met. He had called her beautiful on the dive boat earlier on. The memory caused a stir in her heart, but she certainly wasn't about to relive how she'd got her scars in front of strangers.

She couldn't imagine telling Sebastian about her failure to save Annabel. She wouldn't be able to do it, knowing he had met her twin. She couldn't stand the pity on people's faces when she told them how she'd tried to drag her out, too late, just as the car went up in flames. She'd scarred herself for life, trying and failing to get her out through the windscreen, even though Annabel had already been dead when she'd done it.

Francoise took Mila's hand and dropped a tiny wooden dog onto her palm.

'What's this?' Touched, Mila turned it over in her hand and showed it to Sebastian.

'I wanted to say thank you for helping me. It is to protect you from bad dogs.'

'It's a lucky charm,' Sebastian told her, admiring it in her palm. 'You'll see carvings like this all over Indonesia. This one is exceptionally crafted. That's so nice of you, Francoise.'

'It's beautiful,' Mila agreed. 'Thank you, honey, I'll keep it for ever. It will remind me to be brave in the future, like you were.'

Francesca rocked on her flip-flops, looking shy. 'Is Dr Becker your boyfriend?' she asked Mila innocently.

'No, he's not,' she shot back, trying to laugh.

Sebastian gasped in faux shock to make the kid giggle.

'I think he *should* be your boyfriend,' Francoise volunteered. She gave them both a quick hug, reaching her tiny arms around of them, drawing them together. 'You can help people like me together. You can stop all the bad dogs biting other children. I am going to tell everyone about you.'

Sebastian almost dropped the smoothies as their sides were crushed together. For a little kid, she was strong. They watched her skip her way happily up the dust track with her mother.

70 ENTICED BY HER ISLAND BILLIONAIRE

'Wow.' Sebastian was laughing, resting on one elbow on the bar, even though the tension was a tangible object between them, even bigger than before. 'Looks like you're gathering fans wherever you go.'

'Says *you*. You were really good with her.'

'So were you. Do you really never think about having a family?'

His question caught her off guard and she reacted evasively. 'Me? I'm pretty sure I'd prefer a dog.'

His eyebrows shot up. 'A dog? In that case, maybe you can have Bruno.'

'Bruno needs a permanent home. I'm not here for ever.'

'Shame...' he murmured, and his eyes lingered on her lips just long enough to start a slow simmering burn in her for more of his attention as he sipped his smoothie.

His phone rang then, and saved her having to respond to his obvious flirtation. 'It's Ketut. He'll only just have got home, so something must be wrong. One sec?'

He wandered out to the forecourt with his phone. A couple of twenty-somethings in bikinis looked up at him from the pool, admiring his physique as she did way too often.

His posture quickly told her something bad had happened. She hoped it wasn't serious.

Ketut was a local guy, who worked at the dive shop and drove the boat amongst other things, and she knew Sebastian and Ketut had been good friends since Sebastian had first arrived on the island. He talked about him and Ketut's wife Wayan a lot.

When Sebastian hung up, his mood had done a one-eighty.

'Mila, I have to go,' he said apologetically, slipping into the sandy sandals he'd left by the bar.

He tossed his empty cup expertly into the nearby trash can and hooked his backpack over his shoulder.

'Unless you want to come with me?'

CHAPTER SIX

KETUT FLUNG OPEN the door before they'd even made it up the path. Wayan stood with her arms held out to Sebastian, her belly swollen with their baby, in the doorway of their modest bamboo shack. It was surrounded by terracotta pots and jungle plants, and a moss-covered statue of a Balinese goddess stood to one side. It looked as if it doubled as a bird perch.

'Sebastian! Thank you so much for coming.'

Wayan's voice wobbled and Mila's heart ached as she watched him walk straight into her embrace. It was a real hug, tender and heartfelt, the kind you might give to a family member.

The kind he'd given her on the boat when she'd talked about Annabel's anniversary, she thought, feeling her stomach clench. He must trust her to bring her here. This was personal.

'You know Dr Ricci... Mila? I explained to her a little about the situation on the way over here. Wayan, you should have called me sooner—I would have come.'

Sebastian guided Mila ahead of him across the threshold, kicking off his sandals on the inside mat. She did the same.

'Wayan didn't want to ruin your dive, so she didn't tell me either,' Ketut explained as he closed the door behind them.

The smell of burning scented candles hit Mila's nostrils

as they were ushered into a small, cosy living area. Three dozing cats occupied a tattered pink couch in one corner. Books were stacked haphazardly on chairs, shelves, and even the floor, and soon Ketut was pouring herbal tea from a silver teapot under a whirring fan.

It was simple, but homely. Only the mood was tense.

On the boat on their way over to their house, on a neighbouring island, Sebastian had explained how he spent a lot of time here, so it was almost a second home, and that these two were like his island brother and sister.

Short, fatigued-looking Wayan was likely in her mid-thirties, dressed in a colourful patterned skirt and a white blouse that revealed the lower part of her pregnant belly as she dropped heavily into a tattered armchair. She started biting her nails. On instinct Mila sat beside her just as Sebastian took the wicker chair next to Ketut.

He took the tea cup he was offered. 'So, tell me what's going on, man. What are we dealing with here?'

'I'm hoping you can tell *me*.' Ketut handed Mila a cup too, then pushed a set of ultrasound pictures forward on the coffee table. 'Wayan was given these at Blue Ray. She was too upset to call me, so she came back here and told the cats before she told me.'

'They say the baby will need surgery...' Wayan sniffled.

Her quivering lip turned into a sob and Ketut was beside her in a second, both arms around her shoulders. He was trying to be strong for her, but Mila could tell he was heartbroken. Mila reached for Wayan's hand.

Sebastian pulled his glasses from his backpack, put them on and studied the black and white prints intently.

'Cleft lip and cleft palate,' he confirmed out loud, handing her the X-rays with a deep sigh. 'I'm so sorry, guys, they're right. This is going to have to be fixed in surgery. Usually the procedure's done after about three months...'

'We will love him anyway, of course, Sebastian... Mila.

You know we would, no matter what. Even if you can't help us.'

Wayan's sad eyes broke Mila's heart. She had seen a thousand women broken over babies deformed, wounded, stillborn or killed. Again, she put herself in a mother's shoes. The thought of anything happening to a child of her own made her go icy cold... She just wouldn't know what to do if it was her. She'd already proved that in the worst way.

'Why wouldn't he help you?' Mila asked now, looking from Wayan to Sebastian.

'We don't have medical insurance.'

Sebastian stood up, knelt in front of her, and put a hand reassuringly on her knee, over her bright skirt. 'I told you before, you guys did the right thing calling me. I can help you.'

'*We* can help you,' Mila added.

He had brought her here for a reason. She could see the future of this baby meant the world to him, just as his nephew Charlie did, back in Chicago. And he knew she had a way of injecting a certain calm into a situation... Unless that situation involved saving her twin sister from a burning car, in which case she froze like a useless snowman.

Sebastian thought she was stronger than she was. He would never know how the flashbacks and her guilt over Annabel's death still consumed her.

'What can you do, Sebastian? Mila? Will our baby be deformed for ever?' Wayan was pale now, in spite of Sebastian's comforting words.

'Not if we can help it,' Sebastian said defiantly, taking his seat again.

He was looking at Mila from across the room, dragging his hands through his hair. Behind him, through the window, she saw the daylight fading into twilight.

'The surgery is relatively simple, though it sounds quite complex when you try to explain it,' Mila said, finding her voice. 'Once your child is born we'll do another assessment, and there might be a few operations over time, but as for scarring…'

'Minimal,' Sebastian finished for her, meeting her eyes.

They were on the same page. One of the cats leapt from the chair and started curling around her legs. It purred softly in the silence until Ketut spoke.

'By the time the baby is born you might be gone. Sebastian says you're not with us on the island for very long.'

All eyes were on her now—even the cat's. Mila's throat felt dry in spite of her tea. 'I don't know what to say about that…honestly,' she admitted, putting a hand down to pet the purring animal. 'I'm here for a while yet. I don't have an exact departure date. I gave in my notice in London, so I'm pretty flexible, I guess.'

Suddenly she didn't want to leave the island—at least not until this baby was mended and declared healthy. But what could she do? She might have agreed to an undetermined date for the MAC personnel department to arrange her flight out, but still, her life wasn't here. This wasn't her family—as much as she wanted to help them.

Sebastian was biting the inside of his cheek hard, as if he didn't know what to say either…

'Jared, hey, what's up?'

Sebastian kicked the refrigerator door shut, balancing the phone on his shoulder as he carried a bowl of oats and a carton of milk to the countertop.

He was on the verge of running late for a consultation, followed by a scar revision on a car crash victim who was currently on his way from the mainland. But he needed to eat first. Surgery on an empty stomach was never a good idea. He needed all the brain capacity he could muster—especially now.

'Sorry, bro,' Jared said. 'I know it's early over there, but I really need your confirmation for Mom's birthday thing. I need numbers. Does the world's most exclusive surgeon have a plus one in mind this year, or will you be flying solo like last year?'

'I don't know yet,' he told his brother, pulling a spoon from the cutlery drawer.

He noticed a frangipani flower in the drawer—a gift from his cleaner. She hid them everywhere. He slipped it into his pocket idly. He would re-gift it, like he always did, to one of the women in Recovery at the MAC.

'Hi, Uncle Bas!' Charlie's voice was loud on the end of the line, as if he'd stolen the phone for a second.

Sebastian grinned. 'Hello, trouble. Why aren't you in bed?'

It was a time difference of thirteen hours between Chicago and Indonesia, so he rarely got to speak to Charlie.

He saw his reflection in the glass of the window. He looked tired. He hadn't slept much, worrying about Ketut and Wayan and the not so distant departure of Mila Ricci. She might have a while left on Gili Indah, but he'd been realising lately that he wasn't much looking forward to island life without her.

'He's been on a school trip today—haven't you, bud?' Jared said, taking the phone back. 'He's pretty fired up still...'

'We saw dinosaurs!' Charlie enthused in the background, and proceeded to roar like a T-Rex. 'Listen, Uncle Bas!'

Sebastian sniggered. 'Sounds like fun.'

'Sounds like they gave him E-numbers. We'll get him to bed eventually.'

Sebastian smiled. 'How is everyone else?'

'Good, good...same, same. Wrapping up the season. Mom thinks it should be the last one—did she tell you? I think she's finally getting tired of the show.'

Sebastian sat at the breakfast bar, watching Bruno chasing a bird around the yard outside. Jared had said this before, at the end of the last season. And the one before that, too. He didn't want to tell him he'd believe it when he saw it. The network always came back with a better offer.

'I fully support any decision to make this season the last one, but you already know that,' he said instead.

'I know… I know.' Jared let out a sigh. He knew better than to start that conversation again. 'So, back to the party,' he diverted—predictably. 'I think Mom would like it if you brought someone. Laura's rented the Opal Marquee at the Langford—the one in the orchid garden? It's a surprise for Mom. We've invited all her friends from the badminton club. Actually…if you can't think of anyone to bring from your string of island vixens I can ask Theresa. Remember her? That cute blonde dentist from Smile Right in Lincoln Park…'

Sebastian spooned the oats into his mouth as his brother went on, naming women he couldn't care less about getting to know.

'Jared, I'm not going to take some woman to a party if I'm never going to see her again. And I can only stay three days, remember? I have a lot to do here.'

Jared make a clicking sound with his tongue. 'I get it, bro—your life is there. Can't you think of *anyone* to bring, though? You've come on your own for the last three years.'

'You know why that is.' Sebastian felt his jaw start to tick.

'Yes, I *do* know why. You're paranoid that some pap will catch you doing something shady and make your idyllic island life a misery, But I told you—we don't invite the media to family events, Bas. Any new woman of yours is perfectly safe from prying eyes. None of us wants a repeat of what happened with Klara.'

Sebastian scraped the stool back and dropped his bowl and spoon into the sink—heavily.

Jared's voice softened. 'Sorry to bring it up. I just want to see you happy again, man. You work so hard out there on your own. I hope you're finding time for some fun, too?'

'Actually, there is someone,' he said, before he could stop himself.

'Oh, yeah?'

'I'm not sure she can come with me to Chicago, however. Technically, she's only here on a short-term placement.' He grabbed his backpack and sunglasses, locked the door behind him and patted Bruno in the garden on his way out. 'She's new at the MAC,' he said reluctantly, making sure to close the gates properly.

'Wow. OK…'

Jared drew a breath through his teeth and Sebastian could picture the look on his brother's face.

'You know how I feel about mixing business with pleasure, but I guess that's up to you. Why can't you bring her?'

'For a start we're colleagues—even if it's temporary,' he said, lowering his voice as he walked towards the main MAC building. 'And we're friends too… I think. God, we haven't even been on a date, or anything. I just…'

'You just want to get in her pants before she leaves for good?'

'No, Jared.' He rolled his eyes to the blue sky. 'It's more than that. She's…she's different. Anyway, we have too much to do here, so we can't both be getting on a plane…'

'Stop making excuses, Bas. You deserve a vacation, don't you? And you deserve a decent woman at your side. It's been a long time, bro, since you and Klara broke up.'

'I know.'

'Tell me about this woman! Where's she from?'

Encouraged by his brother's rare enthusiasm for anything that didn't involve the show, Sebastian told Jared a few minor details as he walked—but nothing that would enable him to search for her online. He trusted Jared, of course, but he wouldn't put Mila's privacy in jeopardy for anything.

He spotted Tilda Holt, basking in the sun on a lounger by the swimming pool already. She was recovering from her non-invasive face lift with a cheeky Bloody Mary. He hoped it was a virgin Bloody Mary. He returned her cheery wave and then, remembering the flower in his pocket, turned back and presented it to her with a flourish, his phone still pressed to his ear.

For you, he mouthed in silence.

Her new crease-free eyes shone with delight. She thanked him profusely and proudly placed the tiny white and yellow flower in her hair.

Hugo O'Shea waved enthusiastically from his seat at a table on the sand, looking up from his laptop. He was still hanging around after his enlargement procedure—'working remotely in Recovery,' or so he'd said.

Something about him made Sebastian bristle as he chatted on with Jared. He didn't trust the guy.

But Sebastian's mind was half in the moment, in the MAC's grounds with his patients, and half on the penthouse balcony back home, on showing Mila the views of Belmont Harbour and the lakefront. She'd get a kick out of Charlie, too... He could tell she liked kids a lot, even if she maintained she would prefer a dog herself.

'*Ask* her, bro,' Jared demanded, when he told him he really had to run.

Sebastian swung into the air-conditioned reception area. Mila looked up from the desk, where she and Rachel were studying some papers.

'Hey,' they said at the same time.

Mila was wearing lipstick. He didn't notice anything about Rachel.

God he really wanted to be alone with Mila right now. They'd both been so busy he hadn't seen her much in the last week. But tonight they'd be alone for some of the time. Maybe he should ask her to accompany him to Chicago then.

He pushed the thought aside instantly. He should absolutely *not* do that. They were professional colleagues. Besides, Jared might think the media would leave Sebastian alone in Chicago, and Jared might think he was being exceptionally paranoid, but there were plusses to being paranoid. Being paranoid meant he would never mess up again. Being paranoid meant he would never hurt another woman to the point of her refusing ever to speak to him or see him again.

Sebastian had never said it, and he barely acknowledged it even to himself, but what had happened with Klara had affected him deeply. He would never subject another woman—especially Mila, who clearly had her own vulnerable past to protect—to anything like that again.

'Wayan can really cook,' Mila groaned, putting a hand to her full stomach. 'That veggie *rendang* was probably the best thing I've ever eaten. How do you say delicious again?'

'In Indonesian? *Lezat.*' Sebastian smiled.

He held out an arm to help her step back into the tiny boat and Mila felt the butterflies instantly overpowering her satiated stomach. The water was warm and inviting under her feet, swishing up her legs, almost to the hem of her skirt. The stars were out in force.

With their busy schedules it had taken over a week to arrange another trip for her and Sebastian to see Wayan and Ketut at the same time.

Wayan had made them a *lezat* Indonesian feast that defied all logic, coming from her tiny kitchen, and the conversation had flowed easily—from the cleft palate surgery and scar repair to general pregnancy issues and the brand-new project Sebastian was developing in Bali—a retreat for recovering patients on the mainland.

Mila had also heard countless stories of Sebastian and Ketut's island endeavours, and had been charmed by the way he conducted himself around his adopted family. She'd been about to cancel tonight, out of sheer exhaustion and nightmares three nights running—but, while she needed rest, the thought of being around Sebastian again outside of the MAC was like a comfort blanket somehow.

She admired him and she respected him. Which only served to fuel her growing attraction to him.

She sat on the wooden slats of the tiny fishing boat's seat, watching his muscles flex as he pushed it out from the beach and hopped in. The butterflies swooped in again as he sat down and started the motor. His knee in khaki shorts brushed hers so lightly she might not have felt it if she hadn't been so acutely aware of his closeness.

'Beautiful night,' he said, gesturing up to the stars.

She murmured agreement and looked to the sky. She could feel him watching her. Their mutual attraction was undeniable. She'd seen the looks Ketut had given him, too, and the not so secret smiles between Ketut and Wayan at the dinner table. She knew she lit up in his presence, and that whenever that happened her worries drifted off. But all too often they sprang back unannounced.

Annabel had met him first. Annabel was the one he'd liked first. She had no business entertaining this attraction. Twins did not ever go after the same guy, and those rules hadn't changed just because Annabel was dead.

She shifted slightly, so they were no longer touching. If he noticed her futile attempt at creating distance he said nothing. The boat was skimming the ocean, heading back to the island.

'Did you know the oldest map of the night sky is a map of the Orion constellation?' Mila said, to fill the excruciating silence. 'They found it carved on a mammoth tusk.'

'A mammoth tusk? Really?'

'They think it was carved over thirty-two thousand years ago,' she continued.

Sebastian was looking at her in admiration. She liked it when she taught him things he didn't know.

'So, you're interested in the stars, Doctor?'

'The ones in the sky, yes—not so much the ones on television.'

She was teasing him, and she knew he knew it.

Sebastian grinned at the horizon, one hand steering the boat. 'Are you calling me a star, Dr Ricci?'

'Maybe...'

'A fallen star?'

'Maybe.' She smiled in spite of herself. 'You know how to turn your shine on, though, don't you? Tilda Holt showed me the flower you gave her. She said she was going to press it and put it in a frame.'

Sebastian chuckled. The night was calm and still around the chugging boat. The moon was a thumbnail in the sky. Mila pulled her loose hair over one shoulder to hold it. The wind was tugging it in all directions, along with her white knee-length dress.

'Seriously, we used to study the stars...me and Annabel. But not so much as I did on my own, when I was deployed in the Middle East.'

'Really? You had time to stargaze out there?'

'The quiet nights were the scariest sometimes,' she confessed.

She wondered again why she found it so easy to talk to him about some things, and other things felt impossible to address...like what he might or might not have done with Annabel.

'We never knew what was coming next,' she continued, fighting a vision of Annabel as she pictured her suddenly, right there in the boat with them. 'There wasn't much else you could do on those nights but wish on the stars that the worst would never happen. That's Scorpius—see the long, curving tail?'

She pointed to a constellation above them. Sebastian slowed the boat. It made her heart speed up.

'I see it,' he told her, cutting the engine and shifting on the seat. 'And just to the east...that's what the Balinese call Danau—*danau* means lake. If you want to learn more there's an app. You just point your phone up and it tells you—'

'Stop.' She cut him off.

'What?' He looked alarmed. His knee was back against hers.

'There's an app that you can point at the stars and it tells you what they are? *All* these stars? How is that even possible?'

Sebastian laughed out loud again. The sound was so unexpected it shocked her into laughing herself.

'You're amazing—do you know that?' he said, with genuine affection.

Mila's heart kept on thudding. The way he was looking at her... The engine was still off. They were facing each other now on the seat, so close she could see the lights from the surrounding boats reflected in his eyes.

'I'm not kidding about the app,' he informed her. 'Wait till you see the Zodiacal light.'

'What's that?' she croaked, searching his warm eyes for reasons to back off, to stop this thing before it started. She could feel it coming.

'That's a free show from the skies here that you won't want to miss. It hovers like a cloud over those mountains at sunrise or sunset. It's basically sunlight, reflecting off dust grains that are left over from whatever created our solar system over four and a half billion years ago. They just go round and round, circling the sun in the inner solar system. All these grains...'

Her heart was beating wildly now. The air felt thick and hot, and the back of her neck was damp.

'Sounds like a lot of grains.'

He shifted even closer to her. 'A *whole* lot of grains.'

Sebastian reached a hand to her face and cupped her chin, stroked a thumb softly across her lips. It felt as if time stood still. Her mind went blank.

'You know something?' he said after a pause. His eyes seemed to be clouded over with longing. 'It's not just the fact that I shouldn't have you that makes me want you.'

Mila swallowed. All the hairs on her body stood to attention as he trailed his thumb across her cheek. He made a sound like a strangled groan that spoke straight to her churning insides.

'I know this could be complicated, but…do you even know how hard it is, Mila, keeping away from you…?'

His fingers made tangles in her hair, drawing her face even closer to his with each knot.

'Tell me to stay away and I will,' he whispered, but his lips were so close, and his fingers weren't leaving her hair.

'Don't stay away.'

It was Mila who caved in first and kissed him.

Sebastian's tongue was like his hands—soft at first, then harder, more possessive. His slight stubble razored her chin as her own hands found his hair, felt the delicious softness of it in her fingers. He was urging her closer, as close as they could get on the seat of the bobbing boat. He drew her legs around him, his kisses firing up parts of her that had been dormant way too long.

Mila was so caught up in the thrill of this new connection that she almost forgot who or where she was. So the sound of the swinging boom from an approaching boat and several panicked cries came completely as a surprise.

CHAPTER SEVEN

THE MAN IN the yellow shirt didn't see his boat's boom lunging violently towards him, but Sebastian heard the crack as it hit him in the face and chest.

'Oh, my God…' Mila fists dropped from his hair to the sides of the rocking boat as they were forced apart in a flash. 'What's happened?'

There was blood on the deck of the other boat already. Sebastian saw it glimmering in the floodlights as he restarted the engine and inched closer, standing to see over the side. It was a sailing catamaran, three times the size of theirs, but there looked to be hardly anyone on it.

Mila's knuckles were as white as her dress as she gripped the boat's edge. 'I can't see anyone injured…'

'He's on the floor.'

Sebastian steered the boat as close as he could get. A woman in a long pink dress was shrieking uncontrollably, hunched over the motionless body of her friend, or maybe he was her lover. Three more men and a woman were doing their best to swing the boom back into place and secure it.

'Don't move him!' Mila shouted from their boat.

He watched as she lifted the boat seat and grabbed two medical kits. He made sure all of the MAC's boats had them on board, and he always brought his own.

Unsurprisingly to Sebastian, Mila needed no help climbing over the side of the boat, and in less than three seconds flat she was barefoot on the catamaran, crouched at the man's side.

'Help me, please—he's out cold!' The woman in the pink dress was beside herself.

Sebastian threw a rope onto the other boat's deck, jumped across himself and hurriedly tied the boats together, impressed by Mila's quick action. The medical bag was already open and she was supporting their victim's head on her own lap, instructing someone to get a cushion.

'What's his name?' Mila checked the man's pupils and pulse.

'John—he's John Griffiths, my husband. I'm Janet. Something must have got loose on the boom. Oh, my God... the blood.'

'Get me some clean towels,' Mila ordered the others on deck.

She had sprung into doctor mode so fast it was almost as if the woman Sebastian had just kissed so passionately was another person entirely.

'Where did this glass come from?' she asked next, indicating the broken shards all around them on the hardwood decking.

He had only just noticed them himself.

'We were drinking champagne,' the woman explained, raking a hand through her thick bleached blonde hair. She looked guiltily to Sebastian. Then she lowered her head over her husband, weeping and clutching his lifeless hand.

Sebastian tried not to pass judgement as he prepared for evacuation. They were fairly close to shore. The island's nightlife was still pumping on the tourist side—he could smell the beachfront barbecue dinners from here. Maybe they'd been sailing drunk...maybe they hadn't. But it wouldn't be the first time someone had come to a 'party island' and got a little too complacent about the way the ocean worked.

He pulled out his phone and dialled the Blue Ray, telling Agung where they were.

'Agung's sending help to the harbour—let's get him back quickly,' he told Mila, hurrying to her side.

Mila was strapping an oxygen mask to their patient's head, being careful not to move him any more than was necessary. He was still out cold.

The water was deep out here, rocking the boat as if it was nothing but a fragile toy. With both engines off it was enough to make anyone feel seasick. Maybe that was why Mila looked so ghostly pale.

'Tell him we have a suspected pulmonary contusion, broken nose, and I'm pretty sure a shattered left eye socket,' she said.

He relayed the message, then hung up. He fought the urge to ask if she was OK. Of course she was OK. She was being her usual professional self. But he knew she probably hadn't been involved in an emergency at sea before—she'd been stationed in the desert, after all.

Sebastian had seen a couple of deaths at sea caused by booms. If they didn't sweep people overboard, their lines were trip hazards. In this case he could already agree with Mila. The boom's swinging power had broken this man's nose...at least.

Mila's heart didn't stop its mad pounding the whole time they were transporting their patient to shore.

John's wife, Janet, continued to grip her arm as John was loaded onto a stretcher bound for the clinic. She was seemingly in shock and unable to speak. The petite blonde in her mid-forties wore more dramatic jewellery than Mila had ever seen: bangles, beaded necklaces, earrings shaped like mermaids holding coconuts.

And her wedding ring was just as flashy, Mila noted—a huge sparkling jewel on a silver band. She focused on that as she took her hand in reassurance.

In spite of her being aware of her bare feet sinking into the wet sand, and all the stars and flashlights and equipment beeping around John, Mila felt only half there. First the kiss. Then all that blood on the deck. The swerving of the boat…the way it had all happened so suddenly. Despite her training, it had totally thrown her.

'X-rays show his nose is broken,' Agung confirmed ruefully, soon after they'd arrived at Blue Ray and were all standing in the critical care unit, observing the monitor. Mr Griffiths was on breathing support, but the monitor kept blinking on and off. It was only when Sebastian slammed a hand to the side that the screen stayed lit.

'Damn thing… Don't worry—the new one's been ordered.'

'He's also fractured several bones in his left eye socket,' Agung said. 'Good spot, Dr Ricci.'

Mila caught Sebastian's look of admiration and approval. No doubt they were all impressed with her keen eye, but she wasn't here for compliments. She'd seen worse—much worse. She was trained to see the detail in the fall-out.

If anything, she was embarrassed and annoyed that Sebastian had spotted her ashen face and the way she'd stalled back there, after seeing all that blood. He hadn't asked if she was OK in front of those people, but he'd been about to—she'd seen it in his eyes.

Maybe they should have tried to call out a warning. Maybe this could have been prevented if they hadn't been so lost in kissing each other like that.

She dug her fingernails fiercely into her palms, internalising her self-loathing. Janet Griffiths was looking to her to be strong, and John would need her soon.

'I'm scheduling him for surgery right after the physician's done with the realignment.' Sebastian cut into her thoughts. 'Emergency reconstruction. We'll get him over to the MAC when he's stable. I'll go now.'

'What can I do?' she asked.

Sebastian ushered her into the corner behind the door. His brown eyes were flecked with concern. 'Stay with Mrs Griffiths till her daughter arrives, if you don't mind. Or Nurse Viv starts her shift soon...'

'Yes, of course. I'll stay here till then.'

A volunteer was helping the distraught Janet Griffiths, now wearing a borrowed jacket, over to a seat in the waiting area.

Sebastian lowered his voice, leaning in to Mila. His breath on her ear made her want to reach for him, but she crossed her arms over her chest instead.

'Mila, I'm so sorry.'

'Don't say it, Sebastian.'

He urged her further behind the door, so no one would see or hear. 'Did that freak you out back there?'

'Sebastian, I kissed you too...'

'I meant the boat, the accident—not our kiss...'

'This is my job. I'm used to it.'

His brow furrowed. 'You turned completely white, Mila.'

She looked at her feet, still sandy in her shoes. Guilt raged through her like a fire. It was Annabel's accident all over again. She hadn't been paying attention to her surroundings and she'd been caught totally off-guard. She'd promised herself that would never happen again, and it just had. She'd also promised herself that she wouldn't let her attraction to Sebastian get the better of her.

'It's not me you should be worried about,' she managed.

'John Griffiths will be fine, Mila. You probably saved his life.'

She folded her arms tighter, building a wall, but she knew it was too late for that. She'd kissed him first. The resulting guilt and tension were unbearable, but she wasn't having this conversation here.

'We'll talk later,' Sebastian told her, as Agung called him away.

And it took every ounce of her strength to resume normality for poor Janet Griffiths.

CHAPTER EIGHT

IT WAS FIVE days since their kiss. Sebastian had been trying to get her alone outside of the MAC for dinner, a drink, a dive…but Mila had apparently been trying even harder to ensure they were surrounded by people at all times. She was avoiding him—he knew it. He had crossed a line with that kiss—they both had—and Mila probably felt that being intimate with him…her employer…had been some kind of immoral move.

Or was it something else?

He couldn't think why else she would be acting this way. Maybe it *was* less than ideal to be making out with his employee on a fishing boat after dining with his friends, but so what? He couldn't get her out of his mind.

Today, though, she couldn't avoid him.

'Morning,' he said, as she approached him on the outside terrace of the MAC.

'Morning, Dr Becker.'

She looked around her, pulling her sunglasses down over her eyes. Several patients were looking their way from the breakfast tables and pretending not to. One of them was Hugo O'Shea.

'Ready to set sail to the mainland?' he asked, starting down the steps.

She followed him, light on her feet in brown sandals and a blue striped dress. 'This won't take all day, will it?'

'Not all day, no. I do believe the staff have transported John and Janet Griffiths to the harbour already, with their luggage. They'll meet us at the boat.'

Sebastian had been in the reception area last night when Mila had promised Mrs Griffiths that she would accompany the couple back to the mainland. It was time for them to leave the island, after their ill-fated vacation, and fly home from Bali, but the couple were understandably a little apprehensive about making the crossing after what had happened on the catamaran. Mila had offered to go with them, for company.

He knew Mila probably wanted some time off the island without him. But he'd offered to go with them. In fact he'd told them, he'd do better than that. He would take them all on the MAC's private boat. He had two new monitors to collect from Bali, anyway, along with a few other chores to get done.

Mila had gone quiet when he'd offered, as if she was annoyed. But *he* was annoyed by her refusal to be alone with him—that was what Klara had done before she'd left him. She'd just flat-out refused to talk. Nothing put him more on edge than when people refused to discuss their problems like adults.

It wasn't all his fault, though, this thing with Mila. He'd told her on the boat that he would stay away from her if she wanted him to, but she had kissed him first. Whatever might have changed between them since then, they definitely needed to talk about it.

'Can I ask you a quick question, Dr Becker?'

Hugo O'Shea appeared in front of them suddenly, blocking their exit at the gates. His hair and beard were dyed bright blue again, bluer than ever before. Where on earth had he got that hair dye on an island this size? Sebastian thought, half amused. He must have brought it with him.

'Is everything OK?' Sebastian asked, trying to inch around him.

'You mean with this?' Hugo gestured to his newly enhanced groin area and grinned. 'Couldn't be better, This is about something else. I have a commission, Dr Becker, to write an exclusive story on you and your work here on the island. What drove you from Chicago? What brought you here?' His eyes fell on Mila. 'What keeps you here?'

Mila crossed her arms. Sebastian couldn't read her eyes behind her sunglasses, but her body language suggested she would rather be anywhere than here, with them.

'I have the agreement right here for you to read and sign.' Hugo pulled a piece of paper from the pocket of his shorts and thrust it at Sebastian. 'It's time we got moving. It's great publicity for the MAC. We can do the interview wherever you like. On a boat at sunset, maybe—it doesn't matter. This is your side of the story for *USA World*. It's a big magazine, Dr Becker…think about it. Your chance to explain all about Klara, your ex…'

'I know who Klara is, thank you,' he snapped. 'And my answer is no.' Sebastian folded the paper in one hand against his thigh, then squeezed his fist around it, scrunching it up. 'Now, if you'll excuse us, we have to go.'

'Are you sure you won't just—?'

'No. And I'd like to remind you about the NDA you signed before coming here, Mr O'Shea.'

He gave Hugo the mangled piece of paper, ignoring his look of shock and horror, then put a hand to Mila's back and walked them quickly up the path, to where a horse and cart were waiting to take them to the harbour.

Bali was crazy, loud, and a shock to her senses after weeks on the much quieter Gili Indah. Mila wasn't used to seeing cars or motorbikes any more. Hordes of tourists were crowding the jetty or sitting with their bags on the beach, drinking beers, waiting for their transfers. Catamarans and boats bobbed everywhere, but Sebastian's yacht was catching the most attention.

Bright white and gleaming, with three bedrooms and an indoor lounge bigger than her last apartment, it was clearly the prize of a very rich man. She hadn't said so on the journey over here—she'd chatted to Janet most of the way, and besides he'd seemed distant, probably because of Hugo O'Shea—but she'd felt like a VIP the whole time, reclining in a leather couch while the ocean sped by through the windows.

Everything Sebastian surrounded himself with on the island was modest, and gave no hint of the billionaire lifestyle he probably enjoyed everywhere else. This was like seeing a new side of him—a taster of his old life, maybe. She couldn't help wonder what his place in Chicago was like.

'Do you think we'll make it to the hospital before the rain starts?' Janet asked now, casting her eyes to the heavy, grey sky.

Mila had only just noticed the change. The port was heaving and John was being wheeled towards the waiting ambulance, Sebastian and a paramedic at his side.

'You'll be fine,' Mila told her. 'You're in good hands, and John is making a great recovery. The hospital will arrange for your hotel and airport transfers once they've given him the final go-ahead to fly tomorrow.'

'I can't thank you enough for everything you've done.' Janet took her hands in hers and her bangles jingled on her arms as she squeezed them. 'I know I've said this a hundred times, Dr Ricci. But we might have lost him if it wasn't for you.'

Mila extended a warm smile. 'Well, I'm happy we were there,' she replied.

What else could she say? She was more than happy to have been able to help John Griffiths, of course, in spite of the resulting situation she had put herself in with Sebastian.

Her dreams had changed since then. Annabel was in them all—sometimes alive and dancing, sometimes exactly as she had been when Mila had found her in the car—and sometimes it was herself in the car, Annabel and Sebastian were trying to get *her* out.

It had sent her spiralling into a world of confusion. She'd been hoping for a day to herself over here, to hire a driver and see some of Bali, do some much-needed thinking, but Sebastian had encroached on her plans by coming, too.

'So, forgive me…but I can't not ask you before we go. You and Dr Becker *are* an item, am I right?'

Janet's green eyes flooded with mischief suddenly and Mila realised she'd been gazing absently in Sebastian's direction. He was talking on his phone now, an umbrella tucked under one arm.

She shifted her bag awkwardly onto the other shoulder. 'Not exactly.'

Janet obviously didn't believe her. What the hell?, Mila thought. They were leaving anyway.

She scrunched up her nose. 'There is…something there,' she admitted. 'But it's complicated. And I'm not here for long.'

'Then you'd better get a move on! I met my John at work, by the way. He was a new, arrogant theatre director—I was a new, pushy production manager. We argued like crazy—Shakespearean proportions—till we realised it was actually love and not hate we felt for each other. He proposed on the stage in front of our audience. Over a thousand people saw me cry.'

She held up her big sparkly ring and Mila felt a rush of longing—not for the ring, but for the deep, mutual love Janet had found. It was the kind of love Sebastian had once felt for Klara, she thought, surprising herself with her envy of a woman she had never met.

Janet put a hand to her arm. 'I saw you two out on that dive boat, before the accident. And I've seen the way he looks at you.' Her seashell earrings swung like pendulums and jingled along with her bangles as she leaned in to speak in her ear. 'Everyone adored him on that show—his brother

Jared, too. Quite the handsome partnership. They wrote some terrible things about him when he left…something about his ex-girlfriend…'

'I never watched it.'

Janet looked shocked. 'OK. Well, it was years ago, anyway,' she said flippantly. 'And who knows? Maybe all that had to happen just so he could find his way to *you*.' She flattened a hand to her heart dramatically, then shook her head, smiling. 'Sorry…ever the romantic, me!'

Sebastian was heading towards them through the crowds, head down, baseball hat on, still talking on his phone. A couple of people were trying to take photos without him knowing. Women in particular were staring at him.

Mila realised she had probably underestimated the impact his presence on the show had made, despite him leaving more than three years ago, and how popular it had really been and still was. No one paid him this much attention on the island.

'You're all set Mrs Griffiths.' Sebastian slid the phone into his top pocket, then adjusted his hat on his head. 'We're going to leave you in the ambulance crew's capable hands. Dr Ricci and I have an appointment.'

'Limitations live only in our minds—don't forget that,' Janet quoted conspiratorially in her ear, before she gave Mila a huge hug and left.

Instantly the busy harbour seemed to close in. It was just Mila and Sebastian and the thunder starting to rumble on the horizon.

'Are you ready?'

Mila was still distracted by Janet's words. 'What for? Isn't someone delivering a patient monitor for us to take back later?'

'The plan just changed—that was them on the phone. They can't deliver it for a couple more hours. Bali traffic— you know the deal. There's something I need to do. If you decide to come with me it'll give you a chance to see some of Bali with a driver I trust.' He paused. 'Unless you'd prefer to go your own way and meet up later? It's up to you.'

She deserved the disparaging tone in his voice—she knew she did. She also knew they probably needed to talk about what had happened. And Annabel. She couldn't avoid discussing *that* with him any longer.

Sebastian was inching towards the road, where a shiny chauffeur-driven car with blacked-out windows was pulling up in the dust. He looked as though he was exiting the scene whether she went with him or not.

CHAPTER NINE

SEBASTIAN PULLED ON the crisp white shirt, sleeve by sleeve, and buttoned it up in front of the mirror. He studied his jawline in the light, frowning at his reflection. He should have shaved, but it would have to do. He could use a haircut, too.

'How do I look?' he asked, sweeping the curtain aside dramatically and squaring his shoulders in the tailor-made suit. 'Do you think anyone would guess I spend half my life in scrubs and the other half in a wetsuit?'

Mila stood up from the plush white seat. She put the book of designs down on the table, next to a dish of frangipanis. Her eyes appraised the navy blue pinstripe jacket and he realised, feeling some small element of doubt over his own sanity, that even though he knew he looked good he was still seeking her approval.

She trailed her gaze up his body, from shoes to shirt collar, not giving anything away. 'What's the occasion?' she asked.

'My mother's seventieth birthday party. I have to go back to Chicago.'

He hadn't asked her to accompany him, of course. Maybe he would have done if she hadn't spent most of the last week trying to avoid him.

She raised her eyebrows. 'I recall you mentioning something about that. When is that? Before or after I leave the island?'

'I don't think we've talked about your exact leaving dates yet, have we?' he said evasively.

Mila seemed closed off—distracted, even—so now was clearly not the time to discuss it. She was glancing at the rain outside, and the palms lashing at the tailor's windows. There was a storm on the way, all right. It was only supposed to be a quick downpour, but...

'This is definitely getting worse,' she announced, right as his cell phone buzzed again.

It was the delivery guy, delaying the monitor's arrival yet again.

'They might not get it to us till the morning now,' he told her with a frown.

Mila looked like a deer who wanted nothing more than to run away from his headlights. 'What will we do till then?'

'You stay here. I make something for you,' the tailor cut in. 'Something beautiful. I think blue is your colour!'

Mila turned, holding up her hand. 'Oh, no, that's OK. I don't have anything to...'

'It not take long.'

Sebastian watched Mila in the mirror as Anya, his favourite tailor, bustled off to the storeroom. She came back three seconds later with armfuls of fabric. Before Mila could dissuade her, the tailor was pulling out a tape measure, holding her arms out one by one, whirring around her in her patterned sarong. Then Anya got to her knees and measured each leg, then her hips, waist and bust—quickly, efficiently, enthusiastically.

'You look at designs. I get you samples!'

'Get something made. We can have someone bring it over to the island later,' he told Mila.

He'd been coming here for years, but he'd never brought a woman with him. No wonder they were treating her like royalty.

She shook her head though, resolute. 'No, really... I don't need anything, Sebastian.'

He cocked an eyebrow at her, pulling the shirt off and reaching for another one. This was pale pink. He pulled it on with the curtain still open. He wasn't afraid to wear pink.

He caught Mila in the mirror, biting her lip, watching him dress. 'Have I met the one woman in the world who *doesn't* want a dress made for her?'

'I've never had a dress made for me before, if I'm honest.'

The tailor seemed to notice the way she was covering her arms. 'This one?' She jabbed a finger to a long-sleeved floaty dress in the design book.

Mila let out a defeated sigh. 'OK, fine…yes. I like the ones with long sleeves, actually.'

'Please make whatever dress she wants, Anya. She will find an occasion to wear it.'

Mila looked perplexed. 'Why are you being so nice to me after…?'

'I have no idea,' he grunted. 'Maybe because you're driving me crazy.'

He swiped the curtain closed before she could respond. Anya shuffled quietly into the back room, and he heard Mila stepping closer to his curtain.

She exhaled deeply. 'Look, Sebastian, I'm sorry, OK?'

His irritation faded when he heard the anguish in her voice.

'I'm sorry I've been shutting you out after what happened. You have every right to be annoyed with me. And I know it must be driving you crazy, because you did nothing wrong. I kissed *you* first. It's just…we have to work together, so…'

He stayed quiet. He sat down on the stool in the changing room, put his head in his hands for a moment. This was what he'd wanted to hear—kind of. But he still needed answers she hadn't yet supplied him with.

He couldn't talk with her here. The tailor was tottering in again already.

'I think we should go my place—it's not so far from

here,' he said eventually. 'We can ride this storm out there.' He started unbuttoning the pink shirt and pulling off the dress trousers. 'It's not safe on the yacht right now.'

'You have a place close by?' Mila was standing just behind the curtain. Her silhouette looked stock-still through the fabric.

'He has many house,' the store manager whispered. 'Dr Becker very rich. You very lucky lady. You want dress? I send to island when ready.'

'Yes, she wants the dress—thank you, Anya. And please keep her measurements on file.' He stepped from the changing room, holding his new garments. 'Who knows? We might be needing you again.' He took out his wallet.

'What are you doing? Sebastian, really, I don't need...'

'Just let me do this for you, Mila. You deserve it. We'll take all these, please, Anya—excellent fit as usual. You really do have skills like no other.'

He went about paying for everything and then, holding the store door open for Mila, reached for the umbrella he'd left in the corner and led them back outside into the storm.

'Which is your place?'

Mila was flummoxed. The rain was coming down in thick, hard slashes, turning the hem of her blue-striped dress an even darker blue and whipping up the ocean of palm trees around them. They had hardly seen anything of Bali, even though he'd promised—not that it was Sebastian's fault. The rain had concealed everything through the car windows.

'We need to take the funicular railway up to the top.'

He held the umbrella over her, to protect her as far as possible from the ever-imposing rain, and snaked an arm around her waist so they could both take shelter. The gesture had her tensing slightly, even though she liked it.

'Of *course* you would have the villa on top of the mountain,' she said out loud.

He smiled, walking them towards the small red carriage

on a track. It looked like the start of a rollercoaster, and promised a rickety journey up through the steep green terrain. They were right at the bottom level of some kind of terraced valley. Each level seemed to house a different villa.

'Is it safe?' Mila had travelled in scarier conditions in her time, but she wasn't too thrilled about taking a wobbly funicular in a storm.

'It's perfectly safe. I would never take you anywhere that wasn't safe.'

Sebastian tightened his arm around her protectively and at the waiting carriage flipped the latch, urging her inside ahead of him. Leaves thrashed the Perspex windows, jostling them along with the wind as he slammed the door behind them and dropped to the seat beside her. He pushed a hand through his wet hair. Droplets landed on her arm.

'Maybe someone called the witch doctor,' he said.

'Witch doctor?'

'Practitioners of the dark arts, if you believe in that kind of thing. They're called *dukuns* in Indonesia, and they can control the weather. Amongst other things.'

Mila felt far away from everything and everyone as Sebastian pressed a big red button and the carriage shuddered into motion. They'd already headed past smoky mountains, mystic grey temples covered in carvings, and endless green pastures to get here. He'd told her all about it, even though she hadn't really been able to see any of it though the rain.

They weren't far from the yacht, but now, with the jungle all around them, it felt remote and exclusive.

They were sitting so close on the tiny seat she could make out each of the thick black hairs along his jawline, dotted with grey. She liked it when he didn't shave for a while.

'People hire the *dukuns* to make it rain. And to stop it raining,' he said.

His shoulder brushed hers near the strap of her dress, giving her goosebumps.

'But I hope they don't make it stop just yet,' he went on. 'I think we need to talk about what happened, don't you?'

'I know,' she relented.

His left arm was stretched across the back of the seat behind her. He smelled like a mixture of surgery, incense, musky soap and rain.

A gust of wind rocked the carriage and her hand found his knee. Behind his head the lush green valley stretched for miles under a blackened sky. The thought of the carriage tumbling down into the valley with both of them in it at the whim of a Balinese witch doctor flashed briefly through her mind.

Annabel was there too, suddenly, in the carriage with them—just like she'd been on the boat before Mila had given in to their overwhelming chemistry and kissed him. It felt too small.

'I bet Hugo O'Shea would love a photo of us right now, in here together,' she tested, trying to fill the silence.

Sebastian shook his head, releasing her fingers. A bolt of lightning lit the sky, followed by more thunder. 'Can you believe that guy?' he asked.

'Why is he still on the island?'

'He says he's been working remotely while he recovers, but now I know he really wants a damn story. He's just been hanging about, waiting for the right time to ask.'

'Why don't you just talk to him? Tell him what you want him to print? You can have the final say over it, surely?'

'I don't talk to the media,' he said bluntly. 'Neither should you.'

'I'm not Klara,' she reminded him, before she could think about it. Janet had clearly got to her, talking about Sebastian's ex.

The carriage had stopped on the top level. Sebastian was quiet.

'Sorry,' she said. 'I know you despise the media because of what happened to Klara. But publicity is not *all* bad, is it?

You're doing good things for the island, and people should know about it.'

'Maybe it's none of their business.'

He flung open the door and stepped purposefully from the carriage, opening the umbrella over her as she followed. The subject was clearly closed.

Through the rain she made out the villa. It was smaller than she'd pictured, but undeniably exclusive. A Balinese statue of a lion guarded the carved wooden door. An infinity pool appeared to melt into the jungle all around them.

She was just about to say she'd bet it was beautiful in the sunshine when a dog started to bark uncontrollably. She jumped and her bag fell into a puddle with a thud. The important envelope she'd put in it just that morning drifted straight into the swimming pool...

CHAPTER TEN

'No, NO, NO!' Mila leaned over and fished the envelope out. She looked visibly upset.

'Stay still.'

Sebastian stepped in front of her, making his body a shield between Mila and the growling black dog. It was nothing like Bruno, his docile rescue animal. He suspected it was more like the one who had bitten poor little Francoise. It was flattened to the floor on its belly now, baring its teeth just inches from the poolside.

Mila started shaking the water off the envelope in distress.

'Get on the porch!' he ordered as the dog started snarling again, louder than before.

Mila froze.

'We won't hurt you,' he soothed, holding his hand up to the dog and risking getting closer for a better look.

It was a bitch. She had scruffy pointed ears, thick, coarse fur in tortoiseshell swirls, and what looked like a cut on one paw.

He kept his voice low and his movements slight, crouching down in the rain under the umbrella to retrieve Mila's fallen handbag. 'I know you're just scared.'

He threw the bag towards Mil on the porch. The dog kept on snarling but didn't move.

'She might have been hit by a car on the road at the top

and got lost trying to get down. She might have been attacked by another dog. We should take her inside,' he said.

Mila had pulled something from her bag. She was holding it in the palm of her hand, clenching and unclenching her fist over it.

He tossed her the key. 'Open the door. There'll be treats on the table—bring me something to give her.'

He watched her shake off her shoes, slide the glass door open and enter the apartment barefoot as he braved putting his fingers closer to the dog's nose.

'We won't hurt you,' he said softly.

Mila reappeared with some of the tiny ginger biscuits the housekeeper always left him. 'These?'

'Those will do.'

He unwrapped one quickly and held it out on his palm. The dog sniffed his hand tentatively before taking the biscuit. Her temperament softened instantly. She seemed to have decided to trust them, thankfully.

'Are you hungry, girl? No collar...no obvious owner.'

Sebastian shook his head. It broke his heart that so many animals were abandoned and ignored. He gave her another treat and was rewarded with a lick from her wet pink tongue.

'We should get you cleaned up. Want to come in with me?'

'Is she OK?' Mila flattened her back to the wall, holding the wet envelope to her chest as he carried the dog past her on the way to the bathroom.

'It's not as bad as I thought—just a flesh wound, I think.'

The white marble floor would be good enough for now. He pulled towels from the top drawer of the wicker bathroom storage unit and the first aid kit from the bottom one.

'Help me lay these down. We can clean up the cut, give her a couple of stitches. If it's not looking better by morning we'll take her to a vet.'

Her threw her some towels and she crouched beside him. 'Morning? We'll be here till morning, now?'

'We definitely can't take the yacht back in this weather.'

'I know, but...'

'If you want to stay in another villa I'll give you the keys.'

'That's not what I meant...' She paused. 'How many of the villas do you *own*?'

'All of them. But this is the only one that's furnished beyond the basics right now.'

Mila looked stunned.

'What is that you've got there?' He gestured to the other object she was holding in her hand.

She unclenched her palm reluctantly and he felt his eyebrows shoot to his damp hairline.

'You carried that in your bag this whole time?' It was the wooden dog charm that Francoise had given her at the dive shop.

Mila shrugged. 'She did say it was for protection. It didn't help my bag, though, did it?'

'Sorry... I guess it still worked a little, though. The dog seems OK now.'

The dog's paw must be sore, and she'd likely been scared outside in the storm, but otherwise she really did seem OK. She wasn't barking or growling any more, and she seemed to be appreciative of their help. The licks were now coming thick and fast.

It took them about twenty minutes to stitch and bandage her paw. Then they showered in different bathrooms and changed their clothes. Luckily they'd brought more, in case they wound up swimming somewhere.

The rain was still hammering the pool when Mila met him in the open-plan kitchen. He could see it through the floor-to-ceiling windows. He pulled out cold soda and glasses.

'This place is beautiful,' she told him in genuine admiration. 'I love the walls.'

'Thank you. I had an Indonesian designer do those.' He pointed to his favourite mandala feature wall, and then the carved timber hanging plaques. 'And that rug happens to be the softest rug on earth. Try it.'

Mila walked onto the plush cream rug in her bare feet and moaned in pleasure. He chuckled under his breath.

Much like his other place, he had filled the place with trinkets to make it feel more like a home: wooden and bamboo bowls and baskets, brass and gold utensils, textiles in fabulous colours, gorgeous cushions, glass pineapples...

'What will you do with the other villas?' she asked. 'I'm guessing this is the place you talked about over dinner that night with Wayan and Ketut?'

He nodded, then handed her a glass fizzing with soda. 'I'm hoping Jared will get over here at some point soon. Like I said, this extension of the institute will be more like a health and wellness centre for convalescing trauma patients and people who can't afford the luxury of the MAC. There's a huge building down at the base of the mountain, before you get to the funicular. You wouldn't really have seen it in the rain, I guess. These villas will be the guest quarters. If this really is the last season of the show Jared should have more time, so...'

'They're wrapping up the show for good?'

Mila looked at him in surprise. He hadn't told her this, or anyone for that matter, because he didn't really believe it himself.

'He has said it before and it hasn't happened,' he explained. 'I guess I'll find out more in person when I go home.'

'You didn't say when you were going back to Chicago?'

'I think it's around the time your official term ends at the MAC,' he replied, evading the question again.

Truthfully, he knew it was exactly the same time as her leaving date. He'd tell her soon, but he couldn't bring himself to think about her leaving yet... Or going to Chicago alone and coming back to find her gone.

He poured some dried fruit snacks into a bowl. The housekeeper always kept provisions here.

Their canine patient barked in the bathroom and Mila flinched. 'Is she OK in there?'

'She's just reminding us she's there. You really don't spend much time around dogs, huh?'

'Not as much as you,' she admitted. 'I don't mind them, but I don't particularly trust them as a species. We found a crazy dog once at a military outpost—bit half of my colleague's face off. We were only trying to help it. Annabel got bitten by a dog once, too. When we were kids in Ibiza.' She paused, then added, 'I felt her pain when happened.'

'Physically?'

Mila followed him to the couch, putting her wet envelope down on the table to dry. 'Yes. On my ankle. It felt like I'd got bitten myself. So strange… Personally I try not to have a thing against dogs. We must treat the insurgents, too, am I right?' She gave a wry smile.

Sebastian couldn't help laughing. 'Insurgents?'

'One time a bomb went off, northeast of our base in Helmand. We found two dead—a British soldier and an Afghan interpreter—and two injured soldiers—a Brit and an Afghan. We treated them both, side by side. If local nationals and insurgents were injured as a result of our conflict they were always entitled to a medevac.'

'That must have been…' He blew a sound out through his lips and shrugged apologetically.

'It was the biggest source of conflict out there for some people. But in my eyes if someone is wounded I have to help them—regardless of who they are. There's no first-come-first-served. If someone's dying and I can help stop that happening I'm going to do it. Wouldn't you?'

He stared at her. What else had she seen out there? 'Yes, I would. Of course.'

'I know you would—actually, you're putting Ketut and Wayan first, whenever they need you, even if they're not paying customers.' She paused. 'I wish I was going to be here to see the baby.'

'We don't know for certain that you won't be—babies have a habit of coming when they want to, don't forget.'

Mila shifted awkwardly against the frangipani-printed cushions, sipping on her soda. It was strange having her here in this villa. She hadn't even stepped foot inside his place on the island, and he suddenly regretted never asking her there. He'd been concerned someone might see—someone like Hugo O'Shea—but people were always going to talk anyway. And he was always going to be slightly paranoid. It was just the residual effects of his past life in the spotlight.

He wanted to ask if she really had to leave at the end of her term, but he knew people like Mila didn't stick around in one place too long. She had done too much, seen too much of the world, to want to be cooped up on an island for ever…hiding away with him.

'Is that a twin thing?' he ventured now. 'Feeling each other's pain?'

She curled her legs up on the couch. 'It *was* a twin thing—with us, anyway. I always felt it. Whenever she had a headache, I'd always get one, too. It was the strangest thing…that connection. Sometimes when I get headaches now I still think it might be hers I'm feeling, but then I remember it can't be. The pain is all mine.'

'Talk to me about her,' he said, drawing his legs up on the leather couch opposite hers.

'I'll do one better—I'll show you,' she said. 'If it's not ruined.'

'If what isn't ruined?'

Mila reached for the wet envelope, pulling out a photograph that was damp around the edges. She handed it to him.

'You and Annabel,' he stated.

It shouldn't have surprised him, seeing them both together in the photo, but he found himself staring at it, battling a sudden surge of emotion. He couldn't have told them apart, side by side.

'That was the Christmas we got each other the exact same silly scarf without knowing,' she explained.

The twins were grinning in front of an orange sofa in a cosy living room, both wearing a yellow scarf with the words *Crime Scene* knitted into it. Seeing this image now of them both together made her plight and her grief all the more real.

'You brought this with you?' he asked.

'My mother sent me a package from home recently, and this was in it. We shared a bedroom till we were eighteen, and there are still lots of old photos there in boxes. Mum keeps hinting that I should go home and sort it all out with her…throw some things away. I know I have to do it eventually.'

'I can't even imagine how tough that would be…to have to do that for your twin,' he said, as she took the photo back. 'But have you considered that it also might help?'

She stared at the photo, eyes narrowed. 'Maybe. I still see her everywhere. I dream about her all the time.' She paused then, and took a deep breath. 'Sebastian…what happened when Annabel was here? The two of you…what did you do?'

Mila's words took him completely by surprise. Her eyes were closed now, as if she couldn't even face what he might say.

'I need to know, Sebastian. I should have asked you sooner, but I like you, so I couldn't—no, I didn't *want* to hear it. But I really need to know. Did you kiss her, like we…?' She scrunched up her face, as though the very thought caused her physical pain. 'Did you sleep together?'

'No!'

He put his drink down, took hers away, too. Shuffling up close, he reached a hand to her face. She turned into his palm, exhaling in relief.

'Mila, I thought you already knew that nothing happened with me and Annabel?'

'Nothing at all?'

'No—nothing! Maybe a little mild flirting, but it didn't mean anything to either of us. She was just a typical tourist here—to me anyway. She was drinking and dancing and killing it at karaoke. "Total Eclipse of the Heart" never sounded so adorably terrible as she made it sound. She even missed a snorkelling trip because she couldn't get out of bed one morning. Is that what you wanted to know? Mila, she was just like you—but actually nothing like you at all.'

Mila swiped at her eyes, let out a laugh. 'That sounds like Annabel.'

He put his forehead to hers, both hands to her face. His mind was reeling now. Was this why she'd been distant ever since they'd kissed? Not because she was afraid of putting their working relationship in jeopardy, but because she thought he'd already been intimate with her sister?

'God, Mila, I wish you hadn't carried all this around inside you. You should have talked to me sooner.'

Mila reached for him at the same time as he gathered her into his arms. Their mouths collided, and then all he could do was kiss her till they were stumbling their way together to the bedroom.

Mila let him worship her body and revelled in worshipping his. How could she *not* want to be with this man when he treated her as if she was the only woman he'd ever wanted? It was easy to forget everything, even the horrors she'd seen that kept her up most nights, when they were buried in each other.

They found their way together so easily, so perfectly, time after time on the soft satin sheets of his carved wooden bed—and, when sleep finally came for her, for the first time in a long time Mila had no dreams about Annabel, or the accident, or Afghanistan. None at all.

CHAPTER ELEVEN

THE WOMAN HAVING the mastopexy had a small tattoo of a star on her left shoulder. It seemed to shine under the OR lights as Mila guided her to the wall, where she put her into position on her feet.

'We need you standing up for the markings,' she said. 'I hope you're not feeling too nervous, Mrs Pilkington-Blythe?'

Their patient, a well-to-do forty-four-year-old interior decorator and perfume designer from the UK, didn't look as if she was nervous at all. In fact she looked excited.

'Thank you, Dr Ricci, but it's not exactly a nerve-racking thing to get your boobs out once you've had kids, is it?'

Mila took the marker from Sebastian. 'I suppose not.'

'Mine used to be pert—really up here.' Madison Pilkington-Blythe heaved her breasts upwards for a moment towards her chin, creating a cleavage. 'I miss that,' she moaned.

Sebastian's face was the picture of professionalism as he tapped away at the new touchscreen monitor. It was two weeks now since they'd brought two new monitors back on the yacht—one for the MAC and one for the Blue Ray Clinic. They had almost forgotten to pick them up. They had been more than a little preoccupied the morning after the storm…

It still felt like yesterday that they'd spent hours making

love in every corner of that bedroom in Bali…right up until the dog had jumped on the bed the next morning, wondering what all the noise was about.

The rain had finally stopped and they'd been late to the harbour. There had probably been a thousand more responsibilities she'd ignored, but something big had changed between them. A new lightness had surrounded her. She'd let this new level of intimacy with a man sweep her away with its depth and passion.

Madison Pilkington-Blythe didn't know any of this, of course. Their patient had just been flown in to the island on a private helicopter. But Mila had made love to Sebastian that very morning in the shower at the dive school, and again back at his house before coming in to do this procedure. Making love to him took her to a different place.

'You'll know what breastfeeding does to your nipples too?' Mrs Pilkington-Blythe was still talking. 'Unless you were one of the lucky ones.'

'I wouldn't know about breastfeeding myself—only from what I see in my patients,' Mila returned absently, starting the marking.

'You don't have children?'

'Not me.'

'I suppose it must be hard meeting someone when you live all the way out here…' Mrs Pilkington-Blythe sounded almost sympathetic. 'But don't you worry, Doctor, you've got time. Don't take too long, though—the later you leave it, the harder it is to get your figure back. Trust me—I know. That's why I'm here.'

'Can I interest you in any particular kind of music?' Sebastian cut in—probably to save her.

On this occasion Mila was grateful. She knew he was listening and the topic put her slightly on edge, because she knew Sebastian wanted kids while she…she couldn't think of anything more terrifying.

'What do you two usually like to listen to?' Mrs Pilk-ington-Blythe asked.

'We play all kinds of different things in here,' he an-swered, turning to the old gramophone she knew he'd kept from his father's surgery. 'Dr Ricci has some pretty good moves.' His eyes flicked to hers mischievously and Mila turned her back before her glowing cheeks gave her away.

They worked to the sound of Beethoven, raising their patient's breasts and leaving no hint of the children they'd helped to feed and nourish.

What would it be like, being responsible for someone? A tiny, helpless human? A child who looked a little like her and a little like Sebastian... A child who needed her for food and advice and survival.

It would be...*beautiful*, she thought.

Then Annabel flashed into her head again. Annabel who'd also needed her for survival and who'd died because she hadn't got to her in time.

She had no right even imagining herself with Sebastian's baby, she scolded herself. Not only was she getting too far ahead of herself, but she wasn't fit to be a mother—she hadn't even been able to take care of her sister.

'What's on your mind?' Sebastian asked her, looking at her in mild concern.

'Nothing,' she lied.

'Sebastian? It's me.'

'I know it's you, Jared. I have your number saved in my phone. How's it going?'

He and Mila were on a rare two-hour break from work, and were spending it at his place. He was inside, mixing jasmine tea with ice in a blender, and Mila was outside wearing a red bikini under a see-through sarong. He hadn't anticipated being interrupted.

'I'm calling to find out how you're doing with this photo.'

'Photo? What do you mean?'

Outside, Mila was running the length of the yard with Bruno and the dog they'd rescued on her heels. She'd named her Stormy.

He lowered his voice and crossed to the dish rack for glasses. 'What photo?'

'Social media, bro. Don't you even follow your own hashtags?'

'I try not to.'

'Well, I hate to be the one to break it to you, but some so-called journalist—Hugo O'Shea—has posted a photo of you and some lady. Interesting caption... And you look pretty damn cosy on board your yacht with this... Mila Ricci. Is she the woman you were telling me about before?'

Sebastian saw red. If he hadn't just given Hugo O'Shea a new penis, he'd be very inclined to chop it off...not that he'd say that out loud.

'Yes, that's her,' he said through gritted teeth. 'How the hell did he get photos of us on the boat? He was at the MAC—he can't have known where we were...'

He trailed off and ran the order of events through his head. Hugo had stopped him on the way to the harbour to ask for that interview. He could have asked around, found out where they were going, when they were due back with the new monitors. He could easily have lined up a photographer.

'I can't believe that guy!'

Jared let out a snort. 'Hey, chill... I was going to say you look cute together. You told me she was "different", and you said you liked her. She doesn't exactly look like she hates *you*, standing behind her with your arms out like you're acting out a scene from *Titanic* either. And is that a...a dog with you in the photos? What were you *doing*?'

Sebastian clenched his jaw. He hadn't exactly been mimicking the *Titanic* movie. When the dog had jumped up behind them on the bow of the yacht he'd been trying to maintain balance on a particularly bumpy wave at the request of their skipper.

He closed his eyes, with his back to the countertop. 'What was the caption?'

'Billionaire Doc Re-enacts Titanic with Mystery Brunette.'

'Great. That's just great.'

Jared was laughing.

Outside Mila was calling to Stormy. She loved that dog already.

'Jared, you know I can't stand this kind of thing. You know what happened before…'

'Listen, forget it—it's just one photo. It doesn't matter. Mila's leaving soon anyway, isn't she?'

Sebastian bit his tongue. 'That's not the point.'

He almost felt Jared's sigh in his ear before his brother said, 'I'm sorry about Klara, bro, you know I am. But this is one photo in over *three* years. No one cares about what happened before. You're doing great work out there. But still you refuse to talk to anyone so the media is feeding off scraps. What do you expect? You're an icon.'

Sebastian's heart was thudding at his ribs. He couldn't process it all.

'Just bring her to the party with you, will you?' Jared said.

Sebastian drummed his fingers angrily against the countertop. He had tried his best to avoid this kind of situation—he'd even put up *'No Photography'* signs around the MAC just in case anyone had ideas. But still… Was nowhere safe?

He could see Klara in his mind's eye, slumped distraught on the kitchen floor after reading that email from the parents of the kids at her school. They'd all turned against her. They'd told her she was unfit to be a teacher—when she'd loved those kids more than anything. And now Mila was about to see first-hand what it was *really* like attempting to date a world-famous surgeon.

'Sebastian? Are you bringing her?'

'I haven't asked her yet,' he snapped. 'How can I ask her *now*? The cameras will be waiting for us at the airport.'

'I think you're being way too paranoid. I went ahead and put you down for a plus-one anyway. Mom's excited to see you. I've sent you tickets for the jet—one's blank, so you can fill in her name if you decide to bring her. I'm looking forward to seeing you too, bro, it's been too long.'

Sebastian was fuming. He stood by the kitchen sink under the air-conditioning, watching Mila and Stormy through the window as Jared changed the topic.

From now on he'd have to be even more careful.

CHAPTER TWELVE

'NEARLY A MILLION likes already,' she said as she turned towards the sink and pulled at the strings of her bikini. 'That's impressive.'

'It's not impressive.'

Sebastian's jaw ticked from left to right as if he was grinding his teeth. He was half scrolling through the comments on his phone, half watching her reflection in the mirror from the bathroom doorway.

The sun was streaming in on her body through the trees overhead. At first Mila had felt self-conscious in this outdoor bathroom at Sebastian's place, but the way he worshipped her body in it had shifted her perspective somewhat.

'Those comments, though...' She was determined to lighten the situation. He had a face like a thunderstorm and they didn't have long before they had to get back to the MAC. 'They're not bad. People are just interested in what you're doing out here.'

'I could do without their interest, Mila. So could you. We shouldn't be seen together.'

She pulled the bikini top off completely, dropped it to the floor beside her. He was behind her in a second, folding his arms around her. Her body seemed to attach itself to his like a magnet, and she was shocked for a second by their reflection in the mirror. He looked for a moment as if he never wanted to let her go. Adrenaline flooded her veins.

'Sebastian. Whatever people think or say about me, I can handle myself,' she told him.

The familiar tingle of anticipation had started in her toes. The more she told herself this was just a temporary fling, that they were entirely incompatible on so many levels, the more she craved being with him.

'I don't doubt that you believe that, soldier,' he rasped in her ear.

She shuddered at his intoxicating closeness. 'I don't need you to protect me.'

'What if I need you to protect *me?*'

He was urging her bikini bottoms down now. She stepped out of them, found the button on his shorts, snapped it open, reached into the shower and flipped the lever.

Warm water gushed onto their heads as he sat her on the seat and lowered himself to his knees between her legs. It was moments like this that Mila lived for lately. She hadn't experienced this level of sexual spontaneity till now. Maybe she had just never let herself really trust anyone this much.

A dog barked.

Sebastian pulled away from her in a second, snatching up a towel. 'What was that?'

He stopped the shower, moved to wrap the towel around her shoulders, but she stood up and grabbed his wrist, taking it from his hands.

'Bruno or Stormy must have seen someone go past the gates, that's all. The gates are locked, so nobody can come in,' she said calmly, and dropped the towel again.

He was so on edge after that social media post. She couldn't appear to be affected; he would just get even more jumpy.

'It was nothing,' she promised.

Sebastian looked as if he wanted to leap over the wall, brandishing a baseball bat, but she urged him back into the shower till he stuck his hands up in surrender, groaning under her mouth and her lips.

She knew the gates were locked. And no one could get over them—he'd told her he'd made sure of that himself a long time ago.

'It's only us,' she assured him. 'No one can see us here. Trust me, Dr Becker... I'm a soldier.'

The girl was out cold. Blood had formed dark splotches on her yellow cotton T-shirt and on the hem of her bleached white shorts.

'Female patient, Zuri Lerato, twelve years old. Looks like she's fallen somehow. She was unconscious when her father found her in the hotel bathroom. There was blood on the floor and walls.'

The glucose machine beeped between Mila and Nurse Viv.

'Forty-three,' Viv reported. 'Blood pressure one-six-seven over ninety-three. Pulse one-twenty-three. O2 sat ninety-two...'

Mila put a hand to the girl's chest. This time she stirred and her eyes fluttered open. She blinked up at the ceiling fan, tried to sit up, but Mila encouraged her back down. 'Don't move,' she told her.

The girl looked as if she was lost for words—as if nothing was familiar and it scared her.

'It's OK, sweetie, you're safe,' Mila soothed, stroking her arm softly. We're all here to help you. Do you remember what happened?'

Zuri just groaned and shook her head. She still looked confused. It was worrying, to say the least. She had clearly fallen, and Mila suspected from the girl's father's account that she had hit her head on the bathroom sink and passed out. She was likely to be in shock, but Mila wanted to get this girl a bedside brain scan.

'Another blood pressure reading, please!'

By now Mila was used to having to be in ten places at once on the island, but today of all days she was finding it almost impossible to keep her mind off Annabel. And as her team took care of a dazed young Zuri she couldn't wait to give herself the all-clear and be alone.

It was the day of the anniversary. She had considered taking the day off, as she'd planned, but things were just too crazy.

Sebastian had a facial scarring consultation over on Bali for a guy who was too fragile to be moved to the island yet. He had stayed in his villa on the mainland last night, and although she'd insisted that she would rather they both continue their duties and stay busy, rather than take time off and dwell on what the day meant for her, she was itching to see him later.

They were going to his favourite diving spot off the island: a night dive just for the two of them.

He'd suggested it himself.

'I know you switch off down there too, like I do. Maybe it will help you finally feel at peace with what happened.'

Mila wasn't sure it would be possible not to think of Annabel constantly on a day like this, but she had agreed to the night dive, grateful for his compassion.

When she was finally able to discharge herself, with Zuri stable in Recovery and Nurse Viv on night watch, she realised just how much tension she had been holding in all day. Walking back to her cosy little villa in the MAC grounds she couldn't wait to be under the water. First, however, she had to call her mother.

She reclined in the hammock on her porch with a cup of hot tea. The moon was rising beyond the palms as she dialled the familiar number.

'How are you, Mum?'

'Oh, my darling, I was hoping you would call. I'm as OK as can be expected.'

'I said I would call. I know today is hard, Mum, and I wish I was there with you.'

Mila closed her eyes to the emotions as tears blurred the

trees ahead, feeling the knots start to tighten in her stomach. She'd been doing so well, keeping her cool all day around other people, but her mother's caring voice had the ability to knock the wind from her sails in a heartbeat.

'I'm just about to head out, actually,' her mother informed her.

She swiped at her eyes. 'Where are you going?'

'Just out with a...friend.'

Her mother had paused before the word 'friend' and Mila felt her eyebrows knit together. She stopped swinging the hammock, put her tea on the floor.

'He's taking me to a gallery. There's an exhibition on Tudor England and the reign of King Henry VIII—he knows I'm into that kind of thing.'

'He?' Her mother had never mentioned a male friend— at least not a man who took her to things like art exhibitions. 'Who is "he"?'

'I told you—just a friend. He's good for me, Mila. Today especially.'

Mila decided to store this new information for another day, when they could talk about it without the shadow of Annabel's death hanging over them.

'I'm glad you have company today, Mum.'

'Have you been keeping busy yourself?' her mother asked. 'With your Dr Becker?'

'He is taking me out soon, yes.'

'Does he know what happened? I mean, does he know what day it is?' Her mother's voice faltered suddenly. 'Oh, my... Sorry, Mila, I thought I had this under control.'

Mila swallowed the urge to cry, too. They'd both done well till now, trying to sound strong for each other, like they usually did.

'He knows today is the day Annabel died,' she told her mother apprehensively. 'But he still doesn't really know exactly what happened.'

'What do you mean, "exactly"?'

'He doesn't know that I failed to help her…help her get out of the car in time.'

'Oh, Mila…'

Her mother's voice was faltering now, and Mila cursed herself. She swung her legs from the hammock and paced the porch, taking in a deep lungful of sea air. She was trying to think of something happy to tell her mother, willing the calm to come back.

'We have been over this before, Mila—so many times. I won't let you blame yourself.'

'I know, but I can't help it, Mum.'

She swallowed back her tears. Sebastian was picking her up soon—she couldn't look as if she'd been crying. He was kind, and understanding, and tolerant of her intermittent bouts of PTSD, but he didn't even know how she'd got the scars on her arms. He probably assumed she'd got them in Afghanistan. Maybe he felt asking her about them might upset her—which was true.

She didn't want him to think any less of her for her failure to save Annabel—especially not now she was falling for him.

It hit her like a brick.

She was absolutely falling for him. It was much more than a brief, casual fling to her now—she'd been missing him badly all day.

'When are you coming home, baby?' her mother asked eventually, just as Mila had known she would.

'Soon, Mum. I haven't forgotten about clearing out our old room…the rest of Annabel's stuff. It's the first thing we'll do together when I get back, I promise.'

'You're putting it off as much as I am.' Her mother sighed. 'Or maybe you have another reason not to want to come home now?'

Mila couldn't argue with that. 'You know me too well…' she muttered, casting her wet eyes to the clock through the bedroom window.

It was past eight p.m. Sebastian was supposed to have been here twenty minutes ago.

A small, fuzzy torpedo of love hurtled at her the second she was through the gates. Sebastian had given her a spare key, so she could always get in without ringing the buzzer. Usually it felt like breaking the rules, but tonight she didn't care. He wasn't answering his phone and she was starting to get worried.

'Did you miss me, huh? Did you…?'

Stormy and Bruno barked and nuzzled at her ankles as Mila took the steps up to the front porch. She put her home-made paper lantern down on the table by the hammock, careful not to let the dogs damage it in any way.

'That's for Annabel,' she told the nosy animals, ringing the doorbell. 'We're going to set it off on the water from the dive boat, in her memory. You didn't know Annabel, but you would have liked her.'

Stormy cocked her head with her tongue hanging out and Mila patted her affectionately. Sometimes it was nice not to be answered or buried in questions, just acknowledged by a living creature whose sole responsibility was to give and receive unconditional love.

The house was quiet. It seemed to be all locked up.

Frowning to herself, she peeked through the bottom window into the sitting room. The dogs jumped up at the window too, paws to the glass alongside her, probably anticipating a feed.

'Where is he? He was supposed to be back from Bali by now.'

Stormy let out three barks in quick succession. 'I wish I could understand your language.' Mila sighed, then let herself into the house. 'Sebastian!'

Nothing. There were no sounds coming from his bathroom either.

The couch looked so appealing… She was beyond tired

and could almost have napped on it. Maybe he was just late coming back. She was more than ready for her night dive. She didn't want to be alone with her thoughts. She didn't want to sleep in case the dreams came back. She needed distraction.

'Did he have an emergency that I don't know about?' she asked the dogs, pouring them some kibble from the giant bag under the sink. They wolfed it down hungrily from their bowls.

She picked up the brochure on the coffee table. It was for the Becker Institute. She sank into the couch and flicked through it absently, lingering on a photo of Jared Becker in a white coat. He was handsome, like Sebastian, smiling in a trustworthy fashion with a full set of whiter-than-white American teeth.

She considered whether he was as handsome as Sebastian. Absolutely not, she decided. Sebastian had rougher edges; he looked like he lived on an island in the sun and he looked like he loved it, too.

Where was he?

Two thin pieces of paper fell from the pages of the brochure onto the hardwood floor. Stormy made a run for them.

'Don't eat those!' Mila snatched them up as the dog went to sniff them with her wet nose. 'Tickets to Chicago on a private jet,' she told the dog aloud, realising what they were with a start. 'Sent from Jared for their mother's seventieth birthday, I suppose. One for Dr Sebastian Becker, and one for...'

She trailed off, turning the ticket over and over again, as if it might start to reveal her own name. The spare ticket was blank.

Her hands shook like jelly as she stuffed the tickets back inside the brochure and dropped it onto the table. Jared had sent him a spare open ticket. Was this plane ticket for someone else entirely? If not, why hadn't Sebastian even broached the subject of her accompanying him?

She tried his phone again. Then she tried calling the dive shop, but no one had seen or heard from him.

Panic started setting in. Annabel had left for a party on this day three years ago and never come back. They'd been having dinner when Annabel had announced she had to leave early. Some guy was waiting for her at a party.

Mila tried to fight the creeping paranoia and despair as she walked to the beach. How could he forget her, today of all days? She wasn't even particularly angry about the plane tickets, she realised. She trusted that he was hers for now at least. She just wanted to see him…to know he was safe.

A horse and cart shuttled past on the street behind her as she found a private nook behind some trees and dropped to the sand. The sound of distant music and clanging dishes mingled with the smell of barbecues and incense in the muggy air. The island was alive and the moon was bright for their planned night dive, but there was still no sign of Sebastian.

She drew her knees up, feeling anxiety form around her like a cloak.

She was back in the driveway of her mother's house now, yanking the chain off her bicycle five minutes after Annabel had left for the party. She'd been talking to her sister on the phone when the line had suddenly gone dead.

'Where are you going?' her mother had called from the driveway.

'Me and Annabel got cut off. Wait here!' she'd yelled back to her mother.

She had pedalled so hard down that road. The night had been black, the trees a frenzied mass of bare branches in the wind, and the rain had been threatening to turn from spit and drizzle into a full-blown downpour that would drench her.

But Mila had hardly felt the cold. Not from the weather anyway. She'd had a feeling. It had seeped through to this earthly plain from somewhere else and chilled her bones. *Something wasn't right with her twin sister.*

Then she'd seen the car, wrapped around a tree. She'd seen the smoke pouring from the back and from under the bonnet. She'd seen the motorbike rider, sitting in a crumpled sobbing heap at the roadside. His bike had been a twisted wreck, but the car... It hadn't even looked like a car.

And Annabel... She hadn't even looked like Annabel by the time Mila had came to her senses and tried to heave her out through the broken glass.

Mila's eyes sprang open. She couldn't go there—not again. She could have helped if only she'd been fast enough. She would never forgive herself for freezing up and wasting those precious seconds.

Mila watched the dogs sniffing around the beach for sand crabs, chasing them as if it was the greatest game in the world. If only life were so simple for humans, she thought, wading into the shallows with her lantern.

Both dogs ran over to watch as she pulled matches from her shorts pocket and lit the tiny candle at the centre of her paper lantern.

'I'm so sorry, Annabel,' she whispered as it drifted out to sea on the pull of the tide. 'I miss you so much. Please, if you're out there, send me a sign that you forgive me.'

CHAPTER THIRTEEN

MILA SLATHERED THE jasmine-scented shower gel everywhere, from her fingertips to her toes. Standing in the shower at her place, she scrubbed at her body as if she could scrub away the memories, too.

Annabel wasn't leaving her head now. The night of the accident…all that blood. And that was interspersed with her confusion and frustration over Sebastian, as if one of her nightmares had turned into the real world.

Why hadn't he called?

She was just getting started on the shampoo when the lights flickered out above her.

'Great,' she mumbled. As if the evening wasn't bad enough already, now she had to shower in the dark?

She slid down the wall to the tiled floor. Exhaustion made her bones feel heavy as she watched a yellow butterfly flit against the window outside. All those long nights of delicious sex, losing herself in Sebastian when she should have been sleeping, were taking their toll.

She let the water wash over her, trying to clear her head. They never spent time together outside, where anyone could see them. He was so concerned about her being pictured with him that they were limited to rooms with four walls and total privacy.

At first it had been kind of exciting…even though she knew it wasn't exactly sustainable. Now it was making her think that maybe he'd 'forgotten' tonight for the same reason. Maybe he didn't want to risk being seen out on another boat with her.

Mila blinked back water from her eyelashes as the lights flickered on again.

Those damn island generators.

Something strange caught her eye. The yellow butterfly was still and silent on the glass now—odd—but that wasn't it. She peered closer at the tiny red dots appearing on her bare arms. They were small and strange, blending in with the shower gel…

Wait a second. They were wriggling!

'Oh, my God!'

Mila shrieked and almost slipped as she tried to jump clear of the water. More of the tiny red creatures were landing on her shoulders, trickling down her stomach with the shampoo trails.

Scrambling out of the shower, she grabbed up a towel and broke into a fit of sobs. She reached for the door handle just as a heavy knock on the other side made her jump out of her skin.

'Who's there?'

'Mila, it's me. Are you OK?'

She froze, trying to swallow back tears, but it was impossible.

'Mila? Let me in!'

Her body was heaving with sobs and writhing with shock and disgust—and now with utter embarrassment—but Sebastian was right there on the other side when she finally pulled the door open. He caught her in his arms as she tumbled forward in the towel. Stormy was close behind him, jumping at the doorframe.

'Mila, what's going on?'

She stayed flat against his chest in nothing but the towel, too emotional to move. Sebastian was short of breath, as if he'd run all the way here or something. His arms folded around her instantly and for a moment he just held her while she cried with the force of someone fighting to live through suffocation.

'The front door was open,' he said into her hair. 'I was looking for the dogs and for you. Mila, I'm so sorry I wasn't here for you earlier. I know what today is…'

'I'm not crying because of *you*,' she said, gathering herself together. It was partly true, at least. She forced her body to detach itself from his and pressed a palm to the bathroom door. It swung open in a cloud of hot steam. 'There are *worms* coming out of my shower!'

His brown eyes widened in horror. 'Worms?'

'Go and look,' she told him, running a shaky hand over her eyes.

She wasn't sure what had just happened, but him holding like that, just saying nothing, was making her cry even harder. He hadn't forgotten the anniversary. He'd come to look for her.

Sebastian strode purposefully into the bathroom. She heard the water still running in the shower. Then she heard him curse and turn it off. He strode back into the room, wiping his wet hands on his open blue shirt. She wanted to be touching him again.

'That's not good. It's mosquito larvae…'

'What? That wriggling red stuff is *larvae*?' Mila was repulsed. 'Are you serious?'

His broad frame dominated the room as he walked around the bed towards the door. 'It must be in the water tank. I'll get someone over here…'

'Where *were* you, Sebastian?'

She was still shaking. There was probably still soap in her hair. But Sebastian was in her bedroom after all this time. Usually they went to his place—which probably explained the larvae in her shower. She hadn't used it for a few days.

'There was an emergency,' he told her, taking her hands

now, reaching one hand to her face in concern. 'I left without my phone. I meant to call…'

'I was so worried, Sebastian. I went over all the reasons why you hadn't come. You can't just tell someone you'll be somewhere and then not show up. You can't just leave… That's what Annabel did to me—three years ago on this day!'

As soon as her words were out he seemed to realise the severity of his mistake. 'Baby, I'm so sorry…'

He pulled her to the edge of the bed with him and sat her down. She folded against him in the towel.

'It's my fault Annabel died,' she blurted. 'It's all my fault, Sebastian.'

Silence.

She sobbed into his shoulder till his shirt was wet—but she didn't care and he didn't seem to care either. His arms were still wrapped tightly around her. She had to get it all out now.

'We were on the phone while she was in the car. She was asking me about a guy. I was telling her what to do—or what *not* to do. I don't know… I can't remember. We always did that. We talked on the phone while we drove—hands-free, of course. We always had so much to say…we couldn't stop. She'd only just left the house. Then the phone went dead…'

'It's OK.' He pressed a kiss to the side of her head.

'I just had this *feeling*, like I always did.'

Her voice was as shaky as she felt, even as she tried to pull herself together for his benefit.

'I knew something was wrong. I took my bike and I found the car. There was so much blood…all coming from her…from my *sister.* I couldn't think straight. I completely froze, Sebastian. After all my training, all my combat experience, all the times I'd rescued soldiers from burning convoys and tanks… As soon as I saw my twin sister I couldn't think of anything… Then I tried to pull her out though the windscreen. I couldn't get her through the glass, but I tried anyway. I had to do *something*. But by then I was too late. Those seconds were critical...'

'You did everything you could.'

Sebastian's gentle eyes were making her heart hurt even more.

He reached for her hands and turned her wrists over. 'Your scars,' he stated, running his thumbs along the telltale lines. 'They're not from Afghanistan.'

'They're from trying to pull her out of the car. But I was too late. I was just too late...'

'It wasn't your fault Annabel died, Mila.' He held her at arm's length. 'You of all people should know that. Listen to me—I cannot be the only one ever to have said this to you, but I'm going to say it again. This was *not* your fault. You need to let this go.'

He kissed her nose, her eyes and lips, then looked at her incredulously.

'That's why you didn't get plastic surgery on your arms, isn't it? You felt like you should live with those scars because you deserved them?'

Mila couldn't even answer. He stood up from the bed. For a second she assumed he was so repulsed by her that he was leaving, but he'd picked up the long green dress from the hanger she'd hooked on the wardrobe door.

'What are you doing?' she asked him. 'We've missed the dive. And I already sent my lantern out, too.'

'Get dressed,' he commanded, holding the dress out to her. 'Come with me.'

'Agung? Can we see them?'

'Sure thing, Dr Becker. They're doing really well, in spite of... Well, you know.'

It was midnight now, but Sebastian had known Ketut and Wayan would be awake after what they had been through. The Blue Ray Clinic was quiet, but the sound of a gurgling baby made its way down the hallway as they squeaked along in their shoes.

Mila's eyes grew wide in surprise.

He hadn't told her yet.

'Is that...?'

'Come see.'

After what had happened he wanted to give Mila a surprise and make this awful night a little better—to show her exactly why he'd lost track of time and forgotten his phone.

Later he would give her the other surprise—an offer of a trip to Chicago. He'd been over the pros and cons of asking her so many times, and he'd concluded finally that he would always regret not asking her if he didn't. So he'd been saving it for tonight.

He had the plane tickets on the table...a boxed gift behind the couch... A stomach full of knots.

Agung led them through to the little recovery room which the staff had filled with balloons already.

Mila's hand flew up over her mouth. She stepped to the edge of the bed with him. 'Wayan! You had the baby!'

Wayan was beaming. 'Dr Ricci, it's so good to see you.'

'Meet baby Jack,' Sebastian said, stroking a finger across the tiny boy's cheek.

He had fallen in love with this kid already—all swathes of jet-black hair and crinkled feet and fingers...and a mouth he thought was pretty cute, even if the rest of the world might deem him in need of fixing.

'Oh, Wayan, he's beautiful.'

'Sebastian really helped us tonight,' Ketut told her, adjusting the fluffy white pillows behind Wayan. 'I called him when the contractions got too much and he brought the boat over himself...brought us back here.'

'I left my phone at the MAC when it happened,' Sebastian added.

'It's OK,' Mila told him, touching her fingers to his arm.

He put a hand on top of hers. They were supposed to have

been out diving by now at Shark Reef. He was supposed to have given her the plane ticket and the gift. He'd planned it all for late evening, because he still wouldn't risk them being seen out together where anyone could take a photo of them.

Jared had laughed when he'd told him this earlier.

'You can't keep her all locked up just because of what happened with Klara, bro.'

'I'm not keeping her locked up. It's called being care-ful—for her protection.'

'Didn't you say she was in the Army? Does she really need your protection?'

Sure, let them all think he was paranoid…

But they hadn't seen the look on Klara's face when she'd read that letter from the parents. They hadn't seen her when her whole world fell apart. If anything like that happened to Mila—especially now she'd opened up to him about Anna-bel and shown she trusted him—he wouldn't forgive him-self.

He knew they would have to be extremely careful in Chicago, but he considered it worth the risk to have this woman there at his side.

'I'm so happy for you,' Mila was telling Wayan and Ketut now, extending her finger to stroke the back of little Jack's hand.

The baby only went and took her finger between his tiny ones. Sebastian looked on and felt something strange…a mixture of pride for Ketut and Wayan and envy.

'You decided to join us a few weeks early, huh?' Mila whispered to Jack.

'Maybe he wanted to spend more time with Auntie Mila before she leaves the MAC?' Ketut chimed in.

'Auntie Mila… I kind of like that.' Mila smiled at Se-bastian.

Sebastian reached for the cluster of balloons that had floated between them in the draught from the fan.

'Cleft lip and cleft palate, exactly as shown on the scan,'

he confirmed, seeing the way Mila was studying the baby's mouth. 'Two birth defects: a right unilateral cleft lip and palate with complete deformity.'

'You'll help him, Sebastian, when the time comes,' she said conclusively.

'Of course. My team will take care of everything this little guy needs—no question,' he replied, breaking eye contact and moving the balloons to the corner of the room. His stomach had just twisted at the idea of working on Jack without her.

The trip to Chicago was to be around the same time as her flight to the UK was due. The date of her return had now been confirmed, and it remained an unspoken certainty between them. He was aware that she had things to get home to—her mother included—and asking her to meet his family was a huge decision that could change everything for them.

The media was one monster to slay, but he realised that maybe he hadn't asked her about Chicago yet because he was afraid she might say no. He was already concerned that nothing he could do would keep her in his life…that she would leave him anyway, just as Klara had.

He was totally paranoid, he concluded ruefully.

Wayan was talking again now, looking between them. Holding the baby close against her chest, she looked tired, but elated.

'No matter how many ultrasounds we saw, we couldn't really know what we would see when he arrived. I knew he would be beautiful, though, no matter what. Nothing can prepare you for the love you feel for your unborn child, Dr Ricci. And it's only intensified when it's born.'

'I can't even imagine,' Mila replied with a smile, as Ketut dropped a kiss to his wife's head.

'It's the kind of love you know you've been waiting for your whole life,' she told them, and Sebastian didn't miss the look of awe and wonder in Mila's eyes.

Was that a flicker of sadness he saw too?

CHAPTER FOURTEEN

'OPEN IT,' SEBASTIAN told her, presenting her with the long, rectangular box he'd just pulled from behind the couch.

'You're giving me gifts now?' Mila released Stormy, who had demanded a hug the second they'd walked through the villa door. 'What's this?' she asked as the dog hopped to the floor and sniffed around the couch looking for more surprises.

'Open it!'

She did as she was told, pulling the golden wrapping from the flat box, intrigued. Sebastian threw the paper to the floor, along with the huge red ribbon. Stormy pounced on it straight away, and Bruno soon joined in.

'The dress!' she exclaimed, pulling the soft, floaty light fabric from the box. 'The one from the book at the tailor's in Bali?'

It felt incredible in her hands. She was stunned, and embarrassed because it must have cost so much. But then she remembered he was rich. It was easy to forget, with the way he seemed to treat everyone and everything as an equal.

'I had Anya expedite it and bring it over for you.'

He took her hand and helped her off the couch and out of her wrap. She raised her arms above her head, then slowly he helped slide the dress on, until the soft blue fabric was cinched flatteringly at her waist and floating about her calves. She ran a hand along one almost transparent sleeve.

Adrenaline spiked in her veins as he caught her wrist where the fabric hovered over her scars and brought it to his lips.

'It's beautiful on you,' he said, and kissed her.

He'd remembered that she liked long sleeves, to cover her scars, and even as she kissed him back Mila was mortified by the way she'd broken down in front of him earlier. It was almost two a.m. now, but her eyes were still red from crying. Bless Wayan and Ketut for not saying a word. It had been a rough day for all of them...

'Thank you,' she sighed, putting her arms around his broad shoulders. 'I love it.'

'I want to you wear it in Chicago,' he said.

Mila's heart skipped a beat as he reached down for the brochure on the coffee table—the one she had picked up earlier.

'You're asking me to meet your family?'

'I'm asking you to accompany me to what will undoubtedly be the most lavish, over the top celebration in honour of a seventy-year-old woman you'll have ever seen. My brother and his wife Laura know how to throw a party. They've invited the entire badminton club.'

She didn't smile as she was clearly supposed to. She felt queasy. She hadn't told him she'd already seen the tickets, and she felt a little bad for jumping to conclusions about him not wanting her there.

She turned to him, still in the dress. 'I appreciate you asking me, Sebastian, but I don't think it's a good idea, do you?'

It was the honest truth. How could she go to his home with him, involve herself in his life to that extent, when they were fundamentally different at the core? She'd seen him with baby Jack. At the end of the day he wanted a family of his own here, on the island. If she went with him she would fall for him even harder. And it would only hurt her even more to lose him.

'It's just a few days in Chicago. We'll take the helicopter to Denpasar, then it's a direct flight on the private jet. We'll have our own bedroom on board.' He kissed her passionately, ran his hands through her hair, and his words against her lips gave her tingles. 'Imagine the fun we'll have on the way...'

Mila broke away from him, imagining exactly that—the mile high club...high on each other.

The dress swished heavily around her ankles as she crossed to the doors to the garden. 'I don't know if I should be meeting your family at this point, Sebastian. I mean, I appreciate the offer, but...'

'But what? I know you need to go home and see your mother, Mila, but you can go *after* the party, can't you? And then you can come back here?'

'You mean, extend my contract at the MAC?'

'If you want.'

Her heart raced wildly. He made it all sound so simple. He was sitting there on the couch, holding the brochure and the plane tickets. The night was quiet and still, apart from the dogs, who padded past outside. Stormy was still gripping the red ribbon in her teeth.

Sebastian's jaw started to tic when he realised she wasn't as excited as she should be, but she didn't know what to say. She was so torn.

'I want you in my life,' he said seriously. 'We're good together, Mila.'

'You won't even be seen with me in daylight!'

He wrinkled his nose. 'I wouldn't want to take you home if I didn't think you could handle what might happen there. Jared won't invite the media, so no one will take any photos we don't want them to...'

'I can't live like that, and neither should you. I'm not afraid of what people think or say about me. But that's not the point, Sebastian. I can't give you what you want—not in the long run.'

'What are you talking about?'

'A family, Sebastian. I saw the way you looked at Jack, and I see how you look when you talk about Charlie, too. I *know* that's what you want.'

Sebastian fell silent again and her cheeks flamed. She had pretty much just divulged that she'd both considered and rejected the possibility of having his children—all without him even knowing.

'This thing we have…it's complicated,' he said.

He stood up and crossed to her, and she felt his soft breath on her cheek as his strong hands found her waist from behind, urging her back against him gently.

'And I'm not asking you for anything more than your company right now,' he told her, sweeping her hair aside and dropping kisses along the nape of her neck. 'Just some time off this island together, while we figure out what's going to happen next. What do you say, Dr Ricci? You wouldn't make me listen to the badminton club gossip all alone, would you?'

CHAPTER FIFTEEN

RACHEL CAME FLYING through the MAC reception doors so fast, Mila almost mistook her for the crew bringing an emergency patient in.

'Where's Dr Becker?' Rachel asked excitedly.

Her face was beetroot-red, as if she'd run here from her villa in spite of the blazing heat. She pushed her sunglasses up to the top of her head.

'He's on the mainland again, for consultations,' Mila explained, moving out from behind the desk and closing the window on the computer screen.

She didn't want Rachel to see she'd been looking up the Beckers on the internet, in anticipation of meeting them, as well as double-checking the schedule for the day.

'He'll be back tomorrow. What's happened?'

'*This* has happened.'

Rachel fished an iPad out of her bright pink beach bag. The cover on it matched.

She stepped to Mila's side and showed her the screen. 'It's in French, but you can see what it is,' she enthused. 'I think it's super-exciting! I know Dr Becker doesn't like photos and stuff, especially of you two...'

Mila didn't respond.

'But I think this is something different, right? I mean, it's a *kid*!'

Mila took the tablet in her hands, frowning to herself. What was she talking about? French? A kid?

She was trying not to let on, but she felt sick to the core suddenly. Was it the smell of the detergent they'd just used on the floors? Or maybe it was the eggs she'd had for breakfast? She fought to focus on the tablet. Rachel crossed her arms proudly.

Fatema walked in, and peered over Mila's shoulder. 'What are you looking at?'

'I don't even know,' Mila said, putting a hand to her stomach. 'It's in French.'

Rachel tutted and took the tablet back. 'It translates as "Breakthrough scar surgery saved my face!" It's that French kid...you know, Francoise Marchand? She got bitten by a dog. Dr Becker and Dr Ricci saved her from serious scars with his new laser treatment and now she's written this. She's only eight—can you believe it? Her story's got published in the newspaper—probably because she's so young. Kids who do cool stuff like this always get famous. I wish I was eight years old again... I would do things differently.'

She said it a little wearily, even with a hint of envy, but Mila was only half listening now. She put her hand to the back of a chair and sank slowly onto the seat—just as her next patient glided in through the doors in a full purple sarong.

'Are you OK, sweetie?'

Amita Ahluwalia's perfectly symmetrical eyebrows met in the middle as she crouched in front of her. Mila noticed the smell of the beautiful Indian model's perfume instantly.

'You've gone very pale.'

'I'm OK...don't worry,' she reassured her, swallowing back a slight gag reflex.

This was embarrassing.

'We were just showing her an exciting piece of press coverage,' Rachel explained. 'Anyone would be overwhelmed. This eight-year-old kid has written a story about her dog bite and how our new revolutionary treatment helped her heal. It's a great testament to Dr Becker's work here. We'll get even more appointments after this. No one can resist a kid with a story... Are you OK, Dr Ricci? Do you feel sick?'

They all turned to look at her.

Mila couldn't take it any more. 'Excuse me,' she mumbled, clutching her stomach and bolting from the seat. She couldn't throw up in front of her patient, and the bathroom was just down the hall.

She heard Amita Ahluwalia's voice calling out to her to eat some charcoal as she made her dash down the hallway. Embarrassment coursed through her veins along with the nausea. She almost knocked over a vase of flowers in her hurry.

'Doctor?' Rachel was hot on her heels. 'I'm sorry if I upset you. But the article is *good*! I think Dr Becker will be OK with it. There aren't any photos of you, and it's not like you're in the same boat as his ex...'

'I don't care about that, Rachel.'

Why did everyone think she should care about that? There were far bigger things to be concerned about—like the fact that she was about to be sick at work.

Mila pushed through the door to the ladies' room and half ran, half stumbled to the toilet. With her hands on the porcelain bowl she threw up as quietly as she could—which, she realised in dismay, wasn't particularly quiet.

Rachel was in the bathroom, too. 'Dr Ricci...?'

Mila reached for the lock on the cubicle door and pulled it across. 'Please, Rachel, I'm OK—really. Nothing I can't handle. Can you just go and apologise to Miss Ahluwalia?'

She wiped at her sweaty face with her white coat sleeve, slumping back against the wall. The tiles were cold. And the lights were too bright—they were giving her a headache.

Rachel's sandals shifted beneath the door. Her voice was laced with concern now. 'Is this the first time this has happened to you?'

Mila covered her face with her hands. It was the first time she'd thrown up, but she'd been nauseous before this on a few occasions over the past few days, now that she thought about it.

'I'm… I'm sure it's nothing,' she managed.

'Go home, Dr Ricci, lie down. We'll make sure you're covered here.'

'Thank you.'

'Are you going to tell Dr Becker about this?'

'About the article?'

'No, about you being sick?'

A cold sweat prickled on her back against the tiles. 'No need to tell him anything, Rachel. Like I said, I'm OK.'

Rachel said nothing as she left the bathroom, but Mila knew what she was thinking. Her romance with Sebastian was hardly a secret around here any more. If it wasn't the floor cleaner, or the eggs… She could barely even entertain the notion of what might be causing her nausea.

'Thank you so much for agreeing to do this, Mila!'

Wayan handed over baby Jack, who was gurgling sweetly to himself. He was the epitome of cute, dressed in a little blue onesie. Then promptly put a giant padded bag laden with nappies and toys and bottles of formula over Mila's shoulder. The weight of it threatened to send her toppling sideways onto Sebastian's porch.

'Are you sure you don't mind?'

'Wayan, I told you—I love babysitting,' she enthused, straightening up with the giant bag.

She had never babysat in her life. She'd simply overheard Ketut asking Sebastian if he knew of a good babysitter, and figured it would be a chance to do something nice for the couple while Sebastian was away on the mainland. She also hoped spending some time with little Jack would help her relax, and think things through.

She eyed the paper bag on the dining table, feeling her throat dry up. There was something else she had to do, too…

'You guys just go and enjoy your dinner,' she said to Wayan, plastering a smile onto her face as the dressed-up woman gave her son an extra kiss on his chubby cheek.

Stormy and Bruno bounded ahead of her into the house and, carrying baby Jack under her arm, Mila made herself some tea. It wasn't the easiest thing, holding a baby… But she was doing fine, she told herself, nothing to worry about here.

The paper bag on the table seemed to be calling her.

Take the test! You know it's going to be negative! Just put your mind at rest!

She would do it later. Maybe even tomorrow.

Right now she would continue her research on the Beckers. She might even watch an episode of *Faces of Chicago* and see what all the fuss was about.

She would do anything, she realised quickly, other than take the damn test.

Jack snoozed on the couch next to her as she scrolled through Francoise's article on Sebastian's spare iPad. The kid had written some really sweet things about the MAC and her time on the island, and how she was proud to have been brave like Dr Mila Ricci.

Mila couldn't deny that she was proud to be part of the story. She hoped Sebastian would be proud, too. It wasn't anything close to the kind of 'publicity' that vultures like Hugo O'Shea liked to print. This was only drawing attention to the positive impact his work was having on the island and their patients.

The sharp, shrill ringtone of her phone woke the sleeping baby. He coughed and then started screaming like a banshee. She had never heard a sound quite like it. She bundled him onto her lap and held him close, rocking him.

'No, no, no…it's OK, Jack. I'm sorry.'

Jack's shrieks of discomfort burrowed under her skin,

filling her with dread, as a yellow butterfly flitted in through the open door and came to a stop on the arm of the couch. It sat there even as she reached past it for her phone, to decline the call.

Sebastian. She would have to call him back. She couldn't talk to him when Jack was crying like this.

Something maternal seemed to take control of her body as she rocked and whispered and cooed. 'There you go… you're doing fine, little man.'

But Jack cried and cried, and Mila contemplated singing to him.

What did babies *want*?

She had no clue, but the way he smelled was heavenly. Did all babies smell this nice? His skin was so clear and bright around his little misshapen mouth, and she loved the way his all-seeing eyes shone when he wasn't screaming. He'd have an idyllic life here…seeing the ocean every day, diving in it with his godfather, Sebastian. It must be an incredible privilege to watch a little person grow, to know you'd influenced their life decisions.

She felt a familiar dread creep in again, even as Jack fell silent in her arms. She liked the idea of it…but then she remembered why she wasn't cut out for motherhood—that she'd be terrible at it.

It was all her friends at home who wanted to be mothers, and her mum would've loved to be a grandma, and Sebastian… They all wanted the babies—not her.

Speaking of Sebastian, she should call him back.

Anything to put off taking the test.

CHAPTER SIXTEEN

SEBASTIAN WAS SEATED at a chequered-cloth-covered table between two potential investors who were keen to know more about his plans for the villa complex in the valley. Their waiter was already delivering plates of seafood pasta to their Italian-themed place mats.

'Dr Ricci?' He answered the voice call when the vibration in his pocket didn't stop. 'I have to be fast—I'm in a restaurant. Is everything OK over there?'

Her face flashed onto the screen just as one of his investors peered at it over his spaghetti.

'So this is Dr Ricci? The little French girl painted a wonderful picture of you in her article, but look at you—you're even more delightful in person. Whose baby do you have there?'

'Baby?' Sebastian realised that baby Jack was there, swaddled in a fluffy grey blanket next to Mila. His own *Chicago* shirt was still draped across the cushions on the couch behind her, where he'd left it.

'You're babysitting?' he said in surprise.

The investors were taking in Jack's cleft lip, witnessing Mila with the baby at the same time as him.

'It's my godson,' he explained. He probably shouldn't have picked up her video call—this wasn't looking too professional right now. But he'd thought she would be at the MAC. Mixing business with pleasure was risky...

'What's wrong with his face?' one of them asked.

'He has a cleft lip and palate. I'll be operating in a couple months or so—'

'He's so good, though,' Mila cut in. 'It's almost like he knows Dr Becker is going to help him—so he's being very brave, aren't you, sweetie?'

They all watched as she cuddled him close. Sebastian had never seen her like this. The investors looked truly touched for a moment, and a sudden rush of pride swept over him for both Mila and for Jack.

'Seems you're very close with your staff and your patients,' one of the investors observed. 'Do you open your home to them all like this?'

'Not at all.' Sebastian cleared his throat. 'But things are certainly different on the island. Excuse me just a second...?'

He inched his way past the chairs and tables and the harried waiters, through a waft of parmesan cheese to the door. Outside the air was thick and muggy, reminding him that he was actually still in Bali—not Italy.

'Sorry about that,' he said to Mila. 'I called you earlier to say I should be back by tomorrow, but I need to stay here another night with these investors. I can't get into the base facility till morning and I want to show them around.'

'So the investors have read the article by Francoise?'

He told her he'd been forced to read young Francoise's story that morning, and while he could hardly be angry at the kid for singing his praises, it was a little irritating, putting it in some French newspaper without his consent. More than irritating. Sure, there were no photos of him with Mila, and it wasn't a 'celebrity scandal' angle at all, but the publicity still drew attention where attention wasn't needed.

'Not all press is bad press,' Mila reminded him. 'Sebastian, you have to be OK with people writing things about you if it's done with good intentions. You're doing great work—you deserve to be recognised.'

'Thank you,' he told her sincerely. 'It's sexy when you put me in my place.'

She laughed.

Mila hadn't experienced the extent of the media's wrath enough to appreciate why he despised any hint of attention on him, but he was grateful for her indifference about such things—it was refreshing. It kind of calmed him down.

He told her how these investors from Jakarta were interested in his project there on the mainland. They loved the outside space, the funicular and the villas. They saw incredible potential *and* they were excited.

'I'd prefer Jared to get on board too,' he added quietly. 'He had some great ideas when we talked about it... But I have no choice except to move forward now. There are too many people who can't afford the MAC—we need facilities in both places. So the sooner we can get things moving the better.'

'You love creating more work for yourself, don't you?' she teased him.

He grinned. 'It's how I thrive.'

He turned back to the restaurant, saw the two investors toasting each other through the window. He knew they were likely congratulating themselves on getting involved, even if they hadn't signed anything yet. It was a good sign, he supposed. And he had Mila to thank for this. She had made a lasting impression on Francoise. And vice versa.

'Is everything else OK?' he asked her. 'I should really get back to them.'

Mila looked torn for a moment. She opened her mouth to speak, but then seemed to think better of it. 'Nothing that can't wait,' she said finally.

'You sure?'

'Quite sure.'

He took in the sight of her with baby Jack just for a moment longer before hanging up. She might only want a dog in her family in the future, but it hadn't escaped his attention that she looked pretty hot with a baby.

The clear blue line seemed to darken ominously as Mila studied it from the toilet seat. She was trembling ferociously and her head reeled in the candlelit outdoor bathroom. The crickets seemed to be singing into the night, taunting her from behind the stone wall.

How was this possible? *It couldn't be possible.* She'd been taking her pill the whole time—at the right time.

She would do another test.

Panic strangled her heart as she made her way back to Jack. He was still snoozing soundly, swaddled in his blanket. It seemed so telling, somehow, that the test should come up positive while she was babysitting.

Annabel flashed into her mind. She dropped to the floor beside the couch. She had asked for a sign on the night of the anniversary. Maybe this was Annabel's sign that she'd forgiven her for the accident and was encouraging her to start a family. Stranger things had happened, right?

Mila scowled at the floor, dragging her hands through her hair. She was being ridiculous. This wasn't some divine message from the other side—this was her own fault. She had probably forgotten to take her pill one night, or taken it too late.

You love him. This is the right thing for you.

The voice was in her head, but somehow it came from somewhere else. Mila spun around to Jack. His eyes were open and he was gazing up at the ceiling from the cushions.

Getting to her feet, she put her finger to his little hand, but he didn't stop looking at the ceiling, as if he was seeing something that wasn't there.

'What are you doing, little man?' she whispered, trying not to feel spooked.

Tears prickled her eyes. She wouldn't speak to her twin sister. She wasn't in this room. Annabel was gone and Sebastian had made her feel it was OK to let her go, to forgive herself for not being able to help when she'd still had time.

She rarely had nightmares about Annabel any more—in fact, she'd only had a few since she'd started sleeping in Sebastian's bed—but of course she was still in her every thought. She was part of her.

'We always said we'd have babies at the same time,' she said aloud. What was the harm in talking to her just for a bit...just in case? 'But by no means was an accidental pregnancy ever on the cards—especially one that's the result of a fling with an ex-celebrity doctor from Chicago. You would tell me off, if you were here, Annabel.'

You love him. This is the right thing for you.

She heard it again, loud and clear.

Mila shook her head at herself, petting Stormy when she padded over for some attention.

'Good girl,' she said softly when the dog pressed her nose to Jack's little foot.

She sat there in silence as Jack drifted off to sleep again. What to do?

She couldn't ask anyone at the clinic to test her for pregnancy—it would have to be another kit. It had been tough enough getting the first one from the storeroom without anyone seeing her.

If anyone even suspected she was pregnant they would know without a doubt that Sebastian was the father. It wasn't ideal, showing up as his employee and leaving pregnant with his baby. Besides, he hated attention—and people would surely fix their attention on *this* juicy piece of scandal.

What would he say when she told him, if the second test came back positive too? Would he want this baby with her? And if he did...what if something happened to it?

This was everything she'd been afraid of and all of it was unbearable to contemplate.

'Help me through this, Annabel,' she begged out loud, in spite of herself. 'I don't think I can do this on my own.'

CHAPTER SEVENTEEN

Two weeks later

'WHERE'S THAT NICE female surgeon who was here for the initial consultation?'

The fifty-six-year-old British woman blinking up at Sebastian was nervous without Mila there for her blepharoplasty.

'She had to leave unexpectedly this morning,' he explained, reaching behind him to the gramophone to lay the needle on the vinyl. Beethoven filled the room and he thought of Mila. He hoped she was all right.

'Nothing serious, I hope?'

His patient's eyes were full of genuine concern and so were Fatema's. Mila had clearly touched their patient on some deeper level, in the brief time they'd been in contact, just as she had Francoise.

'Dr Ricci was truly encouraging,' his patient was saying to them now, taking Fatema's arm. 'She said I didn't need this. She said that lines around our eyes are proof of all the times we've smiled, and the more we smile the more beautiful we are to everyone who sees us. Isn't that a nice thing to say? She could have just tried to sell me more plastic surgery.'

'That's not really our policy here,' Sebastian told her, fighting a smile.

It sounded as if Mila had made an even bigger impression that he'd thought. This was the sort of thing he'd been hearing ever since Mila had arrived at the MAC: *'Mila is so wonderful...' 'Mila is so caring...' 'Mila is so good for you...we mean, good for the MAC.'*

Shame she'd left the MAC earlier on today, saying she felt sick.

He was used to the gossip about them by now, of course, and he didn't care about that as long as their photos weren't splashed about the internet. It still gave him chills to think about how it had ended with Klara, and with Mila still set to come to Chicago with him for his mother's birthday party there was always the chance that someone would stick a lens where it wasn't wanted and make things difficult.

He was praying it would all go smoothly. She was well aware he wanted her to stay on at the MAC for various reasons, but they'd agreed that spending some time away from the island to talk about things would be the best course of action before putting it officially on paper.

It was the right thing to do. She had come on board as a temporary employee after all. Neither of them had expected this, and they couldn't exactly keep it a secret with the island itself more like a gossip factory than his last surgery in Chicago, just with more sand and fewer cameras.

Fatema cornered him when he went for the anti-bac. 'Is Mila still sick, then?' she asked him.

'Dr Ricci? I guess so… Maybe she ate something bad.'

'Like before?' Fatema seemed concerned. 'She needs to watch her diet.'

'Before? What do you mean?' He shook the anti-bac from the bottle, then handed it to her.

Fatema looked sheepish. She turned her back to their patient and lowered her voice. A couple of weeks ago— she was sick then, too. I think you were away in Bali. She didn't tell you?'

'Why would she tell me?'

Fatema cocked an eyebrow. 'We *all* know why she would tell you, Dr Becker.'

He grunted. 'Fine. But, no, she didn't tell me.'

The information nagged at his brain even as he forced himself to return to the task at hand. He should be focusing on the fact that he oversaw the most capable and qualified team in Indonesia, instead of wondering if Mila's strange moods and impromptu sick leave were something he should worry about.

She had been sick before today and not told him...?

Fatema was talking to their patient about the procedure. 'So, just to recap, Dr Ricci must have told you to avoid taking any medication that might thin your blood and prevent it from clotting normally prior to this surgery?'

'Yes, Dr Halabi, she explained all that.'

'That includes pain relievers, aspirin and ibuprofen. I trust you stopped those too? And you've only eaten very lightly today, if at all?'

'Dr Ricci told me not to have breakfast or drink anything after midnight the night before my procedure. So I had no margaritas last night—which was such a shame because they were buy-one-get-one-free.'

'You can make up for that later,' Sebastian interjected.

'She also said not to wear make-up—hence this mess you see here before you.'

His patient gestured to her plain face and mascara-free eyes, but he left the make-up chat to Fatema. She was more than capable of handling this.

He couldn't help replaying in his mind an episode from earlier in the week, when he'd taken Mila out on the dive boat. She'd gone for the ride, but she hadn't wanted to dive.

'You don't want to go down?' he'd asked her. 'I was kidding about the sharks. There won't be any sharks, but the manta rays around here—they're something else!'

'I think I'm just liking the feeling of the sun on my skin right now,' she'd told him distractedly.

He'd gone down with the group without her, but he hadn't been able to fully switch off as he usually did.

Mila was being quieter than usual, less involved. Just as she'd been after they'd first kissed, back when she'd pushed him away because she'd thought he'd hooked up with Annabel. She was supposed to be diving with the group tonight, but she'd already told him she couldn't go. He hadn't questioned it because he'd seen she clearly wasn't feeling one hundred percent.

He frowned as Fatema talked details to their patient with exemplary confidence. Mila always went quiet when she had something on her mind. Maybe she was just a little nervous about meeting his family, he mused. They were set to leave tomorrow, so he could understand that. His family could be difficult to handle.

Or maybe she was nervous about finishing her placement at the MAC with nothing set in stone for the future. He couldn't help mulling over that one himself. He hadn't and wouldn't put any extra pressure on her, but the thought of being here without Mila weighed heavy on his heart.

Mila woke from the dream with a jump. She flung her legs over the side of the bed, grabbed the cool pillow beside her and pressed her hot face to the cotton. Thank goodness Sebastian wasn't there—although his comforting arms would be a relief to sink into right now.

In the dream she'd been holding a baby on her lap in a car, but there hadn't been any seatbelts. She'd been forced to travel anyway, as the base camp wasn't safe. They'd been in convoy, cruising by night across the desert plains, taking bumpy secret routes that didn't even exist in reality, dodging insurgents like characters in a video game.

Then the car had been hit—attacked from behind by Afghan soldiers with larger than life AK-47s. The bullets had rained down through the roof and the windscreen and when she'd cried out, begging for the baby's life, the baby had been gone. Vanished.

She'd woken up hotter than fire, still shaking.

Somehow she made it to the bathroom, ran the cold tap and splashed her face. Thank goodness someone had been in to clear the mosquito larvae from the tank, but there were other things wriggling under her skin now: the second test had come back positive and her dreams had returned with a vengeance. They even had a new twist to torture her with.

She studied her face in the mirror as shame washed over her. Would Sebastian comfort her if he knew what she was hiding? It had taken her several days to build up the courage to take the second test, and she still hadn't told Sebastian she was pregnant.

She hadn't told anyone.

The time difference might be a blessing in one way. It would be a good time to talk to her mother in the UK. Surely she could tell her mother?

No. She couldn't tell her—not on the phone anyway.

Every time she so much as thought about telling her mother it became more real in her head. And the more real the baby was for her, the harder it would be to lose it. And she would lose it, surely—because she wasn't a suitable mother. She couldn't care for a baby as a baby needed to be cared for. She just…*couldn't*.

Mila pulled on a T-shirt and shorts. She slipped into her flip-flops and left the room, heart pounding. It was almost five a.m. She realised she was holding her belly protectively as she walked, looking out for dogs that might attack, and when she caught herself doing it she forced her hands away.

She was already looking out for this baby when she didn't even know if she could keep it.

She hadn't been diving, even though she'd wanted to, but Sebastian had gone diving again last night. She'd made another excuse, which she'd felt terrible about. He was worried about her, she could tell. She'd simply told him she would see him the next day. It had bought her more time, but it had brought her nightmares, too.

She had no clue how he'd react to her news, but she had to tell him. The secret was killing her.

It was only the gardener out at this hour, raking leaves from the pathways, and she squared her shoulders at Sebastian's gates and psyched herself up to let herself in. Her legs felt like jelly.

As usual, the dogs greeted her as if she'd just come home from war.

'Hey, Stormy. Hey, Bruno. Oh, it's good to see you, too.'

Sebastian's suitcase was still on the porch—the one he'd half packed for Chicago. He'd spilled milk on it, thanks to Stormy, and left it by the hammock to dry. Just the sight of it made her feel sicker. She'd put this off for so long that they were due to leave tonight and she still hadn't told him.

Was she crazy? She wasn't usually the kind of person who had difficulty speaking up; in fact, the strength to do that had defined her entire career. Why was this any different? You just said it and then it was out…just like the way she'd told him about the car crash that had killed Annabel. Eventually.

But it was so hard.

Maybe she should tell him once they'd left the island. When they'd have more space and time to talk things through privately. That was what they were due to be doing anyway—he wanted her to come back here with him, didn't he, after Chicago? He had told her as much.

He just wasn't anticipating an unplanned baby with the package, Mila!

She stepped up to the porch, but she could tell Sebastian wasn't home. Her instincts kicked in.

There must have been an emergency.

CHAPTER EIGHTEEN

'Is she going to be OK?'

Pedro's eyes were tired and full of panic, and he'd bitten his fingernails almost down to the cuticles. The twenty-eight-year-old from Brazil hadn't left the Blue Ray Clinic or the decompression chamber room all night. He was still wearing his wetsuit. So was Sebastian, under his white coat.

'The team will keep an eye on her, but we've done everything we can up to this point,' Sebastian said, taking the coffee an intern had handed him and peering through the circular window at Pedro's girlfriend, Rose. 'We'll know more when the tests come back.'

What a crazy night. He was utterly exhausted, but he felt it was his duty to stay with the guy; he'd been down there on the dive with him when it had happened. He was glad Mila hadn't gone with them in the end—things hadn't exactly gone to plan.

Pedro's girlfriend, twenty-seven-year-old Rose, had panicked over something under the water at fifteen metres down. He still wasn't sure what it had been, but there had been nothing the team could do to stop her as she'd pushed her way up to the surface without a safety stop. They always did a safety stop at five meters...

'Sebastian?'

Mila's voice made him spin around—Pedro, too. She looked as dazed as he felt. For a moment, in his deep fatigue, he almost went to wrap his arms around her, but he stopped himself. 'Dr Ricci, good morning.'

'Can I see you outside?'

He excused himself and took her out of the room into the hallway, shutting the door behind him. Agung and the resident intern threw them a look, but he signalled with his coffee as if it was perfectly normal to be standing with Mila in his wetsuit at six a.m. in the Blue Ray Clinic's hallway.

'Good *morning*?' she said, lowering her voice to a whisper. She looked him up and down. 'You haven't been to bed, Sebastian.'

'That girl has been in the decompression chamber since we brought her in from the dive.'

Mila looked horrified. 'The dive you were on last night?'

He nodded, noting her pink toenails in her flip-flops. 'We had to call the air ambulance from Lombok to get her back—she might not have made it on the boat. She's still out with decompression sickness... What are you doing here so early?'

Mila's face was pale, he noticed. She was watching the cleaner with her mop and bucket at the other end of the hall, and covering her mouth with her hand.

'Are you feeling sick again?' he asked, resisting the urge to put a hand to her cheek.

She averted her eyes. 'I'm not feeling sick. This is just awful, Sebastian—are *you* OK?'

Sebastian hadn't realised till she'd said it that he probably *wasn't* entirely OK. It was really rare for something like this to happen. It was shocking, to say the least, and he'd been running on adrenaline all night.

'I wasn't her dive buddy—that was Pedro, her boyfriend,' he told her, resting a foot against the wall behind him and tapping the bottom of his coffee cup. 'But we were all there. There were six of us. I guess that's one good thing—we managed to help her pretty fast after she came up.'

'I'm so sorry this happened.'

Mila was studying his face as if she was looking for signs that he might crack. Of course he wouldn't crack, but her eyes were so full of concern. He couldn't remember the last time any woman had cared this deeply about his well-being.

'You must be so tired. We can talk later. I'll let you get back to Pedro.'

She made to turn around, but he caught her arm. 'Wait. What did you want to talk to me about so early in the morning?'

She paused, half with her back to him. She was still looking at the cleaner's mop and bucket as if it was causing her physical pain.

'Mila?'

'Dr Becker?' The obstetrician, Dr Raya, had exited the room opposite. 'Rose's tests are back. Do you have a moment?'

He looked at Mila. 'You can talk to us both,' he said quickly, following Dr Raya back into the room.

Mila had crossed her arms beside him as they waited. Dawn was breaking outside and he could hear the ocean close by through the open window. It didn't calm him down. He was on high alert now—he could tell something was wrong.

Dr Raya looked him right in the eyes and took a long, deep breath. 'Dr Becker, Dr Ricci… The tests show your patient Rose was pregnant. I don't think she knew, as neither she nor her boyfriend mentioned it, I believe?'

Sebastian shook his head gravely as Mila walked over to the window, wrapping her arms around herself. This was not what he'd hoped to hear. 'Pedro didn't mention it, no. Poor guy.'

'Poor Rose,' Mila croaked, metres away now.

'It was four to five weeks, but I'm afraid with the decompression…'

'There's no chance of a pregnancy surviving,' he finished, tossing his coffee cup into the rubbish bin under the desk, hard. 'Damn—could this night get any worse?'

He shoved his hands into his white coat pockets, fists clenched. 'We should tell Pedro, so he can prepare himself before Rose wakes up. We don't want to distress her any more than necessary. She might need a few more sessions in the decompression chamber, so he'll have to decide when to let her know.'

Mila was shifting on her feet now, holding a hand to her mouth again. Before he or Dr Raya could say anything she raced from the window right past them, yanked open the door and stepped into the hallway.

He followed her halfway to the reception area her before she threw up—right into the cleaner's bucket.

Mila was mortified. It was that smell again. If it hadn't been for the smell she might have avoided throwing up—but she couldn't think about it again, she was far too humiliated.

'You should go back inside to Pedro,' she heard herself say as the sea breeze outside caught her hair, cooling her down.

Sebastian had ushered her out, past the stunned cleaner and several patients already in Reception.

'You were the one diving with him—he should hear this news from you.'

'I know,' he said, darkly.

She sat down on the wall outside the Blue Ray Clinic in the shade of a palm tree. It was getting lighter by the second and she felt even more exposed now he was standing in front of her, arms folded.

'You want to tell me what's going on?'

She considered her regrettable timing. This was not the time or place—especially with poor Rose in there in the decompression chamber and her poor boyfriend Pedro about to learn she'd lost a baby he hadn't even know she was expecting.

It was the worst time to tell him she was carrying a baby of her own, and she felt guilty. Why should *she* be pregnant when Rose…?

'Mila, Fatema told me you were sick before…when I was in Bali. Now this?'

Sebastian crouched down to her level. He still had his wetsuit on under his white coat, she realised. He hadn't slept all night and now he was here, trying to take care of her.

It was all too much. Above everything else she despised feeling so trapped and vulnerable; this wasn't who she was.

'And you wouldn't come diving. I mean, I'm happy you didn't come last night—don't get me wrong. Accidents happen, but you never expect a dive student to dismiss every single thing she's learnt in the face of panic…'

He trailed off when he realised what he'd said. His face said it all, though. He blamed Rose for what had happened—just as she still blamed herself for Annabel.

She needed to get away. She needed to be alone.

But Sebastian was holding her hand tight to her own lap. 'Talk to me.'

'I don't know what to say, Sebastian. It's the worst possible time.'

He stood up again. 'You're pregnant, aren't you?'

The world seemed to go white around her. How did he know…? *He's a doctor—that's how*, she told herself wearily.

'Mila? Are you pregnant?'

She still couldn't speak. Instead she just nodded and covered her face for a moment, taking deep breaths. She felt as if she might pass out.

'My God. You are.'

Sebastian sounded devastated and it made her heart ache. If she hadn't already thrown up, she might have done it again.

He turned towards the mountains and watched an early-morning horse trot past with a cart-load of boxes full of beer. This was surreal. She felt as she was looking at herself from outside her own body, hearing someone else saying these things about another person.

'I'm so sorry… I didn't know how to tell you before. It's not exactly something I planned—it's not even what I want…'

'How long have you known?'

'Two weeks.'

'Two *weeks*?' He kicked up the sand at his feet in frustration, then appeared to regret it, but he looked less than happy when he turned back to her. 'You've known for a whole fortnight and you didn't tell me? Mila, we're about to go and see my family—when exactly were you planning to tell me this? This involves me too, doesn't it?' He narrowed his eyes. 'It *is* mine, right?'

'Of course it's yours!' she exclaimed hotly.

'Then when were you going to let me in on this?'

'Today. Now.'

The disappointment on his face at her secrecy brought a lump to her throat. She knew she deserved it, but she felt cold as she struggled for composure. 'I thought we could talk about it when we'd left the island. I realise in retrospect that wasn't the best decision on my part—'

'I have to go deal with Pedro,' he said, cutting her off.

'OK.'

She watched helplessly as he rubbed his tired eyes, a foot away from her. 'We'll talk about this when I'm done. Will you be OK getting back to the house?'

She nodded mutely. Of course she would.

But her heart sank to the pit of her stomach as he strode purposefully back inside without another word. He was furious with her. He would probably end things between them now, seeing as she had basically just taken a firearm to his trust.

Her mind was a running commentary of self-loathing as she hurried back to his house. She needed to cuddle the dogs or something.

She should have told him sooner. She should *not* have told him today, when he'd had no sleep and had something pressing to deal with. Now she'd have to sit on a plane with him, meet his family, with this hanging over them... If he even still wanted her to go with him.

This was all too much. She had to get off this island—think about things rationally and logically somewhere no one could influence her decisions. Not even him.

Mila turned around and made for her consulting room instead. She'd forgotten to tell Personnel to cancel her transfer to the UK because Jared had organised the Chicago trip—she still had her ticket back to Gatwick.

CHAPTER NINETEEN

'WE DIDN'T EVEN know she was pregnant, otherwise we wouldn't have gone diving.' Pedro was slumped over on the leather couch under the ceiling fan with his head between his knees.

'I'm so sorry to have to tell you,' Sebastian said, wringing his hands together on the chair opposite.

He was too exhausted to process anything properly—too sleep-deprived to think about anything beyond the answers to Pedro's questions: *'What happened to the baby? How many more sessions will she need in there? Should we even tell her she was pregnant? Does she need to know? Won't that upset her more?'*

It was almost inconceivable that he was breaking this tragic news to Pedro, hearing him contemplate such a personal dilemma, when he'd just found out about Mila's pregnancy.

What would he do in Pedro's shoes?

He would tell his partner—he knew he would.

But Mila hadn't spoken to him about anything. She'd left it *two weeks* before telling him. And she'd been reluctant even then.

Pedro's phone rang.

'I think I can take over here,' Dr Raya said kindly, taking Sebastian aside. 'You were up all night, Dr Becker, and I'm sure this has been pretty shocking for you, too. And poor Dr Ricci... I hope she gets better soon.'

Dr Raya had offered to help Pedro break the news to Rose about her pregnancy—because of course Rose should know. It was important information. Wasn't it? Someone being pregnant? All parties involved deserved to know.

Instead of going straight back to the house, he went to the rocks off the bay where he'd sat with Mila the night of the fundraiser. He was feeling emotional after last night and because of Pedro's situation. He didn't want to take that out on Mila any more than he already had. He was furious that she'd kept such a secret—he wouldn't deny that—but maybe he was more angry at himself for not noticing the signs.

He should have picked up on her pregnancy. He should have known what was happening right in front of him. He was a doctor, for crying out loud. How could he have been so blind?

He'd been too caught up in their relationship... He hadn't felt this way about anyone before—not even Klara, he realised with a jolt—and now this.

Guilt crept its way in with the sea breeze as he made his way back from the rocks barefoot, relishing the occasional stab of coral to wake him up.

When he'd snapped at Mila before he'd been in total shock. It had been pure self-defence on his part, a grappling for control. He hadn't had the capacity to process everything that was going on and he'd freaked out.

It wasn't as if either of them had been expecting this. This was an accident...

He fixed his stare on the shadows drifting across the mountains. He still couldn't wrap his head around the fact she hadn't told him.

Was it because she really didn't want a baby?

They'd joked about how she would rather have a dog, but he liked to think he knew her better now. Mila was always going to be cut up about Annabel, which meant she was always going to be scared about losing anyone close to her.

She didn't think he knew her at all, but he did.

'Mila?'

Sebastian took the porch steps in one jump with the dogs at his heels. The house was still locked up. It didn't even look as if she'd been inside.

'Damn,' he cursed as he almost fell over his suitcase, right where he'd left it himself.

He wheeled it inside with him, sweat sticking his wetsuit to his back. He was so tired... He hadn't finished packing for Chicago...he hadn't even had time to get changed.

'Don't make me spill anything else on this—I need it,' he said sternly to Stormy, who was sniffing the case as if it was loaded with ice-cream.

The dog wagged her tail and cocked her head. He wondered what it must be like to think only thoughts of food and love all day—certainly a hell of a lot less complicated than being a human.

'Mila!' he called again, dumping the suitcase on the bed.

She wasn't in the upstairs bathroom. She wasn't anywhere.

He pulled out his phone. No missed calls. He kicked off his shoes and heaved himself out of the wetsuit. He needed a shower badly, but he barely even registered being under the water when he stepped into it.

He was mad at himself for the way he'd acted earlier. Why *would* she call him?

He would check her place next...

'Mila!'

He went to knock on her door, then caught himself. He checked in every single direction for anyone who might have followed him with a camera, then pounded it with a fist. His hair was still wet from the shower. A woman passed by and eyed him up and down.

'I know her,' he explained. 'Mila, come out—we need to talk.'

He shot to the window and peered inside. 'No, no, no, no…. Are you kidding me?'

Her bedroom was practically empty. There were barely any clothes left on the hangers she always kept on the wardrobe doors instead of inside it. He loved it that she did that. The dresser was empty, too. Nothing but the hair dryer that had been there before she'd moved in.

When he called her it went straight to voicemail.

He set off at a jog, in the direction of the dive shop. She might have moved to a hotel—somewhere more private, he thought, trying to think of some logical explanation. She might have gone to another part of the island, where she wouldn't have to be around the MAC.

But why would she do that?

They were supposed to be leaving for Chicago in a matter of hours.

He was starting to get a very bad feeling. She had packed all her bags…she hadn't said goodbye…

His phone buzzed, hot in his pocket.

'Mila?' he answered, without checking.

He stopped at the beach shack, sank to a stool in the shade. Someone he knew offered him a coconut and he accepted it gratefully.

'Dr Becker? It's Ava in Personnel—is everything all right?'

His human resources manager and all-round star player. 'Ava? What's going on?'

'Maybe you can tell me…' Ava sounded confused. 'I just had a check-in announcement come through on my email. Dr Ricci has checked in at the airport in Denpasar. Something didn't strike me as right, though. I thought I'd heard her say a while ago that she was going to void the ticket and go to Chicago first.'

Sebastian dug his straw hard into the coconut flesh and

swivelled the stool away from the bar. No one should see his face right now.

'I'll deal with this—thank you, Ava,' he said.

Amelia Ricci's face was a picture of confusion as she flung the front door open seconds after Mila had stepped wearily from a taxi. It was so cold in Rye…the hedges round the lawn were bald. She wasn't used to it.

'Mila, what are you doing here? My God, you must be freezing.'

Mila felt numb inside and out as she was bundled into her mother's soft cardigan-clad arms. She couldn't cry… she'd run out of tears—or at least she'd thought so, until she smelled the scent of her childhood.

'I've missed you, Mum.'

Mila crumpled into the familiar warmth. She had missed this. Even though she had felt this sense of home in Sebastian's arms until she'd messed it all up.

'I think I've done something really stupid, Mum.'

'What's happened?'

Her mother ushered them both inside, wrapped a green woollen blanket around Mila's shoulders and placed her on the sofa. She sank back against the cushions with the elephant covers on—the ones Annabel had brought back from India one time.

'Mila, are you hurt?'

She'd only just realised she was crying again. 'No, I'm not hurt, Mum. I'm pregnant. It's Sebastian's.'

Her mother's hand found hers and grasped it tight. Then she wrapped her arms around her again and held her for a long time.

'It's OK…that's not the end of the world. Here, take your jacket off…'

'I told him—or rather he guessed—and then he freaked out because I'd kept it a secret. I don't want to lose him because of this, but I can't do it.'

'What can't you do?'

Her mother helped her remove her leather jacket, sleeve by sleeve, she was too weak at this point.

'My goodness, look how tanned you are!'

'I can't have a baby, Mum.'

Her mother tutted, shook her head. 'Mila, you *can* have a baby. You're already pregnant.'

Mila took a cushion and pushed a strangled noise out into an elephant. 'It was an accident.'

'But you do you want this baby with him?'

'I don't know… Yes… I shouldn't have left without talking to him properly…it's absolutely the worst way to hurt him. I tried to call him when I got off the plane but his phone's turned off. He's probably halfway to Chicago by now.'

'Chicago?' Her mother placed a hand to her knee.

'I was supposed to go there with him to meet his family.'

'So this is serious? With Sebastian?'

Mila offered a non-committal shrug, but the depth of what she'd done and how she felt was really sinking in now. She might have just run away from the best thing ever to have happened to her.

'Listen, I'm going to make us some tea and then we can talk about this.'

Mila watched her mother fuss around the kitchen through bleary eyes. She must look such a mess—she hadn't slept at all on the plane. She'd sat there listening idly to meditation podcasts, feeling terrible after her snap decision, which she'd made when she'd been in fight-or-flight mode. She hadn't expected the regret to start as soon as the plane took off.

She grimaced into the cushion. She had gone without talking to him first. Just like his ex, Klara, had done. They'd barely ever talked about her—it was a moot point for the most part, because Mila had been able to see he'd moved on…with *her*.

But she knew him well enough by now. She'd been trained to read his body language. His moods had used to darken whenever Klara's name had come up. Her departure and subsequent refusal to talk to him had devastated him, and now *she* had done exactly the same thing.

CHAPTER TWENTY

THE TOURISTS AT the gift shops, the queue for business class… It would usually have been torture. But Sebastian had somehow succeeded in zoning out the drone of chatter and the beeps of loud speakers. If people took photos of him he didn't notice, but he waited till he was checked in and standing by the window in the departure lounge to call Jared.

'I can't come to Chicago. Something's come up.'

He explained the situation as best he could, told him Mila was pregnant and that it wasn't planned, that he had to go and make things right.

He wanted to. He'd booked the next flight out to London. He figured if he could get to her maybe she would listen to him before she decided on anything too rash.

'This is crazy, brother!' Jared was confounded. 'Do you love this woman? I mean, *really* love her enough to have a kid with her?'

'I do—absolutely.'

Jared let out the longest sigh down the phone. 'Then we'll miss you at the party. So will Mom. We have some news for you that would've been better given in person. But I support you.'

Sebastian didn't need his support on this—not that he would tell his brother that.

He'd asked for Jared's opinion once before, when Klara

had left him. Brother to brother, Jared had advised him not to go after her—not to fly over to Thailand, or Kathmandu, or any of the other places she'd gone to teach after humiliation had forced her to abort all form of contact with him. So Sebastian had let her go…until he'd missed her too much.

Then he'd flown to all those places, searching for her—of course he had. He'd just never told anyone. It had been a regrettable set of moves, on reflection. Klara had refused to see him in any of those places either.

Luckily he'd fallen in love with Gili Indah while he'd been flying out from Bali every weekend to try and find her, until eventually he'd never left the island at all—not to look for her, anyway. He'd made a life there at the MAC, he was needed and respected on the island, and there was so much more for him to do.

He wouldn't leave the island now for anyone.

Except Mila.

He was a zombie by the time the flight landed. His phone was dead, but it was probably best not to announce his arrival to Mila; he'd keep it a surprise in case she tried to escape him. He'd been through that before…never again.

Even his bones were cold by the time he was watching the English scenery float past from a car. And it was raining.

He'd found her mother's address on the system at the MAC, told his team where he was going, left the dogs with Ketut and Wayan…

But he still couldn't quite believe it when he found himself standing on the doorstep of the small redbrick house in Rye.

Amelia Ricci stood up from the bed at the familiar *ding-dong* sound and smoothed down her red-striped skirt. Mila hadn't even noticed before that her mother was all dressed up. She'd been too distracted by her perfume. At first it had smelled so good, but now it was abhorrent to her insides.

'That will be Julian.' Her mother glanced at her in the mirror on the dresser and bouffed up her hair.

Mila fought a smile and placed a hand to her belly. She'd been wondering when this would come up.

'Who's Julian?'

'I wasn't sure things would become serious, so I didn't say anything much to you about him before now, but I think that maybe he's a keeper. He's a doctor, like you—a paediatrician down at St Germaine. Come and meet him.'

Her mother hovered in the doorway.

'On second thoughts, meet him later,' she said.

Mila was grateful. She was happy her mother seemed to have acquired a boyfriend in the time since she'd been gone, but she didn't want to meet him right now.

She had slept for a few hours and showered, and booked an appointment with the family obstetrician, but now it was evening in the UK and her jet lag was playing with her mind as much as the thought of Sebastian, whose phone still appeared to be dead or switched off.

'Will you carry on with this while I'm gone?'

Her mother gestured to the open drawers and boxes, shooting her a look of apprehension. They'd been going through Annabel's stuff. Photos, books, rosettes, love letters still in their envelopes.

'I'm OK with it, Mum,' she said. And she was, she realised.

She heard her mother make a strange sound as she opened the front door downstairs. Mila smiled to herself. Her mother deserved someone who treated her like a goddess. She'd been through so much.

She was studying a photo of herself and Annabel on either side of a man dressed as a giant strawberry when the stairs outside the room creaked again.

'Um... Mila?' Her mother looked quite sheepish, peering around the doorway. 'It wasn't Julian.'

The door opened wide.

Mila stood up in her socks and leggings and her heart started crashing against her ribs even before she saw him.

She dropped the photo.

Sebastian stepped into her old bedroom and the familiar scent of him took her hyperactive nostrils by surprise. It did something strange to her insides, where their baby was— something good—and her eyes clouded over with tears. In a second she was falling against his chest as he stood there in the middle of the floor, on the rug where she'd used to play dolls and cars with Annabel.

'You're here...'

'You gave me no choice.'

'I'm so sorry I left you...' She breathed into his jacket, clutching the lapels and kissing his lips. He was cold; she'd never felt his lips so cold. 'Sebastian, I know it was terrible of me, but I totally freaked out.'

'I know,' he said, putting equally cold hands to her face.

She leaned her cheek against one palm; she had missed him.

'And I know why you're scared of this, Mila, but you can't ever do this to me again. This is something we will deal with together from now on, OK?'

Mila had almost forgotten her mother was there until the doorbell rang again.

'That *will* be Julian. It was nice to meet you, Dr Becker,' she said. 'I'll leave you two to talk.'

Before she left she shot a look of approval at Mila, for Sebastian.

'You were meant to be in Chicago by now,' Mila whispered, stepping back and keeping hold of his hands. She never wanted to let him go.

He looked exhausted and unshaven but utterly perfect— even out of context in the house she'd grown up in. He was wearing jeans and a designer sweater, and a brown leather jacket. Her hands found her belly again. He'd brought a ray of hope with him from the island.

'A strawberry man?' he said now, half smiling as he bent to pick up the photo.

'It was a pick-your-own-strawberries day and he was the mascot,' she explained, running a finger over Annabel's face in the photo.

Her twin was here in this room—she could feel her right now…just as she had sometimes felt her on the island, too. Was this what Annabel wanted? To see her happy with a guy she'd unknowingly approved for Mila years ago?

She would have shivered at the thought before, but maybe she just hadn't wanted to allow herself happiness, she realised. She'd been wrapped up in her guilt over the accident for so long… She had someone else to think about now, though. She was going to need to be strong.

Sebastian scanned the items on the floor, taking in the trophies and trinkets, the weird-looking carved camel Annabel had got from Dubai.

'This was the room we shared till we were eighteen,' said Mila. 'And this is me finally moving on.' She sighed, motioning to the half-empty drawer she'd already sorted through. She smiled tentatively at him. 'Can you ever forgive me?'

'Mila…' he said, shaking his head.

He shut his eyes, dragged a hand across his face, and for a second she thought that maybe he had come here to break things off. That she'd damaged something that couldn't be fixed.

'I was angry with you for keeping the news about our baby from me,' he admitted, chewing his cheek.

Her stomach sank.

'I'm not going to pretend you didn't rip me to shreds. You must know how much I love you. You must also know how much raising a kid with you would be…' He trailed off, as if he couldn't find the words.

She covered her mouth with her hand. She had never

heard him tell her he loved her until now. She was utterly shocked at how the words thrilled her.

'It would be the kind of challenge I'm ready for.'

He shook his head again, almost as if he couldn't believe the words coming out of his mouth either. It made her heart soar again.

'I mean, this kid's going to be feral...running about the island with two dogs, all sandy...'

'Let it be feral. I love you, too. Sebastian. I *do* love you. And I know I haven't been the easiest person to deal with, but I'm willing to try and make things work. On the island.'

There was no question in her mind that she'd go back to the island. She missed it already—and the MAC, and little Jack.

'We can do this together if you're really sure it's what you want?'

'*You* are what I want, Mila, and this baby.'

His words were like a confetti bomb going off in her chest and she moved to sit astride him on the edge of the bed, arms and legs wrapped around him.

'I'm so sorry I made you miss your mother's birthday,' she said, kissing him everywhere she could reach, as though he might suddenly disappear in a flash.

She had been through worse, but he was her safe place now. She could feel it—warmth, security and...*home*, she thought. She was home with him.

He let out a sigh into her hair. 'Technically we were supposed to be on that plane to Chicago,' he said, wrapping his hands in her hair, the way he always did. 'But the party's not till Friday, so there's still time for us to get there.'

He kissed her, and the scent of his jacket was driving her hormones crazy.

'You could take me round some of the English countryside, show me off to your friends...'

'Stop talking,' she told him.

She was already sliding his leather jacket off and unbuttoning his shirt.

CHAPTER TWENTY-ONE

SEBASTIAN POPPED THE olive from his virgin martini into his mouth, appreciating Mila from a distance. Her hair was up in a bun again, with soft tendrils framing her face. And she was wearing the fitted blue dress from Bali he'd brought with him—just in case. She looked incredible; she was clearly the best-dressed, most eye-catching woman at the party. But maybe he was biased—she was carrying his baby, after all.

'She seems to have made a good impression on them already,' Jared observed next to him, sipping his own martini. 'Shame you had to move all the way to that island to find her. but still...'

He grinned, slapped his shoulder, and Sebastian shifted on his feet as the box in his jacket pocket dug into his skin.

'I guess this is your way of giving me final brotherly approval,' he said.

'You did the right thing, going to get her,' Jared said seriously.

'I know.'

The party was in full swing. Mila was standing by the buffet table now, chatting happily to Jared's wife Laura and little Charlie, and Sebastian's mother, too. His mother seemed to adore her already.

It hadn't been that tough to convince her to come once he'd shown her a photo of the double bed on the private jet.

They'd slept there, eaten caviar, indulged in some other bed-based activities and even watched *Star Wars*—which he'd remembered neither of them had ever seen.

They'd spent part of yesterday quietly breaking the news of her pregnancy to his family. His mother was so excited about being a grandma again she had already asked her assistant to book her a flight to Bali. She had never even been to visit him on the island before, Sebastian realised, but this was not the moment to feel offended.

The crowds seemed to part as he made his way over to Mila.

'Mila Ricci, do I need to tell you how much I love you in that dress?'

She sighed contentedly and leaned against him as he ran a hand gently across her stomach. He still got a kick out of imagining their baby. Boy or girl, he wasn't bothered which—he knew it would be the love of his life…after Mila.

'I'd better wear it some more, before I get too big for it to fit,' she replied, turning in his arms.

'I'll just get you a bigger one made.'

'I'll wear it every day in surgery.'

'You can wear whatever you like under your white coat… or nothing at all.'

She laughed.

He knew his family and the entire badminton club were watching surreptitiously from their various spread-out social circles around the flower-decorated marquee.

Jared had spared no expense, as usual. There were flowers, multiple musical performers—including a six-piece band—a lavish feast to put an eighteenth-century king to shame, and later there would be fireworks in the gardens by the Japanese koi lake to close the monumental evening.

He could tell Mila had been a little surprised by the extravagance, but there was one more thing to do. It was now or never.

His heart sped up as he lowered himself to one knee in front of her.

'Sebastian, what are you…?'

A crowd started gathering and on the orchid-covered stage the band's jovial tune quivered into quiet.

'Sebastian…' Mila had gone red.

Jared handed him a microphone. He'd considered waiting till they were alone, but there were five hundred people gathered here—he had to give them something worth gossiping about.

Slowly he opened the lid of the little black velvet box.

He heard her gasp, watched her eyes pool with tears as she took in the stunning diamond ring set in platinum. He'd had ten diamonds studded around the main one, so it sparkled the way he knew all women dreamed their engagement ring would sparkle. He'd had to wait till Mila had been whisked off by his mother for an anti-jet-lag massage to go and collect it.

'I can't believe this…'

'Mila,' he said, focusing on her face.

She met his eyes and he knew he'd made the right decision. He wanted to cement this *now*.

'I know this has been crazy, and quick, and God knows neither of us expected any of it, but you are the best thing ever to have walked off the boat onto that island and I want you there with me for the rest of our lives.' He took a deep breath. 'Will you do me the immense honour of becoming my wife? Will you marry me?'

Mila looked as if she couldn't speak. For a second he thought maybe he'd gone too far. Someone pulled out a camera, but he saw Jared put a hand across the lens to stop them.

'Mila?'

'Yes, Sebastian—yes! Sorry, I'm in shock. *Yes!* Of course I will marry you.'

They were kissing now, and she was laughing, crying, hugging him. All before he'd even slid the ring on her finger.

'She said yes!' he yelled needlessly to the crowd, pulling her into him again. Relief flooded through him. 'God, I love you when you're blushing,' he growled into her ear.

'Can I get a photo of the happy couple?' someone asked. And suddenly there were cameras everywhere.

Mila stepped in front of him. 'No, thank you, we don't want any photos.'

'It's OK,' he said, taking her hand.

She squinted up at him. 'What do you mean? You hate all this!'

'This is a moment I'm proud of,' he replied decisively, and they happily posed for the crowd, with Mila's ring the centrepiece.

'You've changed,' she teased him.

He rolled his eyes, smiling. He knew people would always gossip, but he'd learned to let it go a little more since Mila had arrived. If she didn't care about the media, why should he care any more? And that little kid's newspaper article had thrown a positive light on his mounting new reputation as an island entrepreneur.

He knew the negative press—if it ever came again— wouldn't affect his work, or the people he loved. That was all that mattered. He had new priorities now.

Jared was at the microphone suddenly, tapping it. Charlie was gripping his father's pocket, holding a toy dinosaur in his other hand.

'Congratulations to my brother and his fiancée Dr Mila Ricci, everybody!'

The crowd went crazy. His mother was wiping tears from her eyes.

'And, seeing as this is a night for announcements, I have one myself,' Jared continued, clearing his throat. 'I am delighted to say happy seventieth birthday to our wonderful, long-suffering mother!'

The applause was rapturous and their mother performed a curtsey, but Jared wasn't done.

'I would also like to say that that this will be the final season of *Faces of Chicago*.'

The gasps around the marquee were audible.

'From early next year I'll be spending more time in Indonesia, concentrating on getting a new Becker Institute facility for wellness and healing up and running. My brother and I...*and* his fiancée...will let you know more as soon as we can. For now, however, I'm sure he'll be busy with wedding plans.'

Sebastian shot Mila a secret smile. Jared had discussed this with them last night, of course, but it still felt strange to know it was actually happening, after all this time.

He'd turned those investors down already, telling them he was keeping this one in the family, and Jared was coming over for three months initially, to partner him on planning, recruitment and development. He and Laura would also look for schools on Bali for Charlie.

'I have a feeling things will be different around the island pretty soon,' Mila said, admiring her ring again.

'I have a feeling you're right,' he said, drawing her closer for a photo with Charlie and his dinosaur.

One year later

Baby Hope Annabel Becker was watching the tiny turtles on the sand with keen interest as Mila sat with her near the surf.

'Do you want to release one?' she whispered, revelling in the baby-soft curls of Hope's hair against her cheek.

They were sitting at the shoreline, barefoot. The moon was high in the sky. The annual sea turtle fundraiser was the perfect opportunity to introduce Hope to the baby turtles who'd grown from eggs in the sanctuary and were now ready to explore their new ocean home around the reef.

'We've released a hundred so far—thanks to Jack, here.' Sebastian grinned as his sandy feet appeared alongside little Jack's in the water. 'He wants to show you this one.'

Little Jack was learning to walk and talk. Wayan looked on from a seat nearby as her son shoved a baby turtle in Mila's face enthusiastically, and she laughed as Wayan rushed over and swept him up, handing the turtle back.

'Was that ice-cream on his face?' Mila asked Sebastian.

Wayan was wiping some kind of smear from Jack's cheek behind them and Sebastian grimaced.

'What can I say? I'm a bad godfather. Good thing I'm so great at everything else.'

Mila laughed and handed him Hope as he sat down beside her. A wave washed up and soaked them fully to their waists. Hope giggled, the way she always did. She loved the ocean.

'Uncy! Uncy!' Jack's vocabulary was improving. He was calling his Uncle Sebastian back already.

'Just taking a moment with my wife, buddy,' he called back. 'And maybe your future girlfriend?'

He glanced down at Hope, put a finger to her tiny hand and winked.

Mila nudged him playfully. 'Are you setting our daughter up already? We're not the only survivors on this island, you know. She'll be free to make her own choice, just like you were.'

'I wasn't free. You trapped me the moment I met you.'

Mila leaned in to kiss him. She didn't care who saw. No one bothered them, and there was no gossip anyway. They were happy together—just a regular couple with a baby—and to everyone else that was probably boring.

They had worked on Jack's cleft lip and palate, reduced his scarring to a minimum, and now he looked like any other rambunctious one-year-old. He was growing as fast as baby Hope.

Everyone on the island seemed to be charting Hope's progress. And luckily for them there was no shortage of willing babysitters, or people to read bedtime stories in the MAC grounds.

When her mother and Julian had visited, they'd started a children's circle—five p.m. on Wednesdays—and Mila had kept it up when they'd left. She still averaged about twenty kids each time.

Sebastian had teased her. 'For someone who said she'd rather have a dog than a family, you now have two dogs and twenty kids!'

'I'm calling this one Sergeant Major,' Sebastian said now, taking Hope's tiny hand and placing it on the turtle's smooth shell.

Mila watched as he dropped a kiss on their baby's head. *If Annabel was here now she'd be so happy to be an auntie*, she mused, just as a yellow butterfly fluttered down and perched on Hope's nose.

Sebastian looked at her. He didn't say it, and neither did she, but butterflies had a habit of landing on Hope. It was mostly whenever Mila thought about her sister...

* * * * *

THE MAN TO BE
RECKONED WITH

TARA PAMMI

From mathematics class to master's degrees, through crushes on boys to crushing debts, through fights with our mums to marriages and babies – you've always been constant and unflinching in your support and love. This one's for you, Sushma.

PROLOGUE

"He might die any minute of any day or he might live to be a hundred. There's nothing to be done for it."

Nathaniel Ramirez looked up at the snowy, whitecapped mountain peak and gulped in a big breath. The words he had overheard the cardiologist say to his mother all those years ago reverberated inside his skull. The cold air blasted through his throat, his lungs expanding greedily.

Would this be the day?

He raised his face to the sky as his vision cleared and his heart resumed its normal beat.

At some point during the trek, he had realized he couldn't finish the climb today.

He didn't know whether it was because, after almost twelve years of courting death, he was finally bored of playing hide-and-seek with it, or because he was just plain tired today.

For a decade, he had been on a constant go across the world, without planting roots anywhere, without returning home, making real estate deals in corners of the world, making millions.

An image of the roses in the garden his mother had loved, back in California, their color vividly red, the petals so soft that she had banned him from touching them, flashed across his mind's eye.

A stab of homesickness pierced him as he followed the icy path down. Sweat drenched him as he reached the wooden cabin he had been living in since he closed the Demakis deal in Greece six months ago. Restlessness slithered under his skin.

And he knew what it meant. It meant he was thrashing against the cage he had made for himself; it meant he was getting lonely; thousands of years of human nature were urging him toward making a home, to seek companionship.

He needed to chase a new challenge, whether clinching a real estate deal or conquering a new corner of the world he hadn't stamped with his name yet. Fortunately for him, the world was vast and the challenges it presented numerous.

Because staying still in one place was the one thing that made him weak, that made him long for more than he could have.

He'd just stepped out of a hot shower when his satellite phone beeped. Only a handful of people could reach him via this number. He pushed a hand through his overlong hair and checked the caller ID.

The name flashing on the screen brought an instant smile to his face.

He connected the call, and the sound of their old housekeeper Maria's voice coming down the line filled him with a warmth he had missed for too long. Maria had been his rock after his mom passed.

Suddenly he realized he missed a lot of things from home. He clamped down on the useless yearning before it morphed into the one thing he despised.

Fear.

"Nathan?"

"Maria, how are you?"

He smiled as Maria called him a few names in Spanish and then asked after him as if he were still a little boy.

"You need to come home, Nathan. Your father… It's been too long since you've seen each other."

The last time Nate saw him, his father had been the epitome of a selfish bastard instead of a grieving husband or a comforting father. And despite the decade and the thousands of miles that Nathan had put between them, the bitterness, the anger he felt for him was just as fresh as ever.

Maybe there was no running away from a few things in life.

"Is he ill again, Maria?"

"No. He recovered from the pneumonia. They, at least that woman's daughter, she took good care of him."

Praise from Maria, especially for *that woman's daughter*, as she put it, meant Jackie's daughter had slaved to take care of his dad.

Nathan frowned, the memory of the one time he had seen his father's mistress's daughter leaving a sour taste in his mouth. She had been kind even then.

That day in the garage, with the August sun shining gloriously outside with blatant disregard to the fact that Nathan's entire world had crumbled around him. There had been blooms everywhere, the gardeners keeping it up for his mother even though she had stopped venturing into the garden for months.

The grief that his mother was gone, the chilling fear, the cold fist in his chest that he could drop dead any minute like her, and the little girl who had stood nervously by the garage door, a silent witness to the choking sobs that had racked him.

He hated everything about that day.

"I'm so sorry that your mother died. I can share my mother with you if you want," she had said in a small voice.

And in return, he had ripped through her.

"He's getting married, Nathan." Maria's anxiety cut through his thoughts. "That woman," she said again, refusing to even speak Jacqueline Spear's name, the loathing in her voice crystal clear even through the phone line, "she'll finally have what she wanted, after all these years. Eleven years of living shamelessly with him under his roof..."

Nathan grimaced as Maria spouted a few choice words for Jacqueline Spear. Bitterness filled his veins at the thought of his father's mistress, the woman he had taken up with even before Nathan's mother had passed.

"It's his damn life, Maria. He has every right to spend it as he pleases."

"He does, Nathan. But your mama's house, Nathan... she's preparing to sell it. Just two days ago, she asked me to clean out your mother's room, told me to take anything I wanted. Your mama's belongings, Nathan—all her jewelry's in there. She's putting the entire estate on sale—the grounds, the furniture, the mansion, everything."

Every piece that had been painstakingly put together by his mother with love. And now in the hands of a woman who had been everything his mother hadn't been.

"If you don't come back, it will forever be gone."

Nathan scrunched his eyes closed, and the image of a brick mansion rose in front of him. A strange anger gripped him. He didn't want that house to go to someone else, he realized.

He had lived the life of a loner for a decade, and the image of the house he had run away from hit him hard in his gut. "She doesn't have the right to sell it."

The silence on Maria's end stretched his nerves taut. "He gave it to her, Nathan. As a gift."

Nausea rolled around in his mouth. His father had killed his mother, as clearly as if he had choked the life out of her, with his disgusting affair, and after he'd lived in her house with his mistress and now… His knuckles turned white around the phone.

This he wouldn't, couldn't, tolerate.

No matter that he didn't want to live in the house any more than he wanted to put roots down and settle anywhere in the world.

"He's giving away my mom's house as a wedding gift?"

"Not to Jackie, Nathan. To her daughter, from her first marriage. I don't know if you ever saw her. Your father deeded the house to her a few months ago. After he was dreadfully ill that first time."

Nathan frowned. So Jackie's daughter was selling his mother's house. Getting rid of it for the monetary value it would yield, he supposed.

The restlessness that had simmered inside him a few hours ago dissipated, washed away by furious determination.

It was time to go home. He didn't know how long he would stay or if he could bear to even stay there at all after so many years.

Neither could he let the house, his mother's house, fall into some stranger's grubby hands. He just couldn't.

He bid goodbye to Maria and switched on his laptop.

In a few minutes, he was chatting with his virtual manager, Jacob. He gave orders for a local manager to look after his cabin, for his airline tickets to be booked to San Francisco and last but not the least, for any information the man could dig up on his father's mistress's daughter.

CHAPTER ONE

"I HEARD THE investors sold the company to some reclusive billionaire."

"Someone in HR said he's only bought it for the patented software. That he intends to fire the whole lot of us."

"I didn't realize we had value to attract someone of that ilk."

What ilk? What billionaire?

Riya Mathur rubbed her temples with her fingers, slapping her palms over her ears in a gesture that in no way could silence the useless speculation around her.

What had changed in the week she had been gone for the first time in two years since Drew and she had started the company? What wasn't he telling her?

Her chat window from their internal IM program pinged, and Riya looked down at her screen.

A message from Drew: Come to my cabin, Riya.

Riya felt a knot in her stomach.

Things had steadily been going from bad to worse between her and Drew for six months now. Since New Year's Eve to be exact. And she hadn't known how to make it better except to put her head down and do her job.

Stepping out of the small cubicle she occupied, only separated from the open cabins in the huge hall by one movable shelf, she marched past an anxious, almost hyper group of staff amassed in the break room toward the CEO's cabin. She had spent the better part of the morning waiting on tenterhooks, walking around the different teams and trying to persuade them to get back to work while Drew's door remained resolutely closed.

But his continuing silence, even after an email from her, peppered with little tidbits of gossip, was making her head spin. Running her damp palms over her baggy trousers, she came to a halt at the closed door.

She tapped a couple of times cursorily, and every whisper gathered momentum in pitch and volume. Without waiting for an answer, she turned the handle and the pandemonium behind her descended into a deathly silence.

Stepping inside, she closed the door.

Drew's lean frame was molded by the sunlight streaming through the windows, the San Francisco skyline behind him.

He opened his mouth to speak but stopped abruptly. Her heart in her throat, Riya took a step in his direction. He stiffened a little more and tilted his head.

That same awkwardness that had permeated their every conversation filled the air thickly now.

But this was work. Their company truly had been a product of them both. "The whole office is buzzing with rumors…" She came to a stop a couple of steps from him. "Whatever our personal differences, this is our company, Drew. We're in it together—"

"It was your company until you took the first seed capital from an investor," a new voice, every syllable punctured with a sardonic amusement, said behind her.

Riya turned around so fast she didn't see him for a few seconds. Blinking, she brought her focus back to the huge table and the man sitting at the head of it. The chair faced away from the window. With his long legs sprawled in front of him, only his profile was visible to Riya.

The entire room was bathed in midmorning sunlight and yet the man sat in the one area of the room that the light didn't touch. Ungluing her feet from the spot next to Drew, Riya walked across the room so that she could see better.

She felt the newcomer's gaze on her, studying everything about her. Her usually articulate mind slowed down to a sluggish pace. The feeling that he had been waiting to see *her* tugged at her, a strange little premonition dancing in her gut.

"I've been dying to meet you, Ms. Mathur," he said, turning the vague feeling into solid dread. "The smart mind that built the software engine that drives the company," he added silkily. He had left something else unsaid. She knew it, just as surely as she could feel her heart skidding in her chest.

He had even pronounced her last name perfectly, elongating the *a* after the *M* just right. After knowing her since her freshman year at college, Drew still didn't say it right. It was a small thing, and yet she felt as though this stranger knew her entire history.

Taking the last step past the overfilled bookshelf, Riya came to a halt. Her stomach did a funny dive, her sharp exhale amplified to her own ears.

Her first thought was that he belonged in a motorcycle club and not in a boardroom.

Electric eyes, a brilliant shade of ice blue, set deep in a starkly angled face, collided with hers. That gaze was familiar and strange, amused and serious. A spark of recognition lit up inside her, yet Riya had no idea where she had seen him.

Dark blond hair, so unruly and long that her fingers itched to smooth it back, fell onto his forehead. Copper highlights shimmered in his hair. The sunlight streaming in played hide-and-seek with the hollows of his cheekbones, the planes darker than the hollows. Which meant he spent a lot of time outdoors.

His skin, what she could see of it, was sunburned and looked rough. An untrimmed beard covered his jaw and chin, copper glinting in it too.

That beard, those haphazard clothes, his overall appearance—they should have diluted the intensity of his presence in the small room. It should have made him look less authoritative. Except those eyes negated everything.

They had a bright, alert look to them, a sardonic humor lurking beneath the sharp stare he directed at her.

He wore a dark leather jacket that had obviously seen better days, under which the collar of a faded shirt peeked through.

A cough from behind her brought her up short and Riya felt her cheeks heat up.

Amusement deepened in those eyes.

"Who are you?" The awkwardly phrased question zoomed out of her mouth before she realized. Suddenly it was tantamount that she remember him.

Because she did, Riya realized with a certainty.

He leaned back into his chair, not in the least affected by her tone. There was a sense of contained movement about him even though he remained seated. As though he was forcing his body to do it, as though staying still was an unnatural state for him.

"Nathaniel Ramirez."

Riya's mouth fell open as an article she had read just a few months ago in a travel magazine flashed through her mind's eye.

Luxury Travel Mogul. Virtual Entrepreneur. Billionaire Loner.

Nathaniel Ramirez had been called a visionary in developing hotels that were an extension of the environment, a man who had made millions with zero investment. The string of temporary hotels, which he'd envisioned and built with various landowners in different parts of the world, were all the rage for celebrities who wanted a private vacation, away from prying eyes.

He had tapped into a market that not only had met an existing demand but had opened a whole new industry to the local men in so many remote corners of the world.

And more than any of that, he was an enigma who'd traveled the world over since he was seventeen, didn't stay in one place past a few months, didn't own a home anywhere in the world and worst of all, had no family ties or relationships.

Even the magazine hadn't been able to get a picture of him. It had been a virtual interview.

The quintessential loner, the magazine had called him, the perfect personality for a man who traveled the world over and over. The fact that he made money doing it was just a perk, someone had heard him remark.

He'd only said his name, and nothing more about what he was doing here, in San Francisco, in Travelogue, in their start-up company's headquarters.

Why? Why would he give his name instead of stating why he was here?

She threw a quick look behind her and noticed Drew still stood unmoving at the bay windows, his mouth tight, his gaze swinging between her and Mr. Ramirez.

"You make a living out of traveling the world. What can a small online travel sales company do for you?" She shot Drew a look of pure desperation. "And why are you sitting in Drew's chair?"

The intensity of his gaze, while nothing new to Riya,

still had a disconcerting element to it. Men stared at her. All the time.

She had never learned how to handle the attention or divert it, much less enjoy it, as Jackie did. Only painstakingly cultivated an indifference to those heated, lingering looks. But something about him made it harder.

Finally he uncoiled from his lounging position. And a strange little wave of apprehension skittered through her.

"I bought controlling interest in Travelogue last night, Ms. Mathur."

She blinked, his soft declaration ringing in her ears. "I bought a gallon of milk and bread last night."

The sarcastic words fell easily from her mouth while inside, she struggled not to give in to the fear gripping her.

"It wasn't that simple," Nathan said, getting up from the uncomfortable chair. The whole cabin was both inconvenient and way too small for him. Every way he turned, there was a desk or chair or a pile of books ready to bang into him. He felt boxed in.

Walking around the table, he stopped at arm's length from her, the fear hidden under her sarcastic barb obvious. Gratification filled him even as he gave the rampant curiosity inside him free rein.

Like mother, like daughter.

He pushed the insidiously nasty thought away. True, Riya Mathur was the most beautiful woman he had ever seen, and as a man who had traveled to all the corners of the world, he'd seen more than his share.

She was also, apparently, extremely smart and as possessed of the talent for messing with men's minds as her mother, if everything he had heard and Drew Anderson's blatantly obvious craze for her was anything to go by.

But where Jacqueline met the world with a devil-may-care attitude, flaunting her beauty with an irreverent smile, her daughter's beauty was diluted with intelligence and a carefully constructed air of indifference.

Which, he realized with a self-deprecating smile, made every male of the species assume himself equal to the task of unraveling all that beauty and fire.

Exquisite almond-shaped, golden brown eyes, defiant, scared and hidden behind spectacles, a high forehead, a straight, distinctive nose that hinted at stubbornness and a bow-shaped mouth. All this on the backdrop of a golden caramel-colored silky smooth complexion, as though Jackie's alabaster and her Indian father's brown had been mixed in perfect proportions.

She had dressed to underplay everything about herself, and this only spurred him on to observe more. It was like a cloud hovering over a mountaintop, trying to hide the magnificence of the peak beneath it.

A wary and puzzled look lingered in her eyes since she had stepped inside. Which meant it was only a matter of time before she remembered him.

Because he had changed his last name, and he looked eons different from the sobbing seventeen-year-old she had seen eleven years ago.

He should just tell her and get it over with, he knew. And yet he kept quiet, his curiosity about her drumming out every other instinct.

"I had to call in a lot of favors to find your investors. Once they were informed of my intent, they were more than happy to accommodate me. Apparently they're not happy with the ways things are being run."

"You mean disappointed about the bucket loads of money they want us to make?" A flash of regret crossed her face as soon as she said it.

She was nervous, which was what he'd intended.

"And that's wrong how, Ms. Mathur? Why do you think investors fund start-ups? Out of the goodness of their hearts?"

"I don't think so. But there's growth *and* there's risk." She took a deep breath as though striving to get herself under control. "And if it's profits that you're after, then why buy us at all?"

"Let's just say it caught my fancy."

Frustration radiated out of her. "Our livelihood, everything we've worked toward the past four years is hanging in the balance. And all you're talking about is late night shopping, things catching your fancy. Maybe living your life on the periphery of civilization all these years, cut off from your fellow man, traipsing through the world with no ties—"

"Riya, no…." She heard Drew's soft warning behind her. But she was far too scared to pay heed.

"—has made you see only profit margins, but for us, the human element is just as important as the bottom line."

"You make me sound like a lone wolf, Ms. Mathur."

"Well, you are one, aren't you?" She closed her eyes and fought for control. "Look, all I care about is what you intend to do with the company. With us."

Something inched into his features, hardening the look in his eyes. "Leave us alone, Mr. Anderson."

"No," Riya said aloud as Mr. Ramirez walked around the table and toward her. Panic made her words rushed. "There's nothing you have to say to me that Drew can't hear."

Stopping next to her, Drew met her gaze finally. The resignation in his eyes knocked the breath out of her as nothing else could. "Drew, whatever you're thinking, we can fight this. We own the patent to the software engine—"

"Does nothing else matter to you except the blasted company? Statues possess more feelings than you do."

Bitterness spewed from every word, and the hurt festering beneath them lanced through her. She paled under his attack, struggled to put into words why.

"I'm done, Riya," Drew said, with a hint of regret.

"But, Drew, I…"

His hands on her shoulders, Drew bent and kissed her cheek, all the while the deep-set ice-blue gaze of the arrogant man who was kicking Drew out stayed on her without blinking.

Something flitted in that gaze. An insinuation? A challenge? There one minute, chased away by a cool mockery the next.

But Riya didn't look away. Locking her hands by her side, she stood frozen to the spot.

Stepping back from her, Drew turned. "I'll set up something with your assistant, Nathan."

Without breaking her gaze, the hateful man nodded.

"Goodbye, Riya."

The words felt so final that Riya shivered.

Leaving her flailing in the middle of the room, Drew closed the door behind him. It felt as if she were locked in a cage with a wild animal even as her mind was sifting and delving deeper.

Nathan…Nathan…Nathaniel Ramirez. Owns a group of travel and vacation companies called RunAway International, has traveled the world since he was seventeen…

A strange shiver began at the base of her spine, inched everywhere. She pushed her fingers through her hair, a nervous gesture she had never gotten over. "What did Drew mean?"

"Mr. Anderson decided he wanted to move on. From…"

His gaze swept over her, a puzzle in it. "...*Travelogue*," he finished, leaving something unsaid.

Riya felt as if he had slapped her. He had said so much without saying anything, and she couldn't even defend herself against what she didn't understand. She had never felt more out of her depth. "Who the hell do you think you are? And you can't just kick him out. Drew and I own—"

"He sold his share of the stock. To me. I now own seventy-five percent of your company. I'm your new *partner*, Riya. Or boss, or really...there are so many things we could call each other."

CHAPTER TWO

AND JUST LIKE that, her name on his lips, spoken like a soft invocation, unlocked the memory her mind had been trying to grasp from the moment she looked into that ice-blue gaze.

"She's dead. And she died knowing that your trashy mother is just waiting at the gates, ready to come in and take her place. I hope you both rot in hell."

The memory of that long-ago day flashed through her so vividly that Riya had to grab the chair to steady her shaking legs.

Robert's wife had been Anna. Anna Ramirez.

Little shivers spewed all over and she hugged herself. She had brought this on herself. "You're Nathan Keys. You're Robert's son. I read about you and I never realized..."

He nodded and Riya felt her breath leave her in a big rush.

Her little lie had worked and here he was, with the largest of her company's stock, her livelihood in his hand.

Robert's son, the boy who had run away from home after his mother's death, the son of the married man with whom her mother had taken up, the son of the man who had been more a father to her than her own had ever been.

The son she had been trying to bring back to Robert.

She had lied to Maria about selling the estate, hoping it would lure him back home. Thought she would give Nathan a chance she had never had with her own father.

A hysterical laugh rose through her.

Leaning against the far wall, his legs crossed together in casual elegance, he smiled, his tanned skin glinting in contrast against the white of his teeth. "What? No 'welcome home' greeting for your almost stepbrother, Riya?"

There were so many things wrong about his fake greeting, the worst of which was how aware she was of him in the small room. Mortification drenching her inside, Riya glared at him. "You're kidding me, right?"

"My acceptance of your offer for familial solidarity is almost a decade late, but—"

Her chest fell and rose as she fought for a breath. "You… you *waltz* in here, get rid of my business partner, wave the biggest chunk of my company in my face—" she pushed her shaking fingers through her hair "—and you want welcome?"

He stayed silent and her stride ate up the distance between them. Fear was a stringent pulse in her head. "If this is revenge for my mother's affair with your father, let me tell you—"

"I don't give a damn about your mother *or* my father."

The very lack of emotion in his words stilled Riya's thoughts. He was going to be livid when he learned what she had intended. "Then what is this?"

"You refused every offer I had my lawyers put forward for the sale of the estate."

Her gut twisting with fear, Riya flopped into a chair. Hiding her face in her hands, she fought through it. He had moved to acquire her company because she refused his escalating offers for the sale of the estate.

What would he do when he learned she had never intended to sell it in the first place? What had she brought on herself?

Nathan stared at the lustrous swath of dark brown hair that fell like a curtain over Riya. Even as impatience pulled at him, he stood transfixed, stunned anew by the sharpness of his reaction to her.

Every minute they spent in this confining room, his awareness of her grew like an avalanche that couldn't be stopped.

How she wore no makeup and yet the very lack of it only heightened her beautiful skin and sharp features.

How everything about her beauty was underplayed like her professional but bland brown dress shirt and trousers.

And how utterly she failed at masking that beauty.

How exquisitely expressive her wide, almond-shaped eyes were and how she fluttered those long lashes down when she wanted to hide her expression.

Her slender shoulders trembled and he felt a pang of regret. "All I want is the estate. However high I went, you kept refusing my offers. Refused to even give a reason."

She looked up, the flash of fear in her eyes still just as obvious. But now there was a resolve too. "So you made a play for my company?"

"Yes. It's called leverage. Believe me, as innovative as your software engine is, your little company is not Run-Away International material. Sign on the dotted line today and you'll leave here a rich woman. I'll even leave you to run your boring company. Of course, you'll run it into the ground in two years the way you're going, but being the uncaring bastard that I am, I'll let you ruin your and your staff's future."

"What about all the money you spent on acquiring it?"

"A drop in the ocean. I'm sure the stock will be worthless in a couple of years anyway."

Riya chafed at his grating confidence that she would only ruin the company. But she couldn't focus on that now, and there was no good way to put it.

"I didn't accept those offers because I never intended to sell the estate *to anyone*. I still don't."

"Then why did Maria assume that…"

Every inch of his face tightened as if it had been poured over by concrete and had permanently set with the fury in those chilling eyes. He was still leaning against the table, and yet he looked as if the seams of his control would burst any second.

But he didn't move, didn't lose control even by the flicker of a muscle. Only the sheer frost in his gaze was testament to the fury in his eyes. Finally he blinked and Riya felt the tightness in her chest relent infinitesimally.

The most unholy glint appeared in his eye, sending a ripple of apprehension through her.

"You manipulated Maria and me." His words rang with awe and derision, his gaze studying her, as if he was reevaluating and coming to an unsavory conclusion. He moved toward her slowly. "You laid bread crumbs very cleverly to make sure I trailed after you."

"Yes."

The single word sounded like a boom in the wake of his silent chill.

"You took advantage of my attachment to that estate. You knew I would go as high as you wanted."

Forcing a laugh, which sounded as artificial as it felt, she took a step back, her nerves stretching tighter and tighter.

"Actually I took advantage of your hatred for me and Jackie." And because his silence confirmed it, she continued, battling the ugly truth. "I wasn't even sure it would work. Maria just barely tolerates me. How would I know she would come tattling to you?"

Shaking his head, he covered another step. Though it was cowardly, Riya couldn't stop herself from stepping back again. "Don't minimize your accomplishment now. You knew exactly what you were doing."

Heat flamed her cheeks. "Fine. Something she had said a few months ago stuck with me. About how you might have considered coming back long ago if only Jackie and I were gone. About how much you loved the estate, even the staff, and how dare Robert give it to me? About how I was stealing even this from you."

"So you decided luring me here would make you the maximum amount of money on the estate."

"That's not true. I felt guilty. I never asked Robert for the estate. I know it's not—"

"And your guilt, your insecurities give you the right to play games with me?"

The depth of his perception awed Riya. Despite constantly reminding herself that she had been too young to change anything, she had remembered his grief-stricken words again and again, felt guilt carve a permanent place inside her gut.

His gaze met hers, an icy resolve in it, and Riya forgot what she had been about to say. There was not an inch of that grief-stricken boy in him. Only a cold fire, an absolute detachment.

He reached her, and her heart slammed against her rib cage. She couldn't blink, couldn't look away from that piercing blue. And a slow tremor took root in her muscles. Like the time when she'd had the flu. Only in a less hurting and more disconcerting way. As if every fiber of her were a stringent pulse vibrating in tune to his every move.

His lean body neatly caging her against the alcove, his gaze was a fiery frost. "Why are you doing this?"

"You were gone for eleven years. Eleven years during which time I helped Robert with the administration of the estate, with the staff, with everything. You were off doing who knows what and I slogged over every account, every expense and income number, in the face of a staff that hated the very sight of me. I did everything I could to keep that place going." She had tried to be a model daughter to Robert and Jackie, had taken care of him when he fell sick.

Nothing she had done had removed the shadows of guilt and ache in Robert's eyes.

"That's what this is all about? What I offered wasn't enough?" Nathan said, coming closer. Satisfaction practically coated every word. "Name your price."

"I don't want money. I was trying to explain how much that estate means to me...I was—"

"Then what the hell do you want? How dare you manipulate me after your mother turned my mother's last few days into the worst of her life?"

It took every ounce of her will to stand still, bearing the judgment in that gaze. The pain in his words cut through her. "I want you to see Robert."

The silence that dawned was so tense that Riya felt the tension wind around them like a tangible rope. The knot in his brow cleared; the icy blue of his eyes widened. It was the last thing he had expected to hear. That she had surprised him left her only shaking in her leather pumps.

"No."

Fisting her hands behind her, Riya pushed the words that refused to come under his scornful gaze. "Then I won't sign it over. Ever."

She could practically hear him size her up, reassess his assumptions about her in the way disbelief and then pity filled his gaze. He looked at her as though he was seeing her anew.

"Don't lose what you've built trying to alleviate some weird guilt. Don't push me into doing something I don't want to. That estate, it's the one thing in the entire world that means something to me."

His words were laden with emotion and so much more. And she understood that attachment, because she loved the estate too. But she couldn't weaken now, now that he was here in San Francisco, so close to Robert.

"I've already made my decision."

He ran his fingers through his overlong hair, his gaze a winter frost. There was a tremble in the taut line of his shoulders, a hoarse thread in his tone when he spoke. "I'll drag you through the courts. Your company, I'm going to tear it to pieces. Is it still worth it?"

Riya swayed, the impact of what he was saying sweeping through her with the force of a gale. To see her company pulled apart and sold for pieces... Every inch of her revolted at the mere thought. Desperation filled her words.

"I deceived you. My staff has nothing to do with this. Can you be so heartless to take away their jobs?"

Their gazes locked and held. And every second felt like an eternity to her.

Finally he spoke, his mouth a tight line. "Yes."

The fight deflated out of Riya and she held herself together by sheer will. Her company was everything to her. But if Robert hadn't been there for her when she needed an adult with a kind word, Riya couldn't bear to imagine what her life would have been today.

"Fine. The estate, it's rightfully yours, I believe that. And eventually it will be. But a legal battle will take years.

Robert said he made sure the deed was ironclad, exactly to avoid this kind of battle if he died suddenly."

"Because he's determined to rob even this from me?"

"No. You're misunderstanding him. He thought he was going to die. He… A long, drawn-out court battle is what you want for your mother's house? For Maria and the staff who have looked after the house all these years, for your mother's memory?"

His jaw flexed tight, the vein in his temple flickering threateningly. "You have no right to speak of her."

The utter loathing in his words slashed through her. Because he was right. His fury was justified.

She had no right to even speak of his mother, no right to her estate. To this day, she was equal parts amazed and perplexed that Robert had even deeded it to her.

For the first time in her life, she truly wished she was more like her mother—carefree, blissfully ignorant of everything around her but her own happiness. Wished she could turn her back on this man who threatened everything she had built, wished she could turn her back on the shadows that haunted Robert's eyes.

"I've no right to speak of her, true, but I'm sure she would never have wanted you to hate him all your life. Everyone's always talking about what a generous and kind lady she was and—"

He flinched as though she had laid a hand on him. "You have no idea what she'd have wanted." He stood at the window, just as Drew had done, his wide frame blocking the sunlight from coming in. Contrary to the cold, heartless man she had called him, he looked like a volcano of simmering emotions.

"Get out. I have nothing more to say to you."

Riya closed the door behind her, her legs shaking. Panic pounded through her.

Would he break Travelogue into pieces? How could she fight to keep what was hers? How was she to convince him that it was only Robert's haunting pain that had driven her to this?

Her head reeling, she stepped into the huge, open area laid out with open cabins.

The staff had already figured out that Drew was gone. The faint scraping and shuffling of chairs, the concerned glances in her direction—they were looking to her to provide some direction.

But Riya had no way to save the day, no answer to give to those hopeful looks. She grabbed her handbag and left, unable to think of anything else but temporary escape.

Nathan stared at the closed door, still trying to control his raging emotions. One flimsy, fragile woman had so nearly eroded his self-control.

It had taken him a few years to get over the grief of his mother's death, to accept the fatality of his own condition. He'd been so scared, alone and he'd lashed out at the world.

But in the end, he had not only accepted it but also tailored his life to live it without being haunted by the fear of dying every minute. Had made sure he'd not formed an attachment to anyone, made sure that no relationship could leave him weak. Like the way it had left his mother in the end.

Had gloried in each day he had, lived it to the fullest.

Today, he hadn't been able to help himself from taunting the manipulative minx, from pushing her. But for all the steely will with which she had manipulated him, there was a naiveté to her that cooled his interest. In a million years, he wouldn't have expected his father to command such loyalty in anyone. So much that she was risking everything she owned.

But nothing he did or could do would shake that resolve. Despite the very clever way she had manipulated Maria and taken advantage of his attachment to the estate, he had to admire that resolve. And she was right about one more thing.

Engaging his father in a legal battle would gain him nothing but a deadlock for years to come. He would win in the end, but when, he didn't know.

Time was the one thing that Nate didn't have the luxury or certainty of.

He wanted that estate, and convincing Riya to sell it back to him as soon as possible would be the biggest win of his life. He couldn't dismantle her company for no good reason, couldn't just play with the livelihood of so many people.

But he had learned enough about the smart, steel-willed beauty. Just the thought of those beautiful eyes widening with awareness and shock, the way she held herself rigid when he had neared her, brought a smile to his face.

He was going to enjoy convincing her to sell the estate to him.

CHAPTER THREE

By THE TIME Riya drove past the electronically manned gates and along the gravel driveway lined with the tall century-old oaks, she was still wondering what she would say to Jackie or how she would bring up the subject of Nathan. Jackie had the most singular way of looking at the world and the people in it. Only interested in how they affected her own life and happiness.

Riya pulled the window down and took a deep breath. The smell of pine needles and the fragrance of the roses greeted her.

The sight of the mansion emerging just as the driveway straightened always revived her, filled her with an indescribable joy. For her, the brick mansion meant home.

Driving around the courtyard, she pulled into the garage, parked and leaned her forehead on the steering wheel. Disappointment and a perverse anger filled her. Nathan didn't love the estate as she did, had been gone for a decade without a thought for it.

Would probably kick them all out, *her especially*, without a second thought. And to leave this place, to say goodbye finally? The very thought made her chest hurt.

Grabbing her laptop bag and her handbag, she stepped out of her car. All she wanted was to have a bath and sink into her bed and deal with everything tomorrow. She entered the vast, homely kitchen through the back door intending to go up quietly when Jackie called her.

Dressed in a cream silk pantsuit, she looked perfectly put together, as always. Except for the frown marring her brow.

"Riya! I've been calling you for hours and you didn't answer a single time." Her painted mouth trembled. "He's here, just…appeared out of thin air, after all these years."

Riya froze, her gaze flying around the house, her heart ratcheting in her chest. Fighting the rising panic, because of course it had always fallen to her to be the calm one, she straightened her spine. "Mom," she said loudly. "Calm down."

She called her that so infrequently now that Jackie looked at her with alarm.

"Now tell me clearly what happened."

"Nathaniel is here," her mother said, awe coating her words. "Apparently he's some big-shot billionaire who can ruin us with one word or—"

"He said that to you?"

"Of course not. He won't even meet my eyes. It's as if I'm not there, standing right in front of him. That witch Maria said it. He looks so different too, all lean and so coldly distant and arrogant."

Riya nodded, surprised that Jackie had noticed it too. There was something she couldn't pinpoint about Nathan either. A sort of cool detachment, a layer of frost as if nothing or no one could touch him. And yet he had been so angry when she refused to sign over the estate.

"Even Maria took a few seconds to recognize him. He just stood there looking as if he owned the place, when he didn't even ask after Robert all these years." Riya bit the inside of her cheek to keep from correcting her mother that the estate *was* his. "He arrived a couple of hours ago. Showed up at the front door and sent the staff into a frenzy.

They were all crying and laughing, and Robert's not even in town. He won't say why he's here."

How? She hadn't even seen his car in the garage. "Where is he? Did he say what he wants?"

"He's been wandering around the estate, drops in every half hour or so. Maria said he wants to see you."

Riya's heart sank to her feet.

A calculating look emerged in her mother's eyes, her panic forgotten. "Why *is* he looking for you? I'm still shaking from the shock of seeing him, and all this time, if you'd known that he was—"

"Hello, Riya."

Every time he said her name, it was like flipping a switch on inside her. A caress. An invitation. For what, she didn't even want to speculate. Her skin tingling, Riya turned.

He stood at the huge arched entrance into the kitchen.

Once again, Riya felt the impact of his presence like a magnet pulled toward a slab of iron.

The beard was still unshaved, but he had changed. Now his clothes reflected the casual power he exuded so easily. The rumpled shirt had been exchanged for a white dress shirt and a formal jacket this time. The snowy-white collar a contrast against his sunburned skin. His hair gleamed with wetness, looked more black than brown.

He looked knee-meltingly gorgeous. Case in point, her knees practically buckled beneath her.

"You didn't come back to the office, haven't been answering my calls," he said, waving his cell phone.

"I didn't realize I was supposed to be at your beck and call," she retorted, not trusting the invasive intimacy of his smile. In fact, she had liked him better when he was angry and threatening. "Not everything I do is about you."

That small smile turned into a grin, and his teeth gleamed against his tanned skin. It lit up his whole face,

softening the harsh angles of his features. And the mouth…
she had been right. It was made for smiling and something
else that she didn't want to think about.

"From now on, it's going to be all about me," he said,
stretching his arms by his sides. The casual gesture drew
her gaze to the breadth of his shoulders. That jacket was
cut perfectly, following the wide swath of his shoulders and
the narrowing of his waist.

Alarm spiked through her. "No."

"I have a proposition for you." Something glimmered
in his gaze. "You're not chickening out already, are you?"

Jackie gasped, and Riya wondered if her mother could
explode from the tension radiating from her. She infused
steel into her voice. "We don't have a deal."

"We do now. You've…*persuaded* me to take a chance
on you, Riya."

There was no way to arrest the heat blooming up her
face. He was doing it on purpose. Saying her name like that,
insinuating with that smile that there was more between
them than his hatred and her risky gamble. She wanted to
run away and hide in her bedroom, hope it was all a bad
dream.

Next to her, Jackie began again. "Riya, how dare you
not tell me—"

Nathan shot Jackie a look. Pure arctic frost, it was the
only way Riya could describe it. Granted, he probably was
the one man who could shut Jackie up without meaning to,
but Riya had a feeling he would have the same effect on all
of them, even if he had just been Nathaniel Ramirez. And
not the adored heir of the estate.

He had that kind of a presence. Contained and controlled with a violent energy brimming underneath the
calm facade.

How was it possible that she could notice so much, understand so much about him just in a few hours?

"Come," he said in a cajoling tone as if she were a recalcitrant child. When she still didn't move, he caught her wrist and tugged.

Her bare skin tingling at the contact of his rough fingers, Riya followed, past the nonplussed staff, who had gathered in the huge dining hall, and her pale mother, through the door and out into the lush acreage behind the house.

A cold breeze blew her hair in her face, and with a soft huff, Riya pulled it all to the side. The night was inky black, only the moon and carefully placed lights on the ground illuminating the path for them.

But instead of dulling his presence, the dark intensified her awareness of him. The graceful line of his shoulders, the taper of his lean chest to his waist and the corded energy of his thighs when she stumbled and he steadied her.

Her own senses revolted against her mind, determined to observe and absorb every little thing about him. They'd reached the well-lit-up gazebo in the south corner of the estate when Riya realized his long fingers were still wrapped around her wrist.

Dragging her feet on the grass, she tugged her hand away.

The splish-splash of water from another fountain, the relentless whisper of the cicadas, a hundred different fragrances carried around by the breeze greeted her. The very place she had always found blissfully peaceful was now ruined by the man playing a cat-and-mouse game with her livelihood. And something much worse.

Grasping the fear that was the only way to puncture her awareness of him, she lashed out. "You couldn't have given me an evening to brace myself? Let me figure out how and what I'm going to tell my mother, to figure out my future?"

"You left without a word to anyone. Is this how you run the company?"

"The very company that you threatened to tear into pieces?" she threw at him. "You asked me to get out. Very clearly."

"You were blackmailing me."

She bristled at the outrage in his voice. "I was doing no such thing." And because she couldn't bear to simply stop thinking of it as her company, she continued. "Even if your plan is to dismantle the company and sell it for bits, you'll need a skeleton staff to see through the memberships for the rest of the year. I recommend you keep Sam Hawkins on. He's been there from the beginning and Martha Gomez too. She needs this job and she'll be invaluable to—"

All of her panic ground to a halt as his long-limbed stride ate the distance between them.

"I don't remember firing you. Are you resigning, then?"

Riya reached behind her and grasped the wooden column. But there was nowhere to go and he was standing too close.

The lights from around the gazebo cast him in shadows.

Close enough to realize how many different shades of blue his eyes could turn depending on the light. Close enough for her to see the shape of his mouth, which had a hint of gaiety to it. Close enough for her to breathe and learn the scent of him and realize why he affected her so much.

She had never before experienced the weird pull in her stomach, the feverish tremble that gripped her, the constant fascination with every aspect of him.

Fisting her hands by her sides, she clamped down the shaky realization.

His gaze rested on her mouth for a nanosecond. Only an infinitesimal fragment of time, but her lips tingled. "I didn't quit. But have you left me a choice?"

As if the tension became too much even for him, he moved to her side and leaned against the structure. "The staff's murderous glares after you left would have turned me into dust if I hadn't told them you were just having a tantrum."

Her breath left her in a huge whoosh, the sound amplified in the silence. "Building up their hopes that everything's okay is just cruel. Does nothing get to you?"

"No."

His response wasn't threatening or emotional. Scarily, it was honest.

His watch glinted in the light as he folded his hands. "I'll give you and your staff one chance. Prove that Travelogue and you are worth taking on as part of RunAway International."

Catching the immediate thanks that rose to her lips, she turned toward him. Her heart thumped hard in her chest. Whether it was because of how close he was standing or because he was giving her a chance, she had no idea.

Ruthlessly killing her own hopes, she shook her head. "I don't want to work for you."

"Why not?"

"What do you mean *why not*?" She moved away, exasperated by him and her reaction to him. "Because you and I have a history, that's why. And not a good one. Whatever you think of me, I lied because…"

He gave her such an arch look that she backpedaled quickly. "Fine. I manipulated Maria and you with good intentions. Whereas you…you are doing this out of some twisted need for *revenge*. That's it. You want to torture me, guilt me and then—"

He grinned, and his blue eyes glittered. Her knees wobbled. "Have you always been this prone to drama or is it me that brings it out in you?"

How she wanted to say he affected her in no way, but they would both know she was lying. Better instead to focus on fighting it. "Why the sudden change of heart, then?"

"A strong sense of familial duty? A core made of kindness?"

Rolling her eyes, she swatted him. Deftly, he caught her hand in his.

Her breath stuck in her throat. Her fingers moved over his in the dark, registering the different texture of his palm—rough and abrasive, devoid of any softness, so different from her own.

It was his absolute stillness next to her, just as powerful as that latent energy, that made her realize what she was doing.

She jerked her hand away, the air she had been holding rushing out of her.

What the hell was she doing, *pawing* him like that? He was her employer, her enemy…

No man had been so dangerous to her internal balance as him. No man had ever spun her senses so easily.

Rubbing shaking fingers over her face, she struggled to think back to their conversation. "You're agreeing to see Robert, then?"

"If you give me a date now as to when you will sign the deed over to me."

"Stay here in San Francisco until their wedding. See Robert, let him speak to you. And I'll sign over the estate the day after the wedding. Also, none of my staff will be made redundant. When this is all over, I want you to go away and leave Travelogue alone. Forever."

"That depends on if Travelogue stays intact that long."

"If you give us a fair chance, I have no doubt it will."

His eyes gleamed ferociously. "You've got a lot of nerve, setting conditions to sell my mother's house back to me."

"You're a billionaire, you're your own boss and as far as I understand, you have no one in your life that you're answerable to. What's two months in the big picture of your life, Nathan?"

"Everything, Riya." There was no humor in his smile now, only a dark warning. "This is your last chance to let it go."

She didn't take even a beat to think it over. "No. Robert… he…I'll do anything for him."

His curious silence swathed her and Riya felt like the rabbit in the story her father had told her when she was little. The rabbit had gone into the lion's den, determined to change his mind about eating one animal every day.

At that point, she had stuck her fingers in her ears and begged him not to continue. A few days after that, she and Jackie had left. Her father had never seen her again, never called her, never sent a birthday card.

For years, she had wondered if he thought of her, hoped he would write to her, call Jackie to ask about her.

Only utter and absolute silence had greeted her hopes.

Now…now she didn't even remember his face clearly. On the road with Jackie, hearing her crying at night, not knowing where they would go next—it had been the most uncertain time of her life. Until Jackie had met Robert and he had taken them to his estate, Riya had thought she would never know a stable home again.

And to see Robert ache to see Nathan, to speak a few words to him, she couldn't back down now. Not when Nathan was finally here.

"Fine. Come to work Monday morning."

She saw the shadow of something in his eyes—a promise, a challenge.

"I'll stay two months. I'll even dance with you at the wedding."

"I don't want to dance with—"

"You started this, Riya. I'm going to finish it."

She breathed in cold gulps of air, only then seeing the faint shape of a chopper. "Stop saying my name like that," she said, not sure when the words had exactly left her lips.

Frowning, he stepped closer. "Am I saying it wrong?"

There was that strange little tension again. Winding around them, tugging at them.

"No. I just…we're…"

The helicopter blades began whirring, and he bent toward her to make himself heard. A firestorm danced through Riya as his breath played on her nape.

It was a heated brand, a molten caress. The simple touch of his fingers on her waist as she swayed seared through the cotton of her shirt.

"Mr. Ramirez and Ms. Mathur are too formal when we're going to work in close quarters for a couple of months. And calling each other brother and sister, especially when we…" Her heart drummed in her ears, a flash of heat bursting all over her as he paused dramatically. "…*obviously don't like each other* will just earn us a place on a daytime soap opera, don't you think?

"Nathan and Riya, it has to be."

She felt his smile instead of saw it, the faint graze of his beard against her jaw making her hyperaware of him. He lifted his head and Riya stared mutely at the striking beauty of the planes of his face.

All wicked, from the twinkle in his eyes to the dimples in his cheeks. And sexy all the way.

"See you Monday morning." He stepped back, sending

her heart pitter-pattering all over her chest. "And FYI, I'm what they call an exacting boss."

By the time Riya walked the long way around the acreage back to the house, she was hungry and tired and her head hurt.

Turning the gleaming antique handle on the side door into the kitchen, she stepped in. Even though her stomach rumbled, all she wanted was to get into bed and forget that this day had happened.

She couldn't believe that Drew had sold her out so easily, couldn't believe what she had set in motion. And of all things, she couldn't believe the sharp and stringent quality of her awareness of Nathan, of his every word and gesture, of the flash of the same awareness in his. But she had no doubt, where she was floundering and flailing in the wake of it, it was nothing but a game to him.

The overhead ceiling lights came on, bathing her in a blaze of light.

Jackie stood near the curving staircase, her eyes glittering with fear and fury. "If you knew he was coming, why didn't you stop him?"

Guilt settling heavily on her shoulders, Riya sighed. If only life were as simple as her mom thought it was. "It's his estate we're living in. One of these days, he was bound to return."

"Just when Robert has finally agreed to the wedding and—"

Unable to hear another word of her mom's self-absorption, she cut across her. "Robert will be happy to see him. I can't just send him away, even if I wanted to."

Her elegant hands wringing in front of her, Jackie walked around the huge dining table. "What does he want with you?"

"He wants the estate back."

"No," Jackie said, her tone rising, her gaze stricken. "He'll probably just kick us out if you do that. You can't—"

Even as she wished her mother would think of Riya's feelings for once, she softened her tone. Whatever her weaknesses, Jackie had found stability and peace here with Robert and the estate. "I can't stop him from taking what is rightfully his, Jackie."

Jackie's gaze zoomed somewhere far away, and Riya locked out the urge to shake her mom. That look meant nothing she said was going to get through to her now. "I don't care what you have to do. Just make sure he doesn't have the house back. Do something, anything to send him back, Riya."

"I can't take him on," Riya said, looking away. If Jackie found out he was here because of what Riya had done... "If I fight him on this, he threatened to drag us through the courts. I don't have a choice."

"Of course you can. You have Robert on your side. He'll never agree to Nathan taking the estate from you. If there's a long court battle, then so be it. You can't lose the house, Riya. I can't take this uncertainty, this kind of stress at this stage of my life."

And there was the heart of the matter. Bitterness pooled in her throat, but Riya shook it away. As she always did. "Robert will look after you, Jackie. Nothing will happen to you."

"Does it occur to you that maybe it's you I could be worried about?"

"There's no precedent for me to think that, is there?" Jackie paled.

Now Riya felt like the green scum that lived under a rock.

Jackie sighed. "You slogged over the estate for years.

Where was Nathan when he was needed? Do whatever you have to do, but make sure you hold on to this house.

"You have just as much right to this as he. Or even more."

Nathan's dark smile as he'd stood close to her sent a shiver over her skin. His offer for Travelogue was more than she'd hoped for, but she didn't like the look in his eyes.

It wasn't just that ever-present energy between them. It was more. As if he could see through her, into the heart of her. As if he could see her fears and insecurities and found them laughable. As if he knew how to use them to trip her up.

She just had to remember that whatever he threw at her, she could cope with it. The only danger was if he had true interest in her. He didn't. Nathan was a man who traveled the world over.

Like everyone else in her life, she would matter very little to him once he realized she wouldn't budge from her goal. And then he would leave her alone.

For years, she had lived with the knowledge that her father hadn't cared about her. For Jackie, she was nothing but a crutch of safety, the one who would never leave her. For Robert, she had been the means to assuage his guilt about Nathan and his mom. Not that she didn't appreciate his kindness.

But the truth was no one had ever really cared about her, about her fears, her happiness. And Nathan would be no different.

CHAPTER FOUR

WHEN RIYA ARRIVED at work Monday morning, it was to find Nathan leaning against the redbrick building, head bent down to his tablet.

Pulling in a breath, she forced her nerves to calm down. She had agreed to this, actually forced him into this. Now she had to see this through for Robert and for her own company.

The shabby street instantly looked different, felt different. And more than one woman sent him lingering looks as they walked past. But he was unaware of the attention he was drawing.

Today, he was dressed in a V-necked gray T-shirt coupled with blue jeans that hugged his lean hips and thighs in a very nerve-racking way. His hair gleamed with wetness, his beard still hiding his mouth. The veins bulging in his forearms, the stretch of the cotton across his chest. Every time she set eyes on him, something pinged inside her.

So early in the morning, with no caffeine in her system, he was just too much testosterone to stomach.

"You're wasting my pilot's time." His gaze didn't waver from his tablet.

"Pilot? What are you talking about?" Feeling heat in her cheeks, she dug through her bag for her phone.

For the first time in two years since she and Drew had

started Travelogue, she had resolutely refused to check her work email. Now she just felt stupid because she had obviously missed some important communication.

"Not completely together still? Had to abandon the mother ship early today?"

"I need coffee before I can deal with you," she muttered. "I turned off my email client all weekend."

She had hardly finished speaking when his chauffeur appeared by her side with a coffee cup. Nathan's gaze lingered on her as she took a few much-needed sips.

His perception surprised her, but she wasn't going to confide about Jackie to him. Or anything for that matter. For all his generous offer, she didn't trust his intentions.

"I thought you slaved night and day, weekends and whatnot to build Travelogue. Didn't have a life outside of the company and the estate. Apparently you're a paragon of hard work and dedication and every other virtue. Except for the 'small incident' with Mr. Anderson."

Feeling like a lamb being led to slaughter under his watchful, almost indulgent gaze, she gulped too much on her next sip and squealed. He was instantly at her side, concern softening his mouth.

She jerked away as his palm landed on her back, scalded by his touch more than the coffee. Feeling like an irresponsible idiot, she cleared her throat. "Just...tell me what's on the agenda today."

Wicked lights glinted in his gaze. "British Virgin Islands."

Her leg dangled midway over the footpath as if she were a puppet being pulled by strings. "Like going there? Us?"

"Yes."

Alarm bells clanged in her head. "Why?"

He moved closer. She caught the instant need to step back. "A project of mine has come to the execution stages.

It'll suit very well to see what your precious team and you are made of. Sort of a test before I flush you guys."

"A trip to Virgin Islands just to test us seems like the kind of extravagance that adds a lot of overhead to small, itty-bitty companies. I would rather—"

"Didn't I tell you? Your finances, your projects—everything's on probation." Arrogance dripped from his every word, every gesture. "A skeleton crew will keep the website and sales going."

She swallowed the protest that rose to her lips. She'd have to just show him what she and her team were made of. Navigating to the calendar on her phone, she synced it and opened his shared calendar. Tilting her head up, she leveled a direct look at him. "Robert is back tonight. Should I go ahead and block your time, then?"

A mocking smile lingered on his lips as he studied her. Her breath felt tight in her chest as she willed herself to stay still under the devouring gaze. "We won't return for a few days."

"I don't see the need for—"

"I'm beginning to see why your investors were so eager to jump ship. You don't want to make money, and you don't listen to advice or input of any kind. It's almost as though you live and work in isolation."

"That's not true. I…"

Folding his hands, he raised an eyebrow.

Something about the look in his face grated on her. But she didn't want to give him a single reason to back out of their deal. "Fine. I'm ready to go."

Faced with her increasingly unignorable reaction to him, she found it tempting to just accept defeat, sign away the dratted estate and walk away. Except she had heard the stunned silence when Jackie told Robert that Nathan was here. She had heard his hopes, his pain in the one request he had made of her.

"Whatever he wants, please say yes, Riya. I want to see my son."

It was the first time Robert had ever asked anything of her.

Guiding her along with him, Nathan crossed the small, dingy street that housed their office to the opposite side. Every inch of her tautened as the muscled length of his thigh grazed hers.

"Which island are we visiting?" she said pushing her misgivings down. Robert and her company, she must keep her reasons at the center of her mind.

"Mine."

She slid into the limo and crossed her legs as he occupied the opposite seat. "You own one of the Virgin Islands?"

"Yes."

"But you don't even own a home."

Amusement deepened his gaze. "Been reading up on me?"

She shrugged, as if she hadn't devoured the internet looking for every scrap of information on him over the weekend. "There wasn't really much."

"What were you hoping to find?"

"Not the list of your assets," she said, remembering the article he had been featured in in *Forbes* about the youngest billionaires under thirty. It galled her to admit it, but the man *was* a genius investor and apparently also one of the leading philanthropists of their generation.

He donated millions to charity and causes the world over, but there hadn't been a byte about his personal life. What was she to make of him?

"I was looking for something of a personal nature."

He leveled a shocked look at her. "Why?"

"Jackie told Robert you were back and he asked me a thousand questions about you. I had nothing to tell him apart from the fact that you're a gazillionaire and an arrogant, heartless SO..."

He narrowed his eyes and Riya sighed. Antagonizing him was going to get her precisely nowhere.

"So, all this interest in my personal life is only for your precious Robert, right?"

She would jump from the thirteenth story before she admitted to him how scarily right he was. Ignoring the charged air of the luxurious interior, she went through her email. "This whole trip is just an excuse for you to—"

"Excuse for what?" he interrupted, a thread of anger in his voice. He leaned forward, his muscled forearms resting on his thighs. Gaze zeroed in on her with the focus of a laser beam. Lingered over every inch of her face until it was a caress. The decadent sides of the vehicle seemed to move inward until it was as if they were locked in a bubble.

"You're welcome at any time to sign the papers and walk away. And I'll do the same."

Shaking her head, Riya looked away, trying to break the spell he cast around them. She was nowhere near equipped to take him on. On any level.

Soon they arrived at a private airfield. A sleek Learjet with RunAway International's logo, a tangled-up R&A, was waiting. They boarded the aircraft and it was easy to keep her mouth shut, greeted by the sheer affluence and breadth of Nathaniel Ramirez's standing in the world.

The interior of the plane was all cream leather and sleek panels. Her brown trousers and ironed beige dress shirt had never looked quite so shabby as they did against the quiet elegance of her surroundings. While Nathan spoke to the pilot, she took a quick tour and came away with her head spinning.

The master suite in the back was more opulent than her bedroom at the estate.

Still reeling from the sheer breadth of Nathan's wealth, she made a quick call to Jackie and Robert, informing them of her sudden trip.

It took her a few minutes to settle down, to regain her balance that he tipped so easily. Soon they were leveling off at thousands of feet, with nothing but silence stretching in the main cabin.

"Robert asked me to tell you that he can't wait to see you," she said.

His mouth narrowed into an uncompromising line, his whole posture going from relaxed to tense in a matter of seconds. "Tell me what happened between you and Mr. Anderson."

"That's none of your…" Sighing, she tried to collect herself.

The last thing she wanted was to talk about herself and with him of all people. But if he couldn't even tolerate Robert's name, what was he going to say when he saw him? What was the point of all this if he just sat there and glared at Robert with that frosty gaze?

How hardhearted did he have to be not to wonder about Robert all these years?

If the price was that she answer questions about herself, then she would.

"There's nothing much. Drew and I shared a professional relationship. For the most part." Time for attack again. "Where did you go when you left all those years ago?"

Challenge simmered between them. If she went down this road, he was going to make her pay.

"New York City first and then I backpacked through Europe." Promptly came the next shot. "So Mr. Anderson was just a hopeful candidate you were trying on?"

"For the last time, I was not trying him on. I never even went on a date with him."

"That's not the story I've been hearing."

"I have no intention of humiliating myself or Drew just so that you can sit there and play us off against each other."

He leaned back into his seat as they leveled off, and the gray fabric stretched over his chest. "You managed it quite well all by yourself. I reviewed all of last quarter's reports, and he did nothing but run the company into the ground. With his head buried in love clouds and you averse to any risk, Travelogue would have died within a year."

Drew and she had known each other for a while, their relationship always in a strange intersection between friends and colleagues. But things had slowly spiraled to worse in the last few months. "I never expected him to sell me out to you."

"Selling out to me was the wisest thing he did. There hasn't been a lot of financial growth in the last quarter. And anyone who had good ideas, Drew fired them. Like the marketing strategist."

The sparkling water she had ordered came and she took a fortifying sip. "All the marketing strategy suggested was that we increase the cost of membership for customers who have *been* with us since the beginning, and take a bigger cut of the profits from the flash sales for vacations packages.

"These are middle-class families who come to us because we provide the best value for their buck, not international jet-setters who don't have to think twice about buying and sinking companies like a little boy buys and breaks his toys."

Nathan countered without blinking at her juvenile attack. "That marketing strategy is spot-on. Different tiers of membership is the way to go. An executive membership that charges more and provides a different kind of experience. There's a whole set of clientele that Travelogue's missing out on. If you don't grow, if you don't expand your horizons, you'll be pushed out of the market."

"That's a huge risk that might alienate us to our current clientele."

"It is. And it's one I'm willing to take."

Neatly put in place, Riya bristled. It was all her hard work and his risk. And the consequences would be hers to bear. "Does it ever get old?"

"What?"

"That high you're getting from the casual display of your power and your arrogance?"

He laughed, and the deep sound went straight to her heart, as if it were a specially designed missile targeted for her. It seemed every little gesture of his went straight to her heart or some other part of her.

Parts she shouldn't even be thinking about.

How did he get past all of her defenses so easily? Why did he affect her so much?

She had no answers, only increasing alarm that she would never figure out how to resist whatever it was that he did so easily.

"What will you do once I sign over the estate to you? Kick Robert and Jackie out?"

"Maybe. Or maybe we can all live under one roof like a happy family. Would that pacify your guilt?"

The idea of it was so absurd that Riya stared at him, taken aback.

"Horrifying prospect, isn't it? Me and you, me and your mother, me and Robert—it's a disaster every which way."

"This is all so funny and trivial to you…you don't care…" She had to pause to breathe. "You have all these resources, you own a damn plane and yet you couldn't have visited Robert once in all these years?

The cabin resounded with her outburst.

"It's not a one-for-one anymore, Riya."

He slid some papers toward her, and the words *Disciplinary Action* printed neatly on top stole the remaining breaths from Riya's lungs.

She fingered the papers, her heart sinking. "What is this?"

"His mismanagement of the company in the last few months meant Drew was the dispensable one between the two of you, for now. But it doesn't mean you're without culpability. I need to know the source of the problem between you two."

"Ammunition to make me dispensable too?"

"I'm making sure it's documented properly. It's a standard HR policy in my group of companies."

Nathan leaned back into his seat, wondering at the puzzle that Riya Mathur was. The software engine she had built, he'd been told by one of his own architects, was extraordinarily complex. And yet she blanched at using it to its full potential by expanding the client base, at spreading her wings in any way.

"This is your one chance to clear it all up," he said, softening his voice. He wasn't bending the rules, but he was also very curious about what happened between her and her colleague.

"Last year, on New Year's Eve, a week after we had signed up the half millionth member, we had a party. Drew was drunk. I…I had a glass of white wine. We…ended up next to each other when it struck twelve. He…kissed me. In front of the whole company." She looked away. But the small tremble that went through her couldn't be hidden. "I kissed him back…I think. Before I remembered to put a stop to it."

"You think? It's not rocket science."

She glared at him and pushed her hair back. "I don't know what happened or how I let it happen. Just that it was the stupidest thing I've ever done. In my defense, I had got the news that day that Robert was out of danger and with Travelogue making such a big milestone…" She ran shaking fingers over her face. "I've been kicking myself for losing control like that. I never meant to…"

"Enjoy a kiss?"

"Yes. For one thing, it was unprofessional. For another, it was reckless on so many levels. A relationship with any man is not in my plan right now. Career is my focus."

Nathan frowned, seeing embarrassment and something else. He admired her drive to succeed in her career, understood that it might leave very little time for a personal life. If not for the thread of wistfulness in her face.

Every time he had a conversation with her, he was struck sharp by how innocent she was. Yet from everything Maria had told him with grudging respect, Riya had always worked hard, pretty much taken care of herself even when she was a child. Had helped his father every way she could.

The parameters of her life—Travelogue and its current client base, the estate, his father and her mother—they were all so rigidly defined. To step out of any of them, he realized, sent her into a tailspin.

And the one kiss reflected her age, she was calling it a momentary lapse in judgment.

"You have a plan for your life?" he asked, disbelief slowly cycling into something far more insidious.

She fidgeted in her seat. "A road map, yes… Drew is too volatile, unreliable. When I'm ready to settle down in a decade or so, I want a stable man who'll stand by me for the rest of my life, who'll be a good husband and father. Right now I can't allow myself to be sidetracked by—"

Slow anger simmered to life inside him. "It seems your plan allows for everything except living."

Her gaze flew to him.

Nathan uncurled his fist, willing the unbidden anger to leave him. She was of no consequence to him. None.

What did it matter to him if the naive fool spent the rest of her life slaving over the estate and company, wasting her life instead of living it?

"Do you have a list of qualities and a timeline for when you'll meet and mate with this ideal specimen of manhood too?"

Her gaze flashed with warning. "My personal life has no bearing on you. I'm only telling you this because you're questioning my professional behavior."

"Yet you dare ask me questions about my visits, about where I've been all these years."

"That's because I've seen the pain you've caused Robert for so long. Much as I try, I can't help wondering what kind of man stays away from everything he knows for a decade, without once looking back. You didn't even stay for your mother's funeral. You didn't care about what happened to your father for a decade. You didn't come when Maria... If I hadn't realized that she knew where you were—"

"Enough."

He leveled a hard look at her and Riya knew she had crossed a line.

"I want a new software model created within three weeks for an executive membership and a package from your team on the front end. You'll see the launch event."

Her mouth fell open, her stomach dropping into a vacuum. "It can't be ready in three weeks. I'll need to redesign the whole software engine, and we don't have any of the product development team to put the package together. I have only worked behind the scenes till now."

"Then step into the front. Work smarter and learn to delegate. Use your staff as more than your cheerleader. And the next time a colleague professes undying love to you on office premises and continues to harass you, you'll immediately file a report with HR."

She slapped her palms against the table between them, something snapping in her. "How long will you hate me for what my mother did?"

"Don't overestimate your place in my life, Riya." Each word dripped with cutting incisiveness. "Although thanks to your manipulation, I'm veering toward moderate annoyance."

"Then how long will you punish me for lying?"

"Punish you?"

"Yes. Lording it over me, dragging me across the world, setting goals that ensure my failure, enforcing this...this..."

He stood up from his seat and she craned her neck.

"You've got quite the imagination for someone who's determined to live her life by a plan. We made a deal, one that you started. You're bending all out of shape now because I'm holding you to your end of it?"

His voice was soft, all the more efficient for it. The angrier she got, the calmer he grew. And perversely she wanted to ruffle that frosty, still exterior, wanted to make him angry, hurt, feel something.

That scared her more than anything.

"Or is it me personally that you can't deal with?"

She stood up, meaning to get away. "I don't know what you're talking about."

He grasped her arm, the lean breadth of his body too close. "If we're going for all-out honesty, one of us has to state it for what it is."

Panic unfurled in sharp bursts in her belly.

As long as it was unsaid, as long as it was just in her

head, and in their glances and in his knowing, arrogant smile, she could still ignore it, she could still believe it to be just a by-product of how much power he held in her life right now.

"There's nothing to state." She tugged at his fingers but his grip was relentless. Bending down, he neatly trapped her against her seat. His gaze moved over her as if it could touch her. Lingered over her eyes, her nose, her mouth. The sound of their breaths, labored and fast, surrounded her in the silence. She didn't understand where this energy was coming from or why it was so strong.

When she kissed Drew, it had been pleasant, nice. Like a breezy day on the coast, like sitting in front of a warm fire in cold winter.

When Nathan touched her, it felt as if she would come apart from the inside if he continued. Left her feeling shaken when he stopped. Probably how someone would feel when jumping off a cliff. How someone felt when playing with fire.

"Please, Nate, let me go."

A smile wreathed his mouth. It was full of satisfaction, of understanding, even a little glimmer of resignation. The pads of his fingers pressed into her skin. His breath caressed the tip of her nose, his gaze dipping to her mouth. "You didn't wonder what would happen if I came back and turned your life upside down. You didn't expect this current that comes to life when we look at each other. Do you have a plan for what to do in this twisted situation we're in?"

Emotion, that emotion she wanted to see in him, it coated every word. This unbidden fire between them, for all his forcing the matter, he didn't like or want it any more than she did.

"Do you think your life is still completely in your control?" he asked.

"It would be if you weren't so determined to play games with me."

"I haven't done one thing today that I wouldn't have even if you weren't the most beautiful, most infuriating, the strangest creature I've ever met."

A soft gasp left her mouth at the vehemence in his words. The small sound reverberated in the quiet cabin.

Releasing her, he stepped back, his gaze a wintry frost again. Glanced at her with unease. As if he didn't know what had happened.

"You are the problem, Riya. Not me. It rattles you when I come near you, when I lay a finger on you. You fight it by attributing motives to me. Tell me you'll sell the estate, and I'll have the pilot turn the plane around. Tell me you've had enough."

"Why are you fighting me so much on this?" she said, desperation spewing from her. "What do you lose by talking to Robert a few times? What do you have in there, a big hard rock for a heart?"

Her attack took him by surprise. A scornful twist to his mouth, he stared at her. And Riya could literally see the minute he decided she wasn't worth it. Whatever it was.

Perverse disappointment flooded her and she stood immobile in its wake.

"I have no heart. At least not a working one." His mouth barely moved, his jaw clenched tight. "I'll never forgive him for what he did to my mother. He let her down when she needed him. Flaunted his affair with Jackie in her face. Just the mere thought of him fills me with anger, reminds me of my own weakness."

CHAPTER FIVE

RIYA STRAIGHTENED IN her leather seat as they touched down on the runway. She had spent the entire flight alternately staring at the screen and catching sneaky glances of Nathan. He, however, seemed to have very effectively removed her from his mind.

The new software model that he had demanded loomed high at the back of her mind, but she was way too restless to focus.

As much as it galled her, the infuriating man was right.

All these years, she had drowned herself in work, focused on the estate and Robert and Jackie. Had spent it all denying herself a normal life.

What was the point in inviting anyone into her life when all she faced in the end was pain and disappointment? When, inevitably, she would be deserted? A small mistake, and look how easily Drew had walked away from her. Wasn't it better than the hurt that followed if she allowed herself to form any kind of attachment, to constantly look inside and wonder what she was lacking?

For years, she had wondered why her father had given up on her so easily, why she wasn't enough for Jackie as she struggled herself...

Safer to focus on work, to develop her career. At least, the results were dependable. But it also meant she was woefully unequipped to deal with her attraction to Nathan. And all the ensuing little things she was sharply becoming aware of.

Simple things like how different the texture and feel of his hand was against hers. How the scent of him invaded her senses when he stood so close. How there was a constant battle within her between reveling in what he evoked and fear that she was losing control.

How slowly but surely his words were beginning to affect her...

As she followed him down the plane's stairs, she stilled on the second step, taking in the vast expanse of land, a beautiful landscape of beaches and water. Her mouth slack, she blinked at the sheer magnificence of it.

The island was a paradise and apparently Nathan's next billion-dollar venture.

A team of engineers and architects greeted him, all dressed in casual shorts and T-shirts. "Is Sonia still working?" he asked, and was told yes.

Her curiosity about the island and the project he had mentioned trumping everything else, Riya stayed behind him. His attention to detail, his incisive questions...it was like watching a super computer at work.

The island, she learned, was to be rented out as a private retreat to celebrities who wanted a slice of heaven to get away to, at a staggering half a million dollars per day. The tour they had been given, driving around in buggies, had permanently stuck her jaw to her chest.

There were a hundred acres of heaven, with six Balinese-style abodes, a submarine that could be chartered to see the untouched coral reef, a Jacuzzi that could apparently house two dozen people at once and an unnamed attraction that everyone mentioned with sheer excitement. Also included on the island were private beaches, infinity pools that led into the ocean, tennis courts, a wide array of water sports and every single abode came with a personal chef, a masseuse and a housekeeping staff of ten.

No small detail was beneath Nathan's attention. He had even asked after the scientific team dedicated to studying an almost extinct gecko that was native to the island.

The more Riya saw, the more guilt and awe gripped her insides.

He owned all this and he still wanted that small estate. He had chosen to accept her little deal when he could have done anything with her company, with her and not looked back. That didn't speak of a heartless, uncaring man, and Riya struggled to accept what it did mean.

Just the mere thought of him fills me with anger, reminds me of my own weakness.

His words pinged incessantly in her head all afternoon. Beneath the cold fury, there had been so much pain, an ache that she understood. All she knew was that his mother, Anna, had died of a heart condition. But why say Robert reminded him of his own weakness?

Seeing his dynamic interactions with his team, however, his face wreathed into laughter at something, she found it hard to see any weakness in him. He was gorgeous, wealthy and possessed of an incisive mind that had made him a billionaire.

Sometime since they had arrived, he had changed into khaki shorts and a cotton T-shirt. The relentless sun caressed his face, glinted in his beard, reflecting myriad shades of blue in his eyes. The watch on his wrist glinted expensively as he signaled to someone, and his hands and arms caught her attention.

His gaze found her right then, as though he was aware of her fascination, and she dragged her own back to the delicious food that they had been served. They were lunching on the covered terrace of one of the villas.

Fresh water cascaded into a whirlpool on the terrace below and poured into the enormous swimming pool, its water as clear as crystal. The living area was cavernous with tropical sunlight streaming in from every direction.

Using local stone and Brazilian hardwood floors, the villa was an architectural beauty that boasted ten bedrooms. Decorated with priceless antiques, Indian rugs, art pieces and bamboo furniture from Bali, the villa was situated above a hill providing a spectacular view of the beach.

The chocolate soufflé had barely melted in her mouth when Nathan sat down in the chair next to her.

"What do you think?" he asked, and his entire team had come to a grinding halt as though his very question to her demanded utter silence.

Riya had met his captivating gaze, warning herself not to read so much into a simple question. "Everything is brilliant, gorgeous," she replied, feeling his scrutiny like a warm caress. "But you don't need Travelogue to find high-end customers for this place."

She had known he had dragged her along only to make her uncomfortable. Still, disappointment slashed through her. For a few hours, she had forgotten their little deal, had felt like a part of his dynamic team, had realized how much she had been missing living in her own world.

"I have something else in mind for Travelogue. The island is the place we're testing it out. Also, every year, there will be three months when we'll offer up the six villas independently for a deal. A special sale for our low-end customers, a chance for an average man to experience a little slice of heaven."

"And the income from those three months? It goes to a charity, doesn't it?"

The Anna Ramirez Foundation, she remembered, her heart feeling too big for her chest.

"Yes."

"I don't know what to say. Nathan, I—"

"You get to do the work." He cut her off on purpose. "I want you to build a new server plus a front-end package from your team that will tie this to the software model you will be designing. And we'll need—"

"Different tiers for pricing, and packages and even log-in portals for different members," she replied, a keen sense of excitement vibrating through her.

She had a feeling she had scratched not even the surface of the man he was. And yet she had judged him for not seeing Robert all these years. It scared her and excited her, like nothing else, what else she might learn about him in the coming weeks. And there was no way to turn back from this, no way to curb the curiosity that swept through her.

"Maybe you'll last long enough with me, then," he said, standing up.

Riya looked up, hanging between the urge to apologize, why she had no idea, and to leave the status quo. There was something about the tone of his voice that said he had neatly pushed her into the employee box. That he regretted the tiny little fracture in his control earlier.

The easy humor, the carefully constructed indifference, they were all a foil for something beneath, something deeper. Riya wanted to run away and delve deeper at the same time.

"Take a couple of hours off. The island heat can be too strong for newcomers."

She nodded, feeling a strange sense of disappointment as he walked away.

Nathan was e-signing a bunch of documents for his virtual manager when he heard more than one long sigh from his engineering team and a subdued curse fall from the local construction crew they had hired.

Baffled by the sudden change in the tenor, he looked up from his tablet.

His own breath fisted in his chest. Languid energy uncoiled in his belly.

Clad in a white stretchy top that hugged the globes of her lush breasts, and denim shorts that showcased the lean muscles in her long legs, Riya was coming down the steep path. Her hair was tied into a high ponytail and swung left and right with her long stride. She wore flats, the strings of which tied around her ankles in the most sensual way.

He couldn't fault his team for losing their focus, nor fault her for her simple attire. The weather was a combination of damp and stifling heat.

Every inch of him thrummed with tension and anticipation. Locking his jaw, Nathan turned away. Fought the insidious thought supplied by his mind that he could have her if he wanted.

Her skin glistened golden in the sun. And it felt like raw silk, he knew now. And her brown eyes took on the darkest shade when he touched her. The faintest whiff of roses clung to her skin. Two tiny things about her that he would never be able to erase.

Even as he warned himself, his gaze traveled over the modest neckline of the sleeveless T-shirt that draped over her lush breasts and dipped to her waist.

She stopped and looked around her with a smile that only added to her appeal.

The need to run his fingers over that graceful line of her neck, to sink his hands into her hair, to shake loose the safe, sterile world she had built for herself, to be the one to wake her up to her own potential in every way was almost overwhelming.

She was like a beautiful butterfly that refused to leave the cocoon, and he wanted to be the one to lure her out.

With a curse that punctured the stunned silence around him, he shot up from his seat. Turned away from the temptation she presented. Reminded himself that he had conquered obstacles and fears that were far more dangerous.

Things were already too twisted between them. And from her episode with Drew, he knew she could never handle him.

Nathan needed the rule-following, road-map-for-my-life female in his life the way he needed a heart attack.

What he should do was to put her on a flight home immediately and forget her or her little deal.

And yet with the excitement thrumming through her as she reached them, her wide eyes taking in the equipment around, he couldn't find it in him to break his word.

Three more months of this torture, and he was already chafing against his own rules.

Pushing her shades on to keep the orange glare away, Riya looked around herself. All the guesses she had made were off by a mile. It was not a casino, or a resort or a theater or an architectural marvel of any kind.

A huge crane stood behind the working team. An enclosure that was as tall as her surrounded the crane.

Her heart beating with a thunderous roar, she stepped inside and stilled.

A raised platform with an exquisitely designed, waist-high iron railing that went all around sat center stage in the enclosure. The most luxurious little sofa with legroom in the front sat against the back wall, and Riya noted that it was riveted to the wooden floor of the platform. As she watched with spiraling curiosity, tiny little lights, strategically placed around the perimeter of the floor turned on, casting brilliant light around.

Two small tables sat on either side of the sofa. Exotic orchids in vases along with an assortment of other things like expensive chocolate and even a bucket of champagne in ice sat on the tables.

And the final thing she noticed was safety tethers on each side of the sofa.

Her breath hitched in her throat as she realized what the elaborate setup meant.

She turned around, determined to find out if the fantastic idea was really true, when Nathan and a tall brunette stepped inside the enclosure.

Meeting her gaze, Nathan tilted his head toward the newcomer. "This is Sonia Lopez. She's the project manager."

A kind of suspended silence hung in the air where the woman obviously waited for him to say more and then gave up.

"Riya Mathur. She's the software architect on a company I acquired recently."

Relief sweeping through her, Riya shook the woman's hand.

Sonia cast another quick look toward Nathan before stepping out of the enclosure.

Leaving her alone with Nathan.

She jerked as he clasped her wrist and tugged her toward the raised platform. "Let's go."

Her eyes wide, fear beating a tattoo in her head, she shook her head. "No. I would very much like to be a spectator, thank you."

The most unholy delight dawned in his eyes, a wicked fire that turned them into a fiery blue. His mouth curved into a smile; it was the most gorgeous he had ever seemed to her. There was no facade, no frost. Only pure, undisguised laughter at her cowardice. "Not a choice. If you want—"

Surprising him, she took a few steps forward and cast a quick glance at the setup. "It's not fair, Nathan. My going on this has nothing to do with my company's abilities."

"Life's not fair, Riya. But you have to grab your thrills where you can."

With that, he pulled her and they stepped through the railing.

"You sound like a little boy going on an adult ride for the first time."

He clasped her hand and pulled her down to the sofa. Her knees quaking, she managed to stay still as he clipped the safety belt around them. And now, instead of an intangible one, there was a rope binding them together.

Breathe, Riya.

Within minutes, a faint whirring began and the crane unfolded, lifting them up into the sky.

Riya gasped and clasped his hand tighter, at the sheer magnificence of the feeling. Her mouth dry, she laughed giddily as they went higher and higher.

The whole island was laid out beneath them like a glittering jewel. The villas, the infinity pool, the beautiful grounds, she had never seen a more breathtaking sight. Her heart raced at a thunderous speed, a strange pull in her stomach.

When it felt as if she could extend her hand and touch the clouds, they came to a standstill. She found her gaze drawn to Nathan's profile.

His nostrils flaring, he looked around them, his eyes glittering with thrill and energy.

It was the most exhilarating thing she had ever been part of, the most beautiful sight she had ever seen. And the effect of it still paled against the sheer masculinity of the man holding her hand.

Panic surged within her and Riya breathed in greedy gulps. He tightened his clasp on her fingers. "You okay, Riya?"

She nodded and met his gaze. "This is your true thrill, isn't it?"

The safety belts forced them much too close for her comfort. When he turned, his thigh pressed against hers and Riya sucked in a sharp breath through a dry throat. "Yes."

Laughing, because it was just impossible not to when you were hundreds of feet in the sky, Riya nodded. "It's spectacular."

"I think so."

"I hope it's not going to be limited to this island," she said, thinking of how many people, average people like her, would miss it if it were. "Something like this, everyone should have access to it."

He turned to look at her, a warmth in his eyes. "We're aiming for Las Vegas, Paris, Bali, São Paulo, Mumbai, London in the first round. As soon as the approvals are in, we'll launch the new level of membership and also offer an exclusive offer to our low tier members at a discounted price."

Riya glanced around once again, her heart swelling in her chest. "It's going to be magnificent. What's it going to be called?"

He shrugged and smiled. And Riya felt a different kind of pull on her senses. "Haven't decided yet," he said.

Before she could blink, the safety tether loosened. Imagining them plummeting to death, Riya gasped and held on tighter.

Only to realize that Nathan had undone the belt.

"No...no...no...Nate...Please *Noooooo*," she screamed as he tugged her up until they were standing. He dragged her forward to the railing, and the whole setup swung in the air. Her stomach lurched, and Riya plastered herself to him from the side, breathing hard.

He stiffened for an infinitesimal moment even as the ridges and planes of his lean body pressed against her.

Adrenaline pumped through her, her muscles trembling with a thousand little tremors. She was shamelessly plastered against his back, but for the life of her, she couldn't seem to peel herself away from him.

His fingers tugged at her arms around him. His smile dug grooves in his cheeks. His hair was wind-ruffled; his eyes were glowing. "Don't worry, Riya," he whispered, tucking her tight against his side. "I won't let you fall."

Sandwiched snugly against his side, Riya looked around at the magnificent sight.

Her heart boomeranged against her rib cage; her senses spun. It was a moment of utter perfection, of glorious beauty.

When he pulled her back down, she went reluctantly, suddenly loath for it to be over.

Letting her breath out slowly, she settled into the moment, grateful to him for allowing her to be a part of it. They sat like that for a while. Everything about the evening cloaked them in intimacy.

Gratitude that he had given her a chance, that he'd let her be a part of this, and some unknown sensation she couldn't stem welled up inside her. And beneath it, Riya felt a sliver of fear that she was crossing into unknown territory. "Nathan, I'm very sorry for everything that…for all the hurt we caused you. I can't imagine what you must have felt learning about Jackie and me so soon after she died. I'm so—"

His arm around behind her, he turned, and his finger landed on her mouth. "I don't require an apology from you."

Raising her gaze to his, Riya forced herself to focus on

his words rather than the sensation of how her own mouth felt. "Is Maria right? All these years, would you have come back if Jackie and I had been gone?"

"No, I wouldn't have. Leave the past where it is, Riya. Come out of your cocoon, and live your life, butterfly."

The warmth in his endearment caused minute little flutters all over her.

"Just because I don't stand hundreds of feet in the sky and touch the clouds on a regular basis doesn't mean I'm not living," she countered.

His long fingers landed on her jaw, the abraded tips pressing into her skin. Their legs tangled in front of them. He shifted sideways until he was all she saw. Found herself staring into languid pools of molten hunger.

Desire punched through her, every inch of her thrumming with alarm and anticipation.

They were hanging in the sky with a slice of paradise laid out beneath them for as far as she could see. And the man in front of her, the most gorgeous, the most complex man she had ever met. In that moment, something she had held tight inside her, something she hadn't even realized existed, slowly unraveled.

Just a little movement of his head and suddenly his breath feathered over her nose.

Her fingers landed on his chest, to push him back. But the thudding roar of his heart beneath muted any rational thought. A slow fire swirled low in her belly, spreading to every inch of her.

One long finger traced her jawline in reverence, the tips of the others grazing her neck. "I think it's the most terrible thing in the world that you don't know whether you enjoyed a kiss or not, butterfly. The most horrible thing that no man has shown you, without doubt."

Liquid desire darkened the ice blue into the shade of a cloudy sky.

Every other thought faded from her mind except this man, every other sound faded except the loud peal of her own pulse. Every other sensation fled except for the insistent and answering thrum of her skin at the hunger in his eyes.

The brush of his lips against hers was at once cool and hot, testing and assured, bold and yet inviting. His beard rasped against her tender skin, wreaking havoc on her. The contrast of his soft lips and the roughness of his beard... her entire world came crashing around her.

It was her own response to the press of his soft mouth that blew her apart, the strength of the deep longing that jolted to life inside her. Her fingers crinkled against his shirt as he increased the pressure and the back of her head hit the leather.

Heat, unlike any she had ever known, slithered and pooled in every molten muscle as he licked her lower lip. His body teased against her own, a soft invitation to press herself against the hardness.

She purred, like a stroked cat, and gasped at the curl of pleasure and instantly, he pushed on. Only when it vibrated through her did she realize that it was a groan that fell from her mouth. Pleading for more, demanding more.

And it wasn't just their mouths that were touching anymore. His fingers inched into her hair and held her slanted for him; his lean body enveloped her; he was everywhere.

He felt alien, yet familiar. Her thighs trembled, locked against the tensile strength of his; her belly dipped and she groaned.

The tenor of the kiss went from slow, soft appraisal, a testing of fit and sensation to pure, exploding, ravenous heat.

He bit and stroked, nibbled and licked. He kissed her as if they would both drown if he stopped, and that's how it felt. So she let him. Stayed passive and panting under his caresses, let him steal her breath and infuse her with his own.

A freeing desperation joined the molten warmth inside her.

When he stopped, when he sucked in a shuddering breath, everything inside Riya protested that he did. She flushed as he pulled back and locked eyes with her. His gaze was the darkest she had seen yet, his breath coming in and out a little out of sync. The pad of his thumb moved over her lower lip, and she shivered again.

"Did you enjoy that kiss, butterfly?"

Riya fell back against the couch, her fingers on her still-trembling mouth.

That kiss had been beyond perfect. But the mockery in his eyes grated; the laid-back arrogance in it stung. It was nothing but a challenge to him. Whereas the entire foundation of her life had shaken.

"I would have been surprised if I hadn't," she said, dredging up the cool tone from somewhere. Her fingers still on his chest, she glared at him. Her heart still hadn't resumed its normal pace. "Very altruistic of you," she said, a little hollow in her chest, waiting for him to deny.

He grinned instead. "I haven't been called one of this generation's greatest philanthropists for no reason."

"Forgive me if being your charity case doesn't fill me with excitement."

Turning away from him, Riya sought silence. Fortunately for her, she felt them coming down again. They had just stepped out of the enclosure when they saw Sonia waiting there, her gaze stricken, her features pinched with pain.

Mortification came hard at Riya. Had the entire crew

seen them kissing? If Nathan hadn't been satisfied with proving his point and stopped, how far would she have let him go?

Next to her, Nathan turned into a block of ice, and Riya fled fast, wondering what she had stepped into. Reaching the villa, she couldn't help casting a quick look at Nathan and Sonia.

The way they stood close but not touching, the tension that emanated from them, their body language so familiar with each other—it was clear they were or had been lovers. And the pain in Sonia's eyes had been real enough.

Here was one clue to his past, an answer to the unrelenting curiosity that had been eating through her. A streak of jealousy and self-doubt held her still.

Shaking, Riya wiped her mouth with the back of her hand. If only his taste would come off so easily. But her mind rallied quickly enough.

He had stopped so easily when he was done. She was nothing but a naive, curious entertainment to a man who built castles in the sky, to the man who made billions by selling an experience.

Riya avoided Nathan over the next few days. With enough workload to challenge her and the very real threat of losing Travelogue, it was easy. Not that she had been able to get that toe-curling kiss or Sonia and her stricken expression out of her mind.

Determined to assure Sonia, and herself, that there was nothing between her and Nathan, she had gone looking for her the next evening. Only to find that Sonia had left the island that morning.

The fact that Nathan had so neatly, and quietly, dispatched her infuriated Riya. How dare he comment on her conduct when he possessed no better standards? Was this the true Nathan, flitting from woman to woman and walking away when he was done? Why did she even care?

But she kept her thoughts to herself, the very absence of his easy humor over the next few days enough of a deterrent.

He was her employer, and Robert's son.

She spent the rest of her days between work, fixing any defects for Travelogue's software, and her nights, soaking up the sultry beauty of the island. One afternoon the day before they were set to leave, she was working in one of the bedrooms in the villa she was sharing with four other female members of the crew.

The bedroom had open walls, with three-hundred-and-sixty-degree views of the island, bringing cool breezes in. Riya smiled, having finally hit on a solution to a design problem she had been trying to solve for two days.

She stood up and took a long sip of her fruity drink with a straw umbrella when Nathan appeared at the entrance. The cold drink did nothing to fan the flames that the sight of him dressed in a white cotton T-shirt that showcased his lean chest and hard midriff and tight blue jeans ignited.

Wraparound shades hid his expression, but Riya couldn't care. Her gaze glued itself to his freshly shaved angular jaw, traveled over his chin. The beard was gone, although there was already stubble again.

And the mouth it revealed sparked an instant hunger in her.

Men didn't have, *shouldn't* have mouths like his. Lush and sensual with the upper lip shaped like a perfect bow. A cushion of softness that contrasted against the roughness and hardness of the rest of him.

She had the most insane, overwhelming urge to walk up to him and press her lips to his again, to see how it would feel without the beard. She pointed her finger at him and heard the words fall from her mouth. "You shaved it."

Instant heat flared in his gaze, and Riya gasped, only then realizing she had said it out loud.

"What did you say?" he said, coming farther into the room, and she wished she could disappear.

"Nothing," she managed, lifting her gaze to his. "Were we supposed to meet?"

He looked behind her and saw the papers she had been scribbling on and her laptop. "Riya, why didn't you go with the rest of them for the submarine tour? The marine life you get to see here is unparalleled. With your record, it'll be another decade before you leave California again."

His remark grated even as she was aware that it was true. "I was stuck on a tricky design problem and I wanted to resolve it. And I did. I have an initial model ready."

The surprise flashing through his gaze went eons toward restoring her balance. "Already?" he said.

"You did put my life's work under scrutiny and up for assessment," she said sweetly, handing him her laptop.

More than once, her work had come to her rescue. From a young age, she had been comfortable around numbers and equations and then code. Because you could be sure y would come out when you put in x.

Not like people and emotions. Not like the crushing pain of abandonment and the cavern of self-doubt and longing it pushed you into. Nothing like this incessant confusion and analysis their kiss had plunged her into.

He made no reply to her comment. Took the laptop from her and sat down at the foot of the bed. After a full ten minutes, he closed her laptop and met her gaze. Shot her a couple of incisive questions. Finally he nodded. "It's better than I expected." A deafening sound whooshed in Riya's ears.

"Upload the docs into the company's cloud. I'll have my

head of IT take a look too. Travelogue can have this project based on how the rest of your team brings it together for beta testing. But, irrespective of your team, you're Run-Away material."

The whooshing turned into a roar. Exhilaration coursed through her and she damped it down. Too many questions lingered in her, and Riya couldn't untangle professional from personal ones. Only that he would always do this to her…make her wonder about things she shouldn't want. "I don't want another job. I want my company back."

He stood up and faced her, close enough to see the small nick on the underside of his jaw. The scent of his aftershave made her mouth dry. "You're halfway there, then."

"Until you remember why I'm not signing over the estate?"

"Excuse me?"

"I would like to know what you have in store for me, how far you're willing to go for…" When he waited with a grating patience, she said through gritted teeth, "You kissed me."

Nathan frowned, fighting the impulse to kiss that wide mouth again. It was bad enough that damn kiss was all he could think about. Even the incident it had instigated with Sonia hadn't been enough to temper the fire it had started in him. "And you kissed me back. I don't see your point exactly."

Something combative entered her eyes. "What happened to Sonia?"

The question instantly put him on guard. The hurt expression in Sonia's eyes had been haunting him the past few days. And the fact that he had caused her pain, even after he'd been careful not to, scoured through him.

"None of your business," he said, turning away from Riya.

Her hand on his arm stalled him. "Just answer the question, Nathan."

"You think one kiss gives you the right to take me to task?"

"No. I'm trying to understand you."

"Why?"

"You hold the fate of my company in your hand. You hold my fate in your hand. I don't think it's worth killing myself if you're unscrupulous. If you make a habit of taking your employees as lovers and then firing them when things turn sour, I'd rather cut my losses now."

"That's quite a picture you paint of me," he said, laughing at the nefarious motives Riya attributed to his actions.

Even preferred it to the truth. Because the reality of losing a friend who had known him for over a decade was all too painful, the hollow in his gut all too real. The number of people who were constants in his life over the past decade were two—Sonia and his manager, Jacob.

The realization that he was condemning his very soul to loneliness still shook him.

But then Sonia had left him with no choice, giving him an ultimatum between her love and her friendship. One time of seeking comfort with her, of breaking his rule, and she had forgotten he didn't do relationships, forgotten that he lived his life alone by choice, that he'd turned his heart into a stone painstakingly over the years.

That he couldn't let himself become weak by giving in to emotions.

He'd immediately told Sonia that it had been a mistake, that it changed nothing. That they could never repeat it.

It was his fault that he hadn't held her at arm's length like with everyone from the beginning, that she was hurt. His fault that he'd given in to temptation with the woman in front of him, even more ill-suited to handle him than Sonia.

Her fingers bunched in his shirt, Riya's brown eyes blazed with anger and confusion. "How can you be so… so careless about someone's pain? So casual about the havoc you're wreaking?"

"On her?" He gripped her hands with his, feeling a powerlessness course through him. He had punished himself by sending Sonia away, and that Riya judged him for that only fanned his fury. "Or on you and your plan? It was a damn good kiss, Riya, but don't let it distract you from your plan."

She let go of him as if he had struck her. "I know I'm nothing more than an entertaining challenge to you. And that kiss…it's nothing but you proving to me that I'm out of my element with you. But she and you have known each other for a decade, and now no one knows where she is."

He turned toward the stunning vista, his knuckles showing white against the brown of the wood paneling. "No injustice has been done to her. Sonia is a twenty percent shareholder in RunAway. She'll be all right." It was the only thing that gave him solace.

"Then why did she leave?"

"Because I told her in no uncertain terms that she has no place in my life anymore. Pity, because she was my only friend," he said in a low voice.

Riya reeled at how easily the words fell from Nathan's mouth. But the affected disinterest didn't extend to the pain in his eyes. Whatever he had done with Sonia, it hadn't left him untouched. "Why?"

"She messed up at the one thing I asked her not to do."

"What could she have done that you removed her from your life like you would delete a file?"

He smiled at her consternation, but there was no warmth in that smile. There was no mockery, there was no humor in his gaze. Only the shadow of pain, only unflinching honesty. "She fell in love with me. Despite knowing I'm allergic to the whole concept."

The impact of his words came at Riya like a bucket of ice-cold water.

"She knew I didn't want her love. She knew nothing was ever going to come out of it. But she didn't listen. Now she's cost us both a friendship that should have lasted a lifetime."

It didn't matter that it hurt him to lose that. He had still cut Sonia out of his life. He had never turned around for Robert. He was exactly the kind of man who walked away without looking back. The why of it didn't matter in front of his actions.

It was all the proof Riya needed to realize that of all the men on the planet she could have been attracted to, Nathan was the most dangerous of all.

CHAPTER SIX

For three weeks after they returned to San Francisco, Riya slept in one of the extra rooms that had been booked at a downtown hotel in addition to the conference room for the Travelogue team.

Nathan had given her team three weeks to put together a package for the launch event, and for her, to build the software model that would support that package. Even though he could still dismantle them if they didn't come up to scratch, he was definitely giving them a chance first.

It didn't help knowing that his own team from another company was also putting something together at the same time. He expected her company to fail and she was determined to prove him wrong.

Three weeks in which Riya had backed off from pestering him about their deal, in which she had slept only minimum hours to develop the final model for software, in which he had set a relentless pace, driving every member of Travelogue and his own team crazy. Three weeks in which Jackie had figured out somehow that Nathan was back because of Riya, that she had willingly offered to sign away the estate.

Nothing Riya said helped, not that she had a lot of time.

Nathan worked just as hard as they did, putting in long hours, giving much-needed direction and expertise. If they encountered a problem, there was nowhere to go until a solution was found.

As manic as he had been in his energy, he also had tremendous motivating capabilities. With the entire team working together in a conference hall, exchanging ideas and finding instant solutions for challenges they encountered, it had been the best workweek of her life.

There was something to his energy, to his credo of doing everything right then, of implementing an idea as best and as soon as possible.

Now the beta testing they had done of the model had been a spectacular success, and they had entered the next iteration. It was three weeks since Nate and she had struck that deal, and he had yet to see Robert.

She'd been trying to get a word with him for two days and failed. The man was a machine, traveling, working, managing teams all over the world... Knowing that tonight he was just a few floors above her, in the penthouse suite, she had to take this chance.

Squaring her shoulders, Riya took the elevator. The doors swished open and she entered the vast black-and-white-tiled foyer.

For a few seconds, she was lost in the brilliant San Francisco skyline visible through the French doors. Subdued ceiling lights cast a hushed glow over the steel and chrome interior.

She spotted Nathan in the open lounge, clad in gray sweatpants that hung precariously low on his hips, doing push-ups.

The line of his back, defined and pulling tight over stretched muscles, was the most beautiful thing she had ever seen. The copper highlights in his hair glinted and winked in the low lights.

Sweat shone over the smooth, tanned skin of his back,

his breathing punctured by his soft grunts. Warmth uncurled in Riya's belly, her own breathing becoming choppy and disjointed.

In a lithe movement that would have made a wild animal proud, he shot to his feet and grabbed a bottle of water.

Her mouth dry, Riya watched as his Adam's apple bobbed. A drop of sweat poured down his neck and chest, which was lean with sharply bladed muscles. A sprinkle of copper-colored hair covered his pectorals and formed a line down his hard stomach. His shoulder bones jutted out, his throat working convulsively as he swallowed. He wasn't pumped up with bulging muscles, but what was there of him had such sculpted definition that her fingers itched to trace it.

She had the most overwhelming urge to cross the hall and to press her hands against that warm skin, breathe in the scent of him.

Shivering from a heat that speared across her skin like a fire, she was about to clear her throat when she saw him sway. He was so tall and lean that it was like seeing an immovable thing buck against a faint breeze. Her heart lurched into her throat as his knees buckled under him.

Riya didn't know she could move so fast. Working on auto, she grabbed his shoulders just as he sank onto his haunches, his head bent. She tapped his cheek, fear twisting in her gut. "Nathan…Nathan…"

She ran her hands all over him, his shoulders, his neck, her throat aching. "Nate, honey? Please look at me…"

His fingers closed on her upper arm, almost bruising in their grip, and he slowly raised his head. His gaze remained unfocused for a second longer, before it rested on her face. He blinked then. "Did I scare you, butterfly?"

Fear still clawed at her, but she fought it. This was

ridiculous. He was right in front of her, solid and arrogant, as always.

"Riya?"

"Yes?"

His fingers moved from her arm to her wrist, firing neurons left and right. "Don't leave just yet, okay?"

She nodded, the stubble on his jaw scratching against her palm. He didn't look dizzy or disoriented.

Slowly he peeled her fingers from his jaw but didn't let go. "Are you all right?"

Breathing hard, Riya pulled her hand, but his grip was firm. "Me?" She licked her lips and his gaze moved to her mouth. "I'm fine. I thought you…Nathan? You almost fainted."

Something flickered in the depths of his eyes. For a second, Riya could swear it was fear. But it was replaced by warmth.

He flashed a grin that stole her breath. He dragged her hand to his chest.

Skin like rough velvet, hot as if there were a furnace under it, stretched taut over his chest. His nipple poked the base of her palm. His hand covered hers as his heart raced beneath it. "See? In perfect working condition," he murmured, but Riya had no idea what he meant.

And his gaze locked with hers again.

It lingered there with such focus that she wouldn't have known her name then. All she wanted was to sink into his touch, to make sure he was all there. He was always so incredibly focused, so unbearably driven that the seconds-long spell fractured something inside her. Something knotty and hard sat uncomfortably in her throat, and giving in, Riya threw her arms around him. Buried her face in the crook of his neck and closed her eyes. "You scared the hell out of me, Nathan."

He was like a hard, hot statue for a second, and then his hands moved over her back slowly. For a second, his arms were like vines around her, holding her so tight and hard that her lungs struggled to work, and Riya felt her armor shatter.

"Shh. I'm okay," he finally said, releasing her. Pulling her hands forward, he clasped her face with his hands, a burning resolve in his eyes. "I do, however, need a little fortification, butterfly." His breath came in little pants as he made a lithe movement and tugged at her lower lip with his teeth.

A peal of shuddering pleasure rang through Riya and she shivered all over. Gasping at the sharp nip, she braced herself against him. Had every intention of pushing him back. But the moment her palms landed on his shoulders, she was a goner.

With a ragged groan, he covered her mouth again.

He was hot, sweaty, hard, trembling and he was everything she wanted right then. His fingers crept into her hair, held her hard as he stroked her mouth, changed angles and kissed her again.

As if he couldn't stop, as if he couldn't breathe if he did, as if his entire universe was reduced to her.

At least that was how it felt to her.

He pushed her to the floor, and her limbs folded easily.

"Nathan," she whispered as he covered her body with his and claimed her mouth again. He didn't just kiss; he devoured her, ensnared her senses. He made her feel giddily excited and incredibly safe at the same time.

"Please, Riya." His tongue traced the seam of her lower lip; his fingers tightened in her hair. "Open up for me."

The guttural request sent Riya over the edge.

He teased her tongue, nibbled her mouth, bit her lower

lip and when she gasped into his mouth, he stroked it with his tongue. She couldn't breathe with the pleasure as he sucked at her tongue.

This kiss was so different from the first one. It wasn't about give or take. It was about claiming, possessing, about wringing an earthy response that she couldn't deny. It was all about what their bodies did together, how perfectly soft she was against his hardness, how a simple touch and gasp could send them both shuddering.

Her breasts became heavier; her nipples ached. Her spine arched as he locked her hard against him, every inch of him pushing and pressing against her trembling body.

Because lying underneath his shuddering body, lying underneath all the rippling muscle and heated hardness, she felt he was her universe. She opened her legs to cradle him and he moaned against her neck, ground himself into her pulsing heat with a hard grunt.

To feel the hard length of him throb against her aching core, to hear the violent curse that fell from his lips as she moved her pelvis against that unrelenting hardness…it was bliss. It was heaven. And it was nowhere near enough.

"Oh, please, Nate…" Her whisper was raw, close to begging.

She wanted to peel her clothes off, wanted to feel the rasp of his rough skin against her softness, wanted to touch the rigid shaft that was pressing against her sex.

He traced a heated path to her neck and Riya gasped, finding purchase in his shoulders. When he sucked at the crook of her neck while his hand closed over her breast, she bucked off the floor.

And hit the tiled floor with a thud. The impact vibrated through her and she gasped again, her head reeling with pain.

With a curse, Nathan pulled them both up to their knees, his fingers sinking into her hair. Her chest rising and falling, Riya stared at him, shock holding her still under his concern. She felt winded and yet every inch of her also tingled, throbbed. Deprived.

What had she done? What was happening to her? Another few minutes and she would have let him make love to her right there, on the floor. *Begged* him to finish what he had started. A shudder racked through her.

His touch gentle, Nathan clasped her jaw. "Riya, look at me."

Jerking away from his grasp, Riya rose to her feet and straightened her clothes and her hair.

He approached her and she scuttled away again toward the door.

"Stop, Riya." His brow tied into a fierce scowl. "I just want to make sure you're okay."

She shook her head, incredibly frustrated and scared and wound up. "I needed that thud," she said jerkily. "Because it's obvious I've lost all sense. You took my company, you want to take the one place that's ever been home to me, you keep kissing me and I don't stop you and now you've made me bang my head on that hard tile and it hurts like the mother of all…"

Her voice rose on the last few words until she was shouting at him.

"It does seem like you only bring pain to me, so I should be afraid. At least hate you, but why the hell do I not feel either?"

"Don't know." He sounded inordinately pleased with her unwise declaration.

She risked a look at him, saw his mobile mouth twitching and burst into laughter herself. "It's not funny," she yelled at him, even as more laughter was on the way.

She was doubling over then, both laughing and something else, everything piling up on her.

Before she could breathe again, she was in his arms again with his arms locked tight around her, him whispering, "Shh...Riya... You're in shock..."

Male heat, hard muscle, smooth skin...irresistible Nathan. But beneath all that, it felt incredibly good to be just held, to laugh with him, to be in this place that was both strangely intimate and thrilling. A thrill she had had too much of for one evening.

Extracting herself from the cocoon of his arms, she wiped her mouth on her sleeve. "Will you please cover yourself?"

Throwing a strange look at her, he pulled on a sweatshirt and she hurried toward the door.

He appeared between her and the door, his gaze concerned. "You hit your head pretty hard. Check and see if there's a bump."

"I'm fine," she said.

This was not okay; this was not good. Only three weeks in his company and she was ready to throw away all the lessons she had learned, ready to forget all the pain relationships caused, the clawing self-doubt they left.

This heat between them, it was nothing but a challenge for him. He could kiss her and shake it off after a few minutes while the very fabric of her life shook. He would tangle with her and walk away unscathed, while she would wonder and spiral into self-pity and anger. Would forever wonder why it was so easy to walk away from her.

"You're not stepping out until I'm sure you're okay. If you don't check properly, I'll have to do it. And it won't stop there if I lay a hand on you again."

When he stepped toward her, she held him off. Fighting the furious heat climbing up her neck and chest, she poked her fingers under her hair. "There's some swelling."

His pithy curse echoed around them. Riya suddenly remembered.

He had almost fainted, she was sure now. "I thought you were going to collapse. Yet you weren't even surprised. What does it mean? Are you okay? Shouldn't you be the one that should see the doctor?"

Shadows fell over his eyes instantly and Riya knew with a certainty he wasn't going to tell her the truth. Was he unwell? "I think I just overdid it with the exercise." He exhaled in a big rush, ran a hand over his jaw. "I'll be fine. Why did you come here?"

Since they had returned, they danced around each other, avoided even talking to each other without anyone around. And today was a testament to what they had both known.

Apparently even his cold treatment of Sonia wasn't enough to make her see sense.

"I heard that you were leaving for Abu Dhabi. I won't let you leave without seeing Robert."

His hands landed on his lean hips, the bones jutting out at the band of his sweatpants. The hollow planes of his muscles there were the most erotic sight she had ever seen.

"Excuse me?" he said with such exaggerated arrogance that she lifted her gaze to his.

"Yes. To remind you that it's been almost three weeks and you haven't seen Robert yet. You said—"

"Heaven help a man who tangles with you." He shook his head, resignation filling his eyes. "I'll see him tomorrow, fine? Now shut up and sit down."

Switching his cell phone, he rattled off orders for a physician and his chauffeur.

"I don't need to—"

"Doctor or me, Riya?" he challenged.

"Doctor," she said, sinking into the couch.

Even without looking at him, she was aware of his movements at the periphery of her vision. Heard the Velcro rip of his watch. What had happened to his Rolex? Frowning, she turned and saw him look at the display and note down something in a small notepad.

He wiped his face with a towel and Riya pulled her gaze away.

Not that she had missed the rippling muscles or the small birthmark he had on the inside of his biceps. Or that instead of turning her off, even being sweaty, he muddled her senses and filled her with an unbearable longing. Or that he kissed as if he could never stop. Or that he liked having utter control even as he shredded hers.

Or that she had liked it—the way he couldn't stop, the way he took control, the way he just made it hard for her to think, the way he knew exactly what would drive her wild with longing. That she had liked how good it felt to give herself over to him, body and mind, that she trusted him as she had never trusted anyone.

All of them were things she shouldn't know about him. A bunch of things she didn't want to know about herself.

She felt raw, exposed. All she wanted was to run. Far from him, far from herself.

Handing her a chilled bottle of water, he dropped to the couch, and Riya shot up from the couch. He tugged her down. Riya slinked to the edge, her breath coming in choppy bursts. Panic weaved through her.

"You and me, this can't happen, Nathan."

"You can't control everything in life, Riya. I don't want this to happen either, but I've learned the hard way that you can't have everything the way you want it."

She turned to him, desperation raising her tone. "Don't say that, don't just…accept this."

His mouth took on a rueful twist. "What do you want me to do? Wave a wand that'll make it go away? The only solution I can think of is dragging you inside and giving us both what we so desperately want. Maybe we should get it out of the way, and things will be much clearer then."

"This is probably your MO. Seduce a woman, say good-bye and walk away. And cut her out if she doesn't accept your decision. Like you did with Sonia. But I won't fall for you. You have no heart. You're the last kind of man that I should kiss, or want, or…"

Fury dawned in his eyes, turning them into blue fire. "Is it helping, then? If my being here is turning you inside out, how about you give me the blasted estate? I'll leave tonight."

"No. I can't."

"Damn it, Riya. You're not responsible for Jackie or Robert or anyone else. You were what? Twelve? Thirteen, when my mother died?"

"Robert regrets his mistakes. I know he does. He gave Jackie and me a home when we'd have been on the streets. He always had a kind word for me. He gave me shelter, security, food. He treated me like a daughter when my own father didn't bother to even ask after me in a decade."

"Where is your father?"

"How the hell should I know? He never asked about me, never checked how Jackie has been all these years. And this is after he divorced her because she was emotionally volatile. And he let her take me. He let his volatile wife have charge of his eight-year-old daughter.

"For all her weak nature, Jackie at least looked after me in her own way. That's more than I can say for—"

"She didn't do you a favor by doing that, Riya. It was her minimum responsibility. And she failed you in that. She exposed you to her fears, to the staff's hatred at the estate. Don't you see the effects of that in yourself?"

"My life is perfectly fine, thank you. And my professional one even better, thanks to you. The last few days, working with you, have been amazing. I love your energy, I love the way you do things, Nathan. And if Travelogue can—"

"As of this morning, Travelogue has an investment of ten million dollars from RunAway International. I have ordered my lawyers to put the papers together."

RunAway International Group. The brilliant boutique of his companies offering flights, vacations, adventure trips through faraway lands… And now Travelogue was a part of that prestigious group.

Her small company…it was at once the most exciting and breathtaking prospect. She had no words left.

"I'll double the figure you make now and you'll have stock options in RunAway too. I've started the headhunt for a new CEO, and we'll find one by the time I leave."

He was going to leave. That was what she had wanted; that was what she needed. That was their deal.

Then why did the prospect sit like a boulder on her chest? What had changed in a mere three weeks?

Concealing her confusion, Riya forced a smile and thanked him just as the physician knocked on the door.

All the way through him checking on her and the limo ride back to the estate, she couldn't figure out why reaching the goal she had set for herself, why impressing someone of Nathan's vision, why achieving the financial freedom she had always craved was suddenly not enough.

Whatever his behavior toward Robert, Nathan was unlike any other man she had ever met. All her rules, all her fears and insecurities, nothing stayed up when she was around him. He made her want to know him on a visceral level, made her want to abandon her own rules, made her yearn for a connection that she had denied herself for so long.

Nothing mattered with him. Not the pain of the past, not the fear for her future, only the present. And she couldn't let this continue. Already she was in too deep, lost at the thought of him leaving.

Nathan had no idea how long he stood staring at the closed door after Riya left, the silence of his suite pinging on his nerves. Everywhere he looked, he saw her now.

Laughing, smiling, arguing, kissing, moaning, gasping, glaring...even as she denied her nature, there was such an innocence and intensity to the emotions that played on her face.

He wanted her with a sharp, out-of-control need that crossed all lines. Now that he knew how she felt underneath him...

Everything inside him wanted to make her his. Ached to own her, possess her, show her how wild and good it could be between them, longed to make her admit that she felt something for him.

Why not? a voice inside taunted him.

They were both free agents. They were both adults. And she wanted him. There was no doubt about that.

No.

How could he tangle with her knowing what she wanted in life? Even if she was determined to hide from it. How could he touch her knowing that when it was time to leave, she wouldn't be able to handle it?

She hadn't recovered even now from her father's abandonment, from her mother's negligence. Even his father's acceptance and caring of her hadn't been enough to erase that ache from her eyes.

It was in the way she was hiding from life, had slaved herself over her company and the estate, the way she took responsibility for the adults who should have looked after her.

In the way she had risked his wrath and her ruin just to make Robert smile. In the way all the light had gone out of her eyes when she mentioned her father.

And yet she was loyal, she was caring and she was strong. Exactly the kind of woman who could plunge him into his darkest fear if he let her. But by the same token, how was he supposed to walk away without stealing a part of her for himself?

CHAPTER SEVEN

NATHAN PACED THE study in the home he had avoided thinking of for so many years, fighting the surge of memories that attacked him. The study had been one of his favorite rooms with huge floor-to-ceiling shelves covering two walls completely and French doors on the opposite side that opened onto the veranda.

Thick Persian rugs that had been his mother's pride covered the floor. He remembered playing with his toys on those rugs sitting at her feet.

The smell of old books and ancient leather stole through him swiftly, shaking loose things he had forgotten beneath layers of hurt and fear.

Emotions he didn't want to feel surged inside.

They had laughed here, the three of them. Spent numerous evenings in front of the fire—his father reading to him while his mother had sat in the cozy recliner with her knitting. There had been good years, he suddenly realized, years of laughter and joyful Christmases before ruined football games and hospital visits had become the norm. Before fear had become the norm, before fear had infiltrated every corner and nook.

Had it begun with his fainting and near dying at the football game? Had it begun when his mother had been gradually getting worse and worse? Or had it begun when his father had started his affair with Jackie?

Did it matter anymore?

"Hello, Nate," his father said softly, and closed the door behind him.

Even having learned all the details of his father's illness from Maria, Nathan still wasn't prepared for the shock his father's appearance dealt him. As much as he wanted to not give a damn, he found he couldn't not care, couldn't not be affected by how frail he looked.

His blue gaze seemed dulled, haunted by dark circles underneath. His frame, always lean and spare, now looked downright skinny.

Alarm reverberated through Nate.

He didn't want to feel anything for his father. Damn Riya for forcing him to this. The blasted woman was making it hard on herself and him.

"It's so good to see you, Nate. Riya's been telling me all about your ventures and how powerful and successful you are. I'm very proud of you."

Nathan could only nod. He couldn't speak. Was he as big a sap as Riya? Because one kind word from his father and he couldn't even breathe properly.

Fury, betrayal and so much more rose inside him. And that kind of emotional upheaval scared him more than the little fracture in his breathing the other night.

If he let one emotion in, they would all follow. Until all he felt would be fear.

There were too many things out of his control already. And to be in control, he had to remember things he'd rather forget, remember things that had driven him from his home, things that had driven him to live his life alone. "Let's not pretend that this is anything but the fear and regret a man faces once he sees death coming for him, Dad."

His father flinched, and this time, nothing pierced Nathan. Not even satisfaction that he had landed a shot. Tears flooded those blue eyes that were so like his own. "I'm so sorry, Nathan, that you felt you couldn't stay here after she was gone."

He couldn't bear this, this avalanche of fear and love, of need and despair that it always brought. "It was so hard to lose her like that, so hard to see my own fate reflected in her death. But to learn that you were with that woman. Can you imagine what that must have done to her?"

"I made a mistake, Nate, a ghastly one. I couldn't bear to see her wilt away. I let that fear drive me to Jackie. I was so ashamed of myself. And your mother...I instantly told her. And she forgave me, Nate."

Shock waves pounded through Nate. "I don't believe you."

He collapsed onto the settee and buried his head in his hands. There was an ache in his throat and he tried to breathe past it, but his dad's words already stole through him.

Because Jacqueline Spear was the one thing his mother hadn't been in that last year—vivacious, brimming with life, an anchor for a drowning man. He had assumed that his dad had done that to his mom. But what if it was the reverse?

What if seeing his mom lose all her will for life had driven his father to Jackie? It was still the worst kind of betrayal, but didn't Nathan know firsthand what fear could do? How it could turn someone inside out?

His dad reached him. "I don't blame you for not believing me. All these years, I have regretted so many things and the worst of it was that my cowardice drove you away. How many times I wished I had been stronger for you."

"If you were sorry, then why did you bring them here? Jackie and Riya? What was that if not an insult to Mom's memory?"

Wiping his face with a shaking hand, his father met his gaze. "What I did was abhorrent. So much that I couldn't bear to look at Jackie for years after that, much less marry her. She was my biggest mistake given form. But I couldn't do anything to hurt Riya.

"I couldn't turn away from the child who needed a proper parent, and Jackie…she was still reeling from her separation from her husband. It was fear that drove us toward each other, that made us understand each other.

"Riya made me think of what I should have been to you, gave me a chance to rectify the mistake I made."

Nathan nodded, his throat raw and aching, a ray of pure joy relieving the burden in his chest. Something good had come out of all the lies and betrayal.

Because this man who looked at him now, this man who had cared for someone else's daughter, he knew. This was the man he remembered as his father before everything had been ruined. "Is that why you gave her the estate?"

"I had no idea what had become of you. I had no way of reaching you. And when I thought I would die…I thought it a good thing that she have it.

"Riya loves this house, this estate, just like Anna did. Everything she touches blossoms. Jackie and Riya gave me a reason to live for, after I lost everything. I thought it fitting that it went to her."

Nathan shook his head, the most perverse emotion taking hold of him. He should be a bigger man, he knew that. His mother had been generous and kind. She wouldn't have minded the estate going to Riya, going to someone who loved it just as much as she had. But he couldn't just walk away, couldn't sever the last thing that had some emotional meaning to him.

Couldn't let himself become a complete island severed from anything meaningful in the world. "She can have as much money as she wants instead. The estate is mine. If she'll listen to you, ask her to stop playing games with me and sign it over."

His father frowned. "What are you talking about?"

"I asked her to sell it to me, and the condition she put in front of me was that I see you. That I remain here for two months."

"Oh." His father sank to the couch, and Nate reached him instantly.

"What is it? Are you unwell again?"

"No. I…" His father sighed, regret in his eyes. "I ended up being another person who leaned on her too much. When she told me you were back, I told her to do whatever she could to keep you here. After all this, tell me you'll stay for the wedding, Nate."

Nathan didn't want to hear the hope in his father's eyes, fought the sense of duty that he had ruthlessly pushed away all these years. His father had needed him just as much as Nathan had needed him.

But he hadn't been alone. Gratitude welled up inside Nathan for everything Riya had done for his dad.

The more he tried to do the right thing and stay away from temptation, the more entrenched she was becoming in his life.

Lifting his head, he met his dad's gaze. "I had already decided to stay for the wedding."

A smile broke out on his father's face, transforming it. Clasping Nate's hand, he pumped it with joy. "I'm so glad. Will you live in the house again? Anna would have—"

Nathan shook his head.

He wished he could say yes, wished he could let his father back into his life, wished the loneliness that ate at him abated.

The bitterness inside him had shifted today. And the estate was the one place that meant something to him. It was also the one that would forever remind him that his time was always on a countdown, remind him of how his beautiful mother had turned into a shadow because of her fear.

Because Nathan remembered that fear, remembered what his father had left unsaid, realized that he thought he could protect Nathan from the bitter memory. But beneath his anger for his father, his fury toward what Jackie represented, Nate remembered his darkest fear now.

For the last year, his mother had become but a shadow of herself. It was what had driven his father, as deplorable as his action had been. It was what had filled Nathan with increasing fear for his own life. She had willed her heart condition to leach her life away, had only dwelled on being gone, on being parted from Nathan and his dad.

And in the end, she had become a self-fulfilling prophecy. Her fear had leached any happiness, every joy from her life until death was all that had remained.

His father squeezed his shoulder, his voice a whisper. "You've achieved so much, Nate. You won't become like—"

And Nathan swallowed at the grief that rose through him. How perfectly his dad understood him without words.

Turning around, Nathan smiled at his father. "No, I won't. And that's why I can't stay."

"I'm strong enough to face anything, Nate. I would never—"

Clasping his dad's hands, Nate smiled without humor. It was Riya's face that rose in front of his eyes. "I don't know that I am."

Just as he had accepted his own limitations, Nathan

accepted this too. Riya was dangerous to him like no other woman had ever been. Already he had broken so many of his own rules; already he was much too invested in her well-being, in her life.

He couldn't risk more.

He could never care for anyone so much that the fear of being parted would pervade every waking moment. Couldn't let any woman reduce him to that.

Over the next week, Nate arrived at the estate every evening to see his father. As if determined to create new memories for Nathan, his father insisted that he was too weak to leave the estate. And Nathan found a simple joy in indulging him.

The evenings would have been perfect, the most peaceful moments he had known in a while if not for Riya.

Every evening, he found the anticipation of seeing her build inside him. Only to learn that she was out on another errand, one of hundreds apparently and gone all evening. And the couple of times every day that he dropped into the offices of Travelogue, she was nowhere to be seen either.

One evening, he had even walked through the entire grounds and the house itself wondering if she was having his dad and the servants lie to him.

How could she be always out when he was visiting?

It had taken him a week to recognize the pattern.

The woman was avoiding him, going out of her way to make sure they didn't even lay eyes on each other. He remembered the fear that had leaped into her eyes when he suggested he give them both what they wanted.

There were three weeks until the wedding, and Nathan realized, with simmering fury, that she intended to avoid him until that day.

He should have been happy with that knowledge. Riya was not equipped in any way to take him on.

But as another day fell to dusk, he found himself thinking of her more and more. He was working long hours, negotiating a deal with an Arab prince about building a travel resort in his country, and yet every once in a while, he would look up from his laptop in his penthouse and imagine her on the floor, writhing beneath him, her curves rubbing against him, her gorgeous eyes darkened with arousal, her legs clamped around his waist.

His name falling from her lips like a languid caress.

Running a hand through his hair, he slammed his laptop with a force that rattled the glass table.

Pushing away a hundred other warnings his mind yelled at him, Nathan looked at his watch. It was a quarter past noon on Saturday, one where he should be on his private jet in less than half an hour, flying to Abu Dhabi for the weekend.

A fact that Riya was aware of. Switching his cell phone on, Nate called his virtual manager and ordered him to cancel all his plans for the day.

He found her in the grounds behind the house, knee deep in mud, pruning the rosebushes in the paths leading up to the gazebo.

The white sleeveless T-shirt she wore was plastered to her body, her skin tanned and glistened. Her long hair was gathered in a high ponytail while tendrils of it stuck to her forehead.

She looked as though she belonged there.

Nathan swallowed at the sensual picture she presented. Her skin was slick with sweat, and the cotton of her shirt displayed the globes of her breasts to utter perfection.

His reaction was feral, instantaneous, all-consuming.

His mouth dried, all the blood rushing south. Never had deprivation of oxygen to his lungs felt so good. Never had the dizziness he felt just looking at her been so pleasurable before.

He cleared his throat and she looked up. A bead of sweat dripped down the long line of her throat and disappeared into her cleavage.

Nathan fisted his hands and shoved them in his pockets. He wanted to touch her, he wanted to push her down right there on the dirt, spread her out for him and cover her body with his own. He wanted to feel his heart labor to keep up as he plunged himself inside her and pushed them both over the edge.

"You've been avoiding me."

"I've been busy with the wedding preparations. Jackie's been waiting for so long for it and she's so excited that she's practically useless and of course, Robert is ecstatic that you're here. There's a lot to do."

"Then why didn't you ask for my help?"

Her movements stilled. He realized with a pang that she hadn't even considered it.

He got onto his haunches, and her gaze flew to him. "You really think hiding is the solution? Will you hide at the wedding too? Will you hide from everything that threatens to shred your damn rules? One day, you'll be a hundred years old, Riya, and you'll be alone and you'll realize you didn't live a moment of your life."

Her mouth fell open on a gasp, and the shears clattered to the ground. She looked as though he had struck at the heart of her deepest fear. Feral satisfaction filled him.

"Get out, Nathan. This estate is not yours yet. I could dangle it over your head just as you dangled the company over mine."

He laughed and inched closer, the challenge in her gaze playing with his self-control. "You're becoming reckless, butterfly."

"Maybe. Maybe I'm tired of being dictated to by you. I danced to your tunes for my company, for Robert. Now I have a new condition. Stay away from me. Or else—"

"Or else what?" he said, a fierce energy bursting into life in his veins. A hot rush of lust swamped him. "You'll be all alone at the wedding too."

"No, I won't. My plan needed modification, true. And you just happened to be the one that made me realize that. I already found someone I like very much, someone I've known a long time. I even have a date with him tonight."

He tugged her toward him until their noses were almost touching. Until the scent of her, dirt and sweat and something floral, infused his very bloodstream. "With whom?"

"Do you remember Maria's son, Jose? He's stable and nice and dependable."

Clenching his teeth, Nathan released her, awash in burning jealousy. Because that was what it was.

The very fact that the knowledge was sweeping through him with such impact should have warned him. But he didn't heed. He couldn't even see past the red haze covering his vision.

That Jose would kiss that luscious mouth, that Jose would make love to her, that Jose would have her loyalty forever because she would give it all.

"No, you went for him because you think he'll never leave you. Jose might as well be the oak tree in the estate. You're using him. But he'll realize one day that he's nothing but a security blanket for you, that the reason you actually chose him is that you think he'll never leave you. And he'll resent you for it, even hate you for it."

She fell against the dirt, a stark fear in her eyes. "I don't need advice from a man who could cut his best friend out of his life. Now, if you'll excuse me, I have a date to get ready for."

Nathan watched her walk away, his blood boiling in his veins.

He told himself that he had no interest in her. He just couldn't stand by and watch her make a colossal mistake, waste her life like this anymore. If it was up to her, she would never leave this estate, never leave her mother and Robert, never experience anything.

Everything in him wanted to fight the chain of responsibility he felt for her, shackling him.

He made a quick call to his PA and then went back toward the house, intent on finding the woman who was going to marry his father.

He'd first hated her for a decade and then avoided her for the past few weeks. But it was time to talk to Jackie, high time for someone to think of Riya.

CHAPTER EIGHT

TWO DAYS LATER, Riya was rooting through her closet searching for a beige, ankle-length dress she'd once bought in a small designer boutique in downtown San Francisco. It would do very well for the Travelogue Expansion Launch event.

She'd asked Jose if he would come with her after the longest evening of her life. It wasn't Jose's fault that she kept imagining Nathan all evening or that Nathan pervaded her every thought.

In the end, Jose had kindly and laughingly kissed her cheek. With a twinkle in his eyes, he'd told her that, as flattered as he was that she wanted something between them, there was nothing.

She heard a knock at the door and turned around.

Jackie stood at the door. Terrified was not an exaggeration to describe her expression.

Unease clamping her spine, Riya walked around the empty cardboard boxes she had brought for packing. "Jackie, what is it? Is it Robert?"

"No. Robert's fine." She straightened a couple of books on the chest of drawers, her hands shaking.

Her unease deepened. "Jackie?"

"I've been lying to you," she said in a rush, as though the

words wanted to fall away from her mouth. Her arms were locked tight against her slender frame, her words trembling.

Riya clutched the wooden footboard, anxiety filling her up. "About what?"

"About your father."

Her entire world tilting in front of her, Riya swayed. She felt as if she were falling through a bottomless abyss and would never stop. "What do you mean?"

"He didn't abandon you, Riya. Things had begun to go downhill for a couple of years already. But he and I...we tried to work it out for you. Nothing helped. We were just too different. One night, he said he was considering returning to India. I didn't know how serious he was. But I panicked. If he took you, I would lose you forever. So when he went on one of his weeklong conferences, I grabbed you and I ran.

"I'm so sorry, Riya. I never intended it to be permanent. I kept telling myself I would get in touch with him. But then I realized what I had done and I was so scared he would never let you see me again..."

Tears running over her cheeks, Jackie sank to her knees.

Riya heard the hysterical laugh that fell from her mouth like an independent entity. Hurt splintered through her, as if there were a thousand shards of glass poking her insides.

Her father hadn't given up on her. He'd never abandoned her. The biggest truth she had based her life on was a lie.

"You ruined my life, Mom. All these years, you let me think he didn't care about me."

"I'm sorry, Riya. I couldn't bear to part with you then. And every time I thought of telling you, I was so afraid you'd hate me."

Her head hurt so much, and Riya wanted to scream. "You, you, you... It's always about you. My whole life has been about you. You were afraid to be alone, so you ran.

You were afraid I would hate you, so you hid the truth from me all these years."

Jackie clutched her hands and Riya recoiled from her, everything inside her bursting at the seams.

"That's not true. I...I know you must hate me. But I did it only because I was so scared. I...please, Riya, you have to believe me."

"Get out," Riya said, her words barely a whisper. "I don't want to look at you. I don't want to hear a word you have to say."

Casting one last look at her, Jackie closed the door behind her.

Riya sank into a heap on the floor and wrapped her arms around her, every inch of her trembling. Her heart felt as if it were encased in ice. Why else couldn't she shed even a tear?

Everything she had believed about herself had been a lie. She had let the one fact that her father had given up on her permeate every aspect of her life. Had built a wall around herself so that she was never hurt like that again.

"You're a coward, Riya."

Nathan had been right. She had done nothing but hide from life all these years. He'd even been right about her desperate date with Jose. Something even Jose had realized.

Fury and shame pummeled through Riya. And she latched on to the wave of it.

She was done hiding from life.

The launch event for the expansion of Travelogue was being held in the ultra glamorous banquet hall of the luxury hotel where Nathan was staying in the penthouse suite.

He tucked his hands into his pockets and looked out over the crowd. A smile broke out on his face as the Travelogue crew stared around the luxurious hall.

The crystal chandeliers, the uniformed waiters passing out champagne, the vaulted dance floor to the right... he had wanted everything to be on par with RunAway International.

The Travelogue crew had slogged to create the new package and had surprised him and his own team with their dedication and creativity.

He shook his head as a uniformed waiter offered him champagne. Anticipation had never been his thing, but searching for Riya, he felt as if he were looking up at the snowcapped peak of a mountain.

He had set something in motion. Something that couldn't be taken back and he felt the truth of it settle like a heavy anchor in his gut.

The fact that Jackie had told Riya nothing but lies had only urged him on. She had helped Nathan see the truth, hadn't she? He didn't think he could ever forgive his father, but he, at least, understood. Now he was returning the favor.

More than once, he wondered if he was doing it for all the wrong reasons, wondered if he was being incredibly selfish again. Had even considered picking up the phone to stop what he had set in motion. But in the end, he had persisted.

No one had ever looked out for Riya. Her whole life was built on the foundation of a lie.

Running a hand through his hair, he looked at the dance floor. And felt the shock of his life jolt through him in waves.

She was moving to the music, her gaze unfocused. And she didn't look like the Riya he had come to know in the past few weeks.

He heard the soft whispers from the women around, the shocked gasps of the men, and yet he couldn't shift his gaze away from her.

The red dress, the hair, the spiky gold heels that laced around her toned calves…she screamed only one word.

Sex.

The dress was strapless. It cupped and thrust up her breasts to attention, lush and rounded. Her skin glinted under the bright lights, casting shadows of her long eyelashes on her cheekbones.

It cinched at her waist, contrasting the dip of her stomach against the curves of her breasts and hips. Ended several inches above her knees, displaying a scandalous amount of toned thigh.

The dress so scandalously short that he wondered…

And as though as a direct answer to his licentious question, she turned around and Nathan swallowed.

Too much of her back was bare, with only a strip of fabric covering her behind.

And as he watched, she laughed, threw her hands behind her and did a little thing with her shoulders.

His mouth dried up, lust slamming into him from every direction.

Her hair, all that glorious, lustrous hair was combed into a braid that rested on one breast, calling attention to the shadowed crook where her neck met her shoulder.

She wore no jewelry. Her face, usually free of makeup, was made up, and yet not in a garish way. The bloodred lipstick matched her dress perfectly, making her mouth look even more luscious.

Suddenly Nathan was incredibly hot under the collar. His erection turned stone hard as she looked around herself aimlessly, her tongue swiping over her lower lip. It seemed the butterfly had finally come out of the cocoon, and God help the male population.

She moved again, in tune to the soft music, and this

time it was a subtle move of her hips. Threw her head back and laughed.

Her hands above her, she moved in beat to the tune. Rubbed the tip of her nose against her bare arm in a sensual move that knocked the breath out of him.

Where had this woman come from? Where had she been hiding all that sensuality?

Just then, she turned her head and caught his gaze.

Across the little distance that separated them, something zinged between them. Like a juggernaut, he weaved through the crowd toward her.

Their gazes didn't break from each other. And for the first time since she'd stormed into the office that morning a few weeks ago, Nathan saw a challenge, a daring in her gaze.

He moved fast and caught her as she turned in tune to the languid jazzy beat again.

Her breasts pressed against him and he hissed out a sharp breath. Aware that she was beginning to attract unwise attention from colleagues she would have to work with for years to come, Nathan tapped her cheek and tilted it up. "Riya? Riya, look at me."

Her gaze found him instantly and he breathed out in relief. She was only mildly buzzed. He felt her mouth open in a smile against his arm.

Sinking his fingers into her hair, he tugged until her gaze settled on him. Shock, shame and finally recklessness settled into her beautiful brown eyes. Recklessness that had his blood pounding in his veins. "Hi, hotness."

Nate didn't know whether to laugh or throw her over his shoulder and carry her out. Probably both.

She was all toned muscle and soft curves to his touch. His imagination running wild, Nathan swallowed. "This public display is not you, Riya."

"Even I don't know what I'm supposed to be." She sounded sad, wistful. "Anyway, don't be a party pooper, Nathan. I want to do one thing I've never done before the buzz in my head evaporates."

His fingers around her arms, he tugged her toward him.

"Let me go. I'm having fun. For once in my life, I'm behaving the way I should."

"And what is that exactly?"

"To live for the night. And you…you're getting in the way of my fun."

This was going all wrong. It wasn't what he had intended.

Isn't it? a voice mocked him. *Isn't this what you wanted all along?*

For her to throw off the shackles she'd bound herself with? For her to be reckless and wild? For her to realize what it was to truly live? For her to embrace life and make it impossible for him to walk away without giving them both what they wanted without guilt?

Gritting his teeth, he clamped down the questions. It was too late now. For regrets or guilt.

His arm around her waist, he tugged her off the dance floor. "This isn't what you want, Riya."

Her fingers clutched the lapels of his coat. Stretching on her toes, she tilted forward until she could whisper in his ear. Her warm breath feathered over his jaw, making every muscle clench. His entire frame shook with hunger, with lust so hard that he swayed on his feet.

"Do you know what you want, Mr. Ramirez?"

She must have licked her lower lip. But the stroke of her tongue against the rim of his ear burned through him. Turned every drop of blood in him to molten desire.

Keeping his arm around her, he pushed at her chin, until she was facing him again. "I do, Riya, with a blinding clarity. And I know why it would be wrong to take what I want too."

Large, almond-shaped eyes widened. The edge in his voice hadn't gone unnoticed. She would back down now. She would retreat under that hard shell. She always did.

She didn't and Nathan felt something in him unravel.

Long, pink-tipped fingers fanned over his jaw, and their restless wandering drove Nathan crazy. With the tip of her forefinger, she traced his lower lip, sending a shiver down his spine. "You know, you have the sexiest lower lip I've ever seen on a man. The upper one is the mean one, the one that declares to the world that you're heartless. But the lower one betrays you, Nate."

Her gaze caressed him. And Nate struggled to control his own desire under it. "It shows that you're kind underneath, that you have a softer side. Why are you so bent on keeping everyone at a distance?"

Nathan felt like the lowest scum of the world. The trust in her eyes, he didn't deserve it. He didn't even deserve to stand next to her here. "Tell me what happened."

"Why am I finally living my life like a twenty-three-year-old should? Why am I having fun?"

He steered her around. "I'll take you back to the estate."

"No." She shuddered, her balance still precarious. "I don't want to see Jackie. I can't bear to be even near her," she said with such bitterness that it stopped Nathan in his tracks. "I hate her. I didn't know it was possible to hate anyone so much."

He ran his fingers over his eyes, wondering what he had started. To see her turn from a sweet, caring person to this? It was like watching a train wreck happen knowing you had instigated it.

He sighed, fought against the panic rising through him.

Panic because he could see clearly where it was headed and still it seemed he couldn't stop it.

"Riya, you're not yourself. Let me take you back to the estate."

She tugged away from him and stepped back, her mouth pouting. "Leave me here if that suits you. But I won't go back there." She reached out for the pillar and moved toward it. "I've always taken care of myself, did you know? I'm sure I can handle tonight. What's the worst that could happen? I'll fall and land on my rear. The best? I'll go home with some stranger like every other partying twenty-three-year-old over there."

And those words...they sank into Nathan like sharp claws.

The picture they painted, her bare limbs tangled up with some faceless stranger, was enough to root him to the spot.

Nathan clasped her wrist and dragged her behind him. The swish of the elevator doors, the soft ping as it began to ascend. Everything felt magnified. As if every breath was rushing up to the moment where he would have her in his suite, dressed like this, and he and his control and his good intentions in tatters.

He still made one last attempt at keeping his sanity, at doing the right thing. "As soon as I pour some coffee down your throat, I'm taking you home."

She laughed then, her hands tucked tight around her, her entire body trembling. "Home? I have no home, Nathan. That estate belongs to you. I have no one and nothing."

"Riya, it doesn't have to be this way. I understand that you're angry. I understand how it feels when someone who should take care of you betrays you...when someone you—"

"Do you? She lied to me. About my father. She practically stole me from him."

If she had cried, Nathan wouldn't have been so scared for her. But she didn't. It was as though her shock was much too deep for mere tears. "Everything I have believed about myself, everything is a lie. I thought he abandoned me. I thought he didn't love me. I will never forgive her for this. She stole my childhood and she made me into this frozen coward who hid from everything in life. No one has ever cared about my happiness.

"Not her and definitely not my dad. If he had, knowing how emotionally weak she is, would he have threatened her that he would take me from her?"

What the hell had he started?

He had never meant to hurt her. He had never meant to make her feel alone, had never meant to unravel her like this. He understood the weight of it, he knew better than anyone how painful, how awful it felt.

"Shh, Riya. Enough," he said in a stern voice. "Look at me, butterfly."

When she raised her gaze to him, the depth of feeling that filled him scared the life out of him. Her mouth trembled and he jerked his hand back, the urge to touch that soft cushion overwhelming him. "This will pass, Riya. Believe me, let me drive you back to the estate and—"

"Please don't send me away, Nathan. Tomorrow, I'll be back to myself again. Tomorrow, I'll be strong again. Tomorrow, I might even forgive her. Tonight, I want to be selfish. Tonight, I want it to be just about me."

What could he say to that?

His chest was tight with guilt. All she had tried was to make his father smile. And he...he had unleashed nothing but hurt on her.

Because he had coveted something he could never have.

CHAPTER NINE

TIGHTENING HER ARMS around his neck, Riya nudged closer to Nathan, the warmth of his body a cocoon she didn't want to leave. As though sensing her reluctance, he didn't put her down. Not when he lingered outside the sitting area, not when he walked through it into the bedroom.

Finally he sank down in the armchair and settled her in his lap.

How had she never learned how good it felt to be held like this, to be cherished as if she was precious? How many more things had she missed tucked away in her own world?

She had erected a fence around her heart, around herself, and she had missed out on so many things. While other girls had been going on first dates and experiencing first kisses, she had been studying for a place at the university, giving Robert a hand when she could, managing her mother's moods.

She had bound herself so tight that a little truth from the past had splintered through her. Nothing had really changed. And yet everything had.

It felt as if someone had stuck a pin in her side to jolt her awake from a slumbering state. She sucked in a breath and opened her eyes. His gaze clashed with hers, his long fingers splayed out over her bare arm.

An infinitesimal tension spun into life around them.

His other hand tipped her chin up. "Why this dress? Why drinking? Why this route to show your anger, your hurt?"

And just like that, he shot straight to the heart of the matter. "I don't remember when I had decided that no man would ever hurt me like my father's abandonment did, when I decided I would live my life in this frozen state. I wanted to prove to myself that she didn't ruin me forever with her lies."

"And?"

She tucked her head into his shoulder and sighed. "It's not that simple, is it? A lifetime of sticking to the safe side, suppressing any small urge that could be deemed unsafe, that could risk pain, it's a hard habit to shake." She gave a laugh, tinged with sadness. "I was dancing and I had a little to drink, but I realized it wasn't that simple to change myself inside. Like flipping on a switch. I can't suddenly do something I've trained myself not to do."

"No, it's not simple." There was a roughness to his voice, an edge, a desperate sense of being tightly leashed. As if he was forcing himself to laugh instead of...something else.

Her hand clasped in his. Long fingers with blunt nails and hers, slender and pink tipped, coiled around his.

"It takes years to defeat that kind of conditioning, years to conquer that fear. Doesn't take much to trigger it back either." He sounded strained, almost resigned. He squeezed her arm and Riya caught the sigh that rose to her lips.

How did he understand her so well?

"How about you start with small steps, butterfly?"

She smiled and nodded, the scent of his cologne drifting over her. And the huge chasm that she couldn't cross toward living her life suddenly didn't feel so daunting.

In the shifting confusion of her own emotions and thoughts, he was constant, her awareness of him sharp and unwavering.

Nathan, who had brought so much upheaval into her life, felt like an anchor. All he lived for was the thrill, the fun, the moment. Who better to show her what she'd been missing? Who better to show her what it meant to be daring, to be wild, to grab life by the horns and shake it? Who better to start on her path to living than a man who would never affect her in any other way?

With Nathan, there would be no expectations, no disappointments. When it was time to leave, he would, and this fact had nothing to do with her. Therein lay her safety net.

A sharp hunger bursting inside her, Riya slid her fingers toward the nape of his neck. Pressed her mouth to the pulse flickering on his throat. "Is a kiss a small enough step, Nate?"

Instantly he stiffened beneath her. His fingers landed on her jaw, pushed her face away from his neck in a gentle but firm grip. Desire was a relentless peal in her, as if her pulse had moved just from some points to all over her body.

Fear and safety were taboo. Daring and living were her words of the moment.

She clasped his wrist with her hand and laid kisses against the inside of it. His palm was rough and warm, and as she pressed her lips again to the center of it, she felt the rightness of it.

"Tonight's going to be your lucky night," she said, her throat working to get the words out. She had to brazen it out, didn't want him to know how huge this was for her.

A sharp grip at the nape of her neck caused her to look at him. "My lucky night?" he said.

He looked as if his face were carved from pure stone, his blue eyes molten with desire. There was no frost, no ice tonight.

Nathan was all fire and passion, and she wanted that fire;

she wanted to lose herself in him. "Don't make promises you might not be able to keep, butterfly."

Straightening in his lap, she pushed into his touch, determined to have this. "It's okay if you're not up to it, Nate. No one wants to be a pity f—"

His fingers tightened their grip in her hair. His breath landed on her mouth, until there was nothing to do but breathe the same air as him. "You're doing this for the wrong reasons, Riya."

Feeling gloriously alive, she bent and kissed a spot just beside his mouth. The bristle on his jaw rubbed against her mouth. Heat spread everywhere, incinerating a need she had never known. So she did it again. And again. Like a cat rubbing herself against her favorite surface. Until her lips, her cheeks, her chin stung in the most delicious way, scraping against the roughness of his jaw. Until he made a feral sound that in turn scraped against her very senses.

And her desire went from a risk, a dare, to need for him. Only for Nathan.

Finally her mouth landed at the corner of his luscious mouth. And she spoke the words against his lips, felt a shudder vibrate in his lean frame. Reveled that she could do this to him.

He was like a fortress of leashed desire around her.

"I'm doing this for the only reason that it should be done for."

"And that is?" he whispered back against her mouth, and Riya ached. Ached to feel that mouth everywhere, ached to lose herself.

"That it feels so good, Nate." She moved, to get closer to him, and felt the hard evidence of his arousal against her thigh. "From the minute you stepped into my life, this... it's like a fever." She pulled his hand and pressed it to her chest. "And in all the lies and confusion, this is the one thing that's unwavering. Make love to me, Nate. I want to do all the things that I told myself I didn't feel."

She didn't wait for him to deny her. She just jumped off the ledge, hoping he would catch her. Kissed him with everything she had in her.

When her lush mouth touched his, it was all Nathan could do to pull in a breath. There was no hesitation, no doubt in the way she pressed little kisses over the edge of his lips, over his chin, over his lips, her breath coming in little pants all around him, her scent filling his nose, her fingers scraping against his scalp, holding him in place for her pleasure.

No one had ever quite so thoroughly seduced him. No one had even come close.

She was an explosion. She was a revelation. And under her honest, raw hunger he came undone. No amount of honor could compete with the liquid longing coursing through him, could puncture the desire to return her kiss, to give her what she wanted. And to allow himself what he had been craving.

When she stroked his lower lip with her tongue, tentative but still powerfully maddening, he was done being a passive participant.

Clasping her jaw, he sucked her lower lip with his teeth and she shuddered. Gasped into his mouth.

And they were sucking, nipping, their teeth scraping, their tongues licking with a searing hunger that brought the world down to only them. Pasts and futures were forgotten, only the present mattered.

Panting, he moved away from the temptation of her mouth. Sank his hands into her hair and tugged at the lustrous locks until she was looking at him.

Golden skin flushed, pink mouth swollen, beautiful brown eyes dazed with desire and daring, she looked at him without blinking, without hiding. Pushed into his touch. She was inexperienced; her kisses told him as much. But the sensuality of the woman, the way she responded, so hot and fiery. This was a battle he'd already lost.

But this was a defeat he welcomed.

When she thought of him, he wanted her to do so with a smile and a sigh of pleasure.

He leaned forward and dug his teeth into her lower lip. A gasp fell from her mouth and he blew softly over the trembling lip. "This means nothing to me except that I want you with a madness that knows no reason." He could leave no doubt in her mind. And if she wanted to stop, he was going to head straight for a cold shower. But he couldn't take a chance on risking her emotions. "I'll leave when it's time, *butterfly*. And if you want to stop this, do it now. We'll forget about it. You can take the bed and I'll take the couch."

Her gaze flickered to him, a shadow in it. And then she smiled. Her gorgeous, perfect, dazzling smile. "Falling in love, risking my emotions, it's never going to be easy for me. And with you…I could never fall for you. We're really the worst kind of person for each other, aren't we? But that's what makes this easy, that makes one night with you everything I want it to be."

Her honesty stung him, but he slashed the feeling away.

One night to satisfy this craving, desperate need for each other. That was all they could afford of each other.

Pulling her arm to his mouth, he kissed her wrist, licked the vein flickering there. Kissed a path upward, all the glorious skin warm to his touch.

Her soft tremble, her gasp as he reached the crook of her neck swept him away hard. "Shall I shock you and tell you all the different ways I've imagined having you?"

He licked the pulse there, sucked on her skin. She shivered, sank her hands into his hair. Shuddered, writhed, but he didn't let go. He continued until she was panting, moving restlessly in his arms, rubbing her breasts against his chest. He was rock hard, her volatile response tightening his own need, fraying his control.

He fisted his hands, fighting the urge to push her dress up, to drag her on top of him and thrust up into her wet heat.

Sweat beaded on his brow. And that couldn't be borne. He would enjoy this; he would drown himself in the scent of her, but his control couldn't falter.

It was all about release, all about his body. As long as he kept it to that, as long as he didn't think about what this might have meant to her, to him in a different world, beyond tonight, it was good.

Laughing, she tugged her hair away from her shoulder and looked down at herself. A blush spread upward from her neck as she ran a pink-tipped finger over the blemish. A soft pant fell from her mouth, and it was the most erotic sound he'd ever heard.

There was innocence in it and there was a raw hunger in it. For more. He had been right. She had repressed so many things, and that flicker of undisguised hunger now, of playful curiosity, turned him inside out.

Her gaze moved to his mouth and stayed there. "It stings."

Picking her up, he mumbled his apology into her mouth.

She kissed him with a searing hunger that rocked through him. Scraped her teeth against his mouth. Stroked it with her tongue when he groaned.

"Only in the best way," she whispered when he let her breathe. "I want more."

Laying her down on the huge bed, Nathan shucked his jacket and loosened his tie.

Raising an eyebrow, he let his gaze travel all over her. "Unzip, Riya."

Coming to a kneeling position, she reached for the zipper on her dress. Her fingers trembled around it. But she slowly tugged it down.

His mouth dried as the dress came loose around her chest. He was dying to see those lush breasts, those long legs, every inch of her. Just as the fabric flapped down, she held it to herself, her cheeks flushing. "Can we turn off the light, Nathan?"

"Nope," he said so loudly that she smiled. "Those prim dress shirts and trousers have been driving me mad." When she still hesitated, he stilled his hand on his shirt. "You can't see me either, then."

Something flickered in her gaze. Lifting her chin, she straightened to her knees and pulled her dress down. Over her chest, over her midriff. Leaned back onto her elbows and kicked it from around her feet.

Nathan felt his heart pump harder and harder, and for once, something else took precedence over the malfunctioning organ. His breath balled in his throat.

Her slender shoulders bare, her lush, rounded breasts thrust upward, the shadow of her brown nipples visible through her strapless bra, the concave dip and rise of her stomach, the flare of her hips, the V between her thighs hinting at dark curls...

If his heart stopped right then, Nathan would have had no fear, no regrets.

And the lack of fear, the lack of any other emotion except his feral hunger to possess the woman in front of him, was a sensation he reveled in.

Because it made him feel alive as nothing else could.

Riya had never understood what the fuss was about sex, how it drove people to the most unwise decisions.

Until now.

She'd never understood how completely it unraveled you, this desire, how completely it exposed every part of a person, how it connected one so deeply with another.

They hadn't even undressed completely, but the look in Nathan's eyes—so demanding and all-consuming, the possessive challenge that lingered there—would have sent her running to the hills.

He would demand complete surrender, of her body, her mind, even her very soul. And beneath the flicker of fear, there was also a freedom in giving herself over.

The soft fabric of her bra chafed against her nipples and her thong, which had been a necessary evil for this dress, suddenly felt intrusive, making her sharply aware of the ache between her legs, the incessant peal of need there every time his gaze traveled over her.

She was wet there and she was hot all over, and together, the sensation continued to build.

His gaze never leaving her, Nathan unbuttoned his white dress shirt, pushed it off.

All that bronzed, glinting skin, the whorls of copper chest hair, the black string hanging with a pendant over his pectoral muscles, the jut of his shoulders, the flat male nipples so unlike her own, the washboard plane of his stomach, the line of hair that went down below his navel. He was so utterly male.

And all of it was hers tonight to do with as she wished.

With sure movements, he unzipped his trousers and kicked them away. Then his boxers.

Riya licked her lips at the sight of him completely naked. Her heart thudded incessantly, her sex pulsing.

His guttural groan surrounded them, and she raised her gaze to him.

He moved closer, in touching distance. Riya raised her

hand, eager to touch that hardness, eager to learn everything about him. "You won't touch me, is that clear?"

Frowning, she tilted her head up. "Why not?"

He didn't answer.

Pushing her back against the bed, he climbed into the bed and on top of her in such a predatory, masculine way that all of her possessive claims, all of her risky resolve fled.

Leaving nothing but gloriously alive sensations toppling against her, drowning her, demanding her utter enslavement.

He was heavy over her, he was hard against her, he was hot all over and he didn't let her move. His arms cradled her upper body, raising her to him, locking her so tight against him. She was aching to touch him, dying to feel his muscles harden under her fingers...

But he locked her, leaving her no escape but to feel every assault of his fingers, his mouth, his tongue, his breath.

He kissed her until there was no breath left in her. He played with her hair...

Her toes curled into the sheets as he dragged his open mouth down her neck and to the valley between her breasts.

Need knotted at her nipples as he cupped her breasts reverently, kneaded them, lifted them to his mouth. She bit her lip, scrunched the silky sheets with her fingers, bucked against his grip. "Nate, please let me touch you, let me move or—"

"No."

"What do you mean no?" she cried.

He rose above her like a dark god, intent on pulling her under, every inch of his face carved from stone. His icy blue eyes wide, he was panting too. And Riya realized what tremendous control he was exercising, how tightly reined in his desire was. How, even being in the moment, he wasn't truly with her.

But before the thought could take root, he licked her nipple and she lost all coherence again.

"Do you want me to stop, butterfly?" he whispered hotly against her breast, his tongue laving the skin around her eager nipple.

"No," she said so loudly that the word reverberated in the silence.

His fingers tweaked her other breast, pulled at her nipple, while his mouth closed over the first one. Riya kicked her legs against the bed, and still he didn't let her move.

She gasped under the attack, she sobbed, she twisted and turned as he suckled, laved with his tongue. And a frantic pulsing began at her sex.

"I wondered," he whispered against the valley between her breasts, taking a shuddering, reverent breath.

All she could manage between catching her breaths was to say "What?"

"Your nipples," he said, rolling off her and lying on his side. His muscular leg covered her legs, his arm holding her tight against him. He dipped his mouth and suckled the swollen tip again and she arched her spine as sensations rippled and splintered through her.

The heat built intolerably between her legs and she rubbed her thighs restlessly.

His large hands stole between them, denying the friction she needed, and Riya was ready to beg. "I wondered what color they would be." This against the underside of her breasts.

"I guessed it right." This against the planes of her stomach. "Like chocolate."

He looked up then, and Riya looked down, her skin slick with sweat. She saw his gaze move over her face, her mouth and her breasts again, and felt a shyness come over her.

This was so intimate, intrusively so.

This moment when something else arced beneath the simmering chemistry between them was everything she had avoided her entire life. Here, lying naked below him, all of her exposed to his eyes, was the biggest risk she had ever taken.

For a startling second, she wondered what she had started. Wondered how she would face him tomorrow, how she would...

Moving up, he devoured her mouth in a kiss that left no breath in her. Pressed another one at her temple. "You okay, butterfly?"

Riya nodded, not at all surprised at how easily he read her. She had never met anyone who had understood her so well. Grabbing his forearm, she pressed a kiss to his biceps, flicked her tongue over the birthmark that had fascinated her so.

"You're still thinking. And I won't tolerate that, Riya," he said, traveling down her body again, trailing wet heat over her skin. His mouth hovered over the waistband of her thong, his teeth dragging against her skin. His breath sounded harsh. "You're driving me insane and I very much want to do the same to you," he said, sounding almost angry.

She could do nothing but sink her fingers into his hair.

Moan loudly as he tugged the string of her thong tight against her clitoris. And pulled it, up and down.

She bucked off the bed as his fingers explored.

Jerked as he learned her with clever, lingering strokes.

Dug her nails into his shoulders as he tweaked the spot aching for his touch. Dragged her nails over his back as he eased a finger and then two into her wet heat.

The softness of her sex felt amplified around the intrusive weight of his fingers. Every inch of her contracted and pulsed at that spot, and Riya sobbed.

"Nathan!" she said, the invasion of his fingers, the relentless rub of the pad of his thumb, the building pressure, driving her out of her own skin.

She laughed or cried, she didn't know which, her body, her heart careening out of control.

"Look at you!" His hot mouth pressed against her midriff, and her muscles clenched. "You're the wildest thing I've ever seen."

He moved his head between her thighs. The stroke of his tongue against the tight bud was like touching a spark to a building storm. "Let go, butterfly," he said, and without warning, sucked at the slick bundle of nerves.

Screaming and thrashing, Riya shattered around his fingers in a dizzying whirl of such exquisite sensations that she thought she would fall apart. Sobbing, she tried to bring her knees together, but with his fingers still inside her, he clasped her against him. Continued the relentless pressure of his fingers so that the small tremors continued until she was nothing but a mass of sensation and pleasure.

As the tremors slowed down, she opened her eyes, saw the stark need, the possessive pride written in his face. He'd watched her explode and liked it. Took her mouth in a possessive kiss that knocked the remaining breath out of her lungs. "You're a screamer, Riya…"

Fighting the shyness that he had witnessed it with such blatant thoroughness, Riya pressed her mouth to his chest. If she stopped to think, she would stop altogether.

And she didn't want to stop. She wanted all of him.

She moved her fingers down his hard stomach and down farther. Clasped the hard length of him. Flicked the soft head with her thumb, heard the guttural groan that fell from his mouth. His chest was hollow with his breath held.

The most powerful feeling exploded inside Riya. He was

so hard in her palm, and he was big. She felt the sharp need begin in her all over again as she stroked him.

He moaned so loud that she did it harder.

He jerked his hips into her hands, and whispered the filthiest words she had ever heard. Gasping at the renewed urgency in her own body, she moved her fist up and down.

He dug his teeth into her shoulder and she gripped him harder, going hot all over. Sweat beaded his skin, every muscle so tight that she wondered if he would break into a thousand shards.

Moving down, she kissed her way down his body, licking, tasting, reveling in the shudders that racked through him. When she reached his shaft, his fingers tightened in her hair, staying her. Looking up, she jerked her head. "Let go, Nathan."

His eyes were the darkest she had seen yet, his nostrils flaring, his control nearly shredded. "Tonight's about you, Riya."

"No, tonight's about what I want to do," she said boldly. Leaving him no choice, she licked down the long, hard length of him. He cursed.

She closed her mouth over him and sucked experimentally, a wet heat gathering at her own sex. She felt no shame, no shyness, only the gloriously alive feeling coursed through her. Licking the tip, she looked up at him.

And before she could blink, she was on her back and he was lodged between her thighs. "Enough," he said with such vehemence that Riya stared at him.

She watched increasingly boldly as he sheathed himself. She hadn't even given thought to protection. Coloring, she pushed up and kissed the hollow beneath his pectoral, tasted the salt of his skin, breathed in his musky scent.

The head of his shaft rubbed against her entrance. Feeling restless again, Riya met his gaze and held it, wanting all of him in that moment.

He pushed slowly at first, letting her accommodate to his length. Long fingers left deep grooves on her hips, holding her still, the way he wanted her. Kissing her mouth again, he dragged her closer, tilted her hips so she was right for him. And then swept in with one hard thrust.

Her head thrown back, Riya gasped at the sharp sting and the heavy intrusion, every inch of her stiffening. Her hands clasped his shoulders, the bones protruding out of them pressing against her palms.

His head went back in a recoil, the corded length of his neck stiff. Thick veins pulsed in his neck, his face clenched tight in satisfaction. His gaze was unfocused; then he blinked, as though fighting for control. In that moment, he looked savage, like a roaring volcano of emotions and needs, the hard shell he encased himself in falling away by the heat between them.

"Riya, you'll be the death of me," he said in such a grave tone that her focus shifted from the already receding pain.

But instead of being scared, Riya felt like a victor. Because this Nathan who wore his needs and passions in his eyes was the true Nathan.

Hiding his face in her neck, Nathan breathed hard. "You're a virgin." Of course she was. *Damn, damn, damn.*

He heard the accusatory, sinking tone of his words, but for the life of him, couldn't do anything about it.

Couldn't think about anything except the need surging through him, demanding release. She was like a fist around him, smooth and tight, and he was going to burst at the seams if he didn't move. For a man who abhorred having sex merely for the release it provided, this need to plunge into her until she was all he felt...he was drowning in it.

What had he done?

He was truly gone if it had taken him until now for that little fact to filter though.

Somehow he found an ounce of his shredded self-control, and raised his head.

Her pinched look slowly fading, Riya looked up at him. Beads of sweat glistened over her upper lip, and he fisted his hands to stop touching her.

"Do you want me to stop? You should have warned me, slowed me—"

"Would you have done it differently if I had?" the minx demanded. She sounded husky, a ragged edge to her words that seared him. "Would it have stung less? Was there a pain-free way of deflowering that you would have employed?"

Damn it, he had no wish to hurt her. In any way. "No."

This was getting too complicated. He was breaking each and every one of his rules with her. "But I would have resisted you better." *Lies, all lies.*

He saw the hurt in her eyes before she hid it away. "Then I'm glad I didn't."

"Damn it, Riya, this is not what—"

"It's just my hymen, Nate, not my heart. Except it played the gatekeeper to my heart until now."

"If you waited this long, it means you wanted it to be special."

"I waited this long because I was like Sleeping Beauty, except I wasn't sleeping but just functioning. Isn't it better I'm doing it with someone I know than a stranger? With someone I trust?

"You're my best bet, Nate. And I took it. Now it's up to you to make sure I made a good one."

She wiggled her hips experimentally, and Nathan felt

the walls of her tight sex grip him harder, the slow rub of friction driving him out of his own skin.

"Please, Nate. I swear, I won't fall in love with you. Do something. I want—"

He licked her already swollen lower lip, the pleading tone of her words sending him over the edge.

She ran her palms over his thighs and sighed. His thighs turned into hard stones. Wiggled again.

"Stop doing that."

This time, she rotated her hips, and his hips responded of their own accord. He pulled out and thrust into her. Pleasure spiraled up and down his spine. He cursed again. "How do you know how to do that?"

She smiled and winked at him, arched her spine, thrusting those beautiful breasts up, and Nathan felt himself move another inch.

Nothing was in his control anymore, not the situation, not his body and not his heart.

Her fingers moved to his hips, and she scooted closer and sighed. The rasp of it grated against his skin. The blunt tips of her nails dug into his buttocks as though she couldn't wait to be as close as possible. "I think I'm going to be a natural at this. How stupid that I waited this long... ah..."

And that broke the last thread of his control. Grabbing the rounded cheeks of her rump, he tilted her hips up, pulled all the way out and thrust back in. Slow, but letting her feel him every inch. And again. And again.

Until he thought he would die from the pleasure building in his veins, until she was sobbing his name again. But she didn't look away, didn't let him look away, and Nate wondered who was in charge, who was in control, even though he was the one who set the rhythm.

His heart pounded, raced as sensation built and clawed up his spine.

And he wanted her with him. He wanted her as unraveled as she was making him. On the last thrust in, he bent and dragged his teeth on her nipple and she exploded.

As she climaxed around him, Nathan pumped into her heat. And the tremors in her sex pushed him over. His own climax thundered toward him, splintering him into a million shards of pleasure and sensation. And nothing else.

He felt as though he was done for. His heart rushed in his ears, and he smiled, in defiance.

Take that, you useless organ, he challenged it. *Stop this moment and it would all still be worth it.*

Riya was still trembling beneath him, he realized, and he was crushing her with his weight. He meant to move off her, but her fingers clenched around his biceps, holding him still.

"I'm too heavy for you. Let me go."

She hid her face in his chest, and his muscles clenched under her tender kiss. "I can breathe. Just a minute... Please, Nate."

For a few minutes, which actually felt like an eternity, Nate cradled her face in his hands. Rubbed his lips against hers, heard the thundering roar of her heart and her breaths trying to keep up with his.

Lingered in the moment until his heart swelled in his chest.

And slowly, as the haze of the pleasure faded, as his breathing resumed normality, regret and remorse rushed in.

He felt her kiss his forehead, wrap her arms around his shoulders.

Found his own arms moving to wrap around her, to hold

her close, to tell her how explosive it had been. To tell her that sex had never been this personal for him.

"Nate?"

The whisper of his name at his ears was an intimacy that had him hardening inside her again. "Hmm?"

"Is it always like that?"

No, it wasn't always like that. In fact, it had never been like that for him.

Looking into her eyes, he said in a matter-of-fact tone, "With the right partner, it could be."

Her palms traced the ridges of his back. "Oh."

He pushed a lock of hair that fell forward. "And you were right. You're quite the natural at it. You're explosively responsive and any man would…"

The very idea of Riya with another man made him sick to his stomach.

Sudden panic surging up within him, he jerked away from her. Rose from the bed and walked into the bathroom without looking back. Turned the shower on and stood under it.

He never indulged in the intimacy of holding his lover or sleeping with one in his bed. He had never wanted to, if he were honest. In that first year after he left home, all he had done was take, as if the whole world were for his own personal enjoyment, everything in it his prize.

And waking up tangled with a woman whose name he didn't know and would never know, in an unending cycle of seeking comfort and escape from his fate and fears, bitterness had risen in his mouth one day.

Until he'd realized that at the end of all of it, the truth had never changed.

It hadn't made him stronger or smarter or healthier. It had only made him disgusted with himself. And he had realized that even this total loss of control, this gorging on things, was also driven by fear. So instead he'd put rules in place for himself.

Never get involved. Ever. Sex, even as he hated the casual, transient nature of it, had to remain impersonal.

Traveling as he did, working as he did, he'd found it easier to keep to his tenet. He had never had a girlfriend; he had never had a first date or a second date. He'd never taken a woman to dinner, never gotten to know one.

He had never even hugged one or comforted one as he had done tonight. Never let a few minutes of his life be about anyone but himself. Never let anyone get under his skin.

And now everything inside him roared with a savage intensity, raged against an unknown fate. He pummeled his hands against the tiles, bent his head in defeat as the water pounded over him.

A longing like he'd never known burst free inside, spreading through him like an unstoppable virus, and he shivered under the hot spray.

Because he wanted to go back into that bedroom.

He wanted to hold her, kiss her, he wanted to tell her that what they had shared was special. Even his untried heart knew that. He wanted to tell her that he was glad that she'd trusted him for her first time, that for all the hurt she had lived through, there was an intrinsic purity and courage to her emotions.

He wanted to tell her that the thought of her sharing her body with anyone else lanced him like a hot poker, that the thought of her sharing her emotions, her fears and her joys with someone else filled him with a hot fury.

But if he did, he would only make it harder on both of them. Make it awkward for the rest of his stay. Would push her into making more out of it.

He'd never let anyone close in his entire life. And he didn't intend to start now.

Even if she was the most extraordinary woman he had ever met.

He was gone.

Riya opened her eyes and felt the silence around her, touched the empty silk sheets and closed her eyes again. Locked away the sting of his withdrawal. Pulled the sheets up to her neck and scrunched tight into herself.

She ran the tip of her finger against her lips and found them swollen. Her arms trembled, her thighs felt as if she had run a marathon. Her body throbbed and ached after his deep thrusts. Even her scalp tingled, an aftereffect of how tightly Nathan had held her when he climaxed. Her hips bore the evidence of his loss of control, of his passion—pink grooves where his fingers had dug into her.

He had lost control in the end. He'd come as undone as she had. And Riya hugged the fact to herself.

She had known, after all these years of denying herself the simplest touch, it would be strange, weird. But she felt as if she had died and come out alive again.

She gazed at the corridor through which he had walked, his lean frame radiating with tension.

She had broken a rule she hadn't known. That much was clear.

Had it been the kiss? Had it been the way she clung to him? Or had it been her question about it always being that good? Emotions, he didn't do them. She knew that.

But whatever it had been, it was done. In a way, she was glad she had angered him. That left her alone to face what she had done, gave her a reprieve from what she felt around him.

Because nothing, she realized, could take away from the

moment, from the beauty and wonder of what she had experienced. She wasn't going to regret it; she wasn't going to ruin it.

It had been the best few hours of her life, the most alive she had felt. The most fearless she had been. Free to look and touch and taste without wondering about the consequences.

And now it was over.

For a few more seconds, she let herself linger in the moment. Buried her face in the pillow. Breathed in his scent again. Remembered the heady pleasure of being locked under him, her every breath, every moment, every inch of pleasure she felt, all his to give.

Her emotions and herself, under his total control and how good it had felt.

Imagined that he was still there, pulling her into that lean body of his, wrapping those corded arms around her and holding her safe.

This was not a rejection. And even if it was, she couldn't care.

It took only a few moments under the hot spray of the shower for Nathan to realize how heartless he had been. He didn't have to break his self-imposed rules, but he could have at least said a kind word to her. Could have made sure she was okay.

For goodness' sake, it had been her first time.

When had he turned into such a thorough bastard? He felt a distinct unease in his gut. Walking away shouldn't have become this easy. All she'd asked was a simple question.

How could he forget that Riya was new to this, and not just physical intimacy? The hardened cynic that he was, even he'd been moved by the intensity of it.

Wrapping the towel around his hips, he trailed water all over the marble floor as he walked back to the bedroom.

The empty bed felt like a punch to his stomach. He looked around the bedroom and the sitting room and returned to the bedroom again. Her dress was gone. Her sandals were gone. Her clutch was gone.

She was gone.

His phone pinged and he picked it up with a vicious curse. He switched it on, suddenly unsure of where all the anger was coming from. He hated to be so emotional, so unbalanced, and she had done it to him.

"I never asked you to leave," he said.

A short silence reigned before he heard her clear her throat. "I know. I thought it was best. I called to say I found your chauffeur and he's driving me back."

Another silence while Nathan fumed at himself. There was no accusation in her tone. And yet it grated at him.

"Nathan?"

He had taken her virginity and he had forced her into fleeing his bed after the night she had had.

"Nate? Please say something."

Now she sounded wary, tired. And he remembered the emotionally draining day she had had, all thanks to him. "Riya, I'm sorry, I should have—"

"Thank you, Nate," she said, cutting him off. There was no sarcasm or mockery in her tone. Only genuine gratitude.

His throat closed off.

"For...for everything tonight."

"Hell, Riya. You don't have to thank me for sex. I'm not a..."

What? What was he not? And what was he? What was he doing with her?

She laughed, and the ease of the sound only darkened his mood. Had it really been that simple for her? Just been about one night? Had he ruined all her innocence, changed her forever?

"Thank you for being there for me tonight, for your kindness. No one's ever done that for me. No one's ever let it be about me. That's what I meant earlier. I...I will always cherish tonight. And the...sex..."

He had a feeling she was forcing herself to sound breezy.

"...it was more than I would ever have known if left to my own devices. Would never have known how beautiful it could be." Another laugh, self-deprecating this time. "So yeah, thanks for that too, I guess."

He couldn't say a word, couldn't get his vocal cords to work, couldn't manage anything but a stilted silence. He didn't deserve a word she said; he didn't deserve her.

"Good night, Nathan."

She didn't wait for him to speak before she hung up, probably realizing he wasn't going to say anything.

Her face disappeared from his screen, and he clenched his teeth, a soft fury vibrating through him.

He threw his phone across the room, his chest incredibly tight. He sank to the bed and instantly the smell of her, the scent of sex, hit him hard, and he buried his face in his hands. Gulped in a greedy breath.

There was an ache in this throat, something he hadn't felt since his mother told him about his condition.

It was self-pity, it was fear, it was how he felt when his emotions were out of control.

With a curse, he swallowed it back.

No.

She wasn't allowed to do this to him.

No woman was allowed to send him back to being that boy. No woman was allowed to pry this much emotion from him.

With a ruthlessness he had learned to survive without

fear, with the resolve that had turned him from a runaway to a millionaire, he put her out of his mind. Dressed himself and ordered some coffee. Called housekeeping to change the sheets.

He didn't want any reminder of her, of what they had done together, of how he had felt with her beneath him, of how incredibly good the intimacy with her had been. Neither could he focus on how much he wanted to repeat the night, of how he wanted to find her at the estate and sink into her bed, of how much he wanted to hold her slender body in his arms and drift into sleep…

She made him think of Nate Keys, the boy who had been desperately afraid for himself, who wanted to love and live, who wanted to be invincible. But he couldn't be.

He turned on his laptop and went back to being the man he had trained himself to be.

Nathaniel Ramirez—billionaire, survivor and loner.

CHAPTER TEN

OVER THE NEXT couple of weeks, Riya threw herself into the wedding preparations with a rigor that left her with zero headspace. Between her increased responsibilities at Travelogue and the wedding preparations, not to mention the toll it was taking on her to avoid her own mother while living in the same house, it was a miracle she was managing as well as she was.

But she liked it like that. Her days were busy to the point of crammed and when she fell into her bed at night, she was so exhausted that she went right to sleep.

It was only when she was doing some mundane organizational task for the wedding that she found herself thinking of Nathan. She had tried to keep her thoughts free of him. But seeing him every day wasn't conducive to purging him from her mind. After a while, she had just given up.

"Are you well?" he had asked her the following Monday at work, his gaze intent.

She hadn't been able to stem the heat spreading up her neck. "I'm fine," she had said, pleased that she had sounded so steady.

He had tucked her hair behind her ear, clasped her cheek for a moment.

Her heart had thundered in her chest, everything in her yearning to keep his hand there. Because that gesture hadn't been about heat or attraction. It had been about affection, about comfort.

Before she had done anything, however, he had jerked back. He had nodded, looked at her some more and that had been that. And taking his cue, she had thrown herself into work.

Training her mind was still one thing. And absolutely another was her body.

Every time she saw him—either at work or the house, because of course, to her growing annoyance, Nathan apparently couldn't stay away from the house and Robert, she remembered the night they had shared.

Their one night of pleasure. Her one night of freedom from herself. And it was in the most embarrassing and humiliating ways too.

Humiliating because he didn't seem to be facing any such problem. He was back to being the intensely driven slave driver and perfectionist Nathaniel Ramirez. The man really had to have a rock for a heart.

Embarrassing because the memories of that night crept upon her all of a sudden.

The taste of his sweat and skin when she had licked his wrist intruded on her when he extended some papers to her in a meeting full of people. She had stared at his wrist for a full thirty seconds before she grabbed the papers from him.

The velvet hardness of him moving inside her, the stroke of his fingers at her core, the way his spine had arced and the way he had shuddered when he climaxed…she couldn't look at him and not think of what she had let him do to her.

With her late entry into the realm of physical pleasures, she understood her fascination with him. Like how he caught his lower lip with his teeth when he was thinking hard. The way he sometimes placed his palm on his chest and rubbed when he frowned.

But what she missed the most was the man she had come to know. His irrepressible energy around her, his constant teasing of her...now one of them, or both, had erected a wall of politeness. They worked together perfectly, but now they were strangers.

Having finalized the menu once again on the caterer's online website, Riya shut her computer down.

"Riya, I want to speak to you," her mother's voice came from behind her.

Shaking her head, Riya shot out of her chair and grabbed her laptop. "I have nothing to say to you."

"Then why on earth are you doing so much for the wedding?"

"For Robert. I'll do anything for him." Which was why she hadn't packed her stuff and left the estate as her initial impulse had been to do.

Jackie flinched and Riya felt a stab of regret and shock. The fact that anything she said or did could even affect her mom, except in the most superficial way, was a shock in itself. But however hard she tried, she couldn't find it in her to forgive or even forget for a little while.

Her jaw clenching and unclenching, Jackie stopped in front of her, blocking her exit. "I knew it. I knew it from the moment he stepped on the estate that he was going to ruin it all."

Despite every intention not to fall into the guilt trap her mom was so adept at laying, Riya still found herself getting sucked in. "What are you talking about?"

"Nathan. He's doing all this. Robert can't stop talking about him. He wants us to leave the estate without complaint, says we can't have the wedding here anymore because Nathan doesn't want it. And when I argued, he raised his voice to me. Nathan's all he can think about—"

"Robert thought he would never see Nathan again. Can't you be happy for him? For them?"

Because Riya was incredibly happy. For both of them. A little part of her was even envious. Of course, Robert had cared about her. And she was so thankful to him for everything. But the light that came into his eyes when he spoke of Nathan made her a little sad too.

"You're so strong, Riya. Not everyone is so...self-sufficient. I made a bad decision. It doesn't mean I don't love you. You can't give up the estate just because—"

"Are you kidding me, really?"

"I'm telling you the truth. That's what you want these days, right? I love Robert. And yes, I begin to panic when he gets mad at me. Just as I panicked when I thought your father would take you away from me."

Her insecurity was at the root of everything Jackie did. For the first time, instead of helplessness and then anger in the face of it, Riya felt pity for her mother.

"Just because Nathan's back doesn't mean Robert doesn't love you anymore. I don't think it works like that."

"No? Look how he's turned you against me. For years, we've been each other's support, all we've had, Riya. And now, just weeks after he's back, you won't even look at me. All these years of—"

"You were never my support. I was yours. You leaned on me when you shouldn't have. If I've had even a little bit of a carefree childhood, it's because of Robert. And if I've known, even for only a few hours, what it means to live, it's only because of Nathan. So excuse me if I don't—"

"Few hours? What're you talking about?"

At Riya's silence, she became even tenser. "It's none of your business."

Her gaze filled with shock, Jackie shook her. "You slept with him, didn't you? Riya. How stupid are you?"

As dramatic and distasteful as she was making it out to be, Riya refused to let Jackie ruin the most perfect time of her life. "That's grand coming from the woman who fell in love with a married man," she shouted, hating Jackie for reducing her to this.

"At least Robert still stuck with me all these years. Nathan will leave and never look back. He's the wrong man for you."

The fact that Nathan was going to leave was something Riya absolutely refused to think about. But she was aware of it, at the back of her mind, gaining momentum, beginning to rush at her from all sides.

"This has nothing to do with the estate or you, or Robert. It concerns only Nathan and me. No one else. As hard as it is for you to accept it, I have a life. Am going to have a life that's beyond you. I'm leaving after the wedding," she said.

She had been thinking about it, but there was no doubt in her mind now.

She had made to move away when Jackie gave a laugh, and the genuine pity in it rooted Riya to the spot. "Now I see why he insisted. He's planned it all along. And you went straight to his arms."

"What on earth are you talking about?"

"Nathan. He was the one who insisted I tell you about your father. He manipulated you into his bed, Riya. He doesn't care about you."

The urge to slap her hands over her ears was so strong that she dug her nails into her palms. "No," Riya denied, something inside her shaking at the revelation. She closed her eyes and his face, kind and resigned, flashed in front of her. "He didn't manipulate me. He never could." She kept whispering the word, too many things shifting and twisting in front of her.

"He didn't plan anything. He wanted nothing but for me

to know that I was throwing my life away. He's the first person in my life who thought about me, who cared enough to do something about it."

Her mom would never understand. And she needed to be okay with it. It wasn't that she hated Jackie now. Only that she realized that she had a life beyond Jackie, beyond her father, beyond Robert and beyond the estate.

On some level, she knew she should be angry with Nathan. He had been high-handed; he had brought her nothing but hurt. He had set it up without breathing a word to her.

But she couldn't be.

Wasn't it the truth that hurt her? Jackie who had hurt her? Even her father, to some extent, by threatening Jackie to take her away?

Nathan had only liberated her from under the burden of the truth. And then he'd been there to catch her when she was falling. It felt precious, momentous, this molten feeling inside her, this expanding warmth in her chest that he had cared.

She went looking for him later that afternoon when she heard Maria mention that he was visiting. Found him sitting at the gazebo.

He sat with his denim-clad legs stretched in front of him, with his head resting behind him, his face turned up. Sunlight hit his face in rectangular stripes. Kissed the shadows under his eyes. Caressed the planes and hollows of his cheekbones. The breeze ruffled his hair, the copper in it glinting in the sunlight.

His tan was fading a bit and his mouth, not smiling, not teasing, was a tight bow, his lower lip jutting out.

He looked strained, she thought with a pang. He was always such a dynamic, go-go-go, bursting-with-unending-energy kind of man that she didn't like seeing this stillness in him. There was a melancholic quality to that stillness, a dark shadow to the quiet enveloping him.

A sharp need gripped her. Not to feel his touch, although that was there too. But this was a clamoring to reach him, wrap her arms around him, hold him close. For herself, yes, but for him too.

In that moment, there was a loneliness around him. The same one inside her that she had covered up as the need for security.

The realization brought her up short. And she shook her head. It was ridiculous. Just because she felt alone in the world didn't mean Nathan was. It was his choice in life. It had been her choice too, but she hadn't even been aware of it.

As though he could hear her thoughts piling on top of each other, he looked up. His eyes were a different blue in the sunlight, but even the sharp gaze couldn't hide the strain around them.

There was that instant heat between them. He leaned forward onto his knees and frowned. "Is something wrong?"

She shook her head.

For a full minute, she stood there, holding his gaze, not knowing if she wanted to step forward or turn back.

He sighed, a harsh expulsion of breath and anger, she thought. "Come here," he said.

And she went, silencing the clamor inside her. Settled down next to him and stretched out her own legs.

It was a beautiful day with a soft breeze that carried all kinds of fragrances with it. The silence between them, even though a little tense, slowly drifted into a comfortable groove. And she didn't fight it, didn't seek to cover it up or change it.

Was this where they were going to settle? In this place between simmering heat and a strange intimacy?

Slowly she covered the gap between them. Scooted closer until her thigh grazed the hard length of his. Leaned back and sideways until she hit the wall of his chest. Wound her arm around his lean waist. Held herself tight and still, bracing for his rejection.

Seconds piled on top of each other, her breath balled in her throat. He didn't push her away. Her heart thundering just as fast as when she had stripped in front of him, she wrapped her arm around his torso and leaned her head on his chest.

She almost flinched when his right arm came around her shoulders and pulled her closer. Her breath left her in a shuddering whoosh and she settled into his embrace. He smelled familiar, and comforting. He felt like home. And this time, she knew it wasn't the estate. It was the man.

She didn't know how long they sat like that.

"You don't want the wedding to be here?" she finally asked, loath to ruin the peace but needing to. Because if she didn't, she had a feeling she would never let go.

And that was definitely reason to panic.

He tensed, but when he spoke, there was no anger in him. "No."

Feeling his gaze on her, Riya looked up. He ran his thumb over her temple. Pressed a kiss to her forehead. And yet there was no shock in either of them that he'd done it.

Because how could anything that felt so right be wrong?

"I have no anger for her, your mother," he said, and her chest expanded at the kindness in his words, at the rough edge of emotion coating it. "I just want this place to remain my mother's."

Riya nodded, her throat clogging. "Do you miss her very much?"

His mother…she was asking about his mother. The woman who had died with fear in her eyes. She couldn't have jolted him out of the moment better than if she had electrocuted him, reminded him of everything wrong that he was doing. Sitting here, sharing this moment with her, comforting her, finding something in her arms, this was wrong.

All of it, every precious second, every incredible touch.

Nathan jerked away from her and shot up from the bench, fear filling his veins. Every inch of him vibrated with a feral need to ask her to come with him, to show her the world, to have her in his bed for as long as they wanted each other.

And he couldn't let her have this much power over him, couldn't yearn for things he could never have. He steeled himself against her beauty, her heart, and willed himself to become cold, uncaring.

It was the only way to save her from a bigger hurt.

"My manager's taking care of all the arrangements to have the wedding somewhere else. You don't have to redo them. And Robert too. There will be a nurse who will check on him once every day. He and your mother, I'll take care of them, Riya. You've carried their burden long enough."

He had thought of everything. He was making arrangements. Before he... And suddenly she couldn't lock away the questions. "Thanks. So you'll be at the wedding?"

He laughed, and now there was no more easy humor in the sound. The moment was fractured. And she didn't know why. He tucked his fingers into the pockets of his jeans. Looked anywhere but at her. And Riya tried not to show her utter dismay.

It was obvious withdrawal, painful retreat.

"I would like nothing but to leave this very instant and not look back. I've stayed too long already and I'm getting restless. But I did give you my word."

He was not joking and the utter lack of any emotion in

his words shocked her. She had barely made friends, or any other relationship for that matter. And he…he was one relationship she didn't want to lose. "Are we friends, Nathan?"

His jaw tight, he stared at her for several seconds, anger dawning in his gaze. "We are nothing, Riya."

She flinched at the cutting derision in his words. The entire tenor of the conversation had changed. "Why are you acting like this? What did I do wrong?"

"You were fun that night." Her palm itched to knock the derisive curve of his mouth. "Today, you're falling into a pattern that I'm allergic to."

"Because I want us to be friends? I know that it was you that forced Jackie to tell me truth." When he opened his mouth, she put her hand over it to hush him. And felt the contact jolt through her. "I know you did it because you cared. I don't want explanations. I just…I think I would like us to be friends, Nate. I…" She stopped, arrested by the look in his eyes.

"I did what I did because I felt sorry for you, for what your mother and this estate—for what they all did to you."

"Sorry for me?"

"Yes. You manipulated the truth to bring me here, risked everything to patch things up between Dad and me. It has brought me a peace unlike anything. I thought I would pay you back the favor, lift the veil from your eyes, so to speak.

"We're not anything, Riya. We can't even be called a one-night stand. Because you weren't even there for the whole night, right? And we're definitely not friends."

And now she was angry, very angry. And stunned, because there was nothing but finality in his tone. "Why not? Why are you being such a jerk?"

"Because there could be no friendship between us, Riya. Not after that night. When I leave here, you won't see me again, hear from me again. *Ever.*"

Her breath knocked around in her lungs. It didn't feel as though he was stating a fact. It felt as though he was making her a promise. A painful one.

"You never plan to visit the estate that you went to all this trouble for? You'll kick us all out and just let the house be?"

"Yes." The word kicked her in the gut. "I could say otherwise now to make you happy, but it would be a lie. And I can't bear lies."

Something glimmered in his eyes, but Riya had no idea what. He was hurting her with his words. He was aware of it and he was still doing it. Very efficiently even.

Suddenly the cold stranger from the first day was back. Nathaniel Ramirez was back. And the man who had learned more about her in a few weeks than anyone else in her entire life, he was gone.

"Don't do this, Riya. Don't fixate on me because I'm the first man you slept with. Or because I'm the first man who showed a little bit of concern." He clasped her cheek, devouring her as if he were starving, as if he was memorizing every feature, every angle of it. "What you feel for me is only attraction. Only your body asking for—"

"A repeat performance? You think I'm naive enough to sugarcoat my words when all I want is one of those fantastic orgasms you deal out? And for the record, if that's what I wanted, I'm sure you would oblige me, wouldn't you?"

Now there was anger in his eyes. And Riya was glad. She wanted him to be angry, she wanted him to be hurt.

"I think you don't know the difference between a good friend, a great lover and a man who deserves your love. I'm only good for one of those roles. I think you haven't seen enough of the world to know yourself."

"Right. Because Nathaniel Ramirez knows what's best for everyone." She pushed his hand away, hating herself for wanting to revel in his touch. "Will you do me two favors while you're still here, then? Or have I run out of luck with you?"

He looked pale, drawn out. As if there was nothing more left in him. And she was the one who was hurt. "Yes."

"Can you find out where my father is? Put all your power and wealth to use?"

"Yes, I'll put someone on it. What's the second one?"

"There's a week to the wedding. It would make me really happy if you didn't come here. Robert can come see you at the hotel."

"Why?"

Stepping back, she ran her fingers over the wood grain, her throat clogging. "This has been my home for more than a decade. You have the rest of your life here. I only have one week. I want to enjoy it. And if you're around, it'll ruin it for me."

He nodded and then walked away. Riya sank to the bench, her limbs sagging.

For some reason, the tears came then.

They hadn't come so many times when she wished for them, when she needed an outlet for the ache in her heart. They hadn't come when she thought her father had let her go. They hadn't come when she learned that Jackie had lied. But they came now.

Sitting in the gazebo, in the place that had been home to her, Riya cried.

She didn't know why, and she didn't try to understand. Only tucked her arms around her knees and let the tears draw wet paths over her cheeks. She cried for the little girl she had been, for the lost and guarded teenager she had been, for the frozen woman she had become.

She didn't think about Nathan. He had no place in this. This was for her. Only her.

And when the tears dried up and her head hurt, she wiped her cheeks, took a shuddering breath and stood up. Looked around at the lush greenery.

What she had been doing was not enough anymore. That night with Nathan had only been the beginning. Something had to change in her life. She needed to live more. Not that she had any idea how to do that. But she had to start somewhere. After the wedding, she would leave.

She would have to quit her job. She would have to plan her finances, apply for part-time remote-access jobs. To give up all the stability she knew, to leave a job that paid well, the city she had grown up in, to leave Robert and Jackie…the excitement of it all, the fear of it, rocked through her.

There was a whole world out there. And staying still wasn't an option anymore.

Standing at the entrance to the kitchen, Nathan felt every muscle in him clench with a feral ache. Every soft cry that fell from Riya's mouth, every hard breath, landed on him like a claw, raking through him.

But he couldn't go to her. He couldn't hold her as he wanted to, he couldn't promise her that life would get better. That it would hurt less and less. That pain was just as much a part of life as joy.

He didn't make the mistake of thinking she was crying over him. He knew she was saying goodbye. Still, he wished he could be her support even as it was he who was forcing her to leave.

Ask her to come with you, Nate, a voice piped up, catching him unaware.

If he gave in to the longing inside him, if he asked her to come with him temporarily, just until this fire in him was at least blunted… Whether she realized it now or not, when this wave of risk-taking became too much, her natural world would reassert itself. There would be nothing for him except her rejection.

And that rejection would kill him as nothing else had done. To see that fear in her eyes would surely finish him off. And he couldn't blame Riya for being who she was, for the way she had survived.

He would never be the right man for her. And if he wanted to nip this…this yearning, this longing she made him feel, he would have to leave soon. Not risk seeing her again.

Before he forgot, before he started hoping for things that would never be, could never be his. And the distance between hope and fear was not that big.

And so he left, without looking back. As he'd always done.

CHAPTER ELEVEN

THANKS TO THE superefficient event management company Nathan had hired, the wedding preparations went without a hitch. All Riya had to do, even if reluctantly, was to keep her mother calm and turn up to the wedding. More than once, she had indulged in the idea of leaving even before the wedding. But doing that would have hurt Robert and, of course, her mother.

And she wasn't ruthless enough yet just to cut them out of her life.

But the week leading up to it, surprisingly, had been a pleasant one. Grudgingly she accepted that this fact was due to Nathan. She was aware he threw around his wealth as he pleased, but that he had actually cared enough to have the event organized for Robert, that she couldn't overlook.

Since he had kept his word and she had mostly worked from home, she hadn't seen him for the whole week. Having always been the one to take care of the logistics and details of their everyday life, she felt that having it all taken out of her hands had been the best. All she had needed to do was to pick a dress. And even that hadn't been left to her.

She had been presented with three gorgeous ones that a team from a world-famous fashion house, from whose designs she had never been able to afford even a pitiful scarf, had been waiting with for her one afternoon. A stylist and designer along with the dresses.

She had balked at the idea of wearing anything Nathan paid for. Had absolutely refused to even look at the selection picked out for her.

Until he had texted her: Am paying for the wedding. To show my father that I don't resent it.

Can buy my own dress, she had texted back. My boss is a heartless pig, but he pays well.

Thundering silence until…

It's a welcome-to-the-family gift. Accept it or I'll call you sis J

She had laughed, imagined the crinkles he got at the corners of his eyes when he did.

Gross and perverted, that's what you are.

Her heart had run a marathon as she waited. And slammed against her rib cage when her phone pinged again.

Please, Riya.

Her fingers had lingered over her phone's screen. Why? she wanted to ask him. He had rejected her friendship, so why did it matter whether she accepted this from him? Why was he playing games with her? Caring and affectionate one second and a ruthless stranger the next?

In the end, under his relentless will, she had given in. Let them fit her. Fallen in love with the frothy beige silk creation that somehow was almost the same color as her skin and yet stood out against it as if it were made for her.

Whispered sinuously when she moved, outlined her curves without being tacky.

Understated and yet elegant, it had shocked her at how much it suited her, her personality. Not the boring, dowdy clothes she had worn before and not the garish red of her wild night.

But somewhere in between, just perfect for her.

Her hair had been twisted into a sophisticated knot on the top of her head, with soft tendrils caressing her neck and jawline. She had refused the makeup artist's help, however.

The limo that had brought them to the hotel from the estate, the quiet but affluent luxury of the hall they were having the reception in, the delicious buffet—despite all the things clamoring for her awe and attention, despite her heart fisting in her chest with the thought that she was going to leave everything that was familiar to her very soon, Riya couldn't silence her need to see Nathan.

But when she entered the hall, shook hands with friends, he was nowhere to be seen.

And so she waited. Through Robert and Jackie exchanging vows, through their friends toasting them.

She stumbled through her own speech, her eyes still locked on the entrance.

And she waited.

She kissed Jackie's cheek, danced with Robert and only then it dawned on her that her waiting was useless.

Nathan had never planned on attending the wedding.

Riya was fuming when Jackie found her in the quiet corridor that seemed to absorb her anger and the sounds she made.

"Riya." Wary hesitation danced in Jackie's eyes. "I'm so sorry, but this is for the best. Let him go, Riya. It's got nothing to do with you."

Shocked at how perceptive Jackie was being, Riya stared at her. "Please, Jackie. Not today. Just enjoy your day."

"I'm learning, Riya. I've never provided you with security, but I do think of you, worry about you. After all this, you deserve happiness, you deserve someone who'll love you and take care of you for a long time. And Nathan is the last man on earth for you."

Riya didn't like the look in Jackie's eyes. And yet, for the first time in her life, she had a feeling that her mother was speaking the absolute truth. "What do you mean?"

"He doesn't deserve you. Isn't that enough?"

"Just please tell me what you mean."

"He has the same heart condition that Anna had."

Gasping, Riya grabbed the wall behind her. A violent shiver took hold of her, and her teeth chattered in her mouth.

She felt as if someone had pushed her off a cliff and the earth was rising to meet her without a warning, without a safety net.

Anna had been barely into her forties when she died.

No. No. No. It couldn't be true. It couldn't be borne.

Nathan was a force of life.

"I don't have a heart. At least, not a working one."

All the signs had been there right in front of her. That night in his suite, he had almost fainted. Did it happen often? That strap he had worn on his wrist sometimes instead of his watch, it had to be a heart rate monitor.

So many times she had called him heartless, had thrown his mother's name in his face, wondered at how easily he cut everyone out of his life... She shot to her feet and swayed, still feeling dizzy. "I need to see him."

"Riya? What's wrong? You look unwell."

She lifted her gaze to Robert's and swallowed. Tried to rally up her good humor, her strength. Because she had always been strong, hadn't she? They all left, they all deceived her; what else did she have but her strength?

But Nathan hadn't deceived her, hadn't lied to her. In fact, had told her that he would always leave.

"Nathan. Do you know where he is?"

"He went back to the estate. He's leaving in a few hours."

Shock traversed through her, a sudden cold in her chest. "He was here. Today? When? Why didn't he—"

"Yes. But he left just as you and Jackie arrived. Said he couldn't stay any longer. He's leaving tonight."

Let him go, Riya, the part of her that she had painfully trained into place screeched at her. *Let him walk out of your life. End it all before you sink.*

"Oh." It was a miracle Riya managed that, because inside it felt as if someone had pulled the ground from under her. "He didn't even say goodbye, Robert. I... He promised me he would be here tonight." She tried to breathe past the fear and spiraling hurt. "I don't understand any of this. How could I not realize? How could he not tell me? I..."

Wrapping his arms tightly around her, Robert hugged her. And enveloped in the love she had always craved, the lack of which had made her erect a shell around herself, Riya found herself unraveling. One question kept relentlessly pounding against her head.

Why did she care so much?

He had made it clear that they didn't mean anything to each other. Not even friends. Having faced abandonment and rejection all her life, she'd always worn retreat as her armor. She wanted to do that tonight too. But he had left her nowhere to hide.

"I'm sorry it came to this, Riya. But you have to know it has nothing to do with you."

Riya laughed because that was what everyone kept saying. "No?" she said, her voice echoing in the quiet of the carpeted foyer. She was so tired of fighting this, of telling herself that she was strong. "It seems everyone finds it so easy to walk away from me, so easy not to feel even affection for me. So easy to reject me. I hate him for doing this, hate myself for feeling like this. I have to be the stupidest woman in the world—"

Shaking his head, his heart in his eyes, Robert sighed. "It's the way he survives, Riya. He would despise himself if he became like Anna."

"*I don't care* what his reason is. I deserved at least goodbye."

"No, Riya. Wait."

Uncaring of the anxiety in his face, Riya tugged at her arm. Every inch of her was shaking with urgency, the rest of her body scrambling to catch up with her heart. "Let me go, Robert. If he leaves before I can get there, I'll never see him again."

Her throat closed up at the very prospect. "Never again." He'd pretty much promised her that. He'd cut Sonia out like that. And to never see him. "I have to talk to him—"

"Don't make this harder on him."

"What about how I feel?" She screamed the words, wondering how to stem the hurt. She'd been prepared to say goodbye tonight, but knowing what she did now... "I never saw my father again. If Nathan leaves before I see him, if something happens to him, I couldn't bear it, Robert."

It hurt as if someone were ripping out her heart from her chest. Had she and the time they had spent together meant nothing? Hadn't she mattered even a little to him? Shards of hurt and pain splintered through her.

Trembling, she patted her palms down her midriff in a rhythm.

"I'm so sorry, Riya. He had no right to do this to you. I'm sorry I didn't protect you—"

The sob that she had battling rose through Riya and she threw herself into her mom's arms. "He doesn't care, Jackie. He was perfectly willing to walk away…without a word. I wish it didn't hurt so much." She clenched her eyes closed. She couldn't give in to tears now. "This goodbye is just for me. Just for me."

Standing in that softly lit corridor, looking at Robert, who had the exact same eyes as his son, Riya calmed herself down. Her world was changing, slipping from her hands, forever shifting. But even for the fear rattling through her, she couldn't stop.

Only one more night, she reassured herself. Just one more night and she would never think about him again.

"You promised me a dance."

Hearing the soft whisper of her voice, Nathan turned around from the balcony. He hadn't been sure if she would seek him out. With a steely focus, he'd not speculated on whether he wanted her to find him.

Leaning against the wall, he let his gaze rove over her. She looked ethereal tonight, like some beautiful, other-worldly creature come to earth with the express purpose of tormenting him. The beige silk dipped and flared around her lithe body, her hair falling like a silk curtain on one shoulder.

Like a shadow, he had watched her step out of the limo. Hadn't been able to help himself from greedily drinking in her beauty. Had exercised every ounce of will when he saw her gaze wander through the hall, looking for him.

It had taken everything he had in him not to drag her away from the appreciative male gazes and there had been too many of those for his liking. But she wasn't his to pro-tect or even to look at. After so rudely rejecting her small advance for a friendship, after witnessing the hurt flash in those beautiful eyes, he'd known he'd better keep his distance from her.

Not hurting Riya had somehow become the most important thing to him.

"If I remember right, you said you didn't want to dance with me," he said, willing himself to smile. His fingers gripped the railing so tight that the pattern would imprint on his palm. "*Leave Travelogue and go away, forever.* Those were your words."

Something shimmered in her gaze, but for the life of him, he couldn't tell what.

Stepping inside, she closed the door behind her. "I changed my mind. I've decided a lot of things have to change in my life."

"Like what?"

With a shrug, she looked away from him and he saw her chest rise and fall, her spine straighten as though she was bracing herself. For what?

He needed to get her out of here. Before he lost the tenuous thread of his control. Before he forgot how it had felt to have her look at him as if he was her hero, as if there was nothing he couldn't conquer. As if he would always be there for her.

She smiled then. There was fear in that smile, a bravery in it. There was something in her eyes that pulled at him, pierced through him. As if she was fighting to stand, as if she was fighting to keep herself together. And, as it had been from the beginning with her, every atavistic, male instinct in him rose to the fore.

Was she afraid? Of what?

He reached her, lifted her chin, looked into her eyes. "Riya, what is it?"

She shook her head, clasped his wrist, brought his hand closer so that his palm was wrapped around her cheek.

Pressed her mouth to the center of his palm. "I'm quitting Travelogue."

"What?"

"I found a remote-access job. It's a software architect position for a charity based in Bali. A six-month contract."

He frowned, worry for her trumping every other emotion in him. "Bali? Do you even know anyone there? Let me talk to some people I know and get the area checked—"

She shook her head. "No. I'm sure I'll be okay. I've taken care of myself so far, haven't I?"

"Why Bali? Why quit Travelogue?"

"Nothing here...nothing feels enough anymore. This life I've been leading, I want more. I want more excitement, more everything."

"Riya, I don't think you should just up and leave."

"Nathan?"

"Hmm?" He made a sound in his throat, incapable of anything else with her hands moving up his body. Sexual tension and anticipation arced and swelled between them, binding them together.

"A part of me wants to throw caution to the wind and live recklessly. A part of me will always hold me back. You are in between, Nate. Between risk and safety." Her hands clasped his cheek, and she tilted his chin up to meet her eyes. Lust and fire danced in them.

He frowned as her palm pressed against his chest, as if it wanted to confirm the thunderous roar of his heart. The intimacy of the gesture swelled inside him. "What do you want, butterfly?"

"That whole night that you promised me." Stepping back from him, she tugged the zipper of her dress down. With an elegant sensuality that sent lust rollicking through him, she pulled the fabric down, revealing the plump globes of her breasts, pushed it past her hips.

The dress pooled at her feet and she slowly kicked it away. Leaving her voluptuous body in a strapless bra and a thong.

He stepped back from her, only by the skin of his teeth. He couldn't be near her and not take what he wanted. He was painfully aroused, every nerve in him strung to breaking point. It didn't help that he'd had two drinks when he never drank, and now he had a simmering buzz in his head. "No."

She reached him before he could draw another breath. "Yes." She had somehow unbuttoned his shirt and now her palm rested against his hot skin, every line and ridge of it leaving an imprint on him. "You don't have to worry, Nate. I know precisely what I want and what I'll be getting. And come tomorrow morning, I'll bid you goodbye with a smile." Bending, she pressed an openmouthed kiss to his chest, flicked his nipple with her tongue.

Lust slammed at him from every direction.

With a punishing breath, he realized he couldn't send her away. She had come back here, hadn't she? She wanted him, and she owned her desire in a way that reduced him to nothing but heat and hunger.

Maybe with her he would always be weak. With the one woman who needed him to be honorable, strong, maybe he would always be this man who needed more than life had given him, who would always be reduced to the lowest denominator there was of him. Who wanted a few more stolen moments, a few more kisses...

It was exactly as he had feared.

Wasn't that why she was so dangerous to him?

All his armor, all his rules flew out the window when it came to her. She had brought forgiveness into his life. For a few weeks, she had banished the loneliness that was a part of his very bones now. She had brought him peace.

And tonight, it wanted pleasure, hers and his, and it wanted all of her, all night.

So he kissed her. Swallowed her soft gasp. Tasted her with hungry strokes of his tongue, learned her all over again. Drank from her until he was heady with lack of air. He was greedy, he was hot and he didn't grant them both even a breath.

His throat ached; his chest hurt at the sweet taste of her. Her touch, as her fingers wound around his nape, branded him. Her body coiled around his, stamped him forever, owned it, even if she didn't know it. Her breasts grazed him, the taut nipples rasping against his chest like tight buds driving him out of his skin.

And in that minute, he knew he would never again know the touch of another woman, the taste of another woman, the embrace of another woman. His breath harsh, he pressed his forehead against hers, the words rising through him like a tornado that couldn't be contained.

Because, as he had realized all those years ago, it wasn't the fact that his heart didn't work that was the problem. It was that it wanted more than it could ever handle in a lifetime. And all the needs and wants he had suppressed to live his life came rising to the fore when it came to Riya.

Everything he had done, everything he had achieved, felt so small compared to this moment when he couldn't say the words he most wanted to say. They burned on his tongue, fighting to be freed, weighed down on his chest, choking him.

He longed to tell her how much he loved her, how she had forever marked his heart, how she had brought forgiveness to his life, how she had, even if it was only these few minutes that he allowed himself, made him feel.

How alive he felt when he was near her, how much he

wanted to grow old with her, how much he wanted to be the one who would protect her, cherish her, love her.

Their teeth scraped, their tongues tangled. Their breaths mixed and became one. They became one.

The bed groaned as they fell onto it, devouring each other. He pushed his fingers up her thighs until he found her core. Only made sure that she was ready for him. Rubbed the swollen bud there. Let her soft moans surround him.

And she matched him in his hunger, giving as good as she got, digging her teeth into his chest, and there was nothing left in Nate but the desperate need to possess her.

He pushed her legs apart roughly in a frenzy of need. Undid his trousers. Tugged her thong out of the way. Holding her gaze, he entered her in a deep thrust that spoke of his desperate hunger rather than finesse.

Her wet heat clamped him tight, and Nate clenched his jaw to keep the words from spilling out.

Her legs wrapped around his hips; her spine bucked off the bed. She groaned and scratched his biceps with her nails as he pounded into her, only the haze of his approaching climax driving him. He touched the swollen bud at her core, glistening with moisture, calling for his touch.

She exploded around him and he thrust harder, faster, riding the wave of her release, forever changed by her.

His chest still expanding and contracting, he gathered her in his arms and rolled, until she was on top of him. But this time, she shied her gaze away from him and he wondered if she was bracing for his caustic words again. Cursed himself for changing her.

Running his fingers through her silky hair, he pressed a kiss to her temple. Tasted the sweat and scent of her skin. She was all around him, and it was the one place Nate never wanted to leave.

It was a place of belonging, it was home, it was what he

had always wanted in the corners of the heart that he had ruthlessly locked away.

Now, when his heart had found the woman it couldn't have but wanted with so much longing, he knew he would never again look at another woman as a man did.

Because he, Nathaniel Ramirez, apparently was a one-woman man. And he resigned himself to it.

If he couldn't have her, he didn't want anyone. With the realization came desperate need. Tugging her toward him, he pushed her onto her stomach. Breathlessly waited to see if she would protest. Turning her face toward the side, the minx smiled at him. "I'm yours tonight, Nate. To do with as you please."

With a hand under her body, he tugged her up until she was on her hands and knees. Splaying his palm on her lower back, he kissed along the line of her spine. Found the bundle of nerves that was already wet and slick for him.

He plunged his fingers into her and stroked the swollen tissue, a guttural sound escaping him. Felt the shudder that racked her. Bending down, he licked the rim of her ear. "Do you want me to stop, Riya?"

"No, please, Nate. Don't."

And that was all he needed. Holding her hips, he thrust into her. Felt stars explode behind his eyes, felt his body buckle at the waves of sensation.

There was no gentleness left in him. No honor, no control. Only excruciating love for the woman beneath him. It took him every ounce of will he possessed to wait for her before he let his climax take over his body.

Pulling out of her, he turned her face to find her mouth.

The spasms of her climax still rocking through her, Riya shivered, a cold dread pooling in her chest. With his explosive lovemaking, Nathan imprinted himself onto every inch of her, and she felt as if she were drowning in the wake of it.

"Did I hurt you, Riya?" Dragging her close until her skin was slick against his, he pressed his mouth over her temple in a reverent touch. Laced his fingers with hers so tight that a stinging heat rose behind her eyes.

Flushing, Riya shook her head.

"Please, Riya, look at me."

"I'm fine. I just…I think I should go now."

With panting breaths, Riya willed the panic and pain rising through her to abate.

She had meant to say goodbye, thought doing so would give her closure. How could she have left without his touch, his kiss, without feeling his tightly leashed control fray around her one more time? Without feeling the closeness she felt when he made love to her, without feeling the raw edge of his emotion seek her, need her? It was the one time she felt cherished, loved, the one time she felt as though she mattered.

And now she had only dug herself deeper.

She couldn't break down now. If she did she would only end up begging him for another second, another minute, another hour. Of him holding her, kissing her, losing himself in her, of wondering if just another night would make him want her, of eviscerating hope that he would ask her to come with him.

Because another night or a hundred of them wouldn't change him, wouldn't make him care for her. Just as she had a sinking feeling only a lifetime with Nathan would be enough for her. And she couldn't let him see how much he had hurt her. She couldn't bear it if he told her in ruthless words that she was naive and a fool and that he had warned her.

Pushing away from him, she wrapped the sheet around

her nakedness. Picked up the dress she'd discarded in such passion. Padded to the bathroom and splashed water over her face. Swallowed the sharp knot in her throat and sucked in a deep breath.

Even the silky glide of the dress over her skin felt like too much sensation to her hyped-up senses.

Keeping her spine straight, she walked back into the bedroom. Instantly her gaze sought and found him, standing at the French doors, looking up at the sky. It was the darkest of the night, just before dawn. He turned just as she found her clutch.

"Riya, before you go, I know someone in Bali who can—"

"No. I don't want your help. I'd like to get going now," she said, and walked toward the door.

He didn't move or speak. Only stared at her, with that utter stillness of his. His gaze devoured her, a maelstrom of emotions in it.

"Goodbye," she whispered, and turned the knob.

But something in her wouldn't calm down. Adrenaline spiking through her, she felt as if she were standing on a cliff.

"Are you ever coming back, Nathan?" When his mouth tightened, she hurried. "Not for me, don't worry. I know that in the scheme of things I matter very little to you. But for Robert, are you ever going to come back?"

She wished he would lie, wished she could believe him if he did.

"No."

Her stomach lurched, like the time it had on that fantastic ride with him. Only this time, he wasn't going to hold her through it. He was going to let her fall and shatter.

"Dad knows that I won't return." He closed the distance between them, something shimmering in his gaze. "Riya, my leaving has nothing to do with you. Don't make this harder than it has to be."

His words were a soft whisper, but the blaze of emotion in his eyes was unmistakable. And the evidence of his emotion birthed her anger, and it flew through her, an anchor in the drowning storm of hurt and fear.

"Has it become that easy for you, Nathan? Have you become that much of a bastard? Or are you just blind to what you have become?"

His chin reared back as though she had pummeled him with her fists. "I've always warned you that—"

"I know that you have Long QT syndrome like your mom. I know that you fainted and almost died when you were thirteen. I know that that night in the lounge, you almost fainted again. I know that you've cut out every ounce of emotion to survive, that you don't want to go…" Her voice broke. "…go like your mother did. But do you believe you're truly living your life, Nathan?"

"Get out, Riya."

Riya smiled through the tears blurring her vision. They had come full circle. "No, I won't. You pushed the truth on me when I wanted nothing to do with it. You made me hurt, made me feel so much for the first time."

"I already know my truth, butterfly. I've lived with it for more than a decade."

"You think you've conquered your weakness, but you're hiding behind it. You think love makes you weak. You think it'll rid you of your control, leave you at its mercy. You think it will leave you with nothing but fear for yourself and for the ones you love… But you're not your mother, Nathan.

"When I think of what you've achieved, the depth of your generosity…you've allowed yourself everything but happiness. How is it courage if you let it dictate how you live your life? How is it life if it has to be without love?

"You pushed me out of my comfort zone. You made me realize what a sterile life I'd built for myself. When my mother told me about you, I was devastated. I was so scared, Nate. In that moment, if I could erase ever knowing you, I probably would have."

He moved then. Grabbed her arms and hauled her to him. It was like being pulled into a whirlpool of roiling emotions. Like being sucked into the heart of a tornado. "If it scared you so much, then why did you come?"

"I came to say goodbye," Riya said, losing the fight. "I fought the fear that was roiling through me and came to see you. I came despite it, Nathan." She pressed a kiss to his jaw and released the words that she was courageous enough to speak. She knew now he would always plan to leave. But it didn't have to be today. "Tell me not to leave. Ask me to come with you."

Tugging her hands away, he let her go and stepped back. And Riya knew he was putting her out of his mind. "One day, you'll thank me for not taking you up on your offer, butterfly. One day when you find the man who'll love you forever, you'll be glad I left."

CHAPTER TWELVE

Three months later

RUNNING A HAND through his overgrown hair, Nathan waited as the cardiologist checked his heartbeat. It was always hard for him to sit still and even harder when it was this routine checkup.

His chopper was waiting on the roof of the hospital in a remote area of the island of Java. He had stopped seeing world-renowned specialists a long time ago. From day one, he had accepted that there was nothing to be done.

The doctor, who was seeing him for the first time, examined Nathan with warm brown eyes. "You're in remarkably good shape for a man with your condition, Mr. Ramirez," he said in perfect but accented English. "But I guess you know that. Just keep doing what you're doing."

Nathan nodded and thanked him.

"Your next checkup is in—"

"A month," Nathan finished for him.

Thanking the doctor, he was buttoning up his shirt when his cell phone rang. Seeing the face of his virtual manager, he switched it on. "Yes?"

Jacob sounded wary. "Those papers have come back unsigned again."

Nathan caught the fury that rose through him. It wasn't

Jacob's fault. It was that manipulative minx's. What the hell kind of game was she playing? Why was she bent on tormenting him? "From where?"

"From Bali again." So she still hadn't returned. "And there was no reply to our lawyer's question about what she wants."

It had been the same for the last three months. He would send the papers to her and she would send them back, unsigned. Without a reply.

Nathan clenched his teeth, the emptiness he had been fighting for months sucking him in. "Find her number for me."

A few minutes later, Nathan punched in her number and waited. His heart leaped into his throat, his pulse ringing very much like the peal of the phone on the other line.

"Hello?" her voice came across the line, and his stomach lurched. Just hearing her voice was enough to drive him into that crazed, out-of-control need to see her, to touch her, to hold her close, to wake up to her face.

"Hello?"

Stepping back from the sunshine, Nate leaned against the brick wall. Took a deep breath. "Why the hell aren't you signing the papers, Riya? What do you want now?"

The line was silent for a few seconds. And her face popped up in his mind's eye, her expression stricken as she had left him that night.

"I... Nate, how are you?"

"I'm alive, Riya." He heard her gasp and ignored it. At least now there was no need to pretend. "And if I weren't, you would be the first one to—"

"Bastard."

This time, he laughed, chose again to ignore the cutting pain packed into the single word. "Cut the theatrics and tell me why you're refusing to sign away the estate."

"I decided that it should be mine. That I don't want to part with it, after all."

Disbelief roared in his ears. And he let a curse fly. "Have you finally decided to listen to your mother, then?"

"I figured it was mine every which way it counted," she continued smoothly, as though he hadn't just insulted her and *this thing between them*, as though she wasn't tying him up in knots.

"And how did you come to that impossible conclusion?"

"Robert, who's my father as far as I'm concerned, deeded it to me with love. I'm strong enough to accept my right over it now. Of course, that's thanks to you. And more than that, I figured it was mine because it belonged to the man I love with all my heart."

He felt as if a fist had jammed up into his chest. He couldn't breathe as her words sank in. There was no hesitation in her voice. "You've lost your mind," he said, pushing the words out through a raw throat. "Gone over the edge."

"Actually it's the opposite. I've realized that my happiness is in my hands. Not Jackie's or Robert's or even yours. That I have to believe that I deserve love. That I have to risk pain to fight for it." Now she didn't sound that put together. "Admit it, Nate. If I asked you for it right now, you wouldn't fight me. You wouldn't deny me."

His butterfly was getting reckless, coming into her own. Despite the ache in his heart, he smiled. "Why would I do that?"

"Because you love me." She waited, as though she wanted him to feel the full impact of her outrageous announcement. "You can put thousands of miles between us, you can cut all connections from me, you might never even see me again. But you think about me all the time. That estate, that massive fortune of yours, that faulty but generous heart of yours…they are all mine."

"You sound very sure, Riya."

The sound of her laugh pierced through him. "I think I know you as well as I know myself now. I realized that I won't ever have to work a day in my life again and still live like a princess. Because one of the richest and the most wonderful man in the world...I belong to him now. How's that for security, huh?"

She sounded confident, even brazen, but he could imagine the tears in her eyes, her hands fisting at her sides as she forced the words past that beautiful mouth. "But the thing is, I would rather risk my heart for another moment with him than have all the security in the world." He heard her suck in a breath. "That estate is the best waiting place for me when I come back."

With every word she said, she was twisting his insides, unraveling him. And beneath his rules, his honor, his revulsion for fear, Nate saw something else. As if he had been sitting in the dark all this time, mistaking his cowardice for his guts.

He asked the question he knew he shouldn't. "Waiting for what?"

"For you to come home." The ache in her voice was as clear as the ache in his own heart. "For you to come back to me." And she was crying and unraveling, right along with him, even though there were thousands of miles between them.

He rubbed his eyes with his fingers, a stinging heat prickling behind them. Her words gouged a hole through the emptiness he felt. "That's never going to happen, butterfly. You're wasting your precious life. You want a stable life with a steadfast man who'll be with you for the rest of your life, remember? Me? I could be gone any time." His own cheeks were wet now and Nathan didn't feel ashamed or afraid, only ache.

"Yeah, well, you ruined all my plans for my life, Nate. Now I want something else."

"Yeah? What?"

"A decade, a year, a day, or even another moment with the man I adore. With the man who showed me how to live, and love. With the man I'll love for the rest of my life."

He heard her grasping breath, the catch in her voice. Heard her tear-soaked voice as if she were looking at him with those beautiful brown eyes.

"I love you, Nate, with every breath in me. I have been a coward all my life. I was a coward even that night. I let you walk away. But not anymore. I deserve happiness and so do you. My life is empty without you, Nate."

How he wanted to believe her; how he wished he had the courage to be the man she deserved. Because that was what he was lacking. Not the robust heart, not a body that would live for a century. But the courage to grab the love she offered, to trust her love and his, to risk his heart.

Whatever it was that was holding him back now, protecting his heart, this was fear.

He was in that moment he had dreaded his whole life. Fear and pain. And yet it was of not seeing Riya ever again, of not waking up to her, of not seeing her wide mouth split into a smile at the sight of him, of not holding her tight until they couldn't breathe.

"I'm waiting for you, Nate." She was crying now, in soft sobs and broken words. And the pain that caused him was more than any he had ever felt, hurt deeper than any other fear that he didn't want to feel.

"I think I'll always wait for you."

And then she hung up.

Riya sank to her bed in her hotel room, her breaths coming jerkily. Grabbing the edge of the T-shirt she had taken from Nate that night, she buried her face in it. Every inch of her was still vibrating at hearing his voice. Her fingers hurt with how tightly she had fisted them, how she wanted to touch him, feel his arms around her.

Had he known that she was falling apart? How much it had cost her to say what was truly in her heart, even knowing that it might never change his mind? How big a risk she had taken by binding herself to him, by giving him her heart?

But to this new Riya whom he had brought to life, nothing less than what she wanted, what she deserved was acceptable.

Without him, nothing in the world meant anything to her.

CHAPTER THIRTEEN

NATHAN FOUND HER a month later on a beach in Ubud, Bali, in one of the villas RunAway owned, sitting on the deck that offered spectacular views of rolling hills and valleys. The villa was the utmost in privacy and comfort. It perched atop a valley overlooking a lush river gorge.

It had been his very own slice of paradise. When Jacob told him that a request had come in from his property manager that a woman named Riya *Ramirez*, who'd claimed to be his close friend, had wanted to use it, he had laughed for a full minute. The woman was relentless, stubborn, manipulative, and he loved her for all of it.

And yet, with the setting sun casting golden shadows on her striking face, it was loneliness that enveloped her now. And it clawed at his heart.

It had taken him three weeks to consolidate his worldwide holdings, to find and hire efficient managers where he needed, to fight the voice that whispered *no* every second of the day.

But there had also been one that kept counting the time down, telling him that he had wasted enough as it was. And he realized, if he had lived without fear, he had also lived without joy for too long.

Once he had decided, it had taken him a week to find her, and every minute of waiting to hear more had been excruciating. Until the stubborn woman herself had sent him a clue.

Did she love him that much? Would she have stopped at nothing until she got through to him? Could he always prove himself worthy of it?

Feeling a knot of anxiety, he clenched and unclenched his fingers.

She was dressed in a sleeveless, floral dress that rippled around her knees with the breeze.

"Riya?" he said, unable to say anything else past the emotion clogging his throat.

She was off the lounging chair and deck before he could blink. Standing before him with her hair flying in her face before he could draw another breath. Her chest falling and rising, her mouth pinched.

And the love in her eyes undid Nathan as nothing had ever done. "I love you, butterfly," he said, and she swayed, a gasp falling from her lips. Threw herself into his arms like a gale of wind. Knocked the breath out of him, knocked him off his feet.

He buried his mouth in her neck, filling himself with the scent of her.

Her arms wound around him so tight that he laughed. Pulling her head back, she glared at him. "I'm never letting you go, ever. You even talk about leaving me again and I'll chain you to myself." A shudder swept through her in direct contrast to the bravado in her words.

"I love you so much, Nate. I've missed you so much. Every day, every night, wherever I want, I thought about you. It hurt so much that I wanted it to stop for a while. It felt like—"

"Like you were missing an essential part of yourself?" he said, and she nodded.

He tasted her in a rough kiss, needing the fortification,

needing tangible proof of her taste. She clung to him with just as much desperation.

"Do you know what you're signing up for, butterfly?" he said, when his desperation had blunted, when his heart beat normally again. When the shadow of a lifelong fear clasped him tight. "It would kill me much sooner to see—"

Her palm closed over his mouth and she shook her head. "I do feel fear, and sometimes I can't breathe thinking of this world without you. But I'd rather fight that fear every day than live another moment without you. I'll do it, Nate. I'll only ever try to be your strength. And all I ask is that you give me the chance. To love you, to be loved by you, for as long as possible, that's all I want."

Clasping her hand in his, he dragged her to the edge of the deck and looked out into the valley and beyond. Turned her toward him and dropped onto his knees.

"I love you, Riya, with every breath in my body, with every beat of my faulty heart. I was so lonely before I met you. I thought I was protecting you by walking away. When you called me, when you so bravely put into words what you felt for me...to hear you say what I felt for you, to hear you tell me you chose to love me even as you were afraid, it made me realize I wasn't living, merely existing. You've taught me what it is to be brave, butterfly."

Riya kissed him, tears stinging her cheeks. Running her hands over him greedily, she clung to him, fear and joy all bubbling inside her. Her biggest risk had paid off and her heart stuttered in her chest. "All I want is to be by your side for the rest of our lives."

His eyes shining with unshed tears, he kissed her temple. "Will you be my wife, butterfly? Will you tie yourself to me, then?"

Riya nodded, the small doubt in his tone doing nothing to abate the intensity of her own love. He had come for her;

he had shown her his heart. It didn't mean years of protecting himself from fear and hurt would be gone this very second. But she was strong enough for both of them. "Yes."

He dragged her into the cradle of his arms, his lean frame shuddering. "That's the sweetest word I've ever heard, Riya."

For the first time in his life, Nathan felt joy, and he felt complete. With the woman he loved with him, there was no place for fear.

Only love and utter happiness for the rest of his days.

EPILOGUE

One year later

HIS BREATH HITCHING in his throat, every inch of him thrumming with anticipation, Nathan turned around and froze.

With the blue sea and white sand as her background, Riya stilled beneath the arch that was decorated with sheer white lilies and cream-colored silk.

Her gaze met his, her mouth wreathed in a shy smile; she was waiting to see his reaction, he realized.

The red sheer silk sari she wore wound around her striking figure, baring her midriff, inviting his touch. When he had looked at the huge yard of the material and frowned a week ago, she had patiently and laughingly explained to him how it worked, and how much fun she was having with her aunt teaching her how to wear it.

And that she was learning it for him, she had said with a wink.

He was glad she did.

The silk draped over her left shoulder and hung behind her, hiding and showcasing her beautiful body. Her long hair flew in the breeze, but it was the glittering expression in her eyes that arrested him.

He couldn't breathe when he remembered her tears when they'd learned that her father had passed away a few years before they'd tracked him down. He had held her all night, her pain as much as his. And the smile in her eyes, when he'd told her about the aunt his PI had located… the only blood relative of her father still alive.

All his wealth and power, he had truly appreciated it that day. For it had brought such happiness to the woman he loved.

He mouthed, *I love you* and tears shimmered in her gaze as she walked toward him.

Her heart racing as if toward some invisible goal, Riya rubbed her fingers over her face. She blew out a breath, a shadow of fear marring her perfect day.

Beneath the cliff on top of which the villa sat, the sea was dark blue, the horizon where the sky met the sea not visible. It was the most beautiful place she had ever seen.

The wedding on the beach had been her dream come true. Robert, Jackie and her aunt, and the staff from the estate, Riya had never felt more loved or cherished.

And in between all of it was the man she loved.

It had taken all these months for Nathan to believe that she truly wanted this—that she wouldn't change her mind, that she would never stop loving him, that she would never let herself be driven by fear.

And now the truth she had realized just this morning.

Wrapping her arms around herself, she battled both excitement and fear.

She turned when the door of the main bedroom in the villa closed with a soft thud.

Nathan stood leaning against the door, and the raw heat in his eyes instantly sent an answering tremble through her. She wondered if she was betraying herself, if the small thing she had learned this morning was written on her face.

"I don't want you to wear a sari again."

"What?" She ran her hands over the silky folds, distracted by his expression. "You don't like it?"

"As your husband, I command you not to wear it in public," he added with a possessive glint in his eye, and she laughed.

"I've been waiting to say that since I saw you walking down toward me."

He caught the edge that trailed over her shoulder with one hand and tugged hard. And the silky soft material came undone around her and ripped at her waist.

He tugged until Riya was caught in his arms.

"You look utterly gorgeous and scandalously sexy in it. And I don't want any other man but me to see that."

He buried his mouth in the curve of her neck, his hands settling around her bare midriff. "Nate, wait, I want to—"

"It's all I've been wanting to do since I saw you, Riya. Please don't deny me."

Forgetting her own words, she pushed into him and sank her fingers in his hair.

As he whispered words that made her core pulse with spiraling need, his long fingers climbing up her midriff toward her breasts encased snugly in the blouse.

He groaned and pulled the hooks that held it together with a strong tug and Riya gasped as she heard the blouse rip at the hooks. With impatient fingers, he pushed the cups of her bra down.

She shuddered as his abrasive palms covered her breasts, the aching, tight nipples rasping against the roughness. Rubbing her buttocks against his hard body, Riya loosened the petticoat and let it pool at her feet.

His palms moved over her waist and then her thighs. When he picked her up and placed her on an exquisitely crafted sofa table, she laughed and gave herself over to the dark passion lighting up his eyes.

Their lovemaking was swift, desperate, coated with the awareness that they were now joined in the holiest of bonds, exalted by the promises they had made to each other. Sweat cooling on her forehead, she leaned her head against his chest, the superfast rhythm of his heart comforting under her palms.

She kissed the taut skin of his pectorals, breathing in the musky scent of him.

"You always do that," he said, his words a gravelly rasp against her senses.

Looking up, she smiled, her arms still around him. "What do you mean?"

He pushed sweaty tendrils of hair that stuck to her forehead. "Check my heart. Every time after we make love, you put your face to my chest as though you want to—"

Shaking her head, she put her fingers over his mouth. "I'm sorry, I didn't even realize that I did that. I didn't mean to make you feel—"

He laughed and swallowed the rest of her words in a sizzling kiss. "These last few months have been the happiest of my life. Every day, I can't imagine this is my life. I can't believe that I walked away from this. If you hadn't fought for me, for our love…" He sighed against her mouth, a shudder racking through him. "I love you, Riya. I love that you'll forever be mine and I yours."

An ache rose in Riya's throat at his words. Her gorgeous, powerful man never let a day pass without telling her how much he loved her, without showing her how precious she was to him. But they were both still so new to this. He was only now getting used to having her around after living alone for so long.

Underneath that easy humor, there was still a self-sufficiency that wouldn't leave so easily. But he made an effort for her and Riya was so glad for it.

Hiding her face in his chest, Riya gathered the courage to say the words. "Nathan, I have to tell you something."

"What is it, butterfly?"

"I realized yesterday that…I…we've been traveling so much and I lost track of…"

He lifted her chin, his gaze curious. "What's bothering you?"

"I took a pregnancy test this morning, and it's… I'm pregnant, Nate."

Shock flitted in his eyes, cycled to concern. "I don't know what to say."

Riya felt the happiness of her day pop.

"Riya, I know this isn't what we had planned. I mean, we didn't really even plan anything, did we? But, my little butterfly, that's how you came into my life, didn't you?" He tugged her toward him and hugged her so tight that Riya thought she would break under the avalanche of his love. Yet when he spoke, there was a restraint in his voice. "I know it's scary when we're so new to each other. I know that having a child is a huge thing, but, Riya—"

Riya pushed at his shoulders and studied his gaze. He was holding back his reaction for her. She pulled his hands to her stomach and spoke past the raw ache in her throat.

"Please, Nate. Will you be honest with me about this?"

He nodded and clasped her cheek. "It's the perfect gift you could have given me today. You'll have me every step of the way. You—"

And that was when Riya understood. And she laughed and hugged him tight, kissed his face. Looked into his beautiful blue gaze.

"Nathan, you and I made this. We created this with our love. Can you imagine anything more beautiful or wonderful in this world? It's true I'm afraid, I'm nowhere near ready or equipped to be a mom, but if you're with me, I can do anything. Tell me you want this just as much as I do. Tell me you want this baby."

Tears pooled in his beautiful blue gaze and he kissed her again. Now it was he who trembled and Riya hugged him hard to herself. "I do want this, Riya. I'll always want anything you bring into my life, butterfly."

* * * * *

THE SINNER'S
SECRET

KIRA SINCLAIR

There would be no *Bad Billionaires* without my amazing editor, Stacy Boyd. She believed in me and this project from the very beginning. I'm grateful for her support, guidance and vision that helped make this series amazing. Thank you, Stacy!

One

The last two weeks had been surreal, culminating in this moment. Blakely Whittaker stood behind her new desk, staring at the persistent log-in screen waiting for her to input something on her standard-issue laptop.

She had no idea what to do next.

A box of personal belongings waited in her car, which was parked in the basement deck. There was a folder of HR paperwork that Becky had handed her after a quick tour of the building. Blakely should probably read it all.

But her body wouldn't move. Instead, her head kept swiveling between the closed door of her own private office and the huge windows at her back with a view of the city.

A far cry from the dingy, cramped cubicle she'd called home for the last few years.

The people here were so different, too. Everyone she'd encountered, from Finn DeLuca—the charismatic guy who'd approached her about the job—to the receptionist and HR staff had been upbeat, personable and genuinely happy. A huge shift from the depressed, downtrodden lot she'd been working with.

Sure, it was a nice change. One she'd desperately needed, along with the raise that came with her new position as lead accountant for Stone Surveillance.

But something about the whole thing felt off.

Which was why she was still standing, unwilling to take a seat in the very expensive and, no doubt, very comfortable chair waiting beside her.

Blakely could hear the voices in her head—sounding strangely like her parents—fighting like an angel and a devil. Her mother on one shoulder, wary, practical, cynical, warning her that if something looked too good to be true then it most likely was. And her father on the other, eternally optimistic, opportunistic and not to mention criminally inclined, telling her that if someone wanted to give her the world, it was her obligation to take it and run before they figured out their mistake.

Which left her stuck in the middle, a product of both and often paralyzed by indecision.

No, that wasn't true. The decision had already been made. She was here, in her new office, which meant the only path was forward. After pulling out the chair, Blakely dropped into it and let out a deep sigh when her assumptions were confirmed. The thing was real leather. Hell, her last chair squeaked every time she stood up and the underside of the cushion had been held together by duct tape. And not the cute, decorative kind.

Opening the manila folder, she began reading through the packet of information on company policies, leave accrual and insurance plans. She was halfway through when the door to her office opened.

She expected to see Becky walking back in to give her more information, or maybe IT bringing her log-in info so she could access her computer.

But that wasn't who'd come in.

Blakely's belly rolled and her skin flushed hot as she took in the man lounging, bigger than some Greek god, against the now-closed door. Unfortunately, no matter what she thought of him personally, her physical reaction to Gray Lockwood had always been the same. Immediate, overwhelming, bone-deep awareness.

Today, that familiar and unwanted response mixed with a healthy dose of "what the hell?"

Because the last person she expected to saunter into her brand-new office was the man she'd sent to prison eight years ago.

"Bastard."

Gray Lockwood had been called much worse in his life, and probably deserved it.

Hell, he deserved it today, although not for the reasons Blakely Whittaker assumed. She no doubt thought he was a bastard for the past, which he wasn't. He *was* a bastard for maneuvering her into a corner today, though. Unfortunately for her, she hadn't fully realized just how tight a space she was in.

But she was about to learn.

"Is that any way to greet your new boss?"

Incredulity, anger, resentment and, finally, understanding washed across Blakely's face. Gray wanted to be thrilled with the reality he'd just crashed down over her head—like the farce that had rained down over his, the one she'd been an integral part of.

But none of the satisfaction he'd expected materialized.
Dammit.

It was wholly inconvenient. Especially since he still wasn't certain whether Blakely had been an unwitting participant in the deception that had landed his ass in jail, or a willing partner in the fraud.

Eight years ago, he'd been aware of Blakely Whittaker. She was an employee at Lockwood Industries. He'd passed her in the halls a time or two. Seen her in meetings. Been attracted to her in the same distracted way he'd regarded most beautiful things in his life back then.

All that changed the day he sat across from her in a courtroom and listened as she systematically laid out the concrete evidence against him. Blakely had provided the prosecution with a smoking gun.

One he'd never pulled the trigger on. Although, he hadn't been able to prove that. Then.

He still couldn't prove that now, but he was bound and determined to find a way to exonerate himself. It didn't matter that he'd already paid for a crime he never committed. He wanted to get back his good name and the life he'd had before.

And Blakely was going to help him do it, even if she wasn't aware that's why she'd been hired by Anderson Stone as the newest employee at Stone Surveillance.

Stone and Finn had both asked Gray why he was pursuing the investigation. He'd served his time for the embezzlement and was free to live his life. He had enough money in the bank to do anything he wanted—or nothing at all.

Before he'd been convicted, he hadn't given a damn about the family company. And, yes, it stung like hell that his family had disowned him. His father had barred him from Lockwood and refused to speak to him. His mother pretended she never had a son. But he'd learned to live with those facts.

Back then, he hadn't much cared what people thought of him. He'd been lazy, uncaring, spoiled and entitled. Prison had changed him. Connecting with Stone and Finn on the inside had changed him. Now, it bothered him that people whispered behind his back.

Mostly because he hadn't done a damn thing wrong. He might have been a bastard, but he was a law-abiding one.

Blakely shot up from the chair behind her desk. "I work for Anderson Stone and Finn DeLuca."

"No, you work for Stone Surveillance. Stone and Finn are two of the three owners. I happen to be the third."

"No one told me that."

"Because they were instructed not to."

Blakely's mouth set into the straight, stubborn line he'd seen several times. She might be petite, gorgeous and blonde, but she could be a pit bull when she wanted to be. He'd seen her determination firsthand. And not just in the courtroom, when she'd hammered the last nail in his coffin.

He'd watched her in meetings, impassioned about some piece of information she felt to be important. The way her skin flushed pink and her eyes flashed… Gorgeous, enticing and entertaining.

But she was also the kind of woman who placed that same passion into everything. And back then, Gray had been too lazy to want to take on that kind of intensity.

He'd appreciated it from afar, though.

Reaching into a drawer, Blakely pulled out her purse and looped the strap over her shoulder. "Why would you hire me? You hate me."

Gray shook his head, a half smile tugging at his lips. "*Hate* is such a strong word."

"I helped put you in prison. *Hate*'s probably the correct word."

"I wouldn't stake my life on it." Because as much as he wanted to hate the woman standing just feet away from him, he couldn't seem to do it.

Oh, sure, she was an easy target for all of his blame. And, it was still possible—no, probable—that she was up to her eyeballs in the mess that had taken him down. But he wasn't going to learn the truth without her. And she wasn't likely to help him if she thought he blamed her.

"No? What word would you use then?"

Gray tipped his head sideways and studied her for several seconds. "I'll admit, you're not my favorite person. However, I'm not sure you deserve my hate any more than I deserved to be sent to prison."

Blakely scoffed. The sound scraped down his spine, but her reaction wasn't unexpected.

Shaking her head, Blakely scooted around her desk and headed for the doorway. Gray shifted, moving his body between her and the exit.

She stopped abruptly, trying to avoid touching him. Gray didn't miss the way she flinched. Or the way her hand tightened over the strap of her purse.

Smart woman.

Gray had spent the last several years biding his time. Not to mention beating other prisoners in an underground fighting ring that Stone, Finn and he had built. He'd needed a physical outlet, one that didn't constantly land him in solitary.

Those fights had taught him to measure and watch his opponents. To pick up on the subtle physical cues that telegraphed a thought before it became action.

Although, Blakely's intentions were far from subtle. She wanted out of this room and away from him.

Too bad for her.

They were going to be spending a lot of time together in the coming weeks.

"Get out of my way."

The way her eyes flashed fire caused an answering heat that sparked in the pit of Gray's belly. There was something enticing and intriguing about her show of bravado. Even if he didn't want to be impressed.

Gray let his lips roll up into a predatory smile. His gaze swept down her body. It was damn hard not to take in the tempting curves. The way her skirt clung to her pert ass and how the jacket she'd paired it with cinched in at her tiny waist.

A part of him wanted to refuse. To see what she'd do if he pushed a few buttons. Would she put her hands on him? Would his body react with a physical rush at the contact?

Not smart to play that game. Instead of standing his ground, Gray slid sideways, clearing a path for her to exit.

Because he didn't need his body to stop her.

"You're welcome to leave anytime, Blakely."

Her eyes narrowed as she watched him. "Thank… you," she said, her words slow, as if she was sensing danger, but was clearly unable to identify the jaws of the trap.

He let her get one step forward before he hit the pin.

"Although, it isn't like you have anywhere to go. I've taken the liberty of informing your former employer of some questionable activity I recently discovered."

"What questionable activity? I've done nothing questionable."

"Of course you haven't, but that's not what the evidence suggests."

Blakely sputtered, her mouth opening and closing several times before she finally whispered, "Bastard."

"You've already said that. Doesn't feel real great to have lies used against you, huh? Either way, you have no job to go back to. And we both know how difficult it was to find that one after being released from Lockwood."

Blakely's skin flushed hot and her ice-blue eyes practically glowed with fury. God, she was gorgeous when she was pissed.

"What do you want?" she growled. "Is this payback?"

In an effort to keep from doing something stupid, Gray crossed his arms over his chest. "Hardly. I want your help in proving my innocence."

"I can't do that."

"Because you're unwilling?"

Her voice rose in frustration. "No, because you're hardly innocent."

"Maybe you're wrong, Blakely. Have you considered that at all?"

"Of course I have," she yelled, leaning forward and punctuating the words with indignation. "Do you know how many nights I've lain awake, wondering? But I'm not wrong. The numbers and evidence don't lie. I saw proof, with my own eyes, that you embezzled millions of dollars from Lockwood's accounts."

"You saw what someone wanted you to see." Or what she'd maneuvered so that everyone else would see.

"I'm leaving. I'll find another job."

"Sure you will…eventually. But the question is, will you find it here in Charleston or in time to pay your sister's tuition? Or cover the mortgage payment for your mom? Or, hell, your own car payment? It's a little difficult to get a job if you can't drive to an interview."

"Bastard."

"Maybe you should invest in a thesaurus. The job here is real, Blakely. And despite everything, I'm fully aware that you're an excellent accountant. We want you to work for the company. We simply want you to accept another assignment before you begin that work. And we'll pay you handsomely for both."

"For how long?"

"What?"

"How long do I have to work at proving your innocence? Because I think this could turn into a never-ending story."

Gray watched her. It wasn't an unfathomable request. In fact, Finn had asked him much the same question. How long was Gray willing to put his entire life on hold to chase a ghost of a possibility?

"Six weeks."

Blakely growled in the back of her throat. Scrunched her nose up in distaste. And then said, "Fine," before walking out.

Blakely had no idea where she was going…but she needed to get away from Gray before she did something stupid.

Like start to believe him.

Or worse, give in to the invisible tether that pulled her to him whenever the man walked into a room.

The ladies' room down the hall offered her an escape.

The man was walking, talking sin. And always had been. He'd carried the reputation of being hell-bent on pleasure for pleasure's sake. Sex, adrenaline, fast cars and the jet-setting lifestyle.

Gray Lockwood's picture would appear next to the word *sinner* in the dictionary.

Seriously, it wasn't fair. The man had hit the lottery when he'd been born. And not just because he'd been part of a prominent Southern family with good breeding and lots of money. His parents had passed on some amazing genes.

The man was gorgeous, and he knew it. Eight years ago, the most important decision she'd ever seen Gray make was choosing which of the women throwing themselves at him that he would take to bed. He had a confident demeanor, an outgoing attitude and Greek-god good looks.

Sure, Blakely had found him attractive, as did every other female in his vicinity. But he'd been easy to resist because he'd been ungrounded, spoiled and entitled. The man had thrown around money like he was playing *Monopoly*. He had a reputation for buying expensive cars just to drive them fast and crash them. He'd loved to party and had been known for paying for twenty people to have a wicked week in Vegas or Monaco or Thailand. And during the trial, the prosecution had brought into evidence that he'd racked up millions in gambling debts.

Now, he was…different.

The beautiful body had been hardened, probably by some time in the prison gym if she had to guess. And she'd been hard-pressed to miss the puckered skin of a scar running down his left eyebrow into the corner of his deep green eye. Somehow, the imperfection made him even more appealing. Before, Gray Lockwood had been too perfect.

But the biggest change was in his demeanor. While he still had the ability to command any room he walked into, his force was quieter.

The question was, could she work with him for the next six weeks without either wanting to kill him or being tempted to run her hands down his solid body? Or, even more, could she work on a project she didn't believe in simply for money?

She had no doubt, then and now, Gray Lockwood had plenty of secrets to hide. She'd uncovered one and it had derailed her life. Did she really want to risk uncovering more?

Blakely groaned, rubbing her hands down her face before washing them. Leaning over the sink, she stared hard into her own reflection. She'd spent her entire adult life doing the right thing. Because integrity was important to her. As someone raised by a criminal and con artist…you either joined the family business or became straighter than an arrow.

Watching her father bounce in and out of jail her entire childhood, that decision had been a no-brainer. She despised people who took the easy way out—anyone who took advantage of others' weaknesses or misfortunes. As far as she was concerned, Gray Lockwood was the worst kind of criminal.

Because he hadn't needed the money he'd embezzled.

Sure, he'd owed some nasty bookie a few million. But his net worth had been close to a billion. A lot of that wealth had been tied up in assets, but instead of liquidating, he'd decided to dip his hands into the family cookie jar. Probably because the spoiled rich boy thought he'd been entitled to it.

He'd never understood how taking that money had jeopardized the financial position of the company, not to mention the livelihood of all Lockwood Industries employees.

So the question was, could she spend the next six weeks pretending to work on a project she really didn't believe in, in exchange for a salary that she desperately needed?

A knot formed in the pit of her belly. It wasn't like she was lying to Gray. He knew full well she didn't believe him. He had to be aware she wouldn't exactly be the most motivated employee. Not to mention, he'd obviously maneuvered her here—which was something she'd have to talk with Anderson Stone and Finn DeLuca about, the assholes. So, really, she didn't owe Gray anything.

At the end of the day, the question was, could she go to sleep at night with a clear conscience if she stayed?

Today, the answer was yes. She might not like where she was standing, but she had no doubt Gray had backed up his statement and she'd have a hard time finding another job right now. He couldn't blackball her with every company in the country, so eventually she'd find something. But that might entail uprooting her life and moving. And while that didn't necessarily bother her, she couldn't do it right now.

Not when she was concerned her father was back to his old habits.

God, how had her life come to this?

Taking a deep breath, Blakely straightened her spine. She'd stay, take Gray's money and work the six weeks. At least that would give her a cushion to line up something else.

She pulled out a paper towel and dried her hands, then pushed open the door. Two strides out, she jolted to a stop.

She didn't even need to turn her head to know he was there. Her entire body reacted, a riot of energy crackling across her skin. So inconvenient.

Slowly, she turned her head, anyway. Arms crossed over his chest, Gray leaned casually against the wall right between the doors to the restrooms.

"Feel better now?"

Two

Blakely watched him with wary eyes. "No, not really."

He shrugged, dismissing her statement. Because it didn't matter. He wasn't really worried about her comfort.

"Follow me," he said, pushing off from the wall and striding past her. Her tempting scent slammed into him—it was something soft and subtle, but entirely her. Gray remembered it from before.

The one time he'd gotten close enough to pull her enticing scent deep into his lungs had involved a clash in the break room over some creamer he'd "borrowed" from her. After that, he'd purposely kept his distance. She was a vixen, and he'd had to fight the urge to shut down her tirade by kissing the hell out of her. Not smart.

Blakely might be beautiful, but she had a remote, standoffish manner about her. She'd been cordial with her coworkers, but not overly friendly. She wasn't one of the women invited to a girls' night out after work. Everyone appreciated her dedication. However, she didn't exactly give off warmth.

And back then, Gray hadn't just been looking for warm, he'd been looking for red-hot. With no strings. Everything about Blakely screamed serious.

So it hadn't mattered that he couldn't keep his gaze from tracking her whenever she walked down the hallways. Or that he would fall asleep with the phantom scent of her tickling his nose if they'd passed in the lobby.

Hell, he needed to get his head back in the game. Because now, Gray wasn't so certain that the wall she'd put up between herself and everyone else wasn't to hide her own nefarious intentions.

At the end of the hallway, Gray paused. He waited for her to decide what she was going to do. When the click of her heels sounded against the marble floor, he continued to the right.

"Where are we going?" she asked from several paces behind, in no hurry to catch up once she'd made her decision.

Without turning around, he answered, "I've got all the records from my trial in another office. You're going to walk me through the evidence you presented against me."

"Why? You were there in the courtroom."

Yes, he had been. Watching her every move. The way she'd tucked a golden strand of hair behind her ear each time she looked down at the documentation the prosecution was using against him. Or how the sharp tip of her pink tongue would swipe across her lips each time she needed to pause and gather her thoughts before answering.

Had those pauses been her organizing thoughts, or her making certain she told the right lies?

Turning into the empty office beside hers, Gray waited

until she brushed past him, then closed the door. "I sure was, but I didn't know then what I know now."

"And what do you know now?"

Oh, there were so many answers to that question. Most she wouldn't understand or appreciate. Several he had no intention of sharing with anyone, ever. But the only answer he was willing to give her right now was "Let's just say I used my time in prison to broaden my education."

Blakely made a buzzing noise in the back of her throat. "You're one of those."

"One of what?"

"People who go to jail and use the taxpayers' money to get an education they couldn't otherwise afford."

Wasn't that rich. "We both know I could—and did—afford a rather expensive Ivy League education before going to prison." He'd graduated from Harvard Business School. Sure, he'd barely made the cut and hadn't taken any of his classes seriously, but he had the damn degree.

"Little good it did you."

He wasn't going to refute that statement, mostly because he couldn't. "But, considering I'm innocent of the crime I was charged with and spent seven years imprisoned against my will because of it, the least the state owed me was an education in whatever I wanted."

"And what education was that?"

"I got a law degree."

"Of course you did."

At first, his plan was to figure out how to use his degree to help his own cause. Not surprising. However, it became obvious there wasn't much the legal system could do for him. His own attorneys filed every appeal possible, but they were all denied. Short of a call from the governor—not likely since the man had never liked Gray's father—that avenue wasn't going to help.

What he had used it for, though, was helping several of the inmates incarcerated with Stone, Finn and himself. Guys who might have been guilty, but had gotten screwed over or railroaded because they couldn't afford competent representation.

"That wasn't all I accomplished inside."

Blakely crossed her arms, her ice-blue eyes scraping up and down his body. "Oh, obviously."

Gray's lips twitched at her reaction. Her disdain was loud and clear. However, that didn't prevent heat from creeping into her cheeks or her nipples from peaking and pressing against the soft material of her shirt.

He wasn't stupid or oblivious to how women responded to him. He'd simply stopped taking advantage of the ones who shamelessly threw themselves at him. Funny how going without sex for seven years could make you appreciate it even more than having orgasms every day.

But he had no problem giving Blakely a hard time about her reaction. "And what, exactly, do you mean by that, Ms. Whittaker?"

"You know."

Gray hummed, drawing out the low, slow sound. "No, I don't think I do."

Blakely rolled her eyes, then pursed her lips and glared at him. Gray waited, silent, his gaze boring into hers. So he was being slightly juvenile by enjoying the way she shifted uncomfortably under his scrutiny.

Finally, she answered, as he'd known she would if he waited long enough. "It's clear you hit the gym whenever you could."

"How is that?"

She waved her hand in front of him. "You're huge. Broader, more muscular, than you were before."

"I didn't realize you'd noticed my physique before."

The heat in her cheeks deepened. "You made damn sure every woman at Lockwood noticed you. You wallowed in the attention from every female you could snag."

"But not you."

"No, not me."

"Is that because you weren't interested or because I didn't indicate that I was?"

Blakely's jaw clenched and her molars ground together. He could practically hear the enamel cracking from here. This was fun, but not very productive for the work he needed to get out of her. He could hardly expect her to be cooperative if he kept taking digs.

Shaking his head, Gray moved farther into the room. "I'm sorry, that wasn't very professional of me."

"No, it wasn't," Blakely quickly agreed.

"Let's agree that whatever concerns or animosity we had in the past, we both need to set them aside in order to work together right now."

Her eyes narrowed. She was damn smart and had no doubt picked up on the fact that he'd suggested they set them aside, not let them go. He wasn't ready to do that, not while he still questioned her role in the whole mess. Just as she wasn't likely to forget what she knew—or thought she knew—about him.

"Let's pretend we don't know anything about each other and start from square one."

She mumbled something under her breath that sounded suspiciously like "not likely." Gray decided to ignore it.

Pointing to a tower of seven cardboard boxes stacked in the corner of the room, he said, "Here's the data. I also have most of the files electronically, but we need any notes from the attorneys, as well. Why don't we start by tackling the information you presented on the stand and go from there?"

* * *

They'd started three days ago by going over the accounting records the prosecution had entered into evidence. The information she'd uncovered showed a pattern of behavior that had gone undetected for several months. Small amounts had been withdrawn daily from the operating accounts and transferred to a holding account. The amounts had been strategic, varied and below any threshold for automatic review or audit. The final two transactions were transfers of funds out of the company and into offshore accounts.

That first withdrawal was what had finally flagged Blakely's attention. Unfortunately, not until almost four weeks later, when she'd been performing her monthly audit.

The first twenty-million-dollar transfer to Gray's account had been flagged immediately since none of the proper paperwork had been completed. However, considering who was involved, Blakely just assumed he'd failed to follow protocol. At first. Once she'd started digging, she'd discovered a second transaction.

That transfer out had been different. On the surface, it had looked legitimate, with the proper documentation and supporting paperwork in the electronic files. But something about it had still felt wrong. Being a huge international organization, she wasn't always privy ahead of time to large transactions…but more often than not she was aware when the company made large lump-sum purchases.

If anyone else had been auditing, they might not have bothered to look deeper. But she hadn't been willing to let it go. It had taken her a while to pull the threads of the transactions to figure out what had really happened—and that the two transactions were connected.

What she hadn't understood then, and still didn't understand, was why Gray had covered his tracks on one withdrawal but not the other. It made no sense. Unless you took into consideration how lazy the man was. Maybe he just assumed no one would question his actions.

Blakely hadn't been impressed with Gray's work ethic and didn't care whose son he was. The man had stolen millions of dollars from the company. Money they hadn't been able to afford to lose.

She'd turned over the information, never realizing just how instrumental she'd become in the trial process. She'd been inside plenty of courtrooms in her life, all for her father. None of the experiences had been pleasant and neither was Gray's trial. She'd been nervous on the stand, not because she hadn't been confident about the information, but because she'd hated being the center of attention.

Reviewing the documents now brought back all of those emotions. She'd been on edge for days and it was wearing on her.

Or maybe that was being cooped up in an office with Gray. Any other time, she would have said the office was pretty spacious, but put a sexy six-foot-two, two-hundred-and-twenty-pound guy in there, too, and it turned into a closet with all the air vacuumed out.

Letting out a frustrated groan, Gray tossed a bound testimony transcript toward an open box. The sheaf of papers bounced off the edge and clattered to the floor. "I need a break."

Amen. "Okay," Blakely said, seriously hoping he'd leave for a while. Or the rest of the afternoon. Or the week.

Standing up, he put his hands at the small of his back

and leaned backward. The audible pop of his spine made Blakely shiver.

She tried to concentrate on the report in front of her. But it was damn hard not to notice every move he made. Each time Gray passed behind her chair, the tension in her body ratcheted higher. Her neck and shoulders ached with the struggle to ignore the physical awareness she really didn't want. Without thought, Blakely reached around and began pinching the muscles running up into her neck, hoping the knots would loosen.

They were starting to…until Gray brushed her hands out of the way and took over. The minute his grip settled onto her shoulders, Blakely bolted upright in her chair.

"Easy," he murmured. "Is this okay?"

Was it? Heat seeped into her skin. Her body tingled where he touched. Logically, Blakely knew she should say no. Move away. But she didn't want to and somehow found herself slowly nodding.

Gray's fingers dug deep into her muscles. At first, what he was doing hurt like hell…until her muscles started to relax and let go. Then it felt amazing.

Blakely was powerless to stop herself from melting beneath Gray's touch. Delicious heat spread from his fingers, down her shoulders and into her belly. A deep sigh leaked through her parted lips as she sagged against the back of her chair.

"God, you're so uptight."

"Don't ruin this," she groused.

"Admit it. You wouldn't know how to relax if someone gave you a flowchart."

"And you know nothing except how to relax."

Gray let out an incredulous chuckle, his grip on her shoulders tightening for a split second. "You know nothing about me." Then he dropped his hands.

Blakely bit back a cry of protest. Nope, she refused to beg him to touch her.

Scooting around her, Gray headed for the door. "I'm gonna go grab something to eat. Want me to get you something?"

It was well past lunchtime, but she'd been nose-deep in the report and hadn't noticed until now. At Gray's prompting, her stomach let out a growl loud enough for them both to hear.

A teasing smile tugged at the corners of his mouth. "I'll take that as a yes."

He was out the door before Blakely could tell him not to bother. Shrugging, she let him go, grateful for the reprieve so she could get herself back under control.

He'd needed to get out of there.

Never in his life had he gotten so hard from merely touching a woman's shoulders. Although, if he was going to be honest, his physical reaction to Blakely had little to do with actually touching her skin.

It had more to do with the way she'd softened beneath his hands. The way she'd relaxed, letting her head loll back against his belly. The soft sigh of pleasure and relief she'd made in the back of her throat. The way her eyes had slowly closed, as if savoring the sensations he was giving her.

If he hadn't left, he was going to embarrass himself. Or embarrass them both when she noticed his reaction. Food had been a quick, easy excuse.

He was two steps past Stone's office when his friend called out, "Gray."

He backed up, then pivoted inside.

"How's it going?"

There was no need to wonder what Stone was asking

about. The only case Gray was working on right now was his own. "Nowhere."

"I'm sorry, man. Is she cooperating?"

"Yeah." At first, Blakely had appeared to be shuffling papers around more than looking at them. But it hadn't taken her long to actually start reading and digging, which didn't surprise him. Blakely was the kind of woman who couldn't ignore a task once it was placed in front of her. She worked hard and did her absolute best no matter what.

"What are you going to do if there's nothing to find there?"

"Honestly? I have no idea. I mean, it's likely the files won't give us anything, but I have to look, anyway."

"I don't blame you."

"Joker's working his magic, too. Maybe he'll find something."

Their freelance hacker was one of the best on the east coast. Gray had cultivated an introduction through one of the guys he'd fought on the inside. He made damn sure not to ask what else Joker was working on because he didn't want to know. The guy had a reputation for being choosy about his projects and difficult to find.

"We can hope. Let me know if there's anything Finn or I can do."

Stone's offer was unnecessary since Gray already knew the two men would do anything he needed without question. But it was nice to hear, anyway. Especially when he had no one else in his corner.

"Thanks, man," he said, starting to back out of the office.

"A little advice?"

Gray paused, tilting his head and eyeing his friend.

"Don't be a dick," Stone said.

"What?"

His eyebrows rose. "She's gorgeous and I can practically see the sparks you two are striking from my office. You've spent too much time getting her here to screw it up simply because you haven't gotten laid since you've been out."

"I've gotten laid." Okay, that wasn't true. But he wasn't about to admit that to Stone, who'd just give him hell over the fact. Sex wasn't exactly high on his priority list right now. He couldn't move on with his life until he figured out just who had screwed him over. And why.

Because there was no way of knowing when or if it would happen again until he did.

"Not nearly enough."

"I wasn't aware there was an orgasm quota I needed to fill. Perhaps you should put that in my personal development plan."

"Asshole," Stone countered, no heat behind the word.

He was about to make another snide comment when a commotion sounded down the hall.

"Sir, you can't just walk back there," Amanda, their receptionist, hollered down the hall.

Both men headed straight for the doorway. Gray hit it first, fists balled at his sides, his body strung and ready for a fight. Stone was right behind him, no doubt also prepared.

Several of their employees crowded into the hallway, but Gray and Stone both started telling them to get back into their offices and lock their doors. Considering their line of business, it paid to be careful. It wasn't that long ago that Piper, Stone's wife, had been kidnapped and held against her will.

Halfway down the hall, Amanda was chasing after a

man stalking down the line of offices. "I'm just looking for my daughter. I know she's here."

"Sir, if you tell me who she is, I'll be happy to get her for you."

The gentleman waved his hand, dismissing Amanda. "I don't have time for that. They'll be right behind me."

From behind, the man appeared disheveled. Although his clothes were obviously of good quality, his shirt had come untucked from his slacks, the tail of it hanging down past the bottom of his suit coat. The hems of his pants were splotchy with mud and water.

It had been raining earlier in the day, but had stopped several hours ago. However, this guy looked like he'd been tromping through mud puddles and fields.

It didn't take long for Gray to catch up to Amanda. Wrapping a hand around her arm, he pulled her to a stop. "I've got it from here."

"Sir, *who's* going to be right behind you?" Gray asked, his deep voice loud as it echoed against the hallway walls.

The guy glanced over his shoulder, but shook his head instead of answering.

"Who are you looking for?"

"I've already said—my daughter."

At that moment, the office door at the end of the hall, the one he and Blakely had been using for the past several days, swung open. Blakely stepped straight into the path of the man.

Gray cursed under his breath and sped up. He didn't think this guy was dangerous—he didn't appear to be holding a weapon or have one tucked into a holster anywhere on his body—but Gray really had no desire to test that theory with Blakely's safety.

"Get back inside," he said at the exact same time Blakely said, "Dad?"

Three

Oh, God. What was her father doing here? Blakely wanted to scream or curse or both.

"Dad?" Gray's dark, smoky voice floated to her from down the hall. Squeezing her eyes shut, Blakely prayed for strength. And wished her face wasn't currently going up in flames. Which it obviously was, since her cheeks felt like they were on fire.

Of course, he would be right there to witness her father at his absolute worst. She was never going to live this down.

"Baby girl, I don't have much time." Her father was completely oblivious to the people hovering in the hallway, gawking at the spectacle he was making. Or, more likely, he just didn't give a damn.

Her father had never cared what kind of stir he left in his wake, or whether it bothered the people closest to him.

Blakely threw a glance toward Gray, who'd stopped

several feet away, hands balled into fists on his hips and the fiercest scowl scrunching up his handsome face. An unwanted thrill shot through her system. There was something attractive about him, like he'd come ready to swoop in and save her.

Yeah, right.

Not wanting to deal with that thought, Blakely's gaze skipped down to Stone, who was lingering behind Gray, a quizzical expression on his face. She didn't have time to handle either of them right now. Not with her father spouting gibberish.

"Much time before what?" she asked, directing her attention back to her father.

"Before the authorities arrive to arrest me."

Damn, it was worse than she'd thought. *"Dad."*

"I didn't do it."

If she had a dollar for every time she'd heard that... "Uh-huh. What are you being arrested for this time?"

"Conspiracy to commit murder."

Blakely blinked. Her mind blanked. Everything went silent for several seconds before a roar of sound rushed through her. "Excuse me?"

Her dad was a lot of things. A con artist, an idiot, a dreamer and a thief. What he wasn't was a murderer.

"I'm being framed for this. But there's not enough time to explain. I need you to get in touch with Ryan and tell him to come fix it."

Blakely bit back a groan. If she ever heard that name again, it would be too soon. Ryan O'Sullivan had been part of her life since the day she was born...and a thorn in her side for just as long.

"Dad, you promised."

The hangdog expression on her father's face didn't make the pang in her stomach ease any. She was seriously tired of feeling like the parent in their relationship, especially when he gave her that misbehaving, little-boy-caught-with-his-hand-in-the-cookie-jar expression.

Life wasn't supposed to be like this.

"He's my best friend, pet. What was I supposed to do?"

"Stay away from the man who is single-handedly responsible for landing you in prison several times." It appeared, despite everything she'd done to stop the cycle, the man was going to have a hand in sending her father right back. "We agreed when you got out that you were going to cut all ties with Ryan O'Sullivan."

"I tried."

Blakely was quite familiar with the obstinate set of Martin Whittaker's jaw. She wanted to scream. And cry. But neither reaction would help the situation.

"Not hard enough, and now look at what's happening." Blakely flung her hands wide to encompass the Stone Surveillance offices. Other people were now sticking their heads into the hallways to eavesdrop on the juicy gossip.

Wonderful. She might not be thrilled to be working here, but that didn't mean she wanted her family's dirty laundry aired for everyone to judge. "This is where I work, Dad."

Martin let out a sigh and stepped closer, the petulant expression morphing into true regret.

Dammit. That was always how he got her. If there was a single shred of hope, Blakely just couldn't turn her back on him. Her mother and sister both called her ten kinds of a fool. And a softy.

She was probably both.

But when Martin reached for her, Blakely couldn't force herself to stop him. Although, she didn't hug him back. This wasn't the kind of problem that could be solved with some trite Irish quip and a pat on the head.

"I didn't do this, Blakely," he murmured. "I promise. Please, just contact Ryan. He'll take care of everything."

Sure. She wouldn't call that man if he was the sole survivor of the apocalypse. Instead, Blakely started mentally flipping through names of good attorneys. She didn't know many. Her father hadn't ever been able to afford representation, so he'd always stuck with whomever the court appointed. But this time, thanks to Gray and his maneuvering, she had the means to pay for someone who might actually be able to help.

Although, she couldn't quite shake the feeling that it wouldn't make a difference. Her father might not think he was guilty of anything, but that didn't mean he wasn't guilty in the eyes of the law. Especially with a charge like conspiracy.

Who the heck could he have been accused of trying to kill?

Blakely shook her head. One issue at a time.

Before she could open her mouth and ask, another commotion started at the end of the hall. Two officers were stalking toward them, followed by Amanda. They didn't have their guns drawn, but their hands were on the butts ready to pull at the first sign of concern.

In a loud, stern voice, one of the officers demanded, "Mr. Whittaker, put your hands in the air."

Slowly, her father's arms rose over his head. Staring straight at her, his soft blue eyes filled with regret and remorse.

Blakely's throat grew tight and a lump formed. Her body went ice-cold with fear, sadness and frustration.

There was nothing she could do but watch.

One of the officers took another step down the hallway, but before he could reach her father something un-expected happened. Gray moved between them, blocking his path.

"What is Mr. Whittaker being charged with?"

The officer's gaze narrowed. His eyes raked up and down Gray, sizing him up. But that didn't seem to bother Gray. He was perfectly relaxed, his body loose and hands open by his sides.

"Conspiracy to commit murder."

Hearing the words from her father had already sent a shock wave through Blakely. But hearing them from an officer, hand poised on a gun, made her downright terrified.

Because her father wasn't known for being smart or cooperative.

"Now, please step out of the way."

Gray stood exactly where he was, feet unmoving, for what felt like forever. The hallway was silent, the only sound the whoosh of air through the vents in the building. Everyone waited.

Her father was connected to one of the most notorious crime families in Charleston.

Everyone knew Ryan O'Sullivan, mostly because he was the kind of man you wanted to avoid, if at all possible. At least if you were a law-abiding citizen.

There was a time in his life when Gray would have avoided any association with the man. But now... O'Sullivan didn't scare him. He might have connections, but then, so did Gray.

He'd never had any personal experience with the man, or any of his associates. However, the minute they were done here, he'd be making a few phone calls because he was absolutely certain one of his contacts knew O'Sullivan.

And while information on Martin Whittaker might be interesting, what he really wanted to know was just how deep Blakely's ties were to the O'Sullivan family. Because from the sound of things, she knew the man pretty well.

O'Sullivan was definitely connected enough to pull off the kind of theft and cover-up that had landed Gray in jail. Especially with the help of an inside man. Or woman. And twenty million was a big incentive. Especially with a ready-made scapegoat.

Gray folded his arms over his chest, sizing up the officers in front of him. He could continue to block their path, but there wasn't value in doing it. Not only would it not prevent Martin from being arrested and taken in, but it could also potentially land Gray's butt back behind bars.

Nope, not worth it.

However, there might be information to gain and some goodwill to bank. Without glancing behind him, Gray raised his voice and said, "Martin, are you going to leave peacefully with the nice gentlemen waiting to take you downtown?"

"Yes."

Cocking an eyebrow, Gray held up a single finger to ask for a moment, then turned his back to the officers so he could face Blakely and her father.

Gray's gaze skipped across her, as he tried to find a clue that might help him determine something about the state of her mind. But all he could see was a jumbled mess of fear, irritation and determination.

That didn't tell him much, other than that she was a good daughter who loved her father.

"Martin, I'm going to follow the officers and meet you at the station. Take some unsolicited advice and keep your mouth shut until the lawyer I'm about to call gets there."

Blakely made a strangled sound before she opened her mouth to say something. Gray held up a hand, silencing her before she could get out a single word.

Both she and Whittaker shut their mouths. Gray waved behind him for the officers to come forward and then moved out of the way. He didn't bother to watch the commotion in front of him as they cuffed her father. Instead, he watched Blakely.

And because he did, he was probably the only one who noticed the way her body flinched at the sound of the cuffs snapping together around his wrists. Her mouth thinned with unhappiness at the same time her teeth chewed at the inside of her cheek.

Gray didn't even think she was aware that she was doing it.

She started to take a step to follow the officers as they led away her father, but one of them called out behind him, "Stay where you are, ma'am."

Everyone waited and watched. The sound of people shuffling uncomfortably where they stood was like the unsettling scratching of leaves against a window in the middle of the night.

Once Martin was out of view, in unison, all of the spectators turned toward Blakely. And that's when her face flamed bright red.

But Gray had to hand it to her—she didn't bow under the weight of the embarrassment or scrutiny. Instead, she let her gaze travel slowly around the hallway, as she looked each and every person square in the eye. She practically dared them to ask a question or make a snide remark.

No one did.

Dammit, he didn't want to be impressed with her backbone.

Walking up beside her, Gray grasped her arm. She tensed and he could feel her about to jerk away from him.

Pressing close, he murmured low enough so only she could hear, "You probably don't want to make an even bigger scene."

The sound of her breath dragging deep into her lungs shouldn't have had any effect on him. Neither should the way her body brushed against his with the motion. And yet, it did.

"Do you really think I care about making a scene?" she whispered back.

"Yes, I do."

He was close enough to hear her teeth grinding together. But she didn't refute his statement. Because they both knew it was true.

"Now, be a good girl—walk quietly down the hall with me and I'll take you to your father."

A low, growling, frustrated sound rolled through her. "I really don't like you."

Gray laughed, the sound filling the space between them. "Sweetheart, the feeling is mutual."

Propelling her down the hallway in front of him, Gray chose to ignore the pointed expression on Stone's face as they walked past him. No doubt, he was going to hear about this the next time he and his friend were alone.

So Gray would simply avoid Stone for a little while.

Gray and Blakely were both silent as they headed out of the building and into the parking garage. Blakely took the first opportunity to speed up and break the hold he had on her. Which was fine with him. And, no, he didn't flex his hand because it was tingling where he'd touched her bare skin.

Several paces ahead of him, it was clear Blakely intended to take her own car. He could have redirected her, but decided to wait and see how long it took her to realize she didn't have her purse or keys.

She was halfway there when she came to a sudden halt. Her head dropped back and he didn't need a clear view in order to know she was squeezing her eyes shut and probably asking a higher power for strength.

Not that she needed any. For all her faults, Blakely Whittaker was one of the strongest women he'd ever met. Not that he was going to tell her that.

It only took her a few seconds to gather herself, turn and head back toward the entrance to the building.

"Don't bother. I'll take you."

"No, thank you." Her words were formal, but there was no real appreciation behind them. Not that he particularly cared. He wasn't letting her drive. Not because he was worried about her state of mind—or not just because. He wanted to make damn sure he was a fly on the wall.

"Look, you can waste precious time going back inside or you can ride with me to the station. Either way, I'm heading there, and if you don't come with me, I'm going to get there first. And something tells me you'd prefer me not to speak to your father without you."

"Why are you doing this?"

"Doing what? Being nice?"

"No, being a pain in my ass."

"I didn't realize helping your father could be viewed as being a pain in your ass."

Blakely's eyes narrowed. A string of expletives flowed from her lips, some of which were quite inventive. He was impressed and, considering he was a convicted felon and had heard a whole hell of a lot, that wasn't an easy feat.

Stalking past him, Blakely headed straight for his car,

parked a few spaces from the door. It didn't escape his notice that she knew exactly which one was his. Intelligence gathering or something more?

Standing beside the passenger door, she glared at him over the hood. The tap of her foot against concrete rang out, a perfect staccato of irritation and impatience.

If there wasn't a reason to hurry, Gray would have slowed down on principle alone. And because he knew it would bother her. But he wanted to reach her father as quickly as she did. Maybe more.

The drive to the station was silent, the air between them thick with tension and the familiar scent of her perfume. Sweet and exotic. Floral, yet somehow spicy. It had been tempting him for days. The office they were using wasn't exactly small, but when that scent filled the space...

The front seat of his Bugatti was even worse. Normally, it was his sanctuary. The car was the one frivolous, flashy and over-the-top thing he'd allowed himself once he was out of prison. Today, with Blakely so close beside him, it felt just as much like a prison as the cell he'd been assigned.

He couldn't help but wonder if her scent would be stronger if he buried his face between her thighs?

Gray willed away his response. Nope, he wasn't going there.

He might not be naive enough to believe he had to actually like someone in order to be physically attracted to them. But he *was* smart enough to realize his situation with Blakely was complicated enough without adding mindless sex. And that's all that could be between them.

The fifteen-minute drive felt like an eternity. As soon as he pulled into a space in front of the station, Blakely shot from the car. She was halfway across the lot before he'd even turned off the ignition.

Not that her haste would make much difference. She wasn't going to get very far with the officers inside.

Tucking his hands into his pockets, Gray strolled leisurely after her. Once he entered the station he could hear her voice, already raised in frustration.

"I just need to speak to him for a minute. That's all."

"Ma'am, your father is being processed. You can't see him right now."

Gray bypassed the commotion, choosing to approach another officer at the far end of the counter who was protected by a half wall of bulletproof glass.

"Excuse me," he said. "I'm Gray Lockwood, here to see my client, Martin Whittaker. He's just been brought in."

The desk sergeant barely glanced up from a stack of papers. "Are you his attorney?"

"Yes."

He shuffled a few more things. "I'll let them know you're here. Take a seat. Someone'll get you in a few."

"Excellent."

Gray gave the man a polite smile, even though he wouldn't notice it, and turned to sit in one of the chairs lining the far wall. They were hard plastic—no doubt, the cheapest thing the city could buy. The metal legs had been scratched to hell and back. Clearly a lot of people had spent time waiting in them over the years.

With a huff, Blakely collapsed into the chair beside him.

"They won't let me see him."

"Really? How surprising."

Blakely gave him a grimace, her only response to his obvious sarcasm.

"Why did we come here if we weren't planning to see him?"

"I have no idea why you decided to follow your father. And I have every intention of seeing him."

"You do?"

"Yes."

"Oh."

Gray knew exactly what wrong conclusion Blakely had just jumped to. And he had no intention of disabusing her of the notion. At least not until it suited his purposes.

Several minutes ticked by. There was motion and activity all around them, but Gray was content to wait. He'd done a lot of that in his adult life. And he'd learned quickly it was a waste of energy to wish things were different. He'd gotten very good at accepting situations as they were, not as he'd prefer them to be. It saved heartache and disappointment.

Blakely, however, was a bucket of nerves and energy. She couldn't settle and constantly shifted in her seat. Crossed and uncrossed her legs. Cracked her knuckles.

Unable to take any more, Gray reached out and placed a hand on her knee. Blakely immediately stilled. In fact, she stopped moving entirely, not even taking a breath.

Her heat seeped into his skin, making his entire arm hum with unexpected energy.

Shit.

"Mr. Lockwood, please follow me."

Thank God for small favors. Gray looked up at the officer standing at the far doorway. He pushed up from the chair and was halfway across the room before he realized Blakely was following him.

This was gonna be good.

Gray gave the officer a polite smile as he walked past.

"Ma'am, I'm sorry, you're not allowed back here."

Pausing in the hallway, he turned in time to catch Blakely's pointed gesture. "I'm with him."

"Are you part of Mr. Whittaker's legal team?"

"No, I'm his daughter."

The officer shook his head. "I'm sorry. Mr. Whittaker is being questioned. Only legal counsel is allowed into the room."

"Then why is he going back?"

"Mr. Lockwood? Because he's acting counsel."

Blakely stared at him, her gaze narrowing. Gray shrugged. "I mentioned that I have a law degree."

"You don't practice."

"No, I'm fortunate enough that I only take the cases I want to. I'm taking your father's." At least for the moment. Gray had every intention of calling in a few favors to get someone else to actually take Martin's case. While he could do it himself, he had other concerns at the moment and didn't need the distraction.

However, he was going to take this prime opportunity to learn everything he could from Martin about Blakely and her connections to the O'Sullivan family. And whether that could have played into how Gray had found himself framed for embezzlement.

"Tell him I'm with you," Blakely demanded, pointing at the officer standing between them.

"Ah, but you're not."

Four

Blakely wanted to scream. Or find something hard to throw straight at his head. Probably not smart, considering there were at least half a dozen people standing close who could arrest her for assault.

Gray Lockwood was as frustrating as he was sexy. That knowing smirk twisting his gorgeous lips... How could she want to kiss the hell out of him at the same time she wanted to shake him?

What was wrong with her?

Blakely watched him disappear down the hallway, irritation churning in her belly. Dropping back into a hard chair, she stared at the door. And waited.

Conspiracy to commit murder.

God, how could this get any worse? Her father was about to go to jail for a very long time. Sure, he'd been in and out her entire life, but for small crimes. Ten months here, two years there. This would be different.

She wanted to believe him when he said he wasn't guilty…but she just couldn't kill that last spark of doubt taunting her from the back of her brain. Her father had a habit of bending the truth.

And Gray… She didn't trust him further than she could throw him. Like every other criminal she'd ever met—and plenty had marched through her life—they all insisted they were innocent.

She'd yet to meet one who actually was. Especially her father.

But a bigger part of her just couldn't believe he could be responsible for anything close to murder. Her father might be a con man and a thief, but he'd never been violent. Hell, he didn't even own a gun.

Gray, on the other hand, was dangerous as hell. Only he didn't need a gun to be that way. The hum in her blood proved that point nicely. She didn't even like him, but he had the ability to make her body react.

Blakely didn't need the details to know he'd been through a lot. The scar through his eyebrow and the rock-hard muscles he now sported hadn't been earned by doing bench presses and back squats. But there was more to him than his physically intimidating presence. He was quiet and observant. Gray saw too much.

She'd watched him over the last several days, not just as he interacted with her, but with others at the office. He watched and cataloged. Almost as if he was gathering intel on everyone who moved through his existence, even if they only touched his life in the most minor way.

He hadn't been that way when she'd known him before.

Clearly, he brought value to Stone Surveillance. On several occasions Stone and Finn had come to consult Gray's opinion on a case they were working.

She didn't want to see anything good in him. She didn't want to believe he was helping her father. She wanted to see him only as the criminal he was. Without that concerning history, it would be so much more difficult to keep her distance. To pretend she hadn't noticed the layer of humanity and honor. She definitely didn't want to like him. Because right now, she was having a damn hard time keeping her awareness of him in check.

Lucky for her, watching him walk through that precinct door without her was just the reminder she needed.

When she saw him again, he was going to get an earful.

Selfish bastard.

Gray walked into the room and immediately flashbacks assaulted him. A shiver of apprehension raced down his spine, but he refused to let it take hold.

He wasn't the one being questioned here.

Although, being in the small, nondescript, uncomfortable room made it difficult not to let bad memories take over. The barrage of questions he hadn't understood or known the answers to. Feeling blindsided and out of his element. Cut loose without a safety net.

Those first few hours of being questioned had been disorienting because he didn't have a clue what any of the investigators were talking about. And since he'd been innocent, he'd waived his right to counsel. His first mistake.

The detective sitting across the table from Martin glanced up as he entered the room, but didn't say anything. Martin's eyes skipped distractedly over Gray, a puzzled expression filling his face. "Why are you here?"

Gray's first impressions of Martin weren't great. He was the complete opposite of Blakely—scattered, loud and obnoxious. Or at least he had been so far. Although, he also appeared to know exactly who Gray was, which wasn't surprising considering the role Blakely had played in the well-publicized, high-profile trial that had completely turned Gray's life upside down.

"I'm part of your legal team—why wouldn't I be here?"

Martin quirked an eyebrow, but he didn't vocalize the obvious question. Smart man, considering a detective was sitting across from him.

Gray turned to the officer. "I'd like a few minutes with my client, please." The statement might have technically been a request…but it really wasn't.

A frown crunched the corners of the detective's weathered and weary eyes. He stood without saying a word and the door squeaked shut behind him as he left.

Martin opened his mouth, but before he could say anything Gray shook his head. He assumed they were being recorded and watched, and intended to act accordingly.

Taking the vacated chair, Gray folded his hands on the table between them.

"The rest of your legal team should be arriving shortly."

"Why are you doing this?"

An expected question for sure, but one Gray wasn't prepared to answer. At least not here. And not entirely honestly.

"Blakely works for my company and we take care of our own."

Martin scoffed. "Blakely might think I'm gullible, and maybe occasionally I am, but I wasn't born yesterday, son."

Maybe not, but something told him Martin Whittaker wasn't entirely smart when it came to the world, either. Or that was the impression Gray had gotten from Blakely.

And he might not trust her, but she was smart as hell and rather aware of what was going on around her.

"Let's just say I have a vested interest in keeping your daughter focused on a project she's working on with me. I won't have her full attention if she's concerned about you. Money isn't important to me, but right now her assistance is. Buying peace of mind by providing your legal team is a smart strategy for me to get what I want."

Martin slowly nodded. "You could have easily accomplished that without lying to the officers and coming in here to see me."

"Perhaps, but I don't know you."

"True."

"And had no idea whether you'd be smart about what you said until the lawyers I've retained arrive. Besides, I didn't lie. I have a legal degree and specialize in criminal defense."

"But you're not taking my case."

"No, I don't have the luxury of splitting my focus right now, either."

Martin hummed in the back of his throat. "Still doesn't explain why you came all the way down here."

He might be gullible, but Martin Whittaker clearly had enough street smarts to go with his naivete.

"I have a couple questions for you."

"About the charges against me?"

"No."

Martin tugged at the cuffs wrapped around his wrists, rattling the chain connected to the ring bolted to the table. The movement had been instinctive, a gesture he couldn't quite complete.

"Then what?"

"Tell me about your relationship with O'Sullivan. How long have you known him?"

Martin's head tipped sideways as he considered for several seconds before carefully answering. "Ryan and I grew up in the same neighborhood. I've known him for the better part of fifty years."

Interesting. Gray was surprised he'd never heard Martin's name before, all things considered. "And how well does Blakely know him?"

"Not very well." Martin's answer was a little too quick and adamant for Gray's taste.

Perhaps he'd asked the wrong question. "How well does Ryan know Blakely?"

Martin gave him a knowing smile that made Gray wonder whether his scattered persona was all an act.

"Ryan's been in Blakely's life since her birth. Although, my daughter would prefer that not to be the case. He's her godfather and helped put her through college."

Right. Gray stared at the other man, wondering just how to use the information he'd been given to find out if Ryan and Martin had used Blakely's connections at Lockwood Industries in order to steal twenty million dollars and frame Gray. Martin wasn't likely to admit it, especially in the middle of a police station.

And asking outright would tip his hand. Better to have Joker do some digging. The problem they'd run into before was having no real direction to start looking.

Gray began to push up from his chair, but the next words out of Martin's mouth stalled him halfway up.

"My daughter, however, is completely unaware and she'd never speak to me again if she found out Ryan paid for her education. My daughter is proud and honorable to a fault."

While most fathers would say those words with pride in their voices, Martin's tone conveyed disappointment. Gray had to shake his head.

"If Ryan was on fire, Blakely wouldn't cross the street to spit on him. She would, however, cross to throw some gasoline."

Well, that was pretty definitive. And left little room for the idea that Blakely would do anything to help Ryan O'Sullivan. Although, if she really had, no doubt her father would be the first to say whatever he could to deflect suspicion.

So this conversation had done rather little to help Gray decide whether Blakely had been involved in framing him, or had just lucked into information that had been planted.

A knock on the door prevented him from asking any more questions, even if he'd had any.

The detective stood in the open doorway, a very pissed off Blakely glaring from behind him.

Blakely stormed out of the station. She was halfway to Gray's car when he grasped her arm and jerked her to a stop.

Turning to glare at him, she ripped her arm from his grasp. But instead of turning away again, she leaned forward into his personal space and growled, "Don't touch me."

Her blood whooshed in her veins. The sound of it throbbed through her head, along with the tattoo of her elevated breathing.

Seriously, she needed to get a grip.

Logically, she realized the emotion directed at Gray was not entirely his fault. Everything that had happened today was simply coming to a head, crashing down over her at once. And he made a handy target.

But realizing that didn't do her much good.

Glancing around them, Gray frowned. How was it fair

that the man could still manage to look like a Hollywood heartthrob even while irritated?

Ignoring her snarled words, he grasped her arm again and urged her ahead of him and around the corner of the building.

He maneuvered them both into a dark patch of quiet shade. Using his leverage, he set her back against the brick wall and then let her go.

He backed away, putting a few feet between them. "Now isn't the time to lose it, Blakely."

"No joke."

Gray cocked a single eyebrow, silently calling her ten kinds of stupid for doing exactly what she shouldn't be doing.

It stung that he was right. Blakely groaned. Dropping her head back, she let her body sag into the rough surface of the wall. The sharp edges scraped against her skin, but she didn't care.

"I'm pissed at you. I'm pissed at him. I'm just—"

"Pissed. Yeah, I got that."

"He promised me. And I'm such an idiot for believing him because it's not like he hasn't broken a million promises before. But I couldn't stop myself from hoping, even when I knew I shouldn't."

God, she knew better. But it was so difficult to cut those ties. And that's what it would take in order for her to be free of her father's drama and messes. The only way to avoid it all would be to avoid him. And she wasn't to that point yet.

Or she hadn't been.

Her mother and sister had given up on him years ago.

"Perhaps he's being honest and really is innocent."

Blakely stared at Gray, the echo of his words slightly eerie, all things considered. Was he saying that because no one—including her—had believed *him* when he said he was innocent? Was he being just as naive as she was?

"I've heard that before, Gray." And, no, she wasn't just talking about her father.

"Well, I believe him. I've called in a few favors and arranged for a friend to represent him."

"Why would you do that?"

"Funny, he asked me the same question. And I'll give you the same answer. Because I need you fully focused on helping me prove my innocence, and you won't be as long as you're worried about him. I have the money and connections to afford the best representation for Martin."

Blakely shook her head. "No, I won't let you do that. We don't need your money or your help."

The statement, vehement though she tried to make it sound, was a complete lie. She did need his help. And his money, in the form of the salary he was paying her to help him on this wild-goose chase.

"We don't want your charity."

"Too bad, you're getting it, anyway."

"I refuse to accept your help, Gray." There was one sure way she knew to get him angry enough to back down and agree to leave her and her father alone. "You're a criminal, just like Ryan. I won't go to him for help and I won't accept it from you."

Gray's expression went stone-hard. His mouth thinned and his eyes glittered a warning it was too late to heed.

He took a measured step, closing the gap between them. Blakely swallowed even as a frisson of awareness snaked down her spine. Nope, she refused to give in to it.

He shifted. The soft brush of his body against hers made her skin flush hot and a molten center of need melt deep inside her. His voice was low and measured as he leaned close and murmured, "I'm nothing like Ryan

O'Sullivan, although you already know that. Don't get me wrong—I'm ten times as dangerous as he is, only because I have very little left to lose. The difference is I have standards and morals."

The heat of his breath tickled her skin. His lips were so close and she wanted them on her.

No, she didn't.

Blakely tipped her head backward. She tried to crowd into the wall, but there was nowhere for her to go. Nowhere to get away from him. Or get away from her own unwanted reaction.

This close, all she could see were his eyes. His expression. The desolation and hope. The pain and the heat. The intensity centered squarely on her.

The spot at the juncture of her thighs throbbed. The breath in her lungs caught as the warmth of his body invaded every pore of her skin.

Gray Lockwood *was* dangerous. To her sanity. Her peace of mind. The very foundation of her personal morals. She'd spent her entire life avoiding men like him. And she wasn't just talking about his criminal past, although that surely should have been enough to give her pause.

But it was more.

Gray Lockwood was a force to be reckoned with. He was intelligent, observant, dynamic and demanding. In his youth, that combination had manifested in an entitled attitude that had been less than attractive.

Now, those same qualities had the ability to make her panties damp. She shouldn't be turned on by his confidence and domineering attitude. But she was.

Blakely stared up at him, her lips parted. Waiting. Although for what, she wasn't entirely certain.

Gray seemed poised, as well—on the edge of something neither of them wanted to want, but couldn't stop.

So close to her, Blakely could feel the tension coiled in every one of his muscles. He was like a tiger, waiting to spring.

The moment stretched between them. On the far side of the building, a police siren went off. A couple exited the building and chatted, although Blakely couldn't have said what their conversation was about.

She breathed in, filling her lungs with the tantalizing scent that had been taunting her for days. Him.

"To hell with it," he finally murmured right before his body pressed in against her.

All the air whooshed out of her lungs, as if he'd slammed her against the wall, although he hadn't. Excitement flashed through her as his mouth dropped to hers.

Blakely's gasp backed into her lungs as he kissed her, swallowing the sound.

Gray's arm snaked around her, settling on the small of her back as he pulled her closer. His other hand found her face, cupping it and angling her just where he wanted.

The first touch was light, but that didn't last long. Seconds later, Gray was opening his lips, diving in and demanding everything from her.

His tongue tangled with hers, stroking and stoking and driving the need she'd been ignoring into a raging inferno she couldn't deny. Seconds—that's how long it took for him to steal her resolve and leave her a shaking mess of desire.

Her own hands gripped his shoulders, pulling him closer even as her brain screamed that she needed to push him away.

But she couldn't make herself do it.

The angle changed. The kiss deepened. He demanded more. And Blakely didn't hesitate to give it. Going up on her toes, she met him force for force. Need for need.

Somehow her leg raised, hooking up over his hip as she made demands of her own. The overheated center of her sex ached. Blakely moaned in the back of her throat as she undulated against him, looking for relief.

The sound seemed to snap him out of whatever had tangled them together.

Hands gripping her arms, he pushed away, unraveling their intertwined bodies. She leaned into his hold, unconsciously pushing against the invisible barrier he'd placed between them.

"I'm sorry," he said.

"I'm not." Blakely wanted to slap a hand across her wayward mouth, but it was too late. This was his fault. He'd obviously fried her brain.

Shaking his head, Gray gave a soft chuckle. "Thanks for being honest. But I shouldn't have done that."

Blakely wasn't going to argue with him. "You're right."

She expected Gray to walk away, leave her there and let her figure out her own way back to the office.

Instead, he reached out, soft fingers trailing lightly over her cheek. "I've wanted to do that for days." His heated gaze skipped across the features of her face, following his teasing fingertip.

His honesty unnerved her, although it also settled her. It was reassuring to know she wasn't the only one fighting against urges she shouldn't have.

But she also couldn't pretend. "This can't happen." Blakely tried to make the words sound adamant, even if a huge part of her didn't want them to be.

Gray nodded, but his words contradicted the action. "Why not? We're both adults."

"Yes, but you don't like me and I don't like you."

Gray's eyes jumped back to hers, staring straight into her. "That's not true. I like you just fine."

Blakely couldn't stop the scoffing sound that scraped through her throat. "Yeah, right. You hate me. I was instrumental in putting you in jail."

"Maybe."

There was no *maybe* about it. Her testimony had been key to his conviction.

"I'm attracted to you, Blakely. We're working closely together, which makes ignoring the physical pull difficult. You tell me you're not interested and I'll do just that. But knowing you are…"

Blakely understood completely. Her body still hummed with the memory of their kiss. "It's going to be hell to put that genie back in the bottle."

Five

It had been two days since the kiss. Since he'd grabbed her, pressed her against the wall and gotten the first intoxicating taste of her mouth.

Nope, the feel of her hadn't been haunting him.

Gray sat on the opposite side of the room from her, trying to concentrate on a stack of evidence, just as he had for the last two days. Honestly, if Stone walked in right now and asked him what he was doing, Gray couldn't have told him. He hadn't actually absorbed anything he'd read for hours.

This wasn't good. Or productive.

For her part, Blakely had chosen to pretend the kiss never happened. When they'd walked away from the police station, Gray hadn't been entirely certain what her reaction would be. The fact that she hadn't slapped him was promising. And there was no way she could deny being just as into that kiss as he'd been.

But by the next morning, her stiff, perfect facade had been back in place.

Honestly, he preferred Blakely when she was energetic and emotional. Real and authentic. He'd seen the evidence that she could be more than just a disapproving robot who followed all the rules because she was scared of what might happen if she didn't.

His conversation with Martin had been rather enlightening, though. Discovering Blakely had grown up on the outskirts of a major crime family shed some light, for sure.

But after his little meeting at the police station, one thing had become crystal clear—neither Blakely nor Martin were sitting on twenty million dollars. First, if they had been, Blakely wouldn't have been worried about paying for her father's lawyer. She would have called up the best defense attorney money could buy. Second, if they had that kind of money, neither of them would still be in Charleston.

Gray was convinced Martin might act the fool, but was far from it. He used that facade to his advantage. But the man wouldn't stick around near the scene of the crime if he had the means to disappear and live the good life.

While that didn't precisely mean Blakely hadn't been inadvertently involved in the frame job that had sent Gray to prison, it did, at least in his mind, clear her of intentionally setting him up.

Blakely had been just as much a pawn in the whole scheme as he'd been. It was possible that whoever had placed the trail of financial information in the Lockwood Industries books had simply banked on *someone* finding the crumbs.

It really wouldn't have mattered who that someone was. In fact, it might have played better if the someone was completely innocent and unconnected. If the police had done a thorough job—which Gray wasn't willing to concede—they should have investigated every witness just to be certain of their character before they took the stand.

Squeezing his eyes shut, Gray shoved away the file he'd been looking at and dropped back into his chair.

He and Blakely had been pouring over testimony, evidence and notes for a week. And so far, they'd found absolutely nothing.

The only thing Gray had to show for his effort was a growing certainty that Blakely had been unwittingly involved. Which benefited him not at all. It would have been easier if she had been purposely involved. Because then he wouldn't have felt guilty for the way he'd maneuvered her into helping him.

Or for the way he wanted to cross the room, pull her out of her chair, wipe everything off the desk and kiss every inch of her naked skin.

Opening his eyes, Gray glanced across the office. It probably wasn't smart to have his desk facing Blakely's if he wanted to ignore the awareness pulsing beneath the surface of his skin.

Not that it really mattered. He didn't need to be watching her to know she was there. Gray could feel her presence the minute she walked into the room.

Right now, though, it made his lips pull down at the edges to watch her. Because bent over a file spread open on her desk, one hand lodged in her hair and her forehead crinkled with a frown, she looked just as frustrated and unhappy as he was.

And despite everything, he didn't want her to feel that way.

"Let's get out of here." The words were out of his mouth before he even realized he'd meant to say them.

"What?" Blakely looked up at him, blinking owlishly. Her entire body stayed poised over the file, which only made him want to take her away from here even more. It took several seconds for her gaze to clear and focus on him.

"Let's get out of here."

Her head tilted to the side. He was starting to learn she did that when she was weighing things. What she should do against what she wanted to do. Or what everyone else expected of her against what her instincts told her.

He was tired of seeing her calculate every step before taking one. Sure, there was a time in his life when he didn't calculate anything because he knew there were a pile of safety nets—not to mention billions of dollars—to save him if he fell flat on his face.

Trust him to land in a mess that would rip the safety nets out from under him and make his billions worthless in getting him out of the jam.

However, that didn't mean Blakely's approach to life was any better. If there was one thing he'd learned, it was that life was short. You never knew what was going to happen or where you were going to end up. It was your responsibility to make the most of where you were while you were there.

He had a feeling Blakely rarely allowed herself that pleasure.

Gray also knew that if he gave her enough time to come up with a valid excuse, she'd decline his offer simply because he made her nervous. Not because she was scared of him, but because she didn't want to like him.

Or want him.

Well, that wasn't going to work for him anymore.

He wanted her and he wasn't going to let the mess they were trying to unravel stop him from getting what he wanted.

Standing up, Gray walked around to her desk. "Let's go."

"Go where?"

"Does it matter? We both need a break. I haven't seen you eat anything today. You've got to be starving."

She paused. Gray's stomach knotted with nerves that he really didn't want to acknowledge or investigate. And to his surprise, Blakely offered him a small half smile.

"I am pretty hungry."

What the hell was she doing?

For the second time in a few days, Blakely found herself riding in the passenger seat of Gray's low-slung sports car. The leather cupped her body, making her feel snug and safe even as he tore through the city at break-neck speed. Apparently, he wasn't concerned about getting the attention of an officer...or a speeding ticket.

She should have said no and stayed at the office. Not just because avoiding small, enclosed spaces with Gray was just smart. But because she was seriously starting to think the man was innocent of the charges for which he'd been convicted.

And that left her with a nasty taste in her mouth.

They'd spent a lot of time together in the last week. In that time, one thing had become obvious. The man he was now was nowhere near the man he'd been back then.

And, yes, that did nothing to prove he'd been innocent. Gray's reputation back then might have been difficult to surmount. But, honestly, had he really been that terrible?

No. He'd been an entitled prick who'd had everything handed to him on a silver platter, but even as he'd partied and gambled and gone jet-setting around the world, he'd been generous to a fault.

Blakely had also discovered that while he'd been blowing millions on random and pointless things, he'd also established a foundation to assist underprivileged children with college scholarships. He'd been involved in a local fine-arts program, paying to keep art and music in schools that no longer had funding. He'd donated millions to drug-rehabilitation programs and randomly provided money to just about every charitable organization that approached him for a donation.

The information had been brought up in court, which was how she'd discovered the truth. But the prosecutor had implied it was easy to write a check, especially when one needed the tax write-off.

Blakely couldn't dispute that, but something told her the donations had been more than some accountant telling him it was a good money move. The amount he'd donated in the three years leading up to the embezzlement had been significant. In fact, it had been almost half of what he'd been accused of stealing.

Which made no sense. Why would he steal money only to donate it?

He wouldn't. Which had been his argument all along. He didn't need the twenty million. The prosecution had argued need wasn't the only motivation to explain his actions. But Gray hardly struck her as the kind of person who would steal simply to prove he could.

The attorneys also detailed a contentious relationship with his father. Several Lockwood employees testified to arguments and tension between the two in the office. Gray's father was fed up with his irresponsible ways and wanted him to take on more responsibility within the company. Their implied motive for the theft was revenge against his father, but Blakely couldn't see how stealing twenty million from Lockwood had harmed Gray's father. Certainly, the company had struggled for several months, but they'd pulled through just fine.

It all circled back to the fact that Gray hardly needed the money. Which was honestly how she found herself sitting in the seat beside him.

She was starting to like him. Starting to realize the man she'd forced into a round hole was really more complicated than she'd given him credit for.

She'd misjudged him, then and now.

The question was, what was she going to do about it?

"Where are we going?" Blakely finally asked, filling the charged silence stretching between them.

"A little place I know."

That really didn't answer her question. "Where?"

Gray swiveled his head, studying her instead of the road for several seconds. Normally, especially at this speed, that would have made her nervous, but she had no doubt Gray had complete control of his car.

"Do you trust me?"

What a loaded question. Did she? No, but then she didn't really trust anyone. And while she was beginning to think she'd misjudged Gray, that didn't mean she was ready to place her life in his hands.

However, that wasn't necessarily what he was asking.

"To pick a good place to get food? Yes."

Gray's mouth tipped up into a lopsided, knowing grin. He understood precisely what she was saying.

"Excellent. We gotta start somewhere."

Did they?

Blakely's stomach flipped at the idea. She wanted to, that was clear. Even sitting this close to him was doing crazy and unexplainable things to her body. Her skin tingled and heat settled deep in her belly. Her panties were damp and he hadn't even touched her.

He drove her out to a little place near Rainbow Row. It was quaint and small, not exactly what she'd expected him to pick. But even more surprising, she hadn't heard of it.

"I've never been here," she said, staring up at the front as she climbed from the car. Better that than stare at him as he held open her door. Or get tangled up in thinking how easy it would be to lean into the hard planes of his body, press her lips to his and drown in another mind-bending kiss.

Was it her imagination, or did he linger a little longer than necessary before moving out of her way?

"I'm not surprised. It's fairly new, but the food is amazing."

"I guess I'll find out."

It was past the normal lunch rush, but there were still a handful of occupied tables. Mostly older women with their makeup and hair done, obviously out for lunch with friends. There were several affluent neighborhoods close by, so not altogether surprising.

The hostess was pleasant and nice, even if she did stare at Gray a little longer than necessary. But who could blame her? Take away the criminal element and the man was a walking fantasy. Polished, but still with the hint of a few rough edges. He carried himself with a confidence that was both attractive and enviable.

But Blakely wouldn't allow herself to be jealous. Mostly because she had nothing to be jealous about.

The perky hostess showed them to a table in the far corner, beside a window that overlooked a lush garden. The empty tables surrounding them created an illusion of privacy, which might not be a good thing.

Gray held out her chair, brushing his fingers over the curve of her shoulders as he pulled away. All this time, Blakely had assumed holding chairs was simply a polite thing for men to do. Now she realized it was a perfect excuse. That simple touch had sent a low hum vibrating through her body and she was going to spend the next hour fighting to turn it off.

How could she manufacture a reason for him to touch her again?

Nope, she wasn't going there. Picking up the menu, Blakely studied it rather than Gray. After a few moments, the words actually started to make sense.

Their waitress was friendly, and she obviously knew Gray, judging by their conversation. But she was also efficient, as she took their drink orders and highlighted the day's specials. Blakely ordered a pecan-crusted chicken salad that sounded amazing. Gray ordered pimento cheese and homemade pork rinds, followed by pan-seared tuna and asparagus.

Once the menus were taken and some soft rolls appeared on the table, there was nothing left to keep her distracted. Which wasn't necessarily a good thing.

For the first time, Blakely realized Gray had positioned her in a chair with her back to the rest of the room…filling the spot right in front of her with nothing but him. Sneaky man. Had he done that on purpose?

Blakely was trying to decide whether to ask him—because maybe she really didn't want the answer—when Gray's cell, sitting facedown on the table, buzzed. Frowning, he flipped it over. The frown went from a mild crease to full-blown irritation as soon as he read whatever was on the screen. Glancing up, he said, "I'm sorry, I need to get this."

Blakely waved away his apology. They weren't on a date so he didn't need to justify his actions to her.

She expected him to get up and walk away, to gain a little bit of privacy. Instead, he just answered the call, so she could hear his side of the conversation.

"Hello, Mother."

If Blakely hadn't been able to see Gray's expression, the tone in his voice would have clearly conveyed his displeasure. She wondered if that was his normal reaction to his mother, or if there was something specific going on between them. Not that it was any of her business.

Hell, she could identify. It wasn't like she rejoiced whenever her father's name popped up on her cell screen. He never called her when things were going well.

"Calm down." Gray's eyes narrowed, the irritation quickly morphing to something more. "I have no idea what you're talking about." He paused, listening to something on the other end before letting out a sigh. "I'll be there in a few minutes."

Hanging up, he dropped his phone onto the table with a loud clatter that made her concerned for the safety of the screen. "I'm sorry to cut this short, but I need to run over to my mother's house."

"So I gathered."

Waving over their waitress, Gray didn't bother asking for the check. He slipped a hundred into her hand and then stood, holding out an arm for Blakely to go in front of him.

The walk to the car was silent, mostly because she didn't know what to say.

What she didn't expect, once they got inside, was for Gray to head in the opposite direction of the office.

Apparently, she was about to meet his mother.

Six

Gray wasn't looking forward to this confrontation at all. And part of him felt like an ass for dragging Blakely along for the ride. But his mother had been spouting an irate tirade of nonsense and he was afraid to take the time to drop off Blakely at the office, which was in the opposite direction.

With any luck, he could calm his mother and they could be back to work in less than half an hour.

Although, he wasn't holding his breath.

It had been just about eleven months since he'd last spoken to or seen his mother. Before that, it had been seven years. He'd stopped by the estate after getting out of prison. Although he hadn't exactly expected the fatted calf to be slaughtered, an acknowledgment of his place in her life would have been nice.

Instead, she'd followed his father's line and refused to even let him inside the front door.

Who knew if she'd let him inside this time, either. Not

that he particularly cared. His mother hadn't exactly been a warm and loving example of motherhood to begin with. The minute his father disowned him she'd taken that as permission to pretend he didn't exist.

There was a spiteful, vindictive part of him that enjoyed knowing her friends talked about her behind her back because of him. If nothing else, being wrongly convicted of a crime gave him that perk. Although, it hardly outweighed the cons.

It took about five minutes to get to the estate on Legare Street from the restaurant. Not nearly long enough.

He climbed out of the car and headed for the front door. Blakely slowly followed. He purposely hadn't asked her to either stay behind or come with him, instead leaving it as her decision.

He figured, after meeting Martin, she could most likely handle his mother in one of her states, anyway.

Gray didn't bother knocking. Why would he, when the estate had been his childhood home? But it did feel weird walking through the front door after such a long time away. The place looked exactly the same—not a single mirror or piece of artwork on the wall had been changed in almost eight years.

Not surprising, either. His mother was a creature of habit. When given an option, she'd take the path of least resistance every time. One reason she'd made such a perfect trophy wife.

After striding down the hallway, Gray bounded up the wide, sweeping staircase to the second floor and the rooms his mother had claimed as her own long ago. Opening the door to the sunroom, he wasn't surprised to see her pacing furiously back and forth.

She didn't turn when he opened the door, apparently so deep in her own discourse that she hadn't heard him enter. But the minute she spotted him, he became the object of her obvious rage.

Charging across the room, she yelled, "Who does this bitch think she is? Blackmailing me after all these years? I had nothing to do with this, dammit! Nothing. And I'm not paying her a single dollar, let alone twenty million."

Gray shook his head, trying to make sense of his mother's words.

But her rant didn't end there. The words continued to come, punctuated by her slamming fists hitting into his chest and rocking him back on his heels.

Well, that was unexpected.

And so was the way Blakely shot between them, shoving into his mother's face and pushing her backward. "What do you think you're doing?"

"I don't know who the hell you are, but get out of my way."

"Not on your life. Whatever's going on, it doesn't give you to the right to physically assault your son."

His mother laughed, the bitter sound of it sending a shiver down his spine.

"He isn't my son."

"Excuse me?" It was Blakely's turn to be knocked backward. She collided with his chest.

Distractedly, Gray wrapped an arm around her waist, holding her tight against him.

His mother's words startled him, but Gray locked down his reaction and refused to show it. This woman had abandoned him long ago and didn't deserve anything from him.

"What the hell do you mean?"

His mother's eyes jerked up to his. The blind fury clouding them slowly faded. "Shit."

Yeah, that pretty much summed up this whole situation.

Waving a hand in the direction of the sofa in front of the floor-to-ceiling windows, she indicated he should sit. Gray didn't bother following her request. But for the first time, he realized she was holding a piece of paper in her hand.

"What's that?"

Frowning, she waved the thing through the air. Just by sight, it appeared to be cheap copy paper. The shadow of several lines of text could be seen through it, so it wasn't very heavy. "This? This would be a blackmail demand."

"Who sent it?"

"You probably should sit."

"I'm good."

"Your father's going to kill me."

"Since he disowned me several years ago, I find it hard to believe he'll care what you say or do."

His mother shook her head, sadness washing over her expression. "That's where you're wrong."

Somehow, he didn't think so. Not only had his father ignored Gray's insistence that he was innocent, but his father had also gone so far as to cut Gray out of his life entirely. What loving parent did that? Gray had always been nothing more than another pawn to the man. Someone his father could control and move at will. And when Gray became a liability instead of an asset, he was sacrificed.

Unlike Stone, whose parents had stood by him, even before they learned the truth—that he'd murdered their friend's son because he'd walked in on an attempted rape. His friend had kept the details to himself for years, protecting the woman he loved. His family had supported him, accepted him. Hell, they'd thrown him a lavish party when he finally got out.

But despite being innocent, *Gray's* family had disowned him, cut him out of the family business and left him alone in the world.

Sure, he could tell himself that he was better off without his mother and father in his life. And, logically, he realized that was absolutely true. But it still hurt like hell when the people who were supposed to have his back had abandoned him.

His mother gave a grimace. "Oh, don't get me wrong. He wouldn't care because *you* know. But he will care that someone else is privy to the dirty laundry he's so desperate to keep hidden."

Now that sounded more like his father. "Well, then, by all means, tell me. I'd really appreciate having something I could hold over his head."

Especially once Gray had proof of his innocence. Even sweeter to demand access to the company, and also have the means to control the strings on the man who viewed himself as the puppet master.

Blakely, who had taken his mother's suggestion and sat on the sofa several feet away, piped up. "I'm going out on a limb here, but reading between the lines, I'm going to guess that Gray isn't your son, but he is your husband's."

His mother glanced over at Blakely, her gaze moving up and down, taking stock.

What was wrong with him that he wanted his mother to approve of her? Childhood impulses he couldn't control? Wasn't he too old to need parental approval for anything? Especially considering he and his mother hadn't particularly had that kind of relationship to begin with.

Finally, his mother said, "Nailed it in one. She's a smart one."

Yes, she absolutely was. The more time he spent with Blakely, the more he appreciated her quick mind. And he was starting to understand her rock-solid sense of honor, too.

"That note. It's from his biological mother? Demanding money to keep the secret?"

"Pretty much."

"Twenty million. That's what you said earlier?"

"Yes."

Blakely turned her gaze toward him. "Coincidence?"

He knew exactly what she was asking. Was it a coincidence the blackmail demand was the same amount of money that was still missing from the embezzlement? Maybe. It was a nice round figure. Not to mention, the media had been linking that number with his name for years.

But while his release last year had prompted a new flurry of media attention, that had died down in the months since. Partly because both of his friends had taken some of the heat off his back with their own releases and high-profile antics.

But what if it wasn't? They were still looking for that missing twenty million. Maybe his birth mother thought she deserved it? Or maybe she was somehow involved and never got the money she was supposed to get?

"Who is this woman?"

"I don't know."

Yeah, right. That was a lie if ever he'd heard one. His mother might have never gone to college and spent most of her time involved in several charitable organizations coordinating glitzy events, but she was far from ignorant. In fact, she was quite brilliant at gossip and knew exactly how to dig up dirt on just about anyone. There wasn't a snowball's chance in hell she hadn't done—or paid for—a full investigation of her husband's fling. Especially if the woman was the mother of her "child."

He wasn't the only one skeptical. Blakely scoffed. "Please, you don't strike me as stupid."

"Why, thank you, dear." His mother's voice practically dripped syrupy sarcasm all over the floor.

Blakely ignored it. "You know exactly who your son's mother is. You wouldn't be foolish enough to let that important piece of information go until you discovered who it was."

A half smile tugged at his mother's perfect lips. "I like this one. You should keep her around."

"I'll take that under advisement. In the meantime, why don't you answer her question?"

"Fine. I know who she is. Your father wasn't exactly as discreet as he'd like to think."

Gray wasn't entirely certain what to say to that. Sorry? How convenient? So he simply kept his mouth shut and waited.

"She worked at the club. One of those girls that drives a cart around and brings drinks out to the men playing golf. At least, until your father set her up in a nice town house and provided her a monthly stipend to be at his beck and call."

Great, his mother sounded like a winner.

"When she got pregnant, he was pissed. Supposedly, she was on birth control, but the hussy forgot to take it. However, as he always does, your father found a way to make that work in his favor. We'd been trying for years to get pregnant, but couldn't. The doctors weren't hopeful and fertility treatments weren't as advanced back then as they are now. He convinced me that he'd found a woman who'd agreed to a private adoption."

"But you knew."

His mother grimaced. "I knew. I was aware of the affair already. It wasn't the first one and, clearly, wasn't the last. But as long as he was inconspicuous I didn't particularly care."

"You agreed to accept the baby as your own."

With a sigh, his mother walked over to the chair across from Blakely and sat. "I did."

"But you knew," Blakely said. "It wasn't simply that he wasn't yours. It was that he was hers."

His mother looked up at him, regret filling her eyes. "Yes. Every time I looked at you, it was a reminder of your father's infidelity. It was one thing to live with it in the background, but...you look like her."

"I do?"

She nodded. "And him. I tried. I really did, Gray. I wanted you to be my son. And you are."

"But I'm also not."

"It was so hard not to allow you to shoulder the blame for something you had no responsibility for."

Gray nodded. What else could he do? Argue with her? Tell her she should have tried harder? That it wasn't fair for her to agree to accept him as her own, but then not follow through with actually being his mother?

Speaking those truths aloud would change nothing.

"Who is she?"

"Now? She's a showgirl in Vegas. My one requirement was that the adoption be closed and the mother agree to leave the state. Your father paid her a huge sum and she left."

Clearly, his birth mother had been more interested in the money than in her son. And if the letter was any indication, she still was. That was something he'd have to deal with later.

"Do you know how to find her?"

His mother nodded.

"Give me the letter and her information and I'll take care of this."

Reluctantly, his mother handed the letter to him. Without looking, he held it out to Blakely, knowing she'd grab it and keep it safe. When they returned to the office, he'd send it to their forensics team to be analyzed. He'd also contact Joker to see what information he could dig up before heading to Vegas.

Holding out a hand, Gray indicated Blakely should follow him out of the room. She rose, heading in his direction. He stood still, waiting for her to exit first.

And was surprised when her palm landed on his chest and stroked down across his body as she passed. Somehow, that simple touch helped settle the chaos rioting inside him.

He followed her through the house. His mother's footsteps echoed behind his. But before they left, Blakely paused at the front door. Turning, she glanced around him to his mother. "Why did you call Gray instead of your husband?"

"Because Malcolm's indiscretions are the reason we're in this mess in the first place. And I know Gray is part owner of a security firm. I assumed he'd be better equipped to handle the situation than his father."

Blakely nodded. "That's what I thought."

Gray was surprised when she grasped his hand and headed down the wide front steps. Squeezing his hand before she dropped it, Blakely rounded the hood of the car and slid into the passenger seat.

He loved the smooth, graceful way she moved. It was becoming more and more difficult to tear his gaze away from watching her whenever she was close.

Gray slid down into the driver's seat, but before he could put the car in gear, Blakely placed a staying hand over his.

"Are you okay?"

Was he? Gray honestly didn't know. Certainly, his

mother's revelation should have rocked his foundation. But it really hadn't. It wasn't like she'd ever been the demonstrative, loving type. Actually, learning he wasn't her real son added context to his childhood. It helped him understand things that had never made sense before.

And he'd actually lost both of his parents long before now, so learning this new detail changed nothing, although it provided another possible motive for what had happened to him.

Which was a good thing.

"Yeah, I'm good."

Blakely stared deep into his eyes. She didn't try and tell him he wasn't okay. She simply searched for clues that he really meant what he'd said.

After several moments, she gave him a sad half smile and squeezed his hand again. "I'm going with you."

Gray's eyebrows arched up in confusion. "Where?"

"Vegas. Don't pretend you're not going. I'm going with you."

"No, you're not."

"Yes, I am. What would Stone think about you gallivanting off to Vegas by yourself to meet the biological mother you didn't know existed until twenty minutes ago? A woman who may or may not be involved somehow in your embezzlement conviction?"

Oh, she really was good. "That's playing dirty."

Blakely's smile morphed into a megawatt one. "What can I say? I'm learning."

Blakely never expected to find herself sitting across the aisle from Gray on a private plane. Sure, she'd half expected to fly first class for the first time in her life, but this…? Totally unexpected. She was completely out of her element, although tried not to show it.

"Relax."

And she was apparently failing miserably.

"I'm relaxed."

"No, you're not. You're wound tighter than a top. What's wrong?"

Wrong? "Nothing."

Gray arched an eyebrow, silently calling bullshit.

Not that she was going to tell him the truth. When she'd insisted she was going with him, she hadn't completely thought through the implications. It was one thing to be cooped up in the same office with him for ten hours a day, but to be a shadow at his side for the next several days...

At least back in Charleston she had the ability to go home and clear her mind of him. Or attempt to.

"Remind me again, why are we staying so long?"

Another expectation blown to bits. She'd assumed they'd fly up, track down his birth mother and head home. A day at the most. Instead, Gray had told her to pack enough for three or four days. Considering they already had a full rundown on his mother's information, including where she worked and lived, Blakely wasn't entirely certain what he expected to take so long.

"There are a couple other people I want to pay a visit to while we're here."

Blakely couldn't help the suspicion that snaked through her system. She'd been reading enough about Gray's history before he'd gone to prison to know that he'd spent quite a bit of time in Vegas before. And most of that time revolved around gambling, sex and outrageous benders that went on for days.

None of which she was interested in being a part of.

Sure, Gray hadn't done any of those things since he'd been out—at least not to her knowledge—so she didn't think that's what he had in mind, but...

"I'm not down for some wild Vegas weekend, Gray. I'm not interested in the lavish parties or high-roller games."

"Good, since neither of those things are on the agenda. I simply want to check in with some people I used to know."

Blakely's eyes narrowed. Gray looked entirely sincere, his steady gaze holding hers as she watched him. Every fiber of her being wanted to believe him. But she couldn't completely shut down the sneering voice in the back of her head.

She finally shrugged and said, "Great, then I'll leave you to it and take a commercial flight home after we've talked with your mom."

"Nope. I need you here for my meetings."

"Why?"

"Because I'm talking to my former bookie, Surkov."

Nope, that did not sound like something she wanted to be involved with. "You don't need me to gamble."

"Do I look like an idiot to you?"

Blakely didn't understand the question, and seemingly unconnected segue, but answered, anyway. "No."

"Apparently I do if you think I'm here to place a bet. The main reason I spent seven years in prison is because I had a gambling habit. By no means was I an addict, but I wasn't exactly careful, either."

"Why'd you do it? The prosecution's biggest argument was that you were up to your eyeballs in debt to some bad people and didn't want to confess to Daddy to bail you out."

Gray's eyebrows rose. "And what do you think about that now?"

Blakely cocked her head and considered her answer for several seconds. What did she think? At the time, the only information she'd had about Gray was either what the media had told her or based on the limited interactions she'd witnessed at Lockwood Industries, which hadn't exactly painted Gray in the best light.

There was no doubt in her mind the man she knew now wouldn't have hesitated to do or say anything he needed to, including talking to his father, even if their relationship was strained.

But that didn't mean the man he'd been before would have reacted the same way. In fact, she was pretty certain the time he'd spent in prison had fundamentally changed him. And maybe for the better.

"I think I don't know who you were back then, so I can't really say. But I have a pretty good grasp of who you are now, and I don't think you'd be concerned about your father's reaction to anything."

"That's very true."

"However, after pouring over your personal financial records for the last week, I'm well aware that you had more than enough assets to cover the gambling debts without consulting your father."

"Also true."

"But that does raise the question—why did you routinely take out loans in order to gamble?"

Gray frowned and looked away for several seconds. "Because I was young, stupid and lazy."

"Well, doesn't that just explain all sorts of decisions we've all made."

Gray chuckled. "I was spoiled and used to getting what I wanted immediately. On several occasions I found myself in Vegas, enjoying some high-stakes games, and ran out of liquid cash. It's easier to take out a high-interest loan in the middle of the night than contact my portfolio advisor to liquidate assets. Especially when I knew I had the ability to pay back the principal before the interest skyrocketed."

"But the last time…you didn't pay it back immediately."

"No, I didn't. Because my life got blown to bits when officers barged into my home to arrest me for embezzlement. I was a little preoccupied with clearing my name to worry about the latest loan. If I'd known it would be used against me, I would have taken care of it immediately. But, once again, I was spoiled and didn't give a shit. Not even when the gentleman who'd loaned me the money sent an envoy to impress upon me the need to make good on it."

Was he really saying what she thought he was? "They sent someone to rough you up?"

Gray's laughter filled the cabin. "You've been watching too many movies, Ms. Whittaker."

"No, I grew up around organized crime, Gray. I've seen plenty of despicable men do despicable things. Beating someone up over money would be mild in comparison."

Gray's sharp gaze cut to hers and Blakely realized just how much personal information she'd revealed. Personal information she hadn't meant to share with anyone, especially Gray Lockwood. The last thing she wanted was for him to feel sorry for her. Or, worse, ask for more details.

But he didn't. "They actually did just come to have a conversation. At the time, I thought because they knew I was good for the money. I'd paid in full before. But now…"

It wasn't hard for Blakely to connect the dots to what Gray might be thinking.

"Do you really think they had something to do with the embezzlement?"

Gray shrugged. "Logically, it doesn't make much sense. They knew I was good for the money."

No—no, it didn't. But then sometimes crazy people did asinine things.

"It's worth double-checking, though. Especially since we're in town. Turning over all the stones…"

Eight years too late. The guilt she'd been fighting for the last several days swelled inside her. The more she learned about Gray, the more certain she was that he was innocent. Which meant she'd played an instrumental part in sending an innocent man to prison for a significant chunk of his life.

And there was nothing she could do to make up for that.

It was her turn to apologize for something she couldn't change. "I'm sorry."

Gray shrugged, not even attempting to pretend he didn't know what she meant. "Not your fault."

That's where he was wrong, but she wasn't going to argue with him about it. She was going to protest staying, though.

"Considering you don't really expect it to be anything, you don't really need me here for this." Which meant she could escape, and maybe, just maybe, prevent herself from doing something stupid.

Like throwing herself at him and begging him to kiss the hell out of her again.

"Talking to my bookie? I don't."

Well, she hadn't expected him to agree with her. That was easy. Too easy.

Reaching across the aisle, Gray ran his fingers down a strand of Blakely's hair, sending a cascade of tingles from her scalp down to her toes.

"I want you here for me."

Seven

He'd made her nervous, which was actually a little cute. Mostly because from his observations, not much made Blakely Whittaker nervous. He was learning that she might appear small and fragile, but she had a core of straight-up steel.

It was one of the most attractive things about her. Although, he wasn't thrilled knowing she'd built that tough core because of the things she'd seen and experienced in her life.

It was still cute. He liked knowing he could make her off-kilter. Because she certainly had the ability to set his own life on its head.

It might be seriously inconvenient to be dealing with this now, but if there was one thing he'd learned in the last few years, it was that one couldn't control everything. Sometimes, one simply had to roll with the punches, enjoy the experiences and find the lessons.

And like he'd said earlier, he wasn't stupid. When

faced with the opportunity to follow a couple of leads and spend several days in close quarters with Blakely... This was one of those times to take advantage of the opportunities.

Gray breezed through check-in at their hotel, going straight to the penthouse suite. It might have been several years since he'd visited, but the staff was fully aware of who he was and they'd been more than happy to accommodate his last-minute requests when he'd contacted them.

After punching in the code for the private elevator, he led Blakely into the small space. The minute the doors closed, he reached for her. Pulling her tight against his body, he backed them both up until she connected with the shiny chrome wall.

But he didn't kiss her. Yet.

Instead, his gaze raced around her face, taking in her wide, surprised expression. Her soft pink lips parted and a puffed gasp of breath caressed his face.

But she didn't move to break free. Instead, her hands settled at his hips, curling in and pulling him closer. Her pupils dilated as she leaned into him.

She wanted this as much as he did, which was all he needed to know.

Cupping a hand around the nape of her neck, Gray tilted her head and pulled her mouth to his. She tasted like peppermint and sin.

He tried to ease into it, to let them both sink into the connection, but Blakely had something else in mind. With a muffled groan, she rolled up onto her toes, trying to get more. One leg hooked over his hip, widening her stance so he could sink into the welcoming V of her open thighs.

Her heat and scent melted into him as she yanked him closer, grinding his hips against hers. Hers rolled, stroking his throbbing erection through the layers of their clothes.

She was hot as hell. And no doubt someone in security was enjoying the free show. As much as his body begged him to pull off all her clothes and take what she was clearly willing to give, he wasn't thrilled with the idea of having an audience the first time he stripped her naked and feasted on her delectable body.

Reluctantly, Gray put some space between them. But he couldn't make himself completely let her go. His hand still wrapped around her neck, he pressed his forehead against hers.

There was something calming and enticing about the way her body reacted to him. Labored breaths billowed in and out of her lungs, as if she'd just run a marathon instead of kissed the hell out of him. Which was good, since she made him feel the same way—as if he'd had the wind knocked out of him.

Her body arched, trying to find the connection again.

"Shhh," he whispered, nuzzling his lips against her forehead. "If I keep kissing you, I'm not going to be able to stop myself from pulling every stitch of your clothes off. And as much as I want that, the eye in the sky is always watching."

Blakely jerked and then stilled. After several seconds she whispered, "What are we doing? This isn't smart."

A puff of silent laughter escaped his lips. "Enjoying each other's company?"

"We don't like each other."

"You keep saying that. I like you just fine, Blakely. You're sharp, tough and resourceful. You're loyal to a fault and sexy as hell."

Brushing a strand of hair away from her face, Gray stared down at her as she stared up. Both of them paused, teetering on the edge of something. A choice. Potential. An opportunity that could be everything...or nothing more than a few stolen days of a good time.

Gray wasn't sure what would happen, but he knew without a doubt he was willing to take the chance to find out. He'd spent years without choices, without the option of doing and having what he wanted. Tonight, he was damned and determined to take the opportunity in front of him.

But only as long as Blakely wanted the same thing.

"When this elevator stops, I'm going into that room. If you follow me, I'm going to strip you bare, kiss every inch of your naked skin and fuck you until we're both blind with pleasure. If you're not okay with that, don't get off."

Blakely pressed a palm against the cold wall of the elevator. Gray didn't bother turning around to see if she followed when he exited. Was that because he knew she'd follow?

His words rang through her head. There was no question that she wanted what he was offering. Her entire body hummed with the aftermath of that kiss. She could feel the echo of his hands on her skin and needed more.

Following him wasn't smart. It wasn't safe.

But she was tired of being both. God, she'd been smart and safe her entire life. Played by the rules and watched as others who didn't were rewarded. Tonight, she wanted to feel. Real and raw. For once, she wanted to make a stupid, amazing, earth-rocking choice.

The aftermath would come soon enough.

The doors began to shut. Blakely's belly dropped to her toes, as if she'd already taken an express ride back to the bottom floor.

No.

Her hand shot out with inches to spare. The doors touched her skin and immediately bounced back. She slipped through the opening and into the entryway of an amazing suite.

A high ceiling soared above her head. And a massive wall of windows greeted her from the opposite side of the room. Taking several steps, Blakely surveyed the amazing view, a backdrop of light and action against the inky night sky.

Her breath backed into her lungs. Not because of the stunning view, but because Gray stepped up behind her.

The hard length of his body pressed against her. His arms wrapped around her and his palm found the edge of her jaw. Gently cupping her face, he eased her around until his mouth found hers again. The angle of his hold had her arching against him, a little off balance and dependent on him for stability.

Something about that felt uncomfortable and inviting all at once. Because she knew there was no way he'd let her falter.

He held her exactly where he wanted, commanding the moment in a way that made the blood in her veins thick with anticipation. His other hand was busy, as well, methodically popping open the buttons down the front of her shirt.

She'd been purposeful when she'd dressed this morning. Casual, but professional. Determined to set the tone of this trip from the outset.

Spreading open her blouse, Gray let her mouth go long enough to peer at what he'd revealed.

"Please tell me your panties match this bra."

A small smile tugged at Blakely's lips.

She might have been professional on the outside, but

staring at her lingerie options this morning, she just hadn't been able to make herself reach for anything plain. Instead, she'd chosen a mesh-and-lace bra that left almost everything except the bottom edge of her breasts naked. What was that saying? Something about sexy lingerie making a woman feel confident, even if no one else knew she was wearing it?

She'd embraced that school of thought for sure.

"As a matter of fact, they do." Maybe she was gloating. A little. But the appreciation and approval in Gray's voice was absolutely worth it.

"Let me see."

Setting her away from him, Gray took several steps backward.

Turning, Blakely did the same, increasing the space. Without the pressure of his body to keep it in place, the shirt he'd opened slithered off her shoulders to pool at her feet.

Normally, Blakely felt uncomfortable in these types of situations. She was typically a get-naked-get-in-bed-and-have-sex kind of girl. Focused on the end result, because that's what they both wanted, right?

Tonight was entirely different.

Probably because of the way Gray was watching her.

His hungry gaze tripped across her skin. She could feel it, as tempting as any caress. Clearly, he wanted her. Appreciated her. Which only increased her confidence.

"I'm dying here, Blakely. Show me."

Reaching down, she popped the button and zipper on her pants. Rolling her hips, Blakely let them follow the shirt down to the ground.

Gray's sharp intake of breath was worth a million words. His deep green eyes went hot. Kicking off her heels, Blakely stepped closer, standing before him in nothing but her bra and panties.

Her nipples ached and her sex throbbed. She wanted him to touch her. A cool draft of air kissed her over-heated skin, sending a scattering of goose bumps across her body.

"Gorgeous. You're beautiful, Blakely."

Closing the space between them, Gray cupped the nape of her neck and gently pulled her up onto her toes. He eased her into the towering shelter of his body, fus-ing their mouths together.

The kiss was powerful, deep. Drugging.

Languid desire melted through Blakely's body. His clothes scraped against her naked skin, reminding her how vulnerable she was right now. A dangerous edge of anxiety swirled at the fringes of the heat he was building.

Pulling back, she reached for the hem of his shirt, tugging it out of his slacks. Gray let her, somehow sens-ing her need to even the playing field. Lifting his arms, he helped her work the shirt up and off. Blakely didn't even bother tossing it—she simply let it drop to the floor behind him.

His ruffled dark brown hair made her lips curl up in a smile. Gray Lockwood wasn't the kind of guy who let much of anything ruffle him. It felt intimate somehow, to see him that way. More intimate than standing in front of him in her underwear.

Reaching for him, Blakely let her fingers sift through it, smoothing his hair back down. She let her hands drift down his neck, shoulders, torso.

Everything about him was tight and hard. His body swelled with muscle that had not been built in a gym. But what gave her pause was the smattering of scars scat-tered across his body.

Blakely let her fingertips play over them, memorizing the way the puckered skin felt. Gray stiffened beneath her exploration, but didn't pull away. She wanted to ask the questions, but knew he really didn't want to answer them.

And now wasn't the time.

Turning her gaze up to his, she leaned forward and placed her mouth over a particularly ugly one just over the swell of one of his pecs. And then let her mouth trail downward until she found the tight, tiny nub of nipple.

Sucking it into her mouth, Blakely relished Gray's groan. His fingers tangled in her hair, curled into a fist. His hold arched her neck at the same time he pressed into her. Blakely responded with the scrape of her teeth against the distended bud of flesh.

But that patience didn't last long. With a growl, Gray grasped her around the waist and boosted her up onto a kitchen island she hadn't even noticed was there.

The cold surface of the countertop connecting with the warm curve of her ass made her gasp with surprise. Reaching behind her, Gray had the clasp of her bra popped open and his mouth on her breast within seconds.

She arched into him, relishing the way Gray's wet mouth sucked on her skin. His palm spread wide at the base of her spine, keeping her where he wanted. Waves of sensation built in her belly as he tugged and sucked and laved.

His mouth played across her skin. Tingles chased up and down her spine. Pressing her knees wide, Gray stepped into the open V of her thighs. His fingertips caressed the delicate skin at the juncture of her hip and thigh, tracing the edge of her panties. Teasing, tempting her with what she really wanted.

She writhed beneath his touch, needing so much more. "Please."

Gray obliged, slipping a finger beneath the barrier of her panties and finding the moist heat of her sex. Blakely gasped and arched up into his caress, silently demanding more.

"God, you're wet," he groaned.

Urging her down, Gray hooked his fingers into the sides of her panties and tugged them down her legs. Kneeling at her feet, he stared up at her. The expression on his face sent her reeling. Harsh, needy and sexy as hell. She'd never had a man look at her with such desire and intensity.

Naked, spread across the kitchen island, Blakely should have felt exposed. But she didn't. Instead, she felt empowered and sexy.

Hands to her knees, Gray urged her wider as he leaned forward to trail kisses up the expanse of her inner thigh. He licked and nipped, sucked and nuzzled. Until his wicked mouth found the very part of her aching for relief. Blakely's world went dark as his mouth narrowed everything down to that one spot.

His mouth was magic. Blakely groaned, dropping back on her elbows because her body just wouldn't stay upright anymore. Her eyes slipped shut, bursts of color flashing across her brain along with his lightning strokes of pleasure.

The orgasm slammed into her, rocking her entire body. Her hips bucked against him, but his hard hold on her thighs kept her in place. She rode out the relentless waves for what felt like an eternity.

Blakely was breathing hard, her entire body laboring to pull enough oxygen into her lungs. Her elbows were shaky, but somehow she managed to stay mostly upright. It would have been embarrassing to collapse completely onto the kitchen counter in front of him.

Although, he probably wouldn't have cared.

Gray rose between her spread thighs. His mouth glistened with the aftermath of her orgasm. His own lips curled up into a self-satisfied smirk. Blakely had the urge to do whatever it took to wipe that expression off his face.

Starting with stripping him of the last of his clothes.

Blakely curled her hands into the waistband of his slacks, using the hold to jerk him closer. Sitting up, she made quick work of his fly and pushed both the pants and boxer briefs over his hips.

Gray toed off his shoes and stepped out of the pile of clothing, kicking it out of the way.

God, he was gorgeous. Light spilled over his body, highlighting the peaks and valleys of pure muscle. Two grooves sat at the edge of his hips, leading with a V straight to the promised land.

His erection, long and thick, jutted out from his body. A tiny pearl of moisture clung to the swollen tip. Blakely's tongue swept out across her bottom lip. She really wanted to taste him.

A groan reverberated through the back of his throat. "Don't look at me that way."

Startled, Blakely's gaze ripped up to his. "What way?"

"Like I'm a chocolate sundae and you're starving."

A grin played at Blakely's lips. "You're better than a sundae, Gray, and you know it. You're hot as hell."

"You think so, huh?"

Shaking her head, Blakely gestured for him to come closer. "You're walking, talking sin. Shut up and come here."

Gray did what she demanded, stepping back between her open thighs. Blakely started to jump down from the counter, but the solid wall of his body prevented her.

Shaking his head, Gray said, "That's where I want you."

You'd think, considering she'd just had a mind-blowing orgasm, that she might have been a little more malleable and accommodating. Not so much. "Maybe I want to be somewhere else." Like on her knees with him in her mouth. That's really what she wanted.

"Too bad."

Perhaps if she told him her plan he would relent. But she never got the chance. Because the ability to speak left her the minute his fingers found her sex and plunged deep. A strangled sound stuck in the back of her throat and her hips jumped forward, pressing tight against his hand in an effort to get more.

"God, you're so tight."

She nodded, her brain unable to form any other coherent response. Gray's fingers worked in and out, stroking deep. Blakely's brain scrambled, emptying of every thought except for the pleasure he was giving her.

Her body went white-hot as her hips pumped in time with his fingers. She was so close…and then he simply stopped. With his fingers still buried deep in her pussy, he gave a come-hither motion with his other hand that had her eyes crossing.

"Holy…"

"My thought exactly," he said. "Lean back, open the drawer behind you and grab a condom."

Blakely blinked, but did as he asked. Rolling onto one elbow, she reached to the far side and pulled out a drawer. Sure enough, a pile of condoms sat there.

Grabbing one, she asked, "How'd you know?"

"Not my first time staying in this suite."

Blakely tried not to let his statement derail her. She

didn't want to think about him being up here with another woman. Or women.

"And I might have asked the concierge to stock all the rooms with condoms."

Laughter and irritation bubbled up inside her chest. "Asshole."

He shrugged. "I believe in being prepared."

Apparently. Sitting back up, Blakely ripped into the package. Gray held out his hand for the condom, but she shooed him away. This was something she wanted to do.

Reaching for his hips, she guided him closer. Wrapping a hand around the long shaft of his sex, she relished the weight and size of him. Heat seeped into her palm. Friction added to it as she slid her hand up and down the length of him several times.

Blakely relished his groan and the way his hips thrust into her strokes. The walls of her own sex contracted. She wanted to feel him deep inside.

She rolled down the condom over his length and positioned him at the opening to her body. Hands on her hips, Gray paused, holding them both still.

Looking deeply into her eyes he said, "I'm sorry."

"For what?"

"It's been a while. This is probably going to be fast."

"How long is a while?"

"Almost eight years."

"Nope." No way was that possible. Sure, she understood why he was celibate for seven years, but he'd been out of prison for almost a year. Was it really possible he hadn't been with anyone that entire time?

"Why would I lie about something like that?"

He wouldn't. There was no reason to. "That's not what I meant. I just…find it hard to believe someone as handsome and sexual as you has chosen to be celibate."

"I was indiscriminate when I was younger. The past several years taught me what was important. And I haven't found anyone I wanted to be with…until now."

Blakely had no idea what to make of that, but she really didn't have time to consider because Gray took that moment to thrust home.

Blakely's head dropped backward. Her eyes slid closed as she savored the indescribable feel of him. Gray gave her a few moments to adjust.

Hands on her hips, he held her firmly in place as he thrust. In and out, Gray set a pace that had tension and pleasure building steadily inside her.

Sex on the kitchen counter in a penthouse suite should have felt decadent and dangerous. Something completely out of her normal life. And in some ways this moment with Gray did feel like that. Eight years ago, if someone had told her she'd be here with Gray, she probably would have laughed in their face.

But now…

Blakely's hands ran across his body, touching, memorizing, exploring. He was buried deep inside her, and still she wanted him closer. Needed more of him.

This wasn't just physical, although there was no doubt they generated plenty of heat together.

Gray's mouth found hers, fusing them together in a way that mimicked the connection of their bodies. His tongue stroked deep inside even as his sex sank deep.

She felt the flutter of another orgasm teasing at the edges of her senses. Gray's thrusts became harder and deeper, his grip on her hips holding her tightly in place.

And then the world burst open around her again. Just as he let out a roar of relief. His body shuddered against hers. And somehow she found the brainpower to wrap her arms around him and hold him tight. Together, they collapsed, the edge of the kitchen counter the only thing keeping Gray upright.

His labored breaths panted in her ear. The room around her slowly started to come back into focus. And, eventually, Gray pulled away.

She expected him to say something smart. To make some quip to cut the tension and make light of what had just happened between them. Because that's what she needed to keep her head on straight.

Instead, Gray smoothed a hand over her face. He cupped her jaw and brought her close.

"That was everything I ever imagined and more."

Blakely's chest swelled and something soft fluttered deep inside her belly.

But the feeling didn't last long. How could it when he looked at her, his intense gaze trained solely on her and filled with a heat that nearly singed her skin.

"But I'm nowhere close to done with you tonight."

Eight

One night was clearly not enough time with Blakely. Even if that one night had been the best sex of his life… and that was saying a lot.

As closed off as Blakely was in her regular life, she was just as open and free in the bedroom. It was a surprising discovery. One he was grateful for.

But as much as he'd love to take advantage of their surroundings by keeping her in bed all day, that wasn't an option.

Trailing his lips down the curve of her naked spine, Gray murmured, "Rise and shine, sleepyhead."

With a groan, Blakely buried her head farther under the pile of pillows she'd burrowed beneath. An unintelligible mumble floated up from the mound, but he got the gist of it.

"We don't have a few more minutes to spare."

He'd already let her sleep in. After grabbing the pillow shielding her face, Gray threw it onto the floor beside the bed.

Rolling his way, she cracked open a single eye and glared at him. "Go away."

Who knew she could be so cute in the morning?

Grabbing the mug of coffee he'd set on the bedside table, Gray waved it beneath her nose. "I will, if you really want me to. But I'm pretty sure you were adamant about going with me yesterday."

"What kind of monster sets a meeting for the butt crack of dawn?"

Gray chuckled. "It's almost noon."

Blakely bolted upright. If he hadn't acted fast, her elbow would have connected with the mug in his hand, sending hot coffee flying across the bed.

"You're kidding."

"I'm not."

"Why'd you let me sleep this late? I never sleep this late."

Which was one reason he'd done it. He hadn't needed her to tell him to know she wasn't normally the type to sleep in. Blakely was a meet-the-day-at-dawn-and-work-until-well-into-the-evening kind of woman.

But it was also clear she wasn't used to staying up until almost two having sex.

"Letting you sleep was the least I could do after last night."

Blakely's gaze narrowed. Obviously, what he'd thought was a cute quip had hit her entirely wrong.

"Sleep for sex?"

"Uh, no."

Her gaze ran up and down his body, a confusing mixture of heat and disdain filling her eyes. "You obviously didn't feel the need to sleep in."

He'd gotten up a couple hours ago, showered and been handling a few things. "I don't sleep much."

Normally, he would have left the statement as it was, but for some reason more words followed. "Before prison I easily slept until past noon every day because I was up half the night. In prison…everything you do is regimented and controlled by the clock. They tell you when to sleep, eat and even go outside. I have a hard time sleeping in now, even when I want to."

The hard edge that had tightened Blakely's features eased. She collapsed back against the pile of pillows, her mouth twisting into a self-deprecating grimace. "I'm sorry."

"For what?"

"Waking up defensive. I'm not used to this."

Well, that had been obvious without the confession.

"I don't know how I'm supposed to act or what you expect."

Gray set the mug on the bedside table. Shifting, he sat on the bed and settled his hip into the curve of her waist.

"Blakely, I don't expect anything. And the only way you're supposed to act is whatever way feels right to you. You and I get to decide what we're doing and what we want from each other. Nothing else matters."

Her head tipped sideways as she considered him. "You're not at all what I thought."

"You've said that before."

"But I keep getting reminded."

Shifting higher against the headboard, she grasped the covers and tucked them beneath her arms, leaving her shoulders and collarbone bare.

What he really wanted to do was pull them back down again, lean forward and feast on her ripe breasts. Instead, he grabbed the coffee and held it out to her again.

Grasping the mug between her palms, she held it up to her face and pulled in a deep breath. Her eyes closed in bliss, her expression making his half-hard erection stir. She'd looked the same last night when he'd put his mouth on her.

Clearly, she liked her coffee. The look of surprise she sent him when she finally took her first sip was totally worth the extra effort he'd taken to make it just the way she liked it.

"How'd you know?"

Gray didn't pretend not to know exactly what she was asking. Shrugging, he said, "We've been working pretty closely together for the last week. I paid attention."

Her lips twisted into a wry smile. "I didn't."

"That's okay."

"No, I'm starting to realize it isn't."

Leaning forward, Blakely set her mug back on the bedside table. Rolling up onto her knees, she let the covers pool at her waist. "How much time did you say we have?"

"Not enough."

Her hands roamed over her naked body, kneading her breasts. The tight bud of her nipples peaked between her spread fingers. "You're sure?"

Gray groaned. He wanted to be the one touching her. "Unfortunately, I am." Grasping her wrists, Gray pulled her hands away. Leaning forward, he laved one nipple, the rough scrape of his tongue across her soft flesh sending a sharp spike of need through him. "But, trust me, I have plans for you later, Ms. Whittaker."

"Oh, you do, do you?"

"Absolutely."

After a weird and unusual day, Blakely found herself back at the hotel, sitting on the couch with her feet curled up underneath her. She was reading through several emails that had come through on her Stone Surveillance account. Surprisingly enough, she was starting to feel like a real member of the team. In fact, one of the other investigators had sent her a request to review some financial documents on another case.

The case was simple and it had taken her less than an hour to look at what he'd sent...but it was interesting. And when she'd been able to send back a message with her insight, she'd felt like she'd contributed to something important.

That hadn't happened in a very long time.

She was just shutting down her computer when a loud knock on the door startled her. The sound reverberated through the huge suite, reminding her just how alone she was right now. After they'd returned from the meeting with Surkov—which had been unproductive, to say the least—Gray had left her in the suite to "run a couple errands," whatever that meant.

Unfolding from the sofa, Blakely padded across the room, the marble floor cool against the soles of her feet.

"Who is it?" she asked, looking through the peephole. Unfortunately, all she could see was a cart full of bags and boxes and a pair of shiny shoes sticking out from the bottom.

"Ms. Whittaker? Mr. Lockwood sent up some clothes for you from the boutiques downstairs."

Why would he do that? She had a suitcase filled with perfectly good clothes.

Opening the door, Blakely was already shaking her head. "I'm sorry to waste your time, but I don't need anything."

A petite woman stuck her head around the side of

the cart and gave her a disarming smile. "He said you'd say that."

"Did he now?" Blakely wasn't certain what to think about that.

The woman nodded, her bangs flopping into her eyes. With a puff of breath, she blew the hair back out again, uncaring where the strands landed or how they looked. "He also said I wasn't allowed to leave until you let me inside. And he promised me a huge tip. Like a-week-of-salary huge, which I really need. So, please? Let me in?"

Blakely eyed the other woman. She couldn't be more than five-two, a hundred and ten pounds. Her face was round, but skinny. Her features were petite and yet some-how inviting. Maybe it was the disarming, begging smile that stretched her wide mouth. Or the contagious spar-kle of excitement in her brown eyes. Either way, she was hardly threatening.

And there were logos from the shops Blakely had seen downstairs stamped on all the bags.

With a huff, Blakely pulled back and swept her arm wide, indicating the other woman should come in. Far be it for her to deny anyone a chance to make some money.

The other woman was practically bouncing as she wheeled the cart past Blakely. "I'm Desiree." With a gri-mace and a roll of her eyes, she continued, "Yeah, I know. It's awful. My mom was an eighties showgirl, convinced I was going to carry on the family legacy. To her utter shame, I have two left feet and about as much grace as a cactus."

Desiree pushed the cart into the center of the living room, stopped and took a quick turn around. "Nice." With a clap of her hands, she dismissed the opulence of the space and the amazing view outside the windows in favor of the loaded-down cart.

Tapping a finger against her lips, her eyes narrowed as she studied the things. Occasionally, she'd flip a considering glance over at Blakely.

"Not much to go on—"

"Hey!"

Desiree dismissed her indignation with a flip of her hand. "That's not what I meant. You're gorgeous. I meant I can't tell much about your personal style based on the oversize sweatshirt and bare feet you're currently wearing. I'm going to assume that's not your norm."

"You assume right."

"Mr. Lockwood gave me a few parameters and suggestions for what he'd like to see you in, but I'd like to get your input. Sure, we dress to impress the important man in our life, but you should feel amazing in it, too."

Was Gray the important man in her life? Blakely wasn't sure. Her libido definitely wanted a repeat performance of last night. And over the last week she'd come to realize, despite everything, that she might actually like the guy. But it was a huge leap from sex and mutual respect to him being the center of her universe.

A leap she was hardly ready to make.

"He's not important."

Desiree flipped her a disbelieving glance. "Trust me, I know people. He's important."

"Fine, but not to me."

Desiree gave her another expression that said "yeah, right," and shrugged. "If you say so."

"No, really. There's a lot you don't know about him. It's…complicated."

"Sister, it always is. Complicated makes life interesting."

"Interesting is dangerous."

Desiree shook her head. "Interesting is just interesting." Zipping open one of the bags, she revealed a sleek black jumpsuit. "Mr. Lockwood suggested you tend to wear very tailored clothing. Pieces that convey a sense of authority and control."

Interesting. Who knew he'd been studying her wardrobe? And apparently forming many opinions that he'd never voiced.

"He suggested you'd be most comfortable in something tailored and classic. But he also mentioned he'd like to give you the opportunity to try something new. To come out of your shell."

Come out of her shell? What did that mean? Was he passing judgment on her clothing choices? Blakely stared at the cart of things Gray had decided she needed to try.

Embarrassment and anger began to climb up her neck. "There's nothing wrong with the way I dress."

"Oh, I don't think that's what Mr. Lockwood meant."

"And just what did he mean?"

"He said he didn't think you'd had a lot of opportunity to indulge and play in your life, not even as a little girl. Which made me sad. I mean, every little girl should have a chance to play dress-up."

"So he wants me to dress up like a doll now?"

Blakely was lost, uncomfortable and out of her element. But she was also surprised because Gray had pegged her pretty closely. She'd never been the type to play in her mother's makeup or clomp around in her heels. In fact, looking back, she couldn't remember a lot of laughter or happiness in her childhood.

It wasn't that she'd been miserable. Or mistreated. There were plenty of kids who'd had it worse than her, by far. But...

"I think he just wants you to have a chance to feel beautiful."

Blakely blinked at Desiree. She couldn't remember a single time in her life when she'd felt truly beautiful. The suits she preferred to wear to the office made her feel powerful and competent. Prepared to handle anything that came her way.

She hadn't even gone to her high-school prom. Thinking back, she'd never actually owned a ball gown. Or had a reason to want one. And she wasn't exactly sure she wanted a fancy dress now. "I'm not big on pink puffy dresses."

Desiree laughed, the warm, sultry sound surprising Blakely. She'd expected the tiny thing to have a tinkly little laugh. "Good thing I don't have any of those here, then."

With a twinkle in her eye, Desiree began to pull several more outfits from their protective bags. One was a dark red floor-length gown that would no doubt cling to every curve she owned. And make her feel like she was practically naked. Another emerald green gown had a trumpet skirt that kicked out with a row of ruffles.

Nope, neither of those were going to work.

Blakely's eye kept going back to the black jumpsuit Desiree had unwrapped first. It had a subtle sparkle to it and it had taken her several minutes to realize the satin material had iridescent threads running through it.

Desiree revealed a few more outfits, one off-white and another bright purple. There was no way she was wearing either of those colors. She swept her hands across the selection. "Pick your poison—which one do you want to try first?"

"The black one," Blakely stated without hesitation.

"Somehow I knew that's what you'd go for. Are you sure you don't want to try one of the others on just for fun?"

"Not on your life." Nothing about the others appealed to her.

"Okay." After pulling the jumpsuit off the hanger, Desiree handed it to her. "Just slip it on and I'll zip you up."

With a deep breath, Blakely disappeared into the bedroom. She pulled the sweatshirt over her head and dropped it to the floor. Turning her back to the doorway, she put one foot and then the other inside the garment. Pulling it up and over her shoulders, Blakely realized what had looked rather conservative on the hanger was actually sexy as hell. There was no back at all to the jumpsuit.

The waist cinched in, accentuating her hourglass figure. It rode high on her shoulders, cutting shallowly across her collarbone. The edge of the material fell away dramatically in a waterfall that pooled at the small of her back. The drape of the material hugged the curve of her ass and the deceptively long length of her legs.

Because the back was naked, she couldn't wear a bra. Her breasts swung free, brushing tantalizingly against the soft material with each deep intake of breath. She could already feel her body responding at the thought of wearing this in front of Gray.

Her nipples tightened and peaked, rubbing against the fabric.

Blakely reached up, covering both breasts and massaging in an effort to relieve the pressure.

"Well, that's a sexy sight to walk in on."

Blakely jumped and gasped at the sound of Gray's voice. She immediately dropped her hands as if she'd been caught doing something inappropriate.

"Oh, no, you don't. Put those hands right back where they were."

Blakely's gaze tore up to the mirror on the dresser across from her. Gray's penetrating gaze stared back at her, watching her with a predatory gleam that made the ache deep inside her ratchet higher.

He stood in the doorway, one hip propped against the jamb, head cocked to the side studying her. Both hands were tucked into the pockets of his slacks. He was deceptively calm even as his gaze ate her up. At some point he'd shed the suit jacket he'd been wearing earlier. The sleeves of his white dress shirt were rolled up his arms, revealing heavy muscle and bulging veins running up the length of his forearms.

He shut the bedroom door. "We're alone." A single dark eyebrow winged up, silently demanding she do what he'd asked.

Slowly, Blakely's hands rose, settling back over her sensitive breasts.

"What were you thinking about?"

"You." The answer was simple and easy. But that's not what he was looking for.

"What about me? What had that look of pure pleasure crossing your beautiful face?"

There was something freeing about having the conversation through the reflection of the mirror. An added layer of distance that allowed her to be more open than she might have otherwise been.

"I was thinking about you taking me out of this outfit. Your mouth tugging on my swollen nipples. The scrape of the material across them was torture, so I was trying to ease the ache."

"Did it help?"

"Not really."

"Why not?"

"Because it wasn't what I wanted."

A smile played at the corners of his lush lips. "And what is it that you want?"

"You."

He shook his head. "You can do better than that."

"I want you to kiss me like you did last night. Like I was the air keeping you alive. I want you to run your fingers over every inch of my skin. I want your length buried deep inside me, stroking in and out until we're both panting from the need for relief."

Gray pushed away from the door, but his hands stayed firmly where they were. Slowly, she watched him walk forward, closing the gap between them. Blakely's body reacted by drawing tight with anticipation. She wanted him to give her what she'd asked for.

Thinking that was exactly what he was going to do, she braced.

But he didn't. Instead, he sidled up behind her, bending his head down so he could rain kisses across the top of her shoulders. His hands settled on her hips for several seconds, holding her in place.

Slowly, his hands slid up her body, over her breasts and shoulders. One hand curled around her throat, his thumb placing pressure beneath her chin. The hold wasn't hard or demanding. In fact, it was soft and gentle.

He urged her attention to shift from watching his movements in the mirror to looking at herself.

At first, she was uncomfortable, her gaze continuing to slide away. But each time it did, the pressure of his thumb urged her back again. Finally, realizing the faster she complied, the faster he was going to let her go, Blakely gave in and did what he wanted.

"What do you see?"

"Me."

"Tell me more," he coaxed.

Blakely shrugged. "My hair's a mess. The jumpsuit is gorgeous, but not something I'd ever have a reason to wear again. I'm short and should have put on some makeup this morning. I look tired."

"You do look tired, but that's because you were up half the night having passionate sex, which should be a good thing."

"It is a good thing."

"Then why do you say that with regret?"

Because she didn't like looking like something the cat had dragged in. Especially next to him. "You look like you've just stepped off the front cover of some men's fashion magazine. It isn't fair."

Gray chuckled. "I'll take that as a compliment."

Of course he would.

"Would you like to know what I see?"

"Yes."

No. Blakely's shoulders tightened. Did she really want to know?

"You're absolutely gorgeous, Blakely. Your skin is pale and perfectly soft. Those ice-blue eyes draw me in every time I look at you. But it's not just the unusual color. They're so bright with intelligence, curiosity and integrity."

"You mean judgment."

"I meant exactly what I said. Your messy hair reminds me that last night I was the one responsible for making it that way. I remember grabbing a fist of it and holding you exactly where I wanted you. And I remember that you let me. You're a damn strong woman, Blakely. I've known that from the first time we met. But last night… you felt safe enough with me to let go. Which only makes me want to give you more opportunities to do that."

"Is that what this is about?"

"What *what* is about?"

"The clothes?"

"Something like that. And we were invited to attend a VIP event at an exclusive club tonight. I thought it would be fun."

"You were invited." Blakely hadn't been invited to much of anything in her life, let alone a VIP Vegas party.

Gray shrugged. "Only because no one here knows you yet. You're beautiful, intelligent and forthright. Qualities most people appreciate. And when you decide to let go a little, you're amazingly fun. You're going to be a hit tonight."

Blakely scoffed. Now he was just blowing smoke up her ass.

"And with you wearing that outfit, I'm going to have to post a sign of ownership over your head to protect what's mine."

Blakely's eyebrows rose. "Buddy, I'm not yours or anyone else's. No one owns me."

Gray's mouth spread into a wide grin that crinkled the edges of his eyes. "I know. I just wanted to hear your response."

Nine

He was playing a dangerous game, but something told him it would be worth it.

For the past week Gray had studied Blakely. Even when he'd been trying to ignore her, he couldn't help himself. Which meant he'd learned a lot in those days.

But he'd learned even more about her last night.

Watching her relax and let go with him had been… perfection. A gift.

But it had also made him realize he wanted more from her than a stolen weekend in Vegas. However, he wasn't entirely certain she'd be open to the idea of actually being with him.

He hadn't really had a meeting this afternoon, just a need for some space to clear his head. At some point he'd come to the conclusion that it didn't particularly matter what Blakely thought she wanted—it was his job to convince her they could be real and more than just a few stolen moments, even if those moments had been combustible and amazing.

So he was on a mission to seduce her, not just physically, but mentally. And the first step of that was hopefully giving her a chance to loosen up and enjoy herself, something he didn't think she'd had the opportunity to do nearly enough.

Because he wanted to see more of that sparkle in her eyes. The wonder and relief. That easy smile—hard-won, but totally worth the effort.

And right now was the perfect opportunity.

Gray watched Blakely's reflection in the bedroom mirror. She was beautiful even before the team of makeup artists and hairstylists showed up in a bit to do their thing. He'd picked out the jumpsuit himself, knowing it would be perfect for her. He'd also instructed Desiree to give her several other options, just in case he'd been wrong.

But he hadn't been.

He also wasn't wrong that it would look amazing on her.

The outfit was pure class and sophistication, but with a touch of drama at the back. And he couldn't wait to get his hands on the gleaming expanse of satiny skin left bare.

If he touched her right now, though, they'd never leave the suite. And as tempting as that idea was, he wanted to give her a night out first.

"Relax, Blakely, and enjoy the experience."

"Easy for you to say," she grumbled.

"No, it really isn't," Gray countered, his voice filling with wry humor. There was a time in his life that putting on a tux and attending some fancy party was the norm. No, not just the norm. He'd felt a sense of entitlement to be invited. Like the world and everyone in it owed him simply because of who he was.

However, it had been a long time since he'd bothered to enjoy the kind of party they were going to attend. Oh, it would have been easy to revert to old bad behavior once he'd been released. Especially after his father and mother had looked him in the eye and told him they'd be happy to never see him again.

But his time in prison had made him stronger than who he used to be.

That didn't mean he wasn't looking forward to bringing a little glamour and sparkle into Blakely's life. Something told him she'd been seriously lacking in those two things for a very long time.

She might be severely out of her element, but she deserved to have a Cinderella moment.

"You've got about thirty minutes before the rest of the staff shows up to help you get ready."

"Staff? What the heck are you talking about?"

"Hair and makeup."

"You think I can't do my own hair and makeup?" Blakely asked indignantly.

"Of course I know you can. But most women find it fun to let someone else do those kinds of things occasionally."

"I'm not most women."

Gray closed the space between them. Hands to her shoulders, he spun her around so she was facing him. "Of that, I'm keenly aware," he murmured before dropping his head and finding her mouth.

The kiss was deep and hot, a blazing inferno within seconds. Touching her always made him want. Gray let the connection pull him in and under—he relished the taste and feel of her.

It would have been so easy to just give in and let the moment spin out of control. But, somehow, he found the strength to pull back. "Can you do me a favor?" he asked, staring deep into her pale eyes.

Expression glazed with desire and need, she mutely nodded. When she looked at him that way...it was hard to think about anything else.

"Stop fighting me and assuming the worst out of everything I do and say."

"I expect the worst."

A tight band squeezed around his chest. "I know."

Reaching up, he smoothed her soft hair away from the edge of her face. It really bothered him that she'd been taught by everyone in her life to be so wary, including the people who were supposed to protect her the most.

"I have only the best intentions where you're concerned, Blakely. You're a remarkable woman and I simply want to show you how much I value your company."

"I don't need expensive clothes and people waiting on me hand and foot."

No, she didn't. Most of the women who'd been in his life would have accepted his gesture without comment. Hell, they would have expected it. But not Blakely. "Which is exactly why I want to give those things to you. Let me."

She blinked. Slowly, she nodded.

"Excellent. As much as I'd like nothing better than to strip you out of this outfit right now, that's going to have to wait until later. You have twenty minutes to shower before everyone gets here."

After spinning her away from him, Gray pushed her forward. She stumbled a step, but quickly found her footing. Shooting him a perturbed look over her shoulder, he couldn't help but take advantage of the perfect target in front of him.

Reaching out, he smacked her on the rear. "Hop to it."

Blakely yelped and glared at him. No doubt, he'd pay for that later, but he was looking forward to that, too.

Retracing his steps into the living room, he asked Desiree to leave all the accessories that matched the jumpsuit before dismissing her.

Dropping into a chair by the massive wall of windows, he ignored the spectacular view spread out before him. The city was alive with light and activity, but none of that interested him. Instead, he opened his email on his phone and began sifting through the business he'd been ignoring for most of the day.

The dead end with Surkov hadn't come as a surprise. And yet, he'd still left the meeting disappointed. Because he really was no closer today to figuring out who had set him up than he'd been months ago.

The longer he went without a credible lead, the more nervous he was becoming. Because without understanding what had happened, who had set him up and what their motive had been, the possibility that it could happen again lurked around every corner. The damage to his life had blindsided him. And he was willing to do whatever was necessary in order to make damn sure it didn't happen again.

And now, Blakely was involved. Which could potentially put her at risk. A reality he did not like.

With a sigh, Gray zeroed in on the email from Joker that had come in several hours ago. Opening it up, he was hopeful until he realized it was a report on his birth mother, not anything to do with the embezzlement.

Reading the details about the woman who'd given birth to him, basically sold him and then attempted to blackmail his mother did not give him a warm, fuzzy feeling. Apparently, she'd continued to live a high-profile life here in Vegas. At least until the last few years, when her beauty and talent had begun to fade and she couldn't trade on them anymore to support her excessive lifestyle.

She'd gone from having her name featured on the marquee to being a nameless face in the background. Without even meeting her, he had a feeling that hadn't gone over well.

Not to mention, she'd apparently had connections with some questionable people over the years. Joker had discovered that her long-term boyfriend was a well-known criminal.

After reading the report twice, Gray finally closed the document and tossed his phone onto the table in front of him. Nothing inside him wanted to deal with the situation right now. Tomorrow would be soon enough to confront his birth mother and tell her the blackmail wouldn't work; she was going to have to find another cash cow to bankroll her high-roller tendencies.

With a sigh, Gray sank back into the chair. He rubbed his eyes, realizing they were gritty with fatigue for the first time since he'd gotten up this morning. Not surprising, considering he and Blakely had been awake half the night.

He must have fallen asleep, because one moment he was contemplating getting up and taking a shower so he could be ready whenever Blakely was, and the next she was leaning over him, shaking his shoulder and murmuring his name. "Gray…"

Slowly, he blinked his eyes open, his vision bleary and unfocused. A halo of light shone around Blakely's head, like the ring of light depicted in paintings of Mary. Her entire being glowed. It wasn't a description he'd normally use for Blakely. She was many things, but maternally divine wasn't one of them.

However, there was no debating that the glow came from deep inside her. She was radiant in a way that made him want to worship at her feet.

"Gray, are you okay?"

Slowly, everything came into focus. He sat up and Blakely took several steps back, giving him a perfectly unobstructed view of her.

"You're breathtaking."

A deep blush crept up her skin. Clearly, she didn't receive enough compliments. He was going to have to remedy that.

But right now, he needed to get them out of this room, or all the effort the team he'd hired had put into Blakely's appearance would be wasted because they'd never leave the suite.

Standing, Gray texted their driver that they were on the way down, then slipped his phone into his pocket. He held a hand out to her and waited, slightly surprised when she actually twined her fingers with his.

He snagged his suit coat and led them out into the waiting elevator. Wrapping an arm around her, Gray used their joined hands at the small of her back to press her tight against his side. He loved the feel of her there. The way the lush curves of her breasts settled heavily against his arm. The subtle scent of her tantalized his senses. And he could feel the heat of her moist breath against his neck.

"Where are we going?"

"Excess—it's a club downtown."

"Sounds very Vegas."

Gray chuckled. "It's popular enough. I know the owner."

"Partied there often, did you?"

A wry smile tugged at his lips. "Something like that."

The ride in the car was quiet. Blakely would never be the kind of woman to fill a silence with chatter, which was something Gray happened to like about her. When she had something important or profound to share, she did it. Otherwise, she kept her thoughts to herself.

Which intrigued him. Because he really wanted to know what went on behind those intelligent, beautiful eyes.

The drive didn't take long. Less than twenty minutes later they were ensconced in the VIP area on the second floor, overlooking the bustle of the club and the main dance floor below. They had a private waitstaff, dancers and floor of their own.

Gray didn't bother to ask Blakely what she wanted, but ordered drinks for them both. His mission tonight was to get her loosened up enough to see her dance, something he'd hazard Blakely hadn't done much in her life.

A perfect reason for him to want to make it happen.

They'd been sitting there for about fifteen minutes when a heavy hand landed on his shoulder. Gray's heart raced and adrenaline shot into his system. He reacted, snapping a hand down over the wrist and barely checking himself before he could use leverage and power to break the person's arm and throw him over the back of the chair and onto the floor at his feet.

But he wasn't in the middle of a crude fighting ring.

Blakely sat forward, spilling her drink as she settled it on the table in front of them. She was halfway out of her seat, panic in her eyes, before he could stop her.

Shaking his head, he silently told her he was fine. Although, the hitch in his lungs suggested that might be a lie.

"Good to see you back here, my friend," a familiar

voice, clearly oblivious to just how close he'd come to having his arm broken, rumbled from behind him.

Pulling in a huge gulp of air, Gray willed his body to settle. Pasting a smile on his face, he turned and stood in a fluid motion, dislodging the heavy hold from his shoulder.

Clapping a hand across Dominic's shoulder, he said, "It's good to be back."

Blakely's heart was still in her throat as Gray turned to make introductions.

She'd seen the look of shock and involuntary reaction before Gray had shut it down. His body tensed, every vein popping into relief down his muscled arms. His eyes had hardened, turning to the most cold and deadly emerald green she'd ever seen.

A part of her had always recognized Gray had a hidden edge of danger, but there was no doubt she'd almost gotten a firsthand introduction to it right now. Luckily, he had impeccable control over his physical reflexes.

For the first time, Blakely realized she was standing. Her fingers were curled around the edge of the table. Loosening her grip, she held out a hand to the man now standing beside Gray.

"Blakely Whittaker, meet Dominic Mercado."

Dominic leaned forward into the space between them. He grasped her hand in both of his, giving hers a squeeze instead of actually shaking it. "Please tell me you're willing to dump this asshole and spend the evening with me instead."

Gray lifted a single eyebrow. "I'm the asshole? You're the man hitting on my date right in front of me."

Dominic's eyes twinkled as he offered her a wide grin. "I've learned in life, it's folly to ignore the opportunities in front of you. And I'd kick myself if I let this vision walk away without at least taking a shot."

"Too bad for you, she's already taken."

This time, it was Dominic's turn to cock an eyebrow. "Perhaps you should let the lady speak for herself. Are you going to choose this scoundrel over an upstanding citizen and business owner like myself?"

Blakely's gaze bounced back and forth between the two men for several moments. They were clearly friendly, but with an undercurrent of rivalry running beneath their exchange.

Gray simply watched her, waiting for her reaction. Although, his gaze did narrow when it slipped down to take in the way Dominic still had a hold of her hand.

Finally, Blakely turned to Dominic. Tugging gently, she pulled out of his grasp.

"I'm flattered."

Dominic sighed and shook his head. "No, you're not."

Blakely rolled her eyes. "Gray isn't a scoundrel. And something tells me 'upstanding citizen' might be a stretch."

Dominic's grin widened. "Perceptive, isn't she?"

Gray's entire body relaxed. "That she is. Smart as hell, too."

"Lucky bastard."

"You have no idea." Holding out a hand, Gray pulled her into the shelter of his body and she accepted. "Thanks for the info I asked for."

Dominic gave Gray a smile, this one actually genuine. "You're welcome. Anything for you, man, although I don't understand why you're looking into Vegas showgirls with questionable taste in men. Please tell me you're not looking to invest in a show or something stupid."

"Nothing like that. I'm part owner in a surveillance company and she's connected to a case we're working."

Dominic's mouth curled into a grimace. "Not surprising. Her boyfriend has a nasty reputation and I wouldn't be surprised to find out she's up to her neck in the bad shit, too."

"There's plenty of that to be found in this town."

Dominic's gaze scraped over the crowd around them. "Isn't that the truth? Well, I'm going to go back behind the bar and appease my wounded ego with an expensive glass of single-malt scotch." Tipping two fingers to his forehead, he offered them a salute, then said, "Enjoy yourselves. Let my staff know if you need anything."

Gray nodded, his grip around her waist tightening as Dominic turned to leave. Blakely watched as he melted into the crowd, stopping at several tables to speak briefly to people here and there.

From out of nowhere, a tall redhead in a flashy sequined dress stalked up to him. Blakely couldn't hear their words over the roar of music, but clearly the conversation was heated. And the affable, charming, slightly smarmy persona Dominic had been wearing disappeared. His entire body language changed.

Wrapping a hand around her upper arm, he pulled her in so they were practically nose to nose. And then let her go again when she used her other hand to shove him away. Spinning on her heel, the redhead disappeared into the crowd.

And Dominic simply watched her go. But his hands were balled into fists at his sides and his chest heaved as he tried to get ahold of his response.

"Well, that was interesting."

Blakely's attention turned back to Gray. "How so?"

"The redhead? That's his little sister's best friend. I

dated Annalise, his sister, for about two minutes when we were in our early twenties, which is how I met Dominic. Our friendship stuck when the relationship didn't. I didn't realize Meredith was still around."

Shaking his head, Gray's mouth twisted into a wry grimace. "I suppose a lot happened while I was gone. Not that it matters."

The techno music that had been blasting into the space changed. The tempo slowed, even though there was still a thump of bass running beneath the sounds. Several people streamed off the dance floor as others moved on.

Gray didn't bother to ask as he tugged her onto the dance floor.

Grasping her hand, he spun her out and then pulled her back in. Her body settled against the hard planes of his. Thanks to last night, she knew intimately what his Greek-god body looked like beneath the sophisticated layer of his suit.

And she immediately wanted to experience that wonderland again. Her hand snuck beneath his jacket, sliding along the rough texture of his tailored shirt. His body heat warmed her palm. And she loved the way he arched into her touch. Her fingers found the edge of his slacks and teased down as far as they could go. Unfortunately, she couldn't quite reach the bare skin of his ass.

However, his hands could find naked skin. One palm spread wide at the small of her back. His own fingertips tantalized as they dipped into the opening just above the dint of her ass. Pulling her close, he folded his other hand between their two bodies, strategically using the cover of the dance to hide the fact that he was running a fingernail across the distended bud of her nipple.

"I'm pretty sure that's not playing fair," Blakely gasped.

Her entire body began to tingle.

"No, I'm pretty sure this jumpsuit isn't playing fair."

"You're the one who picked it out."

"True. Who knew I was into torture? Knowing you're wearing nothing under this thing has been driving me crazy all night."

Pulling back, Blakely stared up at Gray. "Remind me, why are we still here?"

A grin played at the edges of his lips. "That's a good damn question."

As much as Gray wanted to accept the dare in her heated gaze, there was something they had to do first.

"We have one more stop to make...it's time I met my mother."

Ten

Getting backstage had never been hard for him. Money and notoriety provided access to more than most people wanted to believe. His conviction hadn't simply made the local news, but had hit the national media circuit. On the heels of several high-profile financial scandals, his was just another in a trend...or that's how the media machine had spun it.

Which had pissed off his father. That man did not subscribe to the any-publicity-is-good-publicity mentality.

Gray would admit that for most of his life, walking through doors locked to everyone else gave him a small thrill. A sense of power, right or wrong. Tonight, his stomach just churned when the guard looked at the cash he'd slipped into his hand and then swept them past without so much as a change in his facial expression.

Several steps down the darkened hallway, Blakely pulled him to a stop. Her calming hand rested on his arm as she turned to face him.

"You okay?"

No, he really wasn't. Normally, he'd have kept that confession to himself, but for some reason Gray let the confession free. "I'm a nervous wreck."

A short burst of laughter shot between them. Okay, not the reaction he'd expected.

"You certainly don't look it. I'm starting to realize the calm, reserved exterior you show the world might hide a whole lot."

It was Gray's turn to chuckle, but Blakely wasn't wrong. Long before prison, his father had taught him emotions were something that made you weak. The world rewarded strength, even if it was a facade.

Gray could count on one hand the number of people who recognized that about him, though. And those people were all the most important ones in his life. The idea that Blakely could join that group…made him even more nervous than knowing he was about to meet Cece, his mother.

Leaning back against the wall, Gray wrapped his arms around Blakely and pulled her tight against his body. His mouth found hers in a brutal kiss that gave him the strength he needed.

The feel of her settled him. Centered him in a way only getting in the ring had done before. The way she opened to him, melted against him, made him feel powerful and protective. He let the moment spin, allowing the connection he felt with Blakely to overshadow everything else.

She was the one to finally break the kiss. Pulling back, she whispered, "We need to go."

Shaking his head, Gray knew she was right. But a huge part of him wanted to stay in this dingy hallway with her. To freeze this moment and hold on to it. Hold on to her.

Pressing his forehead to hers, Gray let his eyes drift closed. "Thank you for being here."

Her hands, resting on his hips, squeezed. "I wouldn't be anywhere else. You're not alone in this, Gray."

Damn, it had been a long time since he'd felt that was true. His parents, the people who were supposed to support him and love him unconditionally, had turned their backs when he'd needed them most. They'd believed the lies instead of him.

Sure, Stone and Finn had his back. Of that he was one hundred percent certain. Not just because they said they did, but because they'd proven it time and again. But they both had their own lives. They were married and were hip-deep in building Stone Surveillance. No doubt they'd drop everything if he needed them, but their focus shouldn't be his problems and his life.

And Blakely... Right now, she made him feel like he mattered. She was the most amazing woman he'd ever met, and if she could care about him, maybe that meant he was actually a good person, worthy of someone else caring.

Gray was about three seconds away from saying to hell with it and taking her home without doing what they'd come here to do, when a wolf whistle sounded from down the hall. "Get a room!"

A wry smile lit Blakely's ice-blue eyes as she pushed away from him. Her hand slid down his arm until her fingers were twined with his. She didn't wait for him, but used their connection to bring him along behind her as they continued down the hallway.

The mountain of meat at the door had told him Cece was in the second-to-last room on the left. The closer they got to that end of the long hallway, the more noise could be heard. The tinkle of laughter and rumble of voices.

The ring of hangers against metal rods and the dull thud of things being dropped onto a wooden surface.

They passed one room that was occupied by a group of women. Glancing in, they were half-naked and didn't particularly care the door was standing wide open. Bright, naked bulbs ringed multiple large mirrors. Several women were leaning forward, applying makeup to their faces.

The cacophony didn't surprise Gray. It also didn't hold his attention for anything more than a passing glance. Blakely, on the other hand, slowed, her eyes glued to the sight. Her expression was blank and controlled, so he couldn't tell what thoughts were spinning behind her gorgeous eyes. If he had to guess, though, the thought of being half-naked in a room with twelve other women would give her hives. She wasn't exactly a prude, but she was fairly private.

Later, he'd ask. But right now, he was laser-focused on getting this over with. Something told him his mother wasn't likely to greet him with a teddy bear she'd been carrying around for the last thirty-four years hoping for the opportunity to give it to him.

He didn't live in a Hollywood movie. Not to mention, she'd sent a blackmail demand.

His nerves from before hadn't disappeared, but they'd been joined by a healthy ribbon of anger. Justified or not, it was there and if he wasn't careful, it might color the coming encounter.

The room that the security guy had directed him to was much different from the one they'd just passed. The door was closed, and there was no noise emanating from behind the solid surface.

Gray didn't bother knocking. He simply turned the old round knob and pushed.

The woman in front of the mirror on the far wall spun. Her face was ripe with surprise that quickly morphed into anger. Her eyebrows, clearly exaggerated with stage makeup, slammed down into an angry V.

Gray wasn't certain what he'd expected. Maybe to feel this cosmic connection. Or maybe experience a bone-deep recognition. But there was nothing. The woman looking back at him was a complete stranger.

Oh, certainly, he could recognize features of himself in her. The set of her mouth was familiar. The shape of her eyes, even if hers were brown while his were green. But that was it.

Dispassionately, Gray cataloged her as a woman. Clearly, she'd been beautiful once. Her skin was sagging and lined, but the array of jars behind her suggested she spent time and money to preserve what she could. Her hair was thick and shiny, and hung down her back in lush waves.

She'd also taken time and effort to keep her body in top physical shape. She was slender, and her collarbone jutted out.

Cece stood. The heavy wooden chair she'd been sitting in clattered to the floor. "What are you doing here?"

Gray reached behind him and closed the door. The quiet click reverberated through the room.

"You know who I am." Gray didn't bother to make the statement a question. It was clear from her reaction that she did.

"Of course I know who you are."

Gray huffed with sarcastic laughter. "There's no 'of course' about it, considering I didn't know you existed until two days ago."

"And whose fault is that?"

"I'm going to say yours since you sold me when I was just a few days old."

Her mouth twisted into a nasty expression, and suddenly, Gray realized she wasn't beautiful after all. It was a facade, like everything else about her. "Is that what he told you? Of course he made me out to be the bad guy."

"My father didn't tell me anything. How could he? He hasn't spoken to me in almost eight years."

Her eyes glittered with malice. "That bitch's account wouldn't be any better."

"I assume the bitch you're referring to is my mother."

"No, *I'm* your mother."

Her words made his stomach roll. Oh, he'd known they were true, but hearing her say them out loud, especially with a sneer in her voice, made him want to cringe. Or deck her. But he refused to do either.

"No, you're not. Neither is she, for that matter. But that's none of your business. I'm here to tell you the secret isn't a secret anymore. You can send threatening letters to whomever you'd like, but they're not going to do you any good. No one is giving you more money."

Cece slammed a container of makeup onto the table behind her. It exploded, a puff of powder raining over the surface. "I'm going to kill that little bitch if I ever find her."

Gray took a menacing step forward. Blakely's hand shot out, curling around his bicep and holding him in place. "Did you just threaten my mother?" She might not have been much of one to him, and certainly not when he'd needed her most, but he wasn't about to let this woman get away with threatening her anymore.

"No. I don't give a shit what your mother does. I'm going to kill your sister. Once again, she's managed to ruin everything and she isn't even here."

Out of all the revelations he'd gotten in the last few days, those words actually rocked Gray's world. He went backward on his heels, as if he'd just received an uppercut to the jaw. If Blakely hadn't been standing behind him, he might have fallen to the floor.

"What sister?"

He had a sister.

A sneer twisted Cece's lips. "Half sister."

He had a sister.

"Where is she?"

"That's a damn good question. I haven't seen her in about eight years."

Was it a coincidence his sister had disappeared around the same time he'd gone to jail? Warning bells clanged inside Gray's brain.

"Why?"

Cece stared at him for several seconds, then said, "Screw it." She collapsed back into the chair. "Not much you can do about it, anyway."

Something told him he wasn't going to like whatever she had to say.

"The worthless little shit disappeared the same night she moved twenty million dollars into your bank account. She was supposed to move another twenty million into my account, but obviously that never happened."

His *sister* had set him up. A sister he never even knew existed.

Why? Why would she do that? What had he done that she'd wanted to ruin his entire life? And was she still a threat?

Gray's stomach clenched tight. This conversation had just taken a severe turn he'd not been prepared for.

"Why would she frame me for embezzlement?"

"She wasn't supposed to. She was supposed to frame

your father. My guess is she screwed up and put the money into the wrong account. I didn't even know it had happened until the story hit the news and I realized the mess."

His father had been the original target? They did share a name. Gray was a nickname he'd used since he was a little boy. All of his accounts were obviously set up in his legal name, something he never thought of because he didn't actually use it.

"Why would she frame my father?"

"Because I'd hit a rough patch and he refused to help me out when I went to him."

"So you decided to rob him? What does that have to do with my sister?"

"Your sister is a computer genius. There isn't a system she can't access or a site she can't crash."

His sister was a hacker? And from what his mother said, a talented one.

"How'd she learn those skills?" That wasn't the kind of thing you were born instinctively knowing. Sure, certain people had an aptitude, but they still had to learn. Especially the illegal stuff.

"Michael, her father, recognized her talent when she was young. She was the kind of kid who'd spend hours taking apart the computer I bought her for Christmas just to see what the guts looked like and whether she could put them back together again. It didn't take long to figure out she was just as amazing at breaking codes." His mother shrugged her shoulders. "One puzzle is as good as another. He took her under his wing and trained her. She was seriously beneficial in his business."

His illegal business. Dominic had provided Gray with a bit of information about Michael when he'd passed along some details about Cece. While Joker had uncovered quite a bit, Gray had decided that getting insight from a local was just smart.

His mother had let her boyfriend use her daughter for criminal activity. Gray shouldn't be surprised, all things considered, but he was. "How old was she?"

"When she started?" She shrugged. "Seven or eight. When she screwed you? Sixteen."

Gray saw red. His mother had been exploiting his sister while she was too young to know better. She'd grown up committing crimes and didn't know any other life.

"Framing you was a mistake. She didn't even know you existed. But disappearing with my money—that was all planned."

No doubt. Gray couldn't help but be proud of his sister for her resourcefulness. Even if he'd been the one to pay the price with seven years of his life.

Although, that was assuming his sister wasn't aware of what she was doing. If she'd screwed him on purpose...

"You have no idea where she is?"

"If I did, do you think I'd have sent that note to your mom?"

No, she wouldn't.

Gray let his gaze drift up and down, taking in the woman who'd given birth to him. Even through the heavy makeup he could tell she was tired and worn. Her shoulders were slumped and the caked-on makeup had settled into the deep lines around her mouth.

The only word that came to Gray's mind was pathetic. She'd spent her life trading on her beauty to get what she wanted, but was clearly starting to realize external beauty faded. And now she was screwed because she didn't have a backup plan.

"Don't bother sending any more threatening notes.

You won't be getting any more money from anyone in my family."

"I'll go to the media."

Gray shrugged. "Go ahead. Do you really think a thirty-five-year-old sex scandal will matter to anyone?"

Cece laughed, the sharp sound scraping across his eardrums. "Your name is still big in the media. They'll eat up the story."

"No one will care. I've been out of prison for almost a year. Hell, my parole is finished in a couple months."

Blakely's fingers squeezed his arm again. She hadn't said a single thing during the exchange, but he'd known she was right beside him.

"Go ahead. See how far that gets you. You can only sell the story once."

Gray took a few steps backward. The expression on Cece's face left his belly churning—not because he was concerned, but because she looked utterly devastated and broken.

But that wasn't his problem. She was no one to him.

His sister, on the other hand, was someone he wanted to talk to.

From across the aisle on the plane, Blakely watched Gray. He'd been quiet and distant since they'd walked away from his mother. At first, she'd worried he was about to lose it and tear into the woman. But she should have known better. Gray Lockwood had tight control, even in the midst of utter turmoil.

Hell, she was still trying to digest the information bomb his mother had dropped and it had nothing to do with her.

She'd been quiet for a while, but at some point, they were going to have to talk about it.

"What are you going to do?"

Gray turned to her, his gaze distant and unfocused. "What?"

"What are you going to do?"

His gaze sharpened. He blinked several times. "Find my sister."

Obviously, she never expected anything less. "Are you going to tell the authorities about Cece and her role in everything?"

With a sigh, Gray let his head drop back against the seat. Reaching up, he rubbed his fingers into his eyes. "No, I don't have any proof."

"You have me as a witness."

"Sure, and considering we're sleeping together, that'll go over well."

"No one knows."

Gray's hands fell into his lap. He stared at her for a few seconds. "At the very least, everyone knows we've been working closely together."

"Surely there's a way to make your mother and her boyfriend pay for what they did."

"I doubt it. It's not likely there's a trail to follow, but I'll have Joker see what he can dig up. At least now he knows where to look, which should help. But I'm going to assume they were very careful about getting their hands dirty. And without the trail of money to trace back to them…it's going to be difficult to prove."

"Your sister is the linchpin."

Gray's body sagged against the leather. "She is. I need Joker to track her, as well. Same thing, knowing where to start will hopefully make the job easier."

Maybe, but his mother had said *they* hadn't been able to find her for the last eight years. And something told

Blakely they'd worked at finding her since the girl potentially had twenty million dollars.

Eight years of being missing—that was a long time. Blakely didn't want to say it out loud, but maybe she was dead. His sister had been sixteen, after all, when she'd disappeared. Even with twenty million, it must have been difficult to be on her own.

Blakely might have felt like her father had abandoned her, choosing his friends and a life that took him away from them, but at least she'd always had her mother to count on. To shelter and protect her. It sounded like Gray's sister hadn't had anyone to care about her. Blakely could hardly imagine the woman they'd seen tonight being anything close to maternal.

"When we get back, I'll tell Stone you're available for other assignments. I know he has a couple he could use your help on."

"No."

Gray's eyebrows beetled into a deep frown. "You're not still hell-bent on leaving Stone Surveillance, are you? Not only are you good at this kind of work, you enjoy it. Don't try to deny that."

Why would she deny it? "Yes, I really enjoy it. I enjoy putting the pieces together and solving the puzzle. I love feeling like what I'm doing might make a real difference to someone. But…"

"So why do you want to leave?"

"No one said anything about leaving. I'll stay as long as I have a job."

"I'm confused."

"My assignment with you isn't finished."

Gray shook his head. "Yes, it is. You agreed to help me figure out what happened. Now I know."

"Maybe, but the bread crumbs don't end there, do

they? I owe you a hell of a lot. The least I can do is see this through."

"You don't owe me anything, Blakely."

That's where he was terribly wrong. She owed him seven years of his life, but there was no way she could give those back to him. "You're wrong. My testimony was key to putting you behind bars for a crime you didn't commit."

Gray opened his mouth to protest, but Blakely wasn't having any of it. Holding up a hand, she said, "Don't even bother denying it. We both know it's true. How do you think that makes me feel? Knowing I'm responsible for you losing seven years of your life? Being disowned by your family and barred from the company and your heritage?"

Instead of smoothing out Gray's frown, her words had the opposite effect. Dark anger swirled in the deep green depths of his eyes. "Do you think I want your pity?"

"No, so it's a good thing what I'm feeling is far from pity."

"Ha." Gray let out a growling huff. "Guilt and pity are wafting off you so strongly I'm practically strangling on them. Blakely, what happened to me is not your fault. Nor is it your responsibility to atone for anything."

"Is that what you think? That I'm atoning for some self-assessed sin?"

"Isn't it?"

God, the man was infuriating and a major pain in her ass sometimes.

"No. I'm fully aware the only ones truly responsible for what happened to you are the people involved in framing you—your mother, her boyfriend and your sister."

Gray flinched, which made her regret the words, even if they were the truth.

"We started something. I won't abandon you or what we're doing simply because we got a few of the answers. Especially not when those answers raised more questions."

"Maybe I don't want your help anymore."

It was Blakely's turn to flinch. His words hit her straight in the chest, bruising her just as much as any real punch could have.

"Is that true?"

"Hell, no. I never could have gotten this far without you."

"So why are you trying to push me away?"

Gray closed his eyes. With a groan, he sank back into the chair. "Because you scare the hell out of me."

The confession was just as startling as anything else he'd said to her. "*I* scare you? That's impossible. I'm no one with no significance."

This time, when Gray looked at her with anger in his eyes, the emotion was clearly directed straight at her. "Don't ever say that again. Yes, you scare me. I've truly known you for a little over a week and in that time, you've become the most important person in my life. But my life is utter crap at the moment and I really don't want to drag anyone else into it, least of all someone I actually like and am starting to care a great deal for."

Blakely's mouth opened and closed. Words formed in her head, but wouldn't tumble out. Until she finally said, "Oh."

"Yeah, oh."

What the heck was she supposed to do with that? "I'm past starting to care a great deal for you, Gray. And you've quickly become the most important person in my life, too."

Apparently, she was going to be more honest with him than she'd meant to. Suddenly, a wave of heat washed over her body. What was she doing? Uneasiness filled her, not because she didn't mean what she'd said, but because the truth of her words made her vulnerable in a way she'd never let herself become before.

Relationships had never been her strength. In fact, she'd been accused of being cold and reserved by more than one boyfriend. And, no doubt, they'd all been right. Her father had taught her not to trust, a lesson that had been damn hard to unlearn.

Even now, the thought of letting Gray that close, letting him become important to her, had alarm bells going off inside her head. She was stupid for even considering it, wasn't she?

A week ago, she would have convinced herself that the fact he was a criminal meant he couldn't be trusted… but knowing what she did now, that felt like a cop-out.

But it also didn't make it any easier to let down those protective walls.

"You should take the opportunity I'm giving you and walk away."

Every self-preservation instinct inside her was screaming to do exactly as he suggested. But she couldn't make herself do it.

She didn't want to.

"No."

In the end, uttering that single word was the easiest decision she'd ever made.

Eleven

Gray couldn't decide if Blakely's decision was stupid or noble. Maybe a little of both. She should walk away. There was no doubt in his mind that would be the smartest thing for both of them.

A jumble of conflicting emotions churned in Gray's belly. Anger, frustration, hurt, apprehension. He couldn't shake the feeling of waiting for the other shoe to drop.

And that fear didn't dissipate two days later, when Joker gave them a rundown of what he'd uncovered about his sister.

"You said Kinley, your sister, was sixteen when she ran off on her own?"

Gray, Joker, Blakely, Stone and Finn all sat around the conference table at Stone Surveillance. Everyone who'd been instrumental in getting Gray to this point was there with him.

Why did it feel so monumental? Like another crossroads in his life. An unexpected one.

"That's what my birth mother said."

"I still can't believe you have a sister you never knew about," Stone grumbled. "This is an utter cluster, man. I'm so sorry."

That was Stone, apologizing for something that wasn't his fault. Taking the weight of the world onto his shoulders.

Finn, on the other hand, drawled, "Look on the bright side. At least this sister hasn't disowned you."

Gray laughed. He had to. "No, but she framed me for embezzlement."

"By accident."

So his mother said, but he wasn't convinced.

Joker chimed in, like he could read Gray's mind. "I wouldn't be so positive."

His stomach tightened, the muscles knotting into a tangle it felt like no one would be able to unravel. "Tell me."

Opening a dossier, Joker spread a bunch of papers across the table.

Blakely immediately jumped up, pulling several of them closer for inspection. Gray let her look. But he wasn't entirely certain he was ready to know what they contained.

"This chick is amazing," Joker said. "Who did you say trained her?"

"I didn't." Mostly because he had no clue beyond what his mother had shared. "My mother said she'd shown a natural aptitude at an early age and her father started teaching her."

"That makes sense. Sure, there are some young IT geniuses who could figure this stuff out on their own, but she's really damn slick for someone so young."

It hadn't taken Gray long to do the math. His sister was now twenty-four, give or take a few months. He didn't even know when her birthday was. And that made his stomach tighten even more.

Growing up, he'd desperately wanted someone in his life he could be close to. His father hadn't given a damn about him, unless he could be useful in some way. His father had been too wrapped up in his business affairs. And his mother had been happy to leave Gray's upbringing to anyone else she could pay to fulfill the role.

Maybe that was the problem. He'd gained a sister only to immediately lose her because she'd been instrumental in the worst moments of his life. Karma really was a bitch, although he still wasn't sure what he'd ever done to deserve her disdain.

"Yeah, yeah, she's brilliant. We get it," Finn groused. "Could you hurry this up? I've got things to do and places to break into."

Gray rolled his eyes. Trust Finn to be in a hurry for a little B&E. Luckily, these days his extracurricular activities were wholly sanctioned. Not to mention profitable for their business.

"No, man. I don't think you understand. I've never met another hacker that I couldn't track within a few hours. Everyone leaves a trail, even if they don't mean to. Bread crumbs are easy to follow when you know what to look for. This girl…" Joker looked chagrined. "She's the best. Better than me."

Shit. Gray sat up in his chair. *Joker* was the best he'd ever seen, which was why Gray had cultivated the relationship and convinced the man to work for Stone Surveillance. Joker had single-handedly uncovered information that had been instrumental in saving Piper's life and exonerating Finn from being set up by his wife's grandfather.

"Does that mean you can't find her?"

Joker glared at him. "Of course not. It just means it took me longer than I would have liked. But like I said, everyone leaves bread crumbs...even if they think they're sweeping them all up."

Gray sank into his chair. The comforting weight of Blakely's hand landed on the curve of his thigh. She squeezed, silently giving him her support. He hadn't realized how much he'd needed it until that moment.

Setting his hand over hers, he squeezed back, a silent thank-you.

"It took a while, but I traced her trail backward for the past eight years, right after she left Vegas. Most of that time, she bounced from place to place across the world. A few months in Paris, a couple in Thailand, Venezuela, Brazil, South Africa, Iceland. There was no rhyme or reason, at least none I could figure out."

He was damn good with patterns, so Gray would hazard a guess that if Joker couldn't find one, there probably wasn't one.

"She never stayed long in any place and she rarely came back to the States. She was here during your trial, though. One of her longer periods in one place, actually."

"Here, as in Charleston?"

Joker nodded.

"Why the heck would she be here?" It made no sense. They knew she was responsible for framing him. They also knew she'd stolen another twenty million. Why put herself in jeopardy by coming so close to his trial?

"To make sure it went as she wanted?" Stone mused.

"Or maybe because she felt guilty about what happened," Blakely countered, her eyebrows pulled down into a sharp V of irritation.

"We can speculate all day, but there's no way to know for sure. I think we can all agree it's suspect." At least, that was Gray's take on it. No matter what his sister's motives for coming to Charleston back then…they obviously hadn't been to see he didn't pay for a crime he didn't commit.

"It gets weirder," Joker said.

"Weirder?" Finn's dark eyebrows winged up.

"Once I was able to track her movements, it didn't take me long to uncover several accounts in her name."

"Let me guess—the balance started out at twenty million?"

Joker's mouth twisted into a wry grimace. "Yep."

"How much is left?"

"Just over thirty million."

"Excuse me?"

"And that's in one account."

A sly grin stretched across Finn's lips. "The little minx really is a genius. She's managed to evade everyone and grow her money."

"Oh, she's done more than that."

For the first time since they'd sat down, Gray realized Joker's voice was tinged with respect and pride each time he talked about her. The rascal was impressed.

"Explain."

"Kinley hasn't just been investing your money for the past eight years. She used a little, but each time would eventually replace it with interest."

"And how has she accomplished this?" Stone, who'd been silent and observant much of the time finally asked.

"By stealing money from other people."

Why didn't that surprise him? "Why haven't we heard about these thefts? Did she decide to change her tactics and go after smaller amounts to fly under the radar?"

"Actually, it's the opposite. Your twenty million is

small change. She's managed to steal almost a billion dollars from various people."

"Now I'm less impressed that her bank account has thirty million in it," Finn quipped.

"That's because she doesn't keep the money. Or doesn't keep most of it. She has another account with a few million in it that she appears to use when she needs to disappear again."

"So what's she doing with the rest of the money?"

"Giving it to various charitable organizations."

"Say that again."

"You heard me."

"She's stolen a billion dollars to give it all away?" Finn's incredulity wasn't surprising. The only thing keeping him on the straight and narrow was Genevieve. Without her, Gray's friend would be just as crooked as his sister might be.

"Not only that, but she's managed to keep the thefts out of the media because she's targeted people who can't afford to report the crimes."

"Because the money is dirty."

"Exactly. She's targeted some of the biggest crime syndicates in the world—Russian, Chinese, American, Central and South American. If the money came from human trafficking, selling drugs or trading in weapons, she's taken it."

No wonder Joker was verging on idolizing his sister.

"Let me see if I'm getting this right. My sister, a genius hacker, disappeared eight years ago after framing me for embezzling money from my family's company. She took that money, placed it in an account and hasn't touched it the entire time."

"No, she's touched it, but she treats it like a loan and always pays it back. With interest."

Right, because most criminals worried about interest when they committed a crime like stealing.

"She's spent those eight years targeting and stealing money from criminals around the world and donating the proceeds to charities."

"Most of it. She keeps some money, but not a lot. Not nearly as much as she could. And almost in every instance, the money she does keep funds the next target."

Gray stared at Joker, not really seeing him. Part of him had expected this endeavor would uncover things he might not want to know. Being targeted as a patsy for embezzlement didn't normally happen to people with squeaky clean lives. And he'd hardly been a saint.

But never in a million years had he expected to discover he'd been living a lie and his mother wasn't really his. Or that he had a sister. Who'd framed him, but now operated as the Robin Hood of hackers.

Honestly, he had no idea what to do with this information or how to feel about it all. The hits just kept coming. Like he'd been in the worst fight of his life and was losing, something he wasn't used to and didn't particularly like.

"Where is she now?" Blakely's soft voice filled the silence at the table, asking the question he was too numb to ask.

"Bali. She's been there ever since you were released. It's the longest she's stayed in one place since Vegas."

Gray was too stunned to wonder what that was supposed to mean.

"But there's more."

He wasn't certain he could handle more right now.

"She's been watching you."

That got Stone's attention. Before Gray could even react, his friend's elbows were on the table and he was leaning hard toward Joker. "What do you mean she's been watching him?"

"She has a back door into all of his electronics. She's been monitoring his email and internet traffic. My guess is she's also been listening in and watching through those same devices."

Which explained why Joker had told them to leave their cell phones and electronic devices outside before coming into the conference room. Gray had initially chalked it up to his friend's paranoia.

"You could have told us."

"I wanted to explain before you jumped to conclusions."

"What conclusions would those be? That my sister has been tracking my every movement since I got out of prison? For what purpose? To frame me again? Steal from me again?"

Blakely's hand moved to his arm, tugging. He hadn't realized he'd stood up until he looked down and discovered she was looking up. Slowly, Gray let his legs fold beneath him and he sat back down into his chair.

"I really don't think that's it, man. I think she's been saving the money and is trying to figure out how to give it back to you."

Wonderful. His sister had grown a conscience and was spying on him so she could make amends.

"Why didn't she just send a certified check?" Gray could hear the petty sarcasm in his voice, but couldn't stop it. He was pissed and she was the easiest target right now. Even if his brain told him she might not deserve it.

"Gray," Blakely said, her voice calm and soothing. "That's not going to accomplish anything."

Of course it wouldn't, but it had felt good. At least for a second.

But that feeling was fleeting. Logic, that's what he needed right now. And he knew just who would give it to him.

Turning, he focused squarely on Blakely. "What now?"

Her lips turned up at the corners into a sad, understanding smile that somehow managed to start unknotting the ropes in his belly.

"We go find her. I have a feeling she's waiting for you."

Was she? Gray wasn't sure he was ready for that encounter. But Blakely was right. It's what he needed to do.

This plane ride was much different from the last one. The flight was longer, but it hadn't felt that way.

The moment they soared into the air, Gray unbuckled his seat belt. Reaching across her, he did the same for hers. The metal edges clanged loudly against the seat as they dropped open.

"What are you doing?"

"Taking advantage of the time we have."

Grasping her hands, Gray urged her out of her seat and into the narrow aisle. He led them toward the back of the plane, past a small galley and through a doorway that she'd missed the first time they were on board.

Stepping into the room tucked away, Blakely thought, *Of course it has a full bedroom.*

Gray tugged her inside. And immediately found her mouth with his. The kiss was explosive, going from nothing to red-hot in mere seconds. It was easy to let herself sink into the craving that was always present when he touched her. But tonight, Gray seemed to need more.

Pulling back, he looked down at her, his evergreen eyes filled with passion, but something stronger. Something softer and more enduring.

Something that had hope and uneasiness twisting in her gut.

Slowly, he led her over to the bed. Without saying a word, Gray reached for the hem of her shirt and pulled it up and over. The rest of her clothes quickly followed until she was standing before him entirely naked.

Any other time, she would have felt vulnerable, but not now. Not with a look of such awe and need stamped across his face.

She needed to touch him. To feel him. Now.

Blakely quickly added his clothes to the pile at their feet. An arm wrapped around her back, and Gray urged her to the bed. The coverlet beneath her skin was soft and cool, inviting. But that thought lasted a nanosecond before the blazing heat of his body joined hers.

The drag and pull of his skin against hers made Blakely arch up, searching for more. Always more with him. She could never get enough.

His mouth found her, raining kisses across her entire body. He lingered here and there, nipping and laving, worshipping and teasing. Blakely did the same, letting her mouth and hands explore him with a languid urgency that was both breathtaking and compelling.

Words were unnecessary, but he whispered them, anyway. How beautiful she was. What he planned to do to her body. How he intended to make her writhe with desire, pleasure and passion.

And he was true to each promise.

Blakely's breath caught in her lungs, almost as if her body was too busy with other things to remember that basic function. She wanted to make his body hum with the same rich energy that he was building inside her.

Finding the long, hard length of him nestled between them, she wrapped her hand around the hard shaft and tugged. He growled, the vibration of the sound rumbling through her own body.

Rolling them both, Blakely positioned herself above him and used her hold to guide him home. A sigh of satisfaction and relief left her parted lips. Blakely threw back her head, relishing the joy of feeling him buried deep inside her.

But after a few moments, that wasn't enough.

She began to ride him, rolling her hips back and forth in an effort to get more. Gray's hands gripped her hips, guiding her, moving her, faster and faster until the world began to turn black around the edges.

Blakely's breath panted in and out. Her body burned, heat and need building higher and higher.

One moment she was upright, the next her back was bouncing off the mattress as Gray pounded in and out of her.

Somehow, as he'd flipped them both, he'd managed to find her hands. Twining their fingers together, he used the hold to keep her steady. His mouth found hers, the kiss as deep as the connection between them.

The orgasm exploded through Blakely. Gray's bark of relief was right behind as he thrust deep, once, twice, three more times, before collapsing onto the bed beside her.

Their limbs tangled, bodies sweaty and replete.

After several seconds, Blakely leaned up and stared down into his gorgeous face. His eyes were open, a self-satisfied smile stretching his lips as he watched her.

"Well, isn't it quite handy to have a bed at thirty thousand feet?"

Twelve

Blakely lounged against the pile of pillows. They should probably get up and get dressed, but she wasn't motivated to move, not after the multiple orgasms Gray had just given her. Honestly, she wasn't certain her legs would hold her, anyway, if she tried.

Gray didn't appear to be in too much of a hurry to go back to their seats, either. And she had to admit the view wasn't hard to look at.

He was sprawled across the bed, sheets tangled between his thighs, completely uncaring. Half of his delectable ass was on display. Blakely was tempted to tug at the covers just so she could see the rest. But she knew if she did, they'd end up having sex again, and as much as she enjoyed sex with Gray, her body needed a few more minutes of recovery.

Gray's fingers played across her skin, tracing mindless patterns over her hips, belly and ribs. He had her tucked beneath him, his head resting on the curve of her waist.

He was quiet and a little pensive, just as he'd been earlier when they first boarded the plane.

Threading her fingers into his hair, Blakely gently pulled until his eyes found hers. "Hey, everything's going to be okay."

"I know." His words said one thing, but the darkness lurking in his gaze suggested another.

"You've been hit by so much in the past several years, Gray. I really hope this is the start to everything changing. Your sister could help prove your innocence."

"Sure, but only by admitting to a crime herself."

There was a fly in the ointment for sure. As much as she liked to be able to think most humans were honorable enough to admit to a crime in order to save someone else from paying the price...she knew firsthand that wasn't likely. Most people were selfish and could only see the impact something like that would make on their own lives.

What struck her as surprising was that a few weeks ago she wouldn't have considered it possible at all. But Gray... He was starting to make her feel like there were good people still left in the world.

Maybe his sister would be one of them.

"Why do you think she's been watching you?"

"No idea."

"But you have a theory."

A frown crinkled the corners of his gorgeous green eyes. "Yes."

Blakely smoothed his hair away from his forehead so she could see him better, waiting.

"I'd like to think her guilty conscience means she's been trying to figure out how to fix what she screwed up. But the rest of me..."

Blakely's stomach dropped right along with Gray's voice.

"I keep thinking she's had plenty of time to act if she wanted to. However, if she's been waiting for another opportunity to take from me? To ruin my life some more?"

Blakely shook her head. Something deep inside told her that wasn't what his sister wanted. Maybe she was being naive—a state she'd never been afflicted by before—but it didn't add up.

"To what purpose? You don't have access to the company anymore. Sure, you have plenty of money of your own, but we both know she could have taken that at any point."

"True."

"And the people she's been stealing from have been terrible human beings."

"I'm a convicted felon."

Frustration tinged Blakely's voice. "Because she *framed* you."

Gray's gaze dropped back down to stare at a spot on the bed. He continued to trace patterns on her skin. Goose bumps spread over her arms and legs, but she ignored them.

"You know, going to prison saved my life."

Blakely's own fingers traced across his shoulders, paying special attention to the puckered skin under the ridge of his shoulder blade. She hadn't asked, but assumed he'd gotten the scar during his time inside. He'd told her he'd gotten several others that way.

She couldn't understand how anyone could feel a situation that had left multiple marks across his body had saved him.

"How?"

His mouth twisted into a wry grimace. "I was aimless and spoiled before I went inside."

Blakely couldn't dispute that statement, because it was clearly true.

"I spent my entire life being given everything. I never had to earn anything, not truly. Inside, I had to earn everything. But the most important thing I learned how to earn was respect. Respect for myself and respect from others."

Blakely's stomach clenched. She wanted to wrap her arms around him and hold him close, but something told her this wasn't the time.

"Don't get me wrong, at first I was pissed. Angry at everyone and everything. I was still entitled, wearing the idea that life had treated me unfairly like a chip on my shoulder."

She was surprised he wasn't still pissed. He'd lost seven years of his life because someone else had screwed him over. And no matter how hard she tried, Blakely couldn't forget the role she'd played in putting him there, either.

"But then I met Stone and Finn. Separately, we were vulnerable to the other gangs and groups that formed inside. But together, we had power and quickly discovered how to demand deference from the other inmates.

"The experience stripped away my entitled lifestyle and made me realize I didn't like the person I'd been very much."

That must have been a difficult moment. Not many people had the fortitude to truly evaluate themselves and admit they weren't proud of who they'd become.

"That takes real strength, Gray."

He huffed out a reluctant laugh. "I don't know about that. But it definitely wasn't a comfortable experience.

Stone helped me, though. He's one of the most honest men I've ever met."

Blakely could see that. She'd only had a few dealings with him so far, but he'd seemed very fair and concerned for her comfort and safety.

"It wasn't an easy process. There are things about my time inside I'll never tell anyone, because I'm not proud of them, but also because unless you've been there you can't understand."

Her fingers traced the white, puckered flesh again. Part of her wanted him to be able to share anything with her, but she understood. There were things about her past—her childhood—that she had no intention of sharing with anyone, including Gray.

At the end of the day, the details didn't matter, anyway. What did were the lessons and growth that had come from them.

"It didn't take Stone, Finn or me long to realize in order to stay on the right side of the other inmates, as well as the guards, we needed something that both sides wanted. Inside, boredom is a serious problem. Hours and hours of idleness is a breeding ground for serious issues."

She could absolutely understand how that would be true.

"We ended up running an underground fighting ring. A perfect solution for everyone. Stone managed and arranged things. He handled the details and ensured the guards' buy-in."

"So, basically, he worked the connections and people?" It was the role Stone appeared to fill for Stone Surveillance, as well. He was the face of the company.

"Exactly. Finn handled the books, worked the betting pools and ran the numbers. He also used his charm and personality to stoke friendly rivalries and build hype for whatever fight was coming up."

Blakely had a feeling she knew the answer to her question, but she had to ask it, anyway…even if a huge part of her didn't necessarily want the answer. "And what did you do?"

Gray's mouth twisted into a self-deprecating smile. "I fought."

Of course he had. Blakely's stomach clenched uncomfortably. A spurt of fear shot into her system, as if he was preparing for a fight now.

"I'd never been in a fight before walking into that prison. I was too soft. I'd always used money and status to get myself out of any difficult situations."

"So why did you take on that role? Why couldn't you have been the bookie and let Finn fight?"

Gray's burst of laughter tickled across her skin. "Yeah, right. Finn is a lot of things, but he's too soft to fight. Besides, his dexterous hands are a valuable commodity."

Blakely's eyes rolled. Sure they were. He'd been a jewel thief.

"I was good at it. The training gave me something to focus on outside of my feelings of anger and injustice. I discovered discipline. I finally had to work for something…or risk getting my ass beaten."

"How often did that happen?"

His lips twitched. "A few times in the beginning. By the end…no one could beat me."

Blakely wasn't surprised. Gray might be many things, but the man she knew was driven and determined.

"I learned a lot about myself in the process. But most of all, I grew into a man I could be proud of."

Blakely shifted, using her leverage to roll them both.

He dropped onto the bed, his large body sprawling. Blakely's hips settled over his, their legs tangling together.

The hard ridge of his sex stirred between them, making her own sex pulse with a reminder and demand.

But there was something she wanted to say first.

Wrapping her hands around the base of his skull, Blakely brought her face close to his, making sure she filled his entire gaze.

"You are one of the best men I've ever known, Gray Lockwood. You're honorable, strong, quiet and resourceful. I hate that you went through a terrible time in your life to become the man you are, but the man you are is amazing."

His eyes sharpened, going hot and hard.

His fingers buried deep into her hair, holding her steady as he surged up and found her mouth.

Apparently, words weren't necessary anymore.

They landed in Kuta. Gray was certain the city was gorgeous—they were in Bali, after all. Surprisingly enough, in all his travels during his younger years, Bali had never made it onto the list. Perhaps because he'd been more interested in wild adventures than calming, peaceful vistas.

Unfortunately, the view was still lost on him since his mind wasn't on taking in the sights. Apparently, neither was Blakely's, which shouldn't have surprised him, but did.

She was efficient and focused as they followed the man who greeted them as they disembarked the plane. Striding before him across the tarmac, *that* was the sight Gray couldn't tear his gaze away from. The compact, lithe movements of her body. The lush, rounded globe of her ass hugged by well-worn denim. Hell, he hadn't even realized Blakely owned a pair of jeans until she'd pulled them on when they'd finally decided to climb from the bed.

He liked seeing her relaxed and casual. Something told him not many people got to experience that side of her. He tried not to convince himself it was important she felt comfortable enough to let him in…but it was.

They reached a dark green Jeep, clearly set up for off-roading adventures. The top and doors were off, roll bars showing. Several men who'd followed behind with their luggage quickly stowed everything in the back. Blakely didn't hesitate, but grasped one of the bars and boosted herself up into the lifted vehicle.

Reaching into her bag, she rummaged around until she found a hair band and quickly pulled it into a knot at the base of her skull. Shaking his head, Gray followed her. Beneath his breath he murmured, "Always prepared."

"What?" Blakely turned to him, her eyebrows beetled together in confusion.

"Nothing."

But that was Blakely to a *T*. She hadn't questioned or hesitated. She'd simply seen the vehicle they were taking and adjusted accordingly. It never would have entered her mind to complain and request something else. There had been plenty of women in his life—before—that would have stood outside the Jeep and pitched a fit, refusing to get in because it would mess up their hair.

Climbing up, Gray settled into his seat. Reaching over, he grasped Blakely's hand and pulled it into his own lap. He simply needed to touch her right now.

The drive across the island was beautiful. But the closer they got to the villa he'd rented, the more his stomach churned. After some digging, Joker had finally been able to send him an address. His sister had apparently rented a small place on the beach not far from where they were staying.

In less than an hour he might be confronting the person responsible for his imprisonment. And she was his half sister.

Was he ready for this?

They pulled up at the villa. It was gorgeous, but Gray didn't particularly care. He was used to staying in beautiful places. Often took it for granted.

Blakely didn't.

She hopped out of the Jeep, her feet hitting the ground with an audible thud. And she simply stood there, staring at the place.

It took several moments for her reaction to catch Gray's attention. But when it did, he decided then and there they were coming back to Bali the first chance they got. He wanted to put that look of wonder and surprise on her face every chance he could.

After handing off a bag to the staff that had come out to meet them, Gray walked over to her. Wrapping his arms around her, he pulled Blakely against his body. She willingly went, leaning into him without hesitation.

"It's beautiful."

"Wait until you see the view from the bedroom." The master suite opened out to the pool, which overlooked a stretch of private beach. They could lie in bed and watch the sunset…and sunrise.

Twisting around, she looked up at him. "You didn't have to get a whole villa, Gray. It's just the two of us. Surely they have hotel rooms on the island."

"Of course, but I thought we might want privacy."

Her gaze sharpened. "Because you intend to make me scream your name repeatedly or because you expect things to go badly with your sister?"

Gray huffed out a laugh. "Both."

A smile teased the corners of her lips. "I'm in for the first and I'm going to hope the second doesn't happen."

Gray was going to, as well, but he wasn't holding his breath. Nothing added up where his sister was concerned, so he really had no way of making an educated guess as to how this encounter was going to go.

He was about to say as much when the cell in his pocket buzzed. Pulling it out, he glanced at the number on the screen. His belly tightened, but he answered the call, anyway.

"Joker."

"She's there right now, but she's not planning to stay long. She started moving money a couple of hours ago. Looks like she's getting ready to run."

Because she'd figured out they were close?

Gray had purposely left all of his electronics back in Charleston, including his personal cell. This one was a Stone Surveillance burner he'd grabbed on their way out of town. Not only had he needed to evade his sister's scrutiny, but he was also still on probation technically, and not allowed to leave the country without approval.

"How did she figure out we're here?"

Joker grumbled something unintelligible, but clearly he wasn't happy. Finally, he said, "She didn't. Someone else found her."

Gray let out an expletive. Shitty timing. "Who?"

"A Russian mob boss she screwed over about two years ago."

Perfect. "It going to be a problem?"

"Not if you get to her first."

Grabbing Blakely's hand, he started pulling her back to the Jeep. Whistling to get the attention of their driver, Gray pointed at the Jeep. The guy nodded, then passed off the piece of luggage he'd been carrying. Jogging over, he launched his small frame into the driver's seat.

Gray didn't wait for Blakely to pause, but grabbed her around the waist and boosted her up into the Jeep. Rounding the vehicle, he showed their driver the address before following.

He'd expected to have a little time to prepare for this encounter. But maybe this was better.

Thirteen

Blakely was patient and simply went along for the ride. He hadn't even bothered to tell her what was going on until they were already speeding away from their villa. The whole time Gray's mind raced with what would happen if the Russian muscle arrived first, anxiety gripping his gut.

No one deserved that.

The drive up to his sister's place was severely different from the drive up to theirs. Wild vegetation obscured the view of the house, not just from the road, but from the long, winding drive. Their rental had been meticulously landscaped—the lush vegetation had been tamed to give a sense of tropical decadence.

The house itself was also much different. Small and old, clearly it had seen better days. Their villa screamed affluence and attention, not because Gray cared about stuff like that, but because he could afford the comforts it provided.

His sister could afford the same things. But something told him she'd chosen this place on purpose. Not only because it was well hidden, but also in order to not draw any undue attention.

Before they actually reached the house, Gray leaned forward and tapped their driver on the shoulder, telling him to stop. She might have already heard the Jeep, but in case she hadn't, he didn't want to spook her.

Jumping down, he walked around to help Blakely from the vehicle. Grasping her hand, they quietly walked the rest of the path up to the house.

It was silent and dark. No lights on inside, which made a tight band constrict Gray's chest. Were they too late? Had they missed her?

Rather than knock, he tried the knob, but wasn't surprised to find it locked. No one who made a habit of screwing over powerful people left the front door unlocked. Not if they were smart, and from everything he'd learned, his sister was extremely intelligent.

He could pick the lock, a little skill Finn had shared. But his friend had also imparted another piece of wisdom—don't make a simple job harder than it has to be.

Urging Blakely to follow behind him, Gray circled the house. It might not have much to offer in the way of luxury, but the view was breathtaking. Like most villas here, the back of the house had a huge outdoor area. The living space was open to the breezy outdoor sitting area and a path straight down to the water. There were doors that could be closed for security, but right now they were standing wide open.

Which told him that either his sister had left in a hurry, not bothering to secure the place, or she might be somewhere inside.

Taking a chance, Gray stepped up onto the back deck and raised his voice. "Kinley."

Her name reverberated against the terra-cotta tiles. His instincts hummed. A sound echoed from deep inside the darkened house. A muffled curse.

"Kinley, I'm not here to hurt you. I'm just here to talk."

Slowly, his eyes adjusted to the dark. Moonlight high above washed everything with a ghostly silver gray. He inched forward. And a soft voice floated into the darkness. "Stop."

Blakely's hand clamped down on his arm. Slowly, Kinley materialized out of the shadows as she moved forward into the watery light. "Don't come any closer."

Gray held up his open hands in the universal sign that he meant no harm. "I'm not here to hurt you."

"That's a lie. Why wouldn't you be here to hurt me? I ruined your life."

"You know who I am."

"Of course I know who you are."

Gray took a deep breath, pulling in air and holding it for several seconds before slowly letting it out on a warm stream. Some of the tension that had been tightening his shoulders flowed out with it.

"All I want is to talk."

"Bullshit. You want to make me pay for what I did to you."

Gray tilted his head sideways, really studying his sister. She didn't look a thing like their mother, but that didn't mean she wasn't just as beautiful. In fact, she was even more striking. Her inky hair hung in long, thick curls down her back, contrasting with her creamy skin, making it glow in the moonlight. He couldn't tell their exact color, but her eyes were dark, as well—probably brown. She was tall—he'd guess only a few inches short of six feet. But her body was lean, a runner's build.

Gray wasn't sure what he'd expected, but it wasn't this beautiful, strong woman standing before him. Maybe he'd expected a child. The sixteen-year-old teenager who had influenced his life. Kinley was hardly that. Gray knew within seconds that she was fully capable of taking care of herself. Because she'd had to do it for the last eight years...or even longer than that.

In that moment, Gray realized they had much more in common than a shared parent.

"I want to understand what happened. Yes, I have questions. But I don't want you to pay for anything. I know you were only sixteen when our mother convinced you to steal that money."

Kinley took several steps closer, coming even farther into the light. "Wait, what?" Her dark eyebrows winged down into a deep V of confusion. "*Our* mother?"

Oh, hell. She didn't know.

Gray's mouth opened and closed. Of course Cece had never told Kinley. Why would she?

The job had been about his father, not about him. Kinley had accidentally framed him, pulling him into the mess. Without that mistake, none of it would have touched him, so there'd been no reason to tell his sister that he existed.

Blakely's soft hand landed on his shoulder. She squeezed and then took over when he wasn't sure he had the words to continue.

"Gray is your half brother. Your mother was angry with his father for refusing to give her more money. That's why she had you steal from Lockwood Industries. You were supposed to frame his father for embezzlement, but you put the money in Gray's accounts instead."

* * *

Kinley stared at the woman who'd just rocked her world, dumbfounded by the unexpected revelation. Her gaze jerked to Gray Lockwood, a man who had become as familiar to her as her own reflection. Hell, she'd spent hours watching him over the last several months. A lot more time than the cursory glances she'd taken in the mirror.

How had she missed it?

She'd dug into this guy's background. Read every piece of documentation she could find about his life. She knew he'd been a math whiz as a kid, but hated history. She knew he'd had his appendix out when he was eleven. She even knew the brand of underwear he preferred to buy.

"Not possible."

That was the only conclusion she could come up with. There would have been some paper trail. Some indication.

"I assure you, it's not only possible, it's the truth. My father had an affair with your mother. She got pregnant. My mother couldn't conceive so he paid Cece to give up the baby. My birth certificate was falsified."

Kinley let out a sharp laugh. "Money can buy anything, huh?"

"Something like that."

She stared at him. He was handsome and a little scary. Gray Lockwood reminded her of the men currently chasing after her. Despite the silver-spoon upbringing, he still carried an edge of danger that nothing could hide. He was big and broad and clearly possessed the skills to protect himself if push came to shove.

"Why should I believe you?"

Gray shrugged. "You don't have to. Yet. I'm happy to

get the tests to prove we're siblings…after we get you out of here. We have reason to believe the Russians after you will be here in less than twenty minutes."

Kinley swore under her breath. She'd always known her choices would catch up to her sooner or later. *You piss off enough powerful, vindictive people and eventually you pay the price.*

And she'd been okay with that. In theory. Now that the reality was breathing hot and heavy down her neck…

She'd done a lot of good for a lot of people. She'd righted a lot of wrongs. That was going to have to be good enough. The reality was, there was no one in her life who would give a damn if she disappeared. The Russians could kill her and her death wouldn't be a blip on a single radar.

Which was the life she'd chosen.

But she wasn't ready to give up just yet.

Spinning on her heel, Kinley headed back into the darkened house. She entered the room she'd set up as an office months ago, when she'd settled in Bali. She'd picked the house for very specific reasons, one of which was that despite the run-down appearance and out-of-the-way location, the house was wired like a high-tech ops center. Or at least it was now.

She started placing stuff into the open cases she'd abandoned when Gray had tripped her silent alarm. Most of her computers, servers, racks and equipment were already put away. She only had a few more, and packing them wouldn't take her five minutes. The issue would be getting everything loaded into her car in time.

Next time, she was going to invest in a heavy-duty cart so she didn't have to lug the awkward cases one at a time.

Her brother—she still wasn't ready to accept that— and the woman appeared. They stood in the doorway just watching, without saying anything. Clearly, they weren't there to hurt her, but the Russians would, so that danger was more pressing.

She'd deal with her brother and the woman later. Or not.

Grabbing the first box, Kinley tried to keep in the groan of effort, but couldn't quite make it.

Her brother shot forward, snatching it from her before she could protest. Lifting it like it was nothing, he spun on his heel and headed out the front door. Kinley started to chase after him—he was holding some damn expensive equipment and she really didn't want him to disappear with it.

But she stopped. There was no way she was going to win if they ended up in a wrestling match. Better to grab another box and get it into her car. She had the money to replace anything he took, even if it would be a huge pain in the ass.

Battles and wars and all that. She was picking and choosing.

Kinley headed out behind him, cognizant that the woman who'd come in with Gray had also grabbed one of the boxes stacked in the corner and was following. Great.

Ahead of her, her brother approached a Jeep idling in front of the house. He didn't pause, but lifted up the box and put it into the back. He motioned for her to do the same, but she was in no mood to comply. Instead, she started over to the small SUV she'd bought for ten thousand dollars when she'd arrived to the island.

The woman continued past her and dropped her box into the Jeep before silently returning back to the house for more.

Dammit.

It wasn't worth the breath to argue or try to stop them.

Instead, Kinley popped the door on her car and set the case inside. Gray came behind her and immediately pulled it back out again, then carried it over to the Jeep.

Fed up, she finally turned, put her hands on his back and shoved hard. "What do you think you're doing? Leave my shit alone!"

"Kinley, I'm not letting you deal with the Russians by yourself. Let us help you get out of here. I have a private jet at the airport waiting on standby to take us wherever you want."

Why the hell would he do that?

Kinley stared at the man in front of her, completely dumbfounded. "I ruined your life."

"No, you didn't, but we can talk about that later. Right now, we need to get out of here."

The woman came back with another case and stacked it on the others. Anger, fear, desperation and hope all mixed together in her belly, making her want to throw up. The two of them were certainly acting like they wanted to help.

The faint sound of an engine lifted into the air.

"Shit," Gray said. "They're here. Get in."

"But I don't have everything."

"There's no more time." Grasping her arm, Gray pulled her over to the Jeep, gripped her waist and tossed her into the back seat. The woman with him scrambled up into the other side as Gray vaulted into the passenger seat.

The driver, clearly a local, spun the tires as Gray urged, "Hurry up."

One of the other reasons she'd chosen the house was because there were two paths in and out, something the driver clearly already knew because he headed in the opposite direction of the approaching car.

Everyone was silent as they jolted into the overgrown

vegetation. Anxiety filled the air between them and they all waited to see if the car behind them would stop at the house or follow.

Kinley twisted so she could see out the back. And let out a huge sigh of relief when the wide circle of head-lights stopped, shining straight onto the house. A hand-ful of men jumped out of the two vehicles, swarming up onto the front porch.

That was all she caught before they took a hairpin turn and the house completely disappeared from view.

Turning around, Kinley stared at the back of her broth-er's head. Her world had just gotten very surreal.

The woman beside her leaned forward, catching her attention. Holding out a hand, she said, "Hi, I'm Blakely. I work with your brother."

The Jeep was silent and rife with tension. Blakely wanted to do or say something to cut it, but nothing would help. Gray was only in the front seat, but for some reason he suddenly felt very far away.

Not once since they'd gotten in had he looked back at her. Or at Kinley, for that matter. Blakely's stomach knotted with apprehension and uncertainty.

They pulled into the private entrance at the airport, racing toward the jet sitting on the tarmac.

Several people milled around. A few were loading lug-gage and cargo. Clearly, Gray had instructed someone to pack their things and bring them. She hadn't even seen him send a text or make a call.

But that was Gray, silently taking care of the things that needed attention.

They pulled up close to the jet. Several men raced for-ward, pulled Kinley's cases from the back and rushing them toward the plane.

"Wait," his sister protested, reaching for one. "I'm not going."

The man gave her a look like she'd grown two heads, shook off her hold and then proceeded to do exactly as he'd been instructed.

Gray approached his sister. "Kinley, we'll take you wherever you want to go, but I can't leave you here while the Russians are so close. It's not safe."

Kinley shook her head. "Why are you doing this? Helping me?"

A small smile played at the edges of Gray's mouth. "I know about what you do. You steal money from really bad people and give it to those that need it."

"I stole money from *you*."

"Yes, you did. Did you mean to?"

Kinley threw her hands into the air. "Of course not!"

Gray shifted, rocking on his feet like he wanted to reach out to his sister, but stopped himself before actually touching her. "Trust me, my bank account is fine."

"I have the money. You can have it back. I've been trying to figure out how to put it into your accounts without screwing myself or you even worse than I already did."

"I know."

"You know?"

Gray took another step closer to his sister. "I happen to know a hacker who's almost as good as you are."

"Who?"

Gray's grin widened. "Not my info to share. But I have a feeling you'll have an opportunity to meet at some point."

Blakely watched Gray tentatively reach out a hand to Kinley and set it on her shoulder.

Brother and sister faced off, Kinley with a perplexed

expression and Gray with hope. Blakely's chest tightened. It was a surreal moment, one she was grateful to witness.

Gray had lost so much. The only family he'd ever known abandoned him. He'd learned the woman who'd given birth to him never wanted him and didn't care what happened to him. Sure, he'd found two amazing friends that were as close as brothers, but at the end of the day it wasn't the same as blood.

God, she really hoped Gray was right and Kinley wouldn't screw him over, too. She was hopeful, but it was difficult for her not to let the cynicism of her child-hood color that hope.

"I own a security company. We can always use some-one with your skills."

"No." Kinley didn't even contemplate Gray's tentative offer. "I work alone."

"You still can. I'm just saying, if you ever want to free-lance…" Gray pulled out a cell and handed it to her. "My number is programmed. Call me. Anytime."

"Just like that. You're going to let the twenty million dollars and everything else go?"

Gray shrugged. "It's not like I need it. Use it for some-thing good, Kinley."

"You're not going to turn me in?"

Gray shook his head. "No."

Blakely took a step back. She wasn't surprised to hear him voice that decision, but it still made her heart hurt. He was giving up the one thing he'd been working so long and hard for.

Fourteen

Blakely had been quiet since they'd gotten onto the plane. A few hours ago, they'd made a fuel stop in Hong Kong. They'd also left Kinley there.

It had been difficult to watch his sister walk away. Not just because she was in danger, but because he'd just found her. And a huge part of him wanted the opportunity to get to know her better.

But that wasn't his choice. He'd made the offer of a position with Stone—from there it was up to her what happened next with her life. What he could control was what happened in his.

Gray watched the ground disappear beneath them as they rose higher into the sky. Soon enough, they'd be back in Charleston. He wasn't surprised when Blakely sat down in the chair next to his.

Since they'd boarded the plane, she'd been keeping a distance between them. Maybe she'd sensed he'd needed the space. Or maybe she was avoiding him.

He was so mentally and physically exhausted, at the moment he wasn't sure whether or not it mattered. The result was the same. There was this space between them that hadn't been there before.

"What now?"

Her question was simple. Unfortunately, the answer wasn't. Hell, he wasn't absolutely certain what she was really asking. But he could answer one thing.

"Nothing. We go back to the office and go on with life."

Leaning forward, Blakely put her elbows on her knees and dropped her head. "I was afraid you were going to say that. You're not going to tell the authorities or your father."

It wasn't a question. Clearly, she'd already figured out he wasn't. Not only had he said as much to Kinley, but deep down, he knew it was the right thing to do.

"It would put her in someone else's crosshairs and she's already got plenty of people chasing her."

"What about you?"

"What about me?"

"You deserve your life back, Gray. You didn't do anything wrong and you've lost everything."

Had he? Gray wasn't so sure that was true.

"Getting my life back would mean destroying hers." And he wasn't willing to do that. They might not have shared history, but they did share DNA. And at the end of the day, she was as much a victim in all of this as he was. He refused to punish her for her parents' manipulation and a mistake she'd made when she was sixteen.

"Not necessarily. She's really good at being a ghost. Just because you produce evidence that you were framed doesn't mean you need to give up her trail."

"Maybe, but it's a risk I'm not willing to take. My

father has means and determination. At the moment, he thinks I have twenty million stashed somewhere. If he discovered someone else was in possession of those Lockwood assets…he'd stop at nothing to find the person responsible."

"Kinley's willing to give back the money."

"And that might help, but it won't stop him. I know him, and he's relentless when he's on a crusade. No, it's better if he never knows. I've already paid my debt to society, Blakely. I can't get those years back, no matter what."

"No, but you can get your family back. Your reputation and legacy."

Gray laughed, the sound bitter even to his own ears. "I don't really have a family, do I? And I never did. My father doesn't give a damn about me. He cares about appearances. The woman I thought was my mother couldn't care less what happens to me. And the mother who gave birth to me is only interested in what she can get out of me. No, thank you. I'm perfectly happy with the life I have."

"What life? Gray, I've spent the last few weeks with you. Your existence has been entirely wrapped up in proving your innocence. The last eight years. All I'm saying is, don't make this decision in haste."

A tight knot cramped Gray's stomach. Blakely stared at him through those pale blue eyes that always cut straight through him. He'd seen them filling with passion and heat. Hope and frustration. Right now, they were awash with guilt and disappointment.

"Don't give up the chance to clear your name. Everyone needs to know you're not a criminal. You deserve the chance to shake off that stigma."

In that moment, Gray realized just how important that was to her. Images of her father standing in the middle of the office hallway, everyone staring at the spectacle he'd created, flashed across his mind. Her embarrassment and irritation at the precinct. The tired disappointment in her voice as she'd talked about growing up with a criminal as a father.

Clearing his name had become a crusade for her, as well, and not simply because of the guilt she harbored for her part in putting him in jail.

Blakely had a clear sense of right and wrong thanks to the gray world her father lived in. She'd lived with the taint of that stigma her entire life, and she'd done everything she could to distance herself from it.

And if he didn't clear his name, being with him would taint her once again.

He couldn't ask her to do that. But he also couldn't use the information he had to clear his name.

"I'll think about it." Although he wouldn't. Standing up, Gray gave her a weak smile. "I'm going to make a few phone calls and take care of a few things back home." And he walked back into the bedroom.

This day was about to get worse, but just like the fights he'd been in, sometimes he just had to take a punch.

Gray had spent the rest of their flight in the bedroom, only coming back out minutes before they landed. Blakely almost regretted what she'd said, but she couldn't quite bring herself to get there. He'd worked so damn hard to prove his innocence, she hated to watch him walk away from the opportunity to get back everything he'd lost.

Maybe he just needed time alone to deal with the disappointment of getting so close only to watch the redemption he'd wanted slip through his fingers. She completely understood the decision he was making…but that didn't make it suck any less.

It was late at night when the plane touched down. They disembarked and Blakely tried not to worry about the fact that Gray kept his distance and didn't touch her. He was just dealing with things.

That was, until they reached the tarmac. Two cars waited for them. Blakely caught a glimpse of her bag being loaded into one...and Gray's being put into the other.

Turning, she said, "What's going on?"

"What do you mean?"

"Why are we taking separate cars?"

Gray cocked his head to the side. "Because we're both going home."

Blakely couldn't stop herself, even though she already knew the answer. "Alone?"

"Yes."

"Why?"

He pulled in a deep breath and held it for several seconds before finally letting it out. "Look, Blakely. You held up your end of the bargain. You helped me prove my innocence."

"Even though you're not going to do anything with the information."

His mouth thinned. "Even though. I'm following through with my end. You should be receiving a phone call tomorrow from an accounting firm in town. They're going to interview you, but it's just a formality. You can start your life and career over."

Blakely stared at Gray for several seconds. An anxious pit opened up in the bottom of her belly. This wasn't what she wanted.

"That's it?" Her purse slipped through numbed fingers, dropping to the ground at her feet. She took several steps forward, right into his personal space. Gray didn't flinch—he just stared at her out of cold, remote eyes.

This was not the man who'd rocked her world and spent hours worshipping her body just days ago. The man in front of her was the aloof felon. The intense brawler hell-bent on victory.

"You're going to pretend the last few days didn't happen? That you didn't spend hours with your mouth and hands on my body?"

"No, why would I pretend it didn't happen? I enjoyed every minute of it. You did, too. But that was just proximity and chemistry, Blakely. We were physically attracted to each other."

"Were." The single word fell flat.

"There's no reason for us to see each other again. The job is finished."

"What if I want to stay at Stone?" She'd really enjoyed the work they'd done together. Being part of solving the puzzle had been exhilarating. And it didn't hurt that they'd been trying to find justice, something she prized highly thanks to her childhood. Being part of that had felt…purposeful and important.

"I don't think that's a good idea."

"Why? You're not this asshole, Gray."

His mouth twisted into a self-deprecating smile. "I assure you, I can be as much an asshole as the next guy. It was fun while it lasted, but it's over. Time for both of us to go back to our lives."

Blakely stared up at him, a mixture of hurt, pride, anger and pain making her physically ill. Heat washed over her body, and not the kind that normally filled her when Gray was near. Her stomach felt like she'd swallowed a cup of battery acid.

She refused to beg him, even if her brain was screaming at her to convince him he was wrong. She deserved to be with a man who wanted her, not someone who felt she was disposable as soon as she wasn't useful to him anymore.

Never once had she thought Gray was that kind of man, but apparently, she was wrong.

Taking two steps back, Blakely began nodding her head. "Normal. That's exactly what I need."

She spun on her heel and stalked away. It was either that, or let him see the tears she couldn't hold back silently rolling down her face.

"What the hell is your problem? You've been a right prick the last few days." Finn leaned back in the large leather chair, a single dark eyebrow winged up in that sharp, insolent and questioning way he had.

Gray fought the urge to reach across the table and punch him. Logically, he realized the reaction was way too much. But he was having a very hard time controlling his temper.

"Heartbroken fool." Those two words were Stone's contribution to the conversation.

"O-o-oh," Finn said, drawing out the single word. "Poor bastard."

Stone shrugged. "He did it to himself so I don't have a lot of sympathy."

Finn's lips tipped up at the corners. "Yeah, but you remember both of us had a stupid moment ourselves before we got our heads out our asses."

"Speak for yourself. I don't remember any stupid moments."

Finn scoffed, the incredulous sound echoing through the room and scraping against his last nerve. "Bullshit. Just because you don't want to admit it, doesn't mean it didn't happen. Besides, I'm pretty sure you had more than one."

"No reason to go there," Stone said with a pointed look. "Besides, we were talking about Gray."

"Any bets on how long it takes before he comes to his senses, goes after her and grovels?"

Stone tipped his head sideways, studying him like he was a specimen beneath a microscope. "I'm pretty sure he's close to the breaking point right now. I'd say…two days. Max."

"Nah, I'm going with tomorrow. I hear her dad's case is going before the judge then."

"No fair, you had insider information."

Finn grinned. "Always stack the deck, my friend."

Gray, tired of listening to the banter, growled, "You assholes can stop talking about me like I'm not here."

"Well, look at that, he is paying attention."

"Of course I am." His attention turned to Finn. "Her father's trial is tomorrow?"

This time both of Finn's eyebrows rose. "The high-priced lawyer you hired filed a motion to dismiss. The judge is hearing it tomorrow. Although, I would have expected you to know this already."

And he might have…if he hadn't told the guy who'd called yesterday about Blakely's father's case that he didn't want to hear anything about it. He just wanted the man to do his job. Period.

Dammit, but now he knew. His foot started tapping against the floor. The muscles in his shoulders tightened. Blakely must be stressed out over the outcome.

He needed to get out of here, before he did something stupid. Like call her and see how she was holding up.

Pushing back from the table, Gray said, "You guys will have to finish this meeting without me."

"Please tell me you're going to her."

Gray looked across the table at Stone. "No."

His friend groaned, closing his eyes. "You really are a fool." Waving a hand, Stone added, "Go, we've got this. Do us a favor, though, and don't come back in until you have your shit together. Amanda is afraid to come near you right now. She said you snapped her head off when she brought you some paperwork this morning."

"It was screwed up."

"Maybe so, but that wasn't her fault."

Stone might be right, but Gray wasn't in the mood to acknowledge it. "Whatever."

He was halfway to the door when Finn's voice stopped him. "Would you like some friendly advice?"

Gray paused for several seconds before turning back to his friend. "Not really."

"You're getting it, anyway. I don't know what happened between you. What I do know is that with her you were happier than I'd ever seen you. And that's saying a lot considering everything that was going on. I would have expected the last few weeks to have been some of the most difficult of your life."

And when Gray stopped to think about it, Finn was right. Aside from being convicted for a crime he didn't commit, finding out his mother wasn't really his, that his father had paid someone to cover it up and his birth mother had sold him…not exactly a happy time.

"Still, somehow, you managed to get through that experience without tearing apart someone or something. I saw you smile more often in those weeks than I have in the eight years I've known you. She makes you happy, man. And that's worth a lot."

Stone picked up where Finn left off. "It's worth doing whatever you have to in order to have that in your life.

Whatever the problem is…figure out how to fix it. All of us know, life is too unpredictable. You take the joy where you can find it."

"And when you find a woman worth having in your life, you do what you can to keep her there," Finn added.

Gray stared at both his friends. They watched him with matching earnest expressions, firmly believing what they were telling him.

And he had to admit, the last few days he'd been miserable.

"This is the right thing…for her. It'll get better."

"No, it won't," Stone said, his voice filled with certainty. "I let Piper go before I went to prison. And those feelings never disappeared. They were just as powerful years later. If you love her, tell her."

"Fight for her," Finn chimed in. "You're good at that, man. You know how to fight. So why are you walking away from the most important one of your life?"

Gray's gaze bounced between his two friends. Aside from Blakely, they were the most important people in his life.

What they said both scared him…and gave him hope. Maybe they were right. Stone had been noble, trying to do the right thing just like he was. But in the end, Piper hadn't wanted that sacrifice from him. She'd wanted the man she loved.

Walking away from Blakely was the hardest thing he'd ever done. And Finn had a point. He'd never backed down from a fight before. So why was he doing it now, when it mattered most?

"That's a damn good question."

Fifteen

Blakely sat behind her father. He was at the table in front of her. The lawyer Gray had hired sat next to him. She'd half expected the guy to drop the case, but he hadn't.

She couldn't decide whether to be grateful or pissed. Half of her had hoped Gray would pull an asshole move so she could be angry instead of hurt and heartbroken.

No such luck.

The bastard.

The judge walked into the courtroom and everyone stood. After he was seated, the bailiff instructed everyone else to sit. The registrar began detailing the order of cases. The hearing for her father's motion was first.

Everyone was shuffling papers and murmuring. Getting prepared. Blakely's stomach was in knots. Over the last several days, she'd spent some time with her father, really talking about what had happened. A few weeks ago, she would have gone into that conversation with a completely different mindset. But thanks to Gray...she'd truly listened to her father and decided for herself, and for him, that she believed him. He was far from perfect, but it was clear to her he'd been honestly trying to change his life.

Which made this hearing even more important.

Leaning forward, Blakely placed her hand over her father's shoulder and squeezed. He didn't turn, but brought his own hand up, covering hers. The pads of his fingers were rough with calluses, reminding her that no matter what, her father had worked hard all of his life to provide for his family. Maybe not the way she would have preferred...but the only way he knew how.

The hearing started, and the prosecution began with a brief outline of their case. Blakely listened to the evidence, her throat tightening with each word. They made him sound so guilty.

The defense was about to start when the door at the back of the courtroom opened. Blakely turned at the noise, nothing more than a reflex, but her world stood still when she saw who entered.

Gray.

What was he doing here?

Pausing, he looked straight at her for several moments. His expression was blank and impossible to read. A jumbled mess of emotions tangled into knots inside her already rolling belly. Anger, heartbreak, hope and frustration collided, so coiled together that she couldn't separate them enough to deal with any.

Clamping her jaws together, Blakely purposefully turned away from him, placing her focus back onto her father and the hearing.

She listened to her father's attorney decimate each of the prosecution's points, poking holes in their evidence and making a strong case for dismissing the charges altogether. He also made a compelling argument that her father had been turning his life around, distancing himself from the people who were bad influences and attempting to become a better citizen. He suggested no one should be judged based on their past behavior when they were clearly trying to make the right changes.

The experience was a roller coaster, but optimistic hope came out on top when her father's attorney finally sat. And in that moment, she was proud of her father. Something she'd never been able to say before.

When both sides were done, the judge sat back in his chair. He looked out over the courtroom, his gaze zeroing in on her father.

"Mr. Whittaker, I've heard from both sides. After careful consideration of the facts presented here, I find there isn't enough evidence to hold this case over for trial."

Blakely let out a huge sigh of relief. In front of her, her father sagged into his chair, his shoulders dipping with relief.

"I want to caution you, however. While it might be ideal not to judge people on their past mistakes, ultimately, we're all human and it happens. You have much to atone for in your past, but I'm a firm believer everyone deserves a second chance. So far, you've proven your willingness to make changes in your life. Keep it that way so I don't have to see you in my courtroom again." The judge paused for several seconds. "Because next time, you might not be so lucky."

Her father stood. "Thank you, sir. I understand and I'm so grateful for your decision."

Everyone around her seemed to move at once. Her father's attorney stood and began gathering his files and papers. He turned to her father and murmured several things before clapping him on the back and wishing him the best.

Her father turned to her, a huge grin stretching across his face. Blakely leaned forward, wrapping him in a hug. But she couldn't stop herself from whispering in his ear. "You're lucky, Dad. Please don't blow this second chance."

"I won't, baby girl. I promise not to let you down again."

Pulling back, Blakely looked deep into his eyes. "Dad, don't do it for me. Do it for yourself."

The smile on Martin's face dimmed a little, but he nodded and squeezed her shoulder.

Together, they walked out of the courtroom. Blakely couldn't stop herself from scanning the crowd in front of her, looking for Gray even though she knew she shouldn't.

But he wasn't there.

And for some stupid reason, her heart dropped into her toes when she realized he was gone. He hadn't come for her; he'd come to support her father. To make sure his money had been spent wisely.

In that moment, the last bit of hope Blakely had been clinging to disappeared.

Gray watched as Blakely and her father left the courthouse. Martin got into his car and drove away. His daughter stood for several seconds, watching him disappear.

Her hands were shaking. He wanted to go to her, hold her, and make it stop.

She was so strong for everyone, but for the first time, Gray realized that meant she had no one to be strong for her.

No, that wasn't true. She had him.

To hell with it. He didn't care if she wanted him to be there or not. Didn't care if she was angry with him, or if she didn't like his criminal reputation. They'd figure it out.

Walking out of the shadows, Gray crossed the sidewalk. Reaching out, he grasped her hands and squeezed.

She didn't startle or jerk away. But she also didn't turn to him. Instead, she stared straight ahead and asked, "Why are you here?"

"I wouldn't be anywhere else."

Blakely's head bowed.

Using his grip on her shoulders, Gray gently turned her to face him. Her face was drawn, unhappy and sad. Exactly the way he'd been feeling the past days without her.

"Blakely, I'm miserable without you." Those words were a hell of a lot easier to say than he'd expected. "I miss your laugh, the way you smell. I miss the way you burrow into me in your sleep, like you can't get close enough. I miss the way you argue with me and challenge me. I just miss you."

Blakely's mouth thinned. Her eyes glistened with tears she wouldn't let fall. "You pushed me away, Gray."

"You're right. I did. I was afraid."

"Of what?"

"That you were only with me out of guilt." No, it was more than that. And if there was ever a time to be completely honest with himself and her, it was now. "I was afraid I didn't deserve you. Blakely, I spent seven years in prison. And I might not have been a criminal when I went inside—"

Blakely cut him off, her voice hard and strong when she said, "You're still not a criminal."

And that was where she was wrong. "I've done plenty

of things that are on the gray side of the law. And I know you, Blakely. If you knew everything, you wouldn't be okay with it."

"That's bullshit, Gray. You say you know me, but I know you, too. I don't care what you think you've done. I have no doubt you had perfectly good reasons. Period. I don't need the details to know that, because I know you. Trust you."

Blakely's arm flung out, sweeping across the expanse of the courthouse steps. "I just spent the last hour in a courtroom with my dad. A few weeks ago, dread and disappointment would have sat heavy on my stomach. Because I would have been embarrassed and hurt by what he'd done. Instead, I was hopeful. And not just because you'd spent money on a damn good lawyer. But because I believe that deep down, he wants to change. I believe in him, in a way I never have before. You gave me that." She shook her head. "No, you gave *us* that. Because my support is going to help my dad be successful in making those changes."

Gray's chest tightened. "I'm really happy for you both."

"Then why won't you let me show you the same support you've given me?"

Blakely closed the gap between them, wrapping her hands around his face and bringing her body snugly against his. "I love you, Gray."

Everything inside him went silent at her words. Something sharp lanced through his chest and then warmth expanded, spreading throughout his entire body.

She loved him. Gray wasn't certain what he'd done right in his life to deserve her, but he'd take it. Because he wasn't strong enough not to.

Dropping his forehead to hers, he said, "I love you, too."

"There might have been a time I thought you were the worst kind of man, but I was clearly wrong. Gray Lockwood, you're one of the most honorable, selfless men I've ever met."

Gray's throat tight, he pulled her up until his mouth met hers. The kiss they shared was hot as always, but it was more. Connection, comfort, support and appreciation.

It was a beginning, one they were both anxious to start.

* * * * *

MILLS & BOON

THE HEART OF ROMANCE

A ROMANCE FOR EVERY READER

MODERN

Prepare to be swept off your feet by sophisticated, sexy and seductive heroes, in some of the world's most glamourous and romantic locations, where power and passion collide.

HISTORICAL

Escape with historical heroes from time gone by. Whether your passion is for wicked Regency Rakes, muscled Vikings or rugged Highlanders, awaken the romance of the past.

MEDICAL

Set your pulse racing with dedicated, delectable doctors in the high-pressure world of medicine, where emotions run high and passion, comfort and love are the best medicine.

True Love

Celebrate true love with tender stories of heartfelt romance, from the rush of falling in love to the joy a new baby can bring, and a focus on the emotional heart of a relationship.

Desire

Indulge in secrets and scandal, intense drama and sizzling hot action with heroes who have it all: wealth, status, good looks…everything but the right woman.

HEROES

The excitement of a gripping thriller, with intense romance at its heart. Resourceful, true-to-life women and strong, fearless men face danger and desire - a killer combination!

To see which titles are coming soon, please visit

millsandboon.co.uk/nextmonth

JOIN US ON SOCIAL MEDIA!

Stay up to date with our latest releases, author news and gossip, special offers and discounts, and all the behind-the-scenes action from Mills & Boon...

 @millsandboon

 @millsandboonuk

 facebook.com/millsandboon

 @millsandboonuk

It might just be true love...

GET YOUR ROMANCE FIX!

Get the latest romance news, exclusive author interviews, story extracts and much more!

MILLS & BOON
True Love
Romance from the Heart

Celebrate true love with tender stories of heartfelt romance, from the rush of falling in love to the joy a new baby can bring, and a focus on the emotional heart of a relationship.